DOVER · THRIFT · EDITIONS

Detection by Gaslight

EDITED BY

DOUGLAS G. GREENE

DOVER PUBLICATIONS, INC.
Mineola, New York

DOVER THRIFT EDITIONS

GENERAL EDITOR: PAUL NEGRI
EDITOR OF THIS VOLUME: DOUGLAS G. GREENE

Copyright

Published in Canada by General Publishing Company, Ltd., 30 Lesmill Road, Don Mills, Toronto, Ontario.
Published in the United Kingdom by Constable and Company, Ltd., 3 The Lanchesters, 162–164 Fulham Palace Road, London W6 9ER.

Bibliographical Note

This Dover edition, first published in 1997, is a new anthology of works reprinted from standard sources. A new introductory Note and prefaces to the stories have been specially prepared for this edition.

Library of Congress Cataloging-in-Publication Data

Detection by gaslight / edited by Douglas G. Greene.
     p.   cm. — (Dover thrift editions)
  ISBN 0-486-29928-7 (pbk.)
  1. Detective and mystery stories, English. I. Greene, Douglas G. II. Series.
PR1309.D4D39   1997
823'.08720808—dc21   97-22681
                                                          CIP

Manufactured in the United States of America
Dover Publications, Inc., 31 East 2nd Street, Mineola, N.Y. 11501

The First Golden Age of Detective Fiction

THE OPENING of the First Golden Age of the Detective Story can be precisely dated: It began when *The Strand Magazine* published in its July 1891 issue the first Sherlock Holmes short story, "A Scandal in Bohemia." The creation of a young doctor named Arthur Conan Doyle, Holmes had already appeared in two short novels: A *Study in Scarlet* (1887) and *The Sign of Four* (1890). Together the novels had given flesh and blood to the characters of Holmes and Watson, but as unified tales they were unsatisfactory. Both began with a fairly short detective adventure, but concluded with a lengthy and quite independent novel to explain the motives for the crime. And those motives had little to do with everyday life, associated as they were with the Andaman Islands and with Mormon conspiracies. (Mormons, like communists in more recent times, could always be trotted out to put a scare into late-century Victorians.)

It was only with the introduction of Holmes into the short-story form that the image of the Great Detective came to dominate mystery fiction. This genre had its roots in the short story, starting with the cases of Edgar Allan Poe's C. Auguste Dupin, but Dupin was a reasoning machine rather than a personality. The detectives created by Wilkie Collins (Sergeant Cuff in *The Moonstone*) and Anna Katharine Green (Mr. Gryce in *The Leavenworth Case*) were much more believable, but they both needed full novels to display their skills. Furthermore, for the short story to become the most popular way to present a mystery, the magazines in which these stories first appeared had to change from the stodgy products of mid-Victorian times with tiny type and clumsy illustrations.

When George Newnes founded *The Strand* in 1891, he looked for his readers among the burgeoning middle class. To draw them in, he included an illustration on every page, plenty of human-interest articles, and short fiction for both children and adults. *The Strand* was an immense success, especially after the Holmes stories began to appear.

The short form demanded by the magazine was ideal for Doyle's talents. It forced him to concentrate on the unraveling of the mystery, rather than on the extraneous, exotic story of what had caused the crime. Doyle's Great Detective, with his near infallibility, his eccentricity, and his humanity, was perfect in the short form. A problem was presented, a few deductions revealed to the admiring Watson, the pair dash to the scene of the crime, show the foolishness of the police, make a few more deductions, and solve the crime—all in around ten thousand words. It is remarkable that, until his final Holmes stories, Doyle was able to provide a great variety in the crimes and the details of the investigations, while placing everything into a wonderfully realized world of Hansom cabs, London fogs, gasogenes, railways, and many of the other elements of late-Victorian England.

The Strand was followed by many other magazines—*Windsor, Royal, Ludgate, Harmsworth's, Cassell's, Pearson's,* and so on—which catered to the same market and which published the same sort of material. Sherlock Holmes likewise was followed by many other detectives. Sometimes the arrival of a new sleuth was directly associated with Holmes, as when *The Strand* published Arthur Morrison's cases of Martin Hewitt to replace the Holmes stories after Doyle sent his detective over the falls at Reichenbach. More often, however, authors created detectives who were noticeably different from Holmes but who nonetheless could share the Great Detective aura.

Detection by Gaslight demonstrates how varied the short mystery (and especially its hero or heroine) could be. For example, Catherine L. Pirkis, George R. Sims, and others invented women detectives. Others introduced clerical sleuths, most notably Silas K. Hocking's Latimer Field and G. K. Chesterton's Father Brown. Writers of the highest talent—such as Rudyard Kipling—were attracted to the form, as were authors whose talents were minimal—for example Headon Hill, one of whose few notable tales is included in this book. The form could be stretched to include pure scientific detection, as with R. Austin Freeman's Dr. Thorndyke, and to investigations into the paranormal—as with K. and H. Prichard's Flaxman Low. An examination of the monthly magazines of the Victorian and Edwardian eras leaves the reader with the feeling that almost every profession could produce a detective—from the woman reporter created by the Baroness Orczy to the butterfly collector who investigates a crime in a story by Robert W. Chambers.

   Detection by Gaslight is a tribute to those days when Sherlock Holmes and his contemporary sleuths dominated fictional crime: when, as the great bookman Vincent Starrett wrote, "it is always eighteen ninety-five."

DOUGLAS GREENE

NORFOLK, VIRGINIA
AUGUST 1996

Table of Contents

Sir Arthur Conan Doyle

(1859–1930)

THE CREATOR of Sherlock Holmes was a bluff, honorable physician who always thought that his most important work was in his historical novels (like *The White Company* and *Sir Nigel*), rather than in his detective stories. Almost no one has ever agreed with Doyle. Born in Edinburgh, he received a Master's degree in Medicine in 1881 and a doctorate in 1885. From 1882 to 1890 he practiced in Southsea, and it was there—because having few patients meant empty hours—that he wrote his first stories, including the earliest case for Sherlock Holmes. He was knighted by King Edward VII in 1902 for his service during the Boer War, and he also became a Knight of the Order of St. John of Jerusalem. In later life, probably because of the loss of his son during World War One, Doyle became a determined advocate of spiritualism. His biographer, John Dickson Carr, recalled that the author's family believed that long after his death Sir Arthur still wandered about the estate, seeking his pipe and so on.

"The Adventure of the Copper Beeches" was published in the June 1892 issue of *The Strand*, as the final story in the first series of Holmes adventures. It shows Holmes at his most testy, his most active, and his most contemplative. Doyle often depicted strong women in his stories, and Violet Hunter is one of the most resourceful.

1

The Adventure of the Copper Beeches

To THE MAN who loves art for its own sake," remarked Sherlock Holmes, tossing aside the advertisement sheet of the *Daily Telegraph*, "it is frequently in its least important and lowliest manifestations that the keenest pleasure is to be derived. It is pleasant to me to observe, Watson, that you have so far grasped this truth that in these little records of our cases which you have been good enough to draw up, and, I am bound to say, occasionally to embellish, you have given prominence not so much to the many *causes célèbres* and sensational trials in which I have figured but rather to those incidents which may have been trivial in themselves, but which have given room for those faculties of deduction and of logical synthesis which I have made my special province."

"And yet," said I, smiling, "I cannot quite hold myself absolved from the charge of sensationalism which has been urged against my records."

"You have erred, perhaps," he observed, taking up a glowing cinder with the tongs and lighting with it the long cherry-wood pipe which was wont to replace his clay when he was in a disputatious rather than a meditative mood—"you have erred perhaps in attempting to put colour and life into each of your statements instead of confining yourself to the task of placing upon record that severe reasoning from cause to effect which is really the only notable feature about the thing."

"It seems to me that I have done you full justice in the matter," I remarked with some coldness, for I was repelled by the egotism which I had more than once observed to be a strong factor in my friend's singular character.

"No, it is not selfishness or conceit," said he, answering, as was his wont, my thoughts rather than my words. "If I claim full justice for my art, it is because it is an impersonal thing—a thing beyond myself. Crime is common. Logic is rare. Therefore it is upon the logic rather than upon the crime that you should dwell. You have degraded what should have been a course of lectures into a series of tales."

It was a cold morning of the early spring, and we sat after breakfast on either side of a cheery fire in the old room at Baker Street. A thick fog rolled down between the lines of dun-coloured houses, and the opposing windows loomed like dark, shapeless blurs through the heavy yellow wreaths. Our gas was lit and shone on the white cloth and glimmer of china and metal, for the table had not been cleared yet. Sherlock Holmes had been silent all the morning, dipping continuously into the advertisement columns of a succession of papers until at last, having apparently given up his search, he had emerged in no very sweet temper to lecture me upon my literary shortcomings.

"At the same time," he remarked after a pause, during which he had sat puffing at his long pipe and gazing down into the fire, "you can hardly be open to a charge of sensationalism, for out of these cases which you have been so kind as to interest yourself in, a fair proportion do not treat of crime, in its legal sense, at all. The small matter in which I endeavoured to help the King of Bohemia, the singular experience of Miss Mary Sutherland, the problem connected with the man with the twisted lip, and the incident of the noble bachelor, were all matters which are outside the pale of the law. But in avoiding the sensational, I fear that you may have bordered on the trivial."

"The end may have been so," I answered, "but the methods I hold to have been novel and of interest."

"Pshaw, my dear fellow, what do the public, the great unobservant public, who could hardly tell a weaver by his tooth or a compositor by his left thumb, care about the finer shades of analysis and deduction! But, indeed, if you are trivial, I cannot blame you, for the days of the great cases are past. Man, or at least criminal man, has lost all enterprise and originality. As to my own little practice, it seems to be degenerating into an agency for recovering lost lead pencils and giving advice to young ladies from boarding-schools. I think that I have touched bottom at last, however. This note I had this morning marks my zero-point, I fancy. Read it!" He tossed a crumpled letter across to me.

It was dated from Montague Place upon the preceding evening, and ran thus:

DEAR MR. HOLMES:

I am very anxious to consult you as to whether I should or should not accept a situation which has been offered to me as governess. I shall call at half-past ten to-morrow if I do not inconvenience you.

Yours faithfully,
VIOLET HUNTER.

"Do you know the young lady?" I asked.

"Not I."

"It is half-past ten now."

"Yes, and I have no doubt that is her ring."

"It may turn out to be of more interest than you think. You remember that the affair of the blue carbuncle, which appeared to be a mere whim at first, developed into a serious investigation. It may be so in this case, also."

"Well, let us hope so. But our doubts will very soon be solved, for here, unless I am much mistaken, is the person in question."

As he spoke the door opened and a young lady entered the room. She was plainly but neatly dressed, with a bright, quick face, freckled like a plover's egg, and with the brisk manner of a woman who has had her own way to make in the world.

"You will excuse my troubling you, I am sure," said she, as my companion rose to greet her, "but I have had a very strange experience, and as I have no parents or relations of any sort from whom I could ask advice, I thought that perhaps you would be kind enough to tell me what I should do."

"Pray take a seat, Miss Hunter. I shall be happy to do anything that I can to serve you."

I could see that Holmes was favourably impressed by the manner and speech of his new client. He looked her over in his searching fashion, and then composed himself, with his lids drooping and his fingertips together, to listen to her story.

"I have been a governess for five years," said she, "in the family of Colonel Spence Munro, but two months ago the colonel received an appointment at Halifax, in Nova Scotia, and took his children over to America with him, so that I found myself without a situation. I advertised, and I answered advertisements, but without success. At last the little money which I had saved began to run short, and I was at my wit's end as to what I should do.

"There is a well-known agency for governesses in the West End called Westaway's, and there I used to call about once a week in order to see whether anything had turned up which might suit me. Westaway was the name of the founder of the business, but it is really managed by Miss Stoper. She sits in her own little office, and the ladies who are seeking employment wait in an anteroom, and are then shown in one by one, when she consults her ledgers and sees whether she has anything which would suit them.

"Well, when I called last week I was shown into the little office as usual, but I found that Miss Stoper was not alone. A prodigiously stout man with a very smiling face and a great heavy chin which rolled down in fold upon fold over his throat sat at her elbow with a pair of glasses on his nose, looking very earnestly at the ladies who entered. As I came in he gave quite a jump in his chair and turned quickly to Miss Stoper.

"'That will do,' said he; 'I could not ask for anything better. Capital! capital!' He seemed quite enthusiastic and rubbed his hands together in the most genial fashion. He was such a comfortable-looking man that it was quite a pleasure to look at him.

"'You are looking for a situation, miss?' he asked.

"'Yes, sir.'

"'As governess?'

"'Yes, sir.'

"'And what salary do you ask?'

"'I had £4 a month in my last place with Colonel Spence Munro.'

"'Oh, tut, tut! sweating—rank sweating!' he cried, throwing his fat hands out into the air like a man who is in a boiling passion. 'How could anyone offer so pitiful a sum to a lady with such attractions and accomplishments?'

"'My accomplishments, sir, may be less than you imagine,' said I. 'A little French, a little German, music, and drawing——'

"'Tut, tut!' he cried. 'This is all quite beside the question. The point is, have you or have you not the bearing and deportment of a lady? There it is in a nutshell. If you have not, you are not fitted for the rearing of a child who may some day play a considerable part in the history of the country. But if you have, why, then, how could any gentleman ask you to condescend to accept anything under the three figures? Your salary with me, madam, would commence at £100 a year.'

"You may imagine, Mr. Holmes, that to me, destitute as I was, such an offer seemed almost too good to be true. The gentleman, however, seeing perhaps the look of incredulity upon my face, opened a pocket-book and took out a note.

"'It is also my custom,' said he, smiling in the most pleasant fashion until his eyes were just two little shining slits amid the white creases of his face, 'to advance to my young ladies half their salary beforehand, so that they may meet any little expenses of their journey and their wardrobe.'

"It seemed to me that I had never met so fascinating and so thoughtful a man. As I was already in debt to my tradesmen, the advance was a great convenience, and yet there was something unnatural about the whole transaction which made me wish to know a little more before I quite committed myself.

"'May I ask where you live, sir?' said I.

"'Hampshire. Charming rural place. The Copper Beeches, five miles on the far side of Winchester. It is the most lovely country, my dear young lady, and the dearest old country-house.'

"'And my duties, sir? I should be glad to know what they would be.'

"'One child—one dear little romper just six years old. Oh, if you could see him killing cockroaches with a slipper! Smack! smack! smack! Three gone before you could wink!' He leaned back in his chair and laughed his eyes into his head again.

"I was a little startled at the nature of the child's amusement, but the father's laughter made me think that perhaps he was joking.

"'My sole duties, then,' I asked, 'are to take charge of a single child?'

"'No, no, not the sole, not the sole, my dear young lady,' he cried. 'Your duty would be, as I am sure your good sense would suggest, to obey any little commands my wife might give, provided always that they were such commands as a lady might with propriety obey. You see no difficulty, heh?'

"'I should be happy to make myself useful.'

"'Quite so. In dress now, for example. We are faddy people, you know—faddy but kind-hearted. If you were asked to wear any dress which we might give you, you would not object to our little whim. Heh?'

"'No,' said I, considerably astonished at his words.

"'Or to sit here, or sit there, that would not be offensive to you?'

"'Oh, no.'

"'Or to cut your hair quite short before you come to us?'

"I could hardly believe my ears. As you may observe, Mr. Holmes, my hair is somewhat luxuriant, and of a rather peculiar tint of chestnut. It has been considered artistic. I could not dream of sacrificing it in this offhand fashion.

"'I am afraid that that is quite impossible,' said I. He had been watching me eagerly out of his small eyes, and I could see a shadow pass over his face as I spoke.

"'I am afraid that it is quite essential,' said he. 'It is a little fancy of my wife's, and ladies' fancies, you know, madam, ladies' fancies must be consulted. And so you won't cut your hair?'

"'No, sir, I really could not,' I answered firmly.

"'Ah, very well; then that quite settles the matter. It is a pity, because in other respects you would really have done very nicely. In that case, Miss Stoper, I had best inspect a few more of your young ladies.'

"The manageress had sat all this while busy with her papers without a word to either of us, but she glanced at me now with so much annoyance upon her face that I could not help suspecting that she had lost a handsome commission through my refusal.

"'Do you desire your name to be kept upon the books?" she asked.

"'If you please, Miss Stoper.'

"'Well, really, it seems rather useless, since you refuse the most excellent offers in this fashion,' said she sharply. 'You can hardly expect us to exert ourselves to find another such opening for you. Good-day to you, Miss Hunter.' She struck a gong upon the table, and I was shown out by the page.

"Well, Mr. Holmes, when I got back to my lodgings and found little enough in the cupboard, and two or three bills upon the table, I began to ask myself whether I had not done a very foolish thing. After all, if these people had strange fads and expected obedience on the most extraordinary matters, they were at least ready to pay for their eccentricity. Very few governesses in England are getting £100 a year. Besides, what use was my hair to me? Many people are improved by wearing it short, and perhaps I should be among the number. Next day I was inclined to think that I had made a mistake, and by the day after I was sure of it. I had almost overcome my pride so far as to go back to the agency and inquire whether the place was still open when I received this letter from the gentleman himself. I have it here, and I will read it to you:

"The Copper Beeches, near Winchester.

"DEAR MISS HUNTER:

"Miss Stoper has very kindly given me your address, and I write from here to ask you whether you have reconsidered your decision. My wife is very anxious that you should come, for she has been much attracted by my description of you. We are willing to give £30 a quarter, or £120 a year, so as to recompense you for any little inconvenience which our fads may cause you. They are not very exacting, after all. My wife is fond of a particular shade of electric blue, and would like you to wear such a dress indoors in the morning. You need not, however, go to the expense of purchasing one, as we have one belonging to my dear daughter Alice (now in Philadelphia), which would, I should think, fit you very well. Then, as to sitting here or there, or amusing yourself in any manner indicated, that need cause you no inconvenience. As regards your hair, it is no doubt a pity, especially as I could not help remarking its beauty during our short interview, but I am afraid that I must remain firm upon this point, and I only hope that the increased salary may recompense you for the loss. Your duties, as far as the child is concerned, are very light. Now do try to come, and I shall meet you with the dog-cart at Winchester. Let me know your train.

"Yours faithfully,
"JEPHRO RUCASTLE.

"That is the letter which I have just received, Mr. Holmes, and my mind is made up that I will accept it. I thought, however, that before taking the final step I should like to submit the whole matter to your consideration."

"Well, Miss Hunter, if your mind is made up, that settles the question," said Holmes, smiling.

"But you would not advise me to refuse?"

"I confess that it is not the situation which I should like to see a sister of mine apply for."

"What is the meaning of it all, Mr. Holmes?"

"Ah, I have no data. I cannot tell. Perhaps you have yourself formed some opinion?"

"Well, there seems to me to be only one possible solution. Mr. Rucastle seemed to be a very kind, good-natured man. Is it not possible that his wife is a lunatic, that he desires to keep the matter quiet for fear she should be taken to an asylum, and that he humours her fancies in every way in order to prevent an outbreak?"

"That is a possible solution—in fact, as matters stand, it is the most probable one. But in any case it does not seem to be a nice household for a young lady."

"But the money, Mr. Holmes, the money!"

"Well, yes, of course the pay is good—too good. That is what makes me uneasy. Why should they give you £120 a year, when they could have their pick for £40? There must be some strong reason behind."

"I thought that if I told you the circumstances you would understand afterwards if I wanted your help. I should feel so much stronger if I felt that you were at the back of me."

"Oh, you may carry that feeling away with you. I assure you that your little problem promises to be the most interesting which has come my way for some months. There is something distinctly novel about some of the features. If you should find yourself in doubt or in danger——"

"Danger! What danger do you foresee?"

Holmes shook his head gravely. "It would cease to be a danger if we could define it," said he. "But at any time, day or night, a telegram would bring me down to your help."

"That is enough." She rose briskly from her chair with the anxiety all swept from her face. "I shall go down to Hampshire quite easy in my mind now. I shall write to Mr. Rucastle at once, sacrifice my poor hair to-night, and start for Winchester to-morrow." With a few grateful words to Holmes she bade us both good-night and bustled off upon her way.

"At least," said I as we heard her quick, firm steps descending the stairs, "she seems to be a young lady who is very well able to take care of herself."

"And she would need to be," said Holmes gravely. "I am much mistaken if we do not hear from her before many days are past."

It was not very long before my friend's prediction was fulfilled. A fortnight went by, during which I frequently found my thoughts turning in her direction and wondering what strange side-alley of human experience this lonely woman had strayed into. The unusual salary, the curious conditions, the light duties, all pointed to something abnormal, though whether a fad or a plot, or whether the man were a philanthropist or a villain, it was quite beyond my powers to determine. As to Holmes, I observed that he sat frequently for half an hour on end, with knitted brows and an abstracted air, but he swept the matter away with a wave of his hand when I mentioned it. "Data! data! data!" he cried impatiently. "I can't make bricks without clay." And yet he would always wind up by muttering that no sister of his should ever have accepted such a situation.

The telegram which we eventually received came late one night just as I was thinking of turning in and Holmes was settling down to one of those all-night chemical researches which he frequently indulged in, when I would leave him stooping over a retort and a test-tube at night and find him in the same position when I came down to breakfast in the morning. He opened the yellow envelope, and then, glancing at the message, threw it across to me.

"Just look up the trains in Bradshaw," said he, and turned back to his chemical studies.

The summons was a brief and urgent one.

Please be at the Black Swan Hotel at Winchester at midday to-morrow [it said]. Do come! I am at my wit's end.

HUNTER.

"Will you come with me?" asked Holmes, glancing up.

"I should wish to."

"Just look it up, then."

"There is a train at half-past nine," said I, glancing over my Bradshaw. "It is due at Winchester at 11:30."

"That will do very nicely. Then perhaps I had better postpone my analysis of the acetones, as we may need to be at our best in the morning."

By eleven o'clock the next day we were well upon our way to the old English capital. Holmes had been buried in the morning papers all the way down, but after we had passed the Hampshire border he threw them down and began to admire the scenery. It was an ideal spring day, a light blue sky, flecked with little fleecy white clouds drifting across from west to east. The sun was shining very brightly, and yet there was an exhilarating nip in the air, which set an edge to a man's energy. All over the countryside, away to the rolling hills around Aldershot, the little red and gray roofs of the farm-steadings peeped out from amid the light green of the new foliage.

"Are they not fresh and beautiful?" I cried with all the enthusiasm of a man fresh from the fogs of Baker Street.

But Holmes shook his head gravely.

"Do you know, Watson," said he, "that it is one of the curses of a mind with a turn like mine that I must look at everything with reference to my own special subject. You look at these scattered houses, and you are impressed by their beauty. I look at them, and the only thought which comes to me is a feeling of their isolation and of the impunity with which crime may be committed there."

"Good heavens!" I cried. "Who would associate crime with these dear old homesteads?"

"They always fill me with a certain horror. It is my belief, Watson, founded upon my experience, that the lowest and vilest alleys in London do not present a more dreadful record of sin than does the smiling and beautiful countryside."

"You horrify me!"

"But the reason is very obvious. The pressure of public opinion can do in the town what the law cannot accomplish. There is no lane so vile that the scream of a tortured child, or the thud of a drunkard's blow, does not beget sympathy and indignation among the neighbours, and then the whole machinery of justice is ever so close that a word of complaint can set it going, and there is but a step between the crime and the dock. But look at these lonely houses, each in its own fields, filled for the most part with poor ignorant folk who know little of the law. Think of the deeds of hellish cruelty, the hidden wickedness which may go on, year in, year out, in such places, and none the wiser. Had this lady who appeals to us for help gone to live in Winchester, I should never have had a fear for her. It is the five miles of country which makes the danger. Still, it is clear that she is not personally threatened."

"No. If she can come to Winchester to meet us she can get away."

"Quite so. She has her freedom."

"What *can* be the matter, then? Can you suggest no explanation?"

"I have devised seven separate explanations, each of which would cover the facts as far as we know them. But which of these is correct can only be determined by the fresh information which we shall no doubt find waiting for us. Well, there is the tower of the cathedral, and we shall soon learn all that Miss Hunter has to tell."

The Black Swan is an inn of repute in the High Street, at no distance from the station, and there we found the young lady waiting for us. She had engaged a sitting-room, and our lunch awaited us upon the table.

"I am so delighted that you have come," she said earnestly. "It is so very kind of you both; but indeed I do not know what I should do. Your advice will be altogether invaluable to me."

"Pray tell us what has happened to you."

"I will do so, and I must be quick, for I have promised Mr. Rucastle to be back before three. I got his leave to come into town this morning, though he little knew for what purpose."

"Let us have everything in its due order." Holmes thrust his long thin legs out towards the fire and composed himself to listen.

"In the first place, I may say that I have met, on the whole, with no actual ill-treatment from Mr. and Mrs. Rucastle. It is only fair to them to say that. But I cannot understand them, and I am not easy in my mind about them."

"What can you not understand?"

"Their reasons for their conduct. But you shall have it all just as it occurred. When I came down, Mr. Rucastle met me here and drove me in his dog-cart to the Copper Beeches. It is, as he said, beautifully situated, but it is not beautiful in itself, for it is a large square block of a house, whitewashed, but all stained and streaked with damp and bad weather. There are grounds round it, woods on three sides, and on the fourth a field which slopes down to the Southampton highroad, which curves past about a hundred yards from the front door. This ground in front belongs to the house, but the woods all round are part of Lord Southerton's preserves. A clump of copper beeches immediately in front of the hall door has given its name to the place.

"I was driven over by my employer, who was as amiable as ever, and was introduced by him that evening to his wife and the child. There was no truth, Mr. Holmes, in the conjecture which seemed to us to be probable in your rooms at Baker Street. Mrs. Rucastle is not mad. I found her to be a silent, pale-faced woman, much younger than her husband, not more than thirty, I should think, while he can hardly be less than forty-five. From their conversation I have gathered that they have been married about seven years, that he was a widower, and that his only child by the first wife was the daughter who has gone to Philadelphia. Mr. Rucastle told me in private that the reason why she had left them was that she had an unreasoning aversion to her stepmother. As the daughter could not have been less than twenty, I can quite imagine that her position must have been uncomfortable with her father's young wife.

"Mrs. Rucastle seemed to me to be colourless in mind as well as in feature. She impressed me neither favourably nor the reverse. She was a nonentity. It was easy to see that she was passionately devoted both to her husband and to her little son. Her light gray eyes wandered continually from one to the other, noting every little want and forestalling it if possible. He was kind to her also in his bluff, boisterous fashion, and on the whole they seemed to be a happy couple. And yet she had some secret sorrow, this woman. She would often be lost in deep thought, with the saddest look upon her face. More than once I have surprised her in tears. I have thought sometimes that it was the disposition of her child which weighed upon her mind, for I have never met so utterly spoiled and so ill-natured a little creature. He is small for his age, with a head which is quite disproportionately large. His whole life appears to be spent in an alternation between savage fits of passion and gloomy intervals of sulking. Giving pain to any creature weaker than himself seems to be his one idea of amusement, and he shows quite remarkable talent in planning the capture of mice, little birds, and insects. But I would rather not talk about the creature, Mr. Holmes, and, indeed, he has little to do with my story."

"I am glad of all details," remarked my friend, "whether they seem to you to be relevant or not."

"I shall try not to miss anything of importance. The one unpleasant thing about the house, which struck me at once, was the appearance and conduct of the servants. There are only two, a man and his wife. Toller, for that is his name, is a rough, uncouth man, with grizzled hair and whiskers, and a perpetual smell of drink. Twice since I have been with them he has been quite drunk, and yet Mr. Rucastle seemed to take no notice of it. His wife is a very tall and strong woman with a sour face, as silent as Mrs. Rucastle and much less amiable. They are a most unpleasant couple, but fortunately I spend most of my time in the nursery and my own room, which are next to each other in one corner of the building.

"For two days after my arrival at the Copper Beeches my life was very quiet; on the third, Mrs. Rucastle came down just after breakfast and whispered something to her husband.

"'Oh, yes,' said he, turning to me, 'we are very much obliged to you, Miss Hunter, for falling in with our whims so far as to cut your hair. I assure you that it has not detracted in the tiniest iota from your appearance. We shall now see how the electric-blue dress will become you. You will find it laid out upon the bed in your room, and if you would be so good as to put it on we should both be extremely obliged.'

"The dress which I found waiting for me was of a peculiar shade of blue. It was of excellent material, a sort of beige, but it bore unmistakable signs of having been worn before. It could not have been a better fit if I had been measured for it. Both Mr. and Mrs. Rucastle expressed a delight at the look of it, which seemed quite exaggerated in its vehemence. They were waiting for me in the drawing-room, which is a very large room, stretching along the entire front of the house, with three long windows reaching down to the floor. A chair had been placed close to the central window, with its back turned towards it. In this I was asked to sit, and then Mr. Rucastle, walking up and down on the other side of the room, began to tell me a series of the funniest stories that I have ever listened to. You cannot imagine how comical he was, and I laughed until I was quite weary. Mrs. Rucastle, however, who has evidently no sense of humour, never so much as smiled, but sat with her hands in her lap, and a sad, anxious look upon her face. After an hour or so, Mr. Rucastle suddenly remarked that it was time to commence the duties of the day, and that I might change my dress and go to little Edward in the nursery.

"Two days later this same performance was gone through under exactly similar circumstances. Again I changed my dress, again I sat in the window, and again I laughed very heartily at the funny stories of which my employer had an immense repertoire, and which he told inimitably. Then he handed me a yellow-backed novel, and moving my chair a little sideways, that my own shadow might not fall upon the page, he begged me to read aloud to him. I read for about ten minutes, beginning in the heart of a chapter, and then suddenly, in the middle of a sentence, he ordered me to cease and to change my dress.

"You can easily imagine, Mr. Holmes, how curious I became as to what the meaning of this extraordinary performance could possibly be. They were always very careful, I observed, to turn my face away from the window, so that I became consumed with the desire to see what was going on behind my back. At first it seemed to be impossible, but I soon devised a means. My hand-mirror had been broken, so a happy thought seized me, and I concealed a piece of the glass in my handkerchief. On the next occasion, in the midst of my laughter, I put my handkerchief up to my eyes, and was able with a little management to see all that there was behind me. I confess that I was disappointed. There was nothing. At least that was my first impression. At the second glance, however, I perceived that there was a man standing in the Southampton Road, a small bearded man in a gray suit, who seemed to be looking in my direction. The road is an important highway, and there are usually people there. This man, however, was leaning against the railings which bordered our field and was looking earnestly up. I lowered my handkerchief and glanced at Mrs. Rucastle to find her eyes fixed upon me with a most searching gaze. She said nothing, but I am convinced that she had divined that I had a mirror in my hand and had seen what was behind me. She rose at once.

"'Jephro,' said she, 'there is an impertinent fellow upon the road there who stares up at Miss Hunter.'

"'No friend of yours, Miss Hunter?' he asked.

"'No, I know no one in these parts.'

"'Dear me! How very impertinent! Kindly turn round and motion to him to go away.'

"'Surely it would be better to take no notice.'

"'No, no, we should have him loitering here always. Kindly turn round and wave him away like that.'

"I did as I was told, and at the same instant Mrs. Rucastle drew down the blind. That was a week ago, and from that time I have not sat again in the window, nor have I worn the blue dress, nor seen the man in the road."

"Pray continue," said Holmes. "Your narrative promises to be a most interesting one."

"You will find it rather disconnected, I fear, and there may prove to be little relation between the different incidents of which I speak. On the very first day that I was at the Copper Beeches, Mr. Rucastle took me to a small outhouse which stands near the kitchen door. As we approached it I heard the sharp rattling of a chain, and the sound as of a large animal moving about.

"'Look in here!' said Mr. Rucastle, showing me a slit between two planks. 'Is he not a beauty?'

"I looked through and was conscious of two glowing eyes, and of a vague figure huddled up in the darkness.

"'Don't be frightened,' said my employer, laughing at the start which I had given. 'It's only Carlo, my mastiff. I call him mine, but really old Toller, my groom, is the only man who can do anything with him. We feed him once a day, and not too much then, so that he is always as keen as mustard. Toller lets him loose every night, and God help the trespasser whom he lays his fangs upon. For goodness' sake don't you ever on any pretext set your foot over the threshold at night, for it as much as your life is worth.'

"The warning was no idle one, for two nights later I happened to look out of my bedroom window about two o'clock in the morning. It was a beautiful moonlight night, and the lawn in front of the house was silvered over and almost as bright as day. I was standing, rapt in the peaceful beauty of the scene, when I was aware that something was moving under the shadow of the copper beeches. As it emerged into the moonshine I saw what it was. It was a giant dog, as large as a calf, tawny tinted, with hanging jowl, black muzzle, and huge projecting bones. It walked slowly across the lawn and vanished into the shadow upon the other side. That dreadful sentinel sent a chill to my heart which I do not think that any burglar could have done.

"And now I have a very strange experience to tell you. I had, as you know, cut off my hair in London, and I had placed it in a great coil at the bottom of my trunk. One evening, after the child was in bed, I began to amuse myself by examining the furniture of my room and by rearranging my own little things. There was an old chest of drawers in the room, the two upper ones empty and open, the lower one locked. I had filled the first two with my linen, and as I had still much to pack away I was naturally annoyed at not having the use of the third drawer. It struck me that it might have been fastened by a mere oversight, so I took out my bunch of keys and tried to open it. The very first key fitted to perfection, and I drew the drawer open. There was only one thing in it, but I am sure that you would never guess what it was. It was my coil of hair.

"I took it up and examined it. It was of the same peculiar tint, and the same thickness. But then the impossibility of the thing obtruded itself upon me. How *could* my hair have been locked in the drawer? With trembling hands I undid my trunk, turned out the contents, and drew from the bottom my own hair. I laid the two tresses together, and I assure you that they were identical. Was it not extraordinary? Puzzle as I would, I could make nothing at all of what it meant. I returned the strange hair to the drawer, and I said nothing of the matter to the Rucastles as I felt that I had put myself in the wrong by opening a drawer which they had locked.

"I am naturally observant, as you may have remarked, Mr. Holmes, and I soon had a pretty good plan of the whole house in my head. There was one wing, however, which appeared not to be inhabited at all. A door which faced that which led into the quarters of the Tollers opened into this suite, but it was invariably locked. One day, however, as I ascended the stair, I met Mr. Rucastle coming out through this door, his keys in his hand, and a look on his face which made him a very different person to the round, jovial man to whom I was accustomed. His cheeks were red, his brow was all crinkled with anger, and the veins stood out at his temples with passion. He locked the door and hurried past me without a word or a look.

"This aroused my curiosity; so when I went out for a walk in the grounds with my charge, I strolled round to the side from which I could see the windows of this part of the house. There were four of them in a row, three of which were simply dirty, while the fourth was shuttered up. They were evidently all deserted. As I strolled up and down, glancing at them occasionally, Mr. Rucastle came out to me, looking as merry and jovial as ever.

"'Ah!' said he, 'you must not think me rude if I passed you without a word, my dear young lady. I was preoccupied with business matters.'

"I assured him that I was not offended. 'By the way,' said I, 'you seem to have quite a suite of spare rooms up there, and one of them has the shutters up.'

"He looked surprised and, as it seemed to me, a little startled at my remark.

"'Photography is one of my hobbies,' said he. 'I have made my dark room up there. But, dear me! what an observant young lady we have come upon. Who would have believed it? Who would have ever believed it?' He spoke in a jesting tone, but there was no jest in his eyes as he looked at me. I read suspicion there and annoyance, but no jest.

"Well, Mr. Holmes, from the moment that I understood that there was something about that suite of rooms which I was not to know, I was all on fire to go over them. It was not mere curiosity, though I have my share of that. It was more a feeling of duty—a feeling that some good might come from my penetrating to this place. They talk of woman's instinct; perhaps it was woman's instinct which gave me that feeling. At any rate, it was there, and I was keenly on the lookout for any chance to pass the forbidden door.

"It was only yesterday that the chance came. I may tell you that, besides Mr. Rucastle, both Toller and his wife find something to do in these deserted rooms, and I once saw him carrying a large black linen bag with him through the door. Recently he has been drinking hard, and yesterday evening he was very drunk; and when I came upstairs there was the key in the door. I have no doubt at all that he had left it there. Mr. and Mrs. Rucastle were both downstairs, and the child was with them, so that I had an admirable opportunity. I turned the key gently in the lock, opened the door, and slipped through.

"There was a little passage in front of me, unpapered and uncarpeted, which turned at a right angle at the farther end. Round this corner were three doors in a line, the first and third of which were open. They each led into an empty room, dusty and cheerless, with two windows in the one and one in the other, so thick with dirt that the evening light glimmered dimly through them. The centre door was closed, and across the outside of it had been fastened one of the broad bars of an iron bed, padlocked at one end to a ring in the wall, and fastened at the other with stout cord. The door itself was locked as well, and the key was not there. This barricaded door corresponded clearly with the shuttered window outside, and yet I could see by the glimmer from beneath it that the room was not in darkness. Evidently there was a skylight which let in light from above. As I stood in the passage gazing at the sinister door and wondering what secret it might veil, I suddenly heard the sound of steps within the room and saw a shadow pass backward and forward against the little slit of dim light which shone out from under the door. A mad, unreasoning terror rose up in me at the sight, Mr. Holmes. My overstrung nerves failed me suddenly, and I turned and ran—ran as though some dreadful hand were behind me clutching at the skirt of my dress. I rushed down the passage, through the door, and straight into the arms of Mr. Rucastle, who was waiting outside.

"'So,' said he, smiling, 'it was you, then. I thought that it must be when I saw the door open.'

"'Oh, I am so frightened!' I panted.

"'My dear young lady! my dear young lady!'—you cannot think how caressing and soothing his manner was—'and what has frightened you, my dear young lady?'

"But his voice was just a little too coaxing. He overdid it. I was keenly on my guard against him.

"'I was foolish enough to go into the empty wing,' I answered. 'But it is so lonely and eerie in this dim light that I was frightened and ran out again. Oh, it is so dreadfully still in there!'

"'Only that?' said he, looking at me keenly.

"'Why, what did you think?' I asked.

"'Why do you think that I lock this door?'

"'I am sure that I do not know.'

"'It is to keep people out who have no business there. Do you see?' He was still smiling in the most amiable manner.

"'I am sure if I had known——'

"'Well, then, you know now. And if you ever put your foot over that threshold again'—here in an instant the smile hardened into a grin of rage, and he glared down at me with the face of a demon—'I'll throw you to the mastiff.'

"I was so terrified that I do not know what I did. I suppose that I must have rushed past him into my room. I remember nothing until I found myself lying on my bed trembling all over. Then I thought of you, Mr. Holmes. I could not live there longer without some advice. I was frightened of the house, of the man, of the woman, of the servants, even of the child. They were all horrible to me. If I could only bring you down all would be well. Of course I might have fled from the house, but my curiosity was almost as strong as my fears. My mind was soon made up. I would send you a wire. I put on my hat and cloak, went down to the office, which is about half a mile from the house, and then returned, feeling very much easier. A horrible doubt came into my mind as I approached the door lest the dog might be loose, but I remembered that Toller had drunk himself into a state of insensibility that evening, and I knew that he was the only one in the household who had any influence with the savage creature, or who would venture to set him free. I slipped in in safety and lay awake half the night in my joy at the thought of seeing you. I had no difficulty in getting leave to come into Winchester this morning, but I must be back before three o'clock, for Mr. and Mrs. Rucastle are going on a visit, and will be away all the evening, so that I must look after the child. Now I have told you all my adventures, Mr. Holmes, and I should be very glad if you could tell me what it all means, and, above all, what I should do."

Holmes and I had listened spellbound to this extraordinary story. My friend rose now and paced up and down the room, his hands in his pockets, and an expression of the most profound gravity upon his face.

"Is Toller still drunk?" he asked.

"Yes. I heard his wife tell Mrs. Rucastle that she could do nothing with him."

"That is well. And the Rucastles go out to-night?"

"Yes."

"Is there a cellar with a good strong lock?"

"Yes, the wine-cellar."

"You seem to me to have acted all through this matter like a very brave and sensible girl, Miss Hunter. Do you think that you could perform one more feat? I should not ask it of you if I did not think you a quite exceptional woman."

"I will try. What is it?"

"We shall be at the Copper Beeches by seven o'clock, my friend and I. The Rucastles will be gone by that time, and Toller will, we hope, be incapable. There only remains Mrs. Toller, who might give the alarm. If you could send her into the cellar on some errand, and then turn the key upon her, you would facilitate matters immensely."

"I will do it."

"Excellent! We shall then look thoroughly into the affair. Of course there is only one feasible explanation. You have been brought there to personate someone, and the real person is imprisoned in this chamber. That is obvious. As to who this prisoner is, I have no doubt that it is the daughter, Miss Alice Rucastle, if I remember right, who was said to have gone to America. You were chosen, doubtless, as resembling her in height, figure, and the colour of your hair. Hers had been cut off, very possibly in some illness through which she has passed, and so, of course, yours had to be sacrificed also. By a curious chance you came upon her tresses. The man in the road was undoubtedly some friend of hers—possibly her fiancé—and no doubt, as you wore the girl's dress and were so like her, he was convinced from your laughter, whenever he saw you, and afterwards from your gesture, that Miss Rucastle was perfectly happy, and that she no longer desired his attentions. The dog is let loose at night to prevent him from endeavouring to communicate with her. So much is fairly clear. The most serious point in the case is the disposition of the child."

"What on earth has that to do with it?" I ejaculated.

"My dear Watson, you as a medical man are continually gaining light as to the tendencies of a child by the study of the parents. Don't you see that the converse is equally valid. I have frequently gained my first real insight into the character of parents by studying their children. This child's disposition is abnormally cruel, merely for cruelty's sake, and whether he derives this from his smiling father, as I should suspect, or from his mother, it bodes evil for the poor girl who is in their power."

"I am sure that you are right, Mr. Holmes," cried our client. "A thousand things come back to me which make me certain that you have hit it. Oh, let us lose not an instant in bringing help to this poor creature."

"We must be circumspect, for we are dealing with a very cunning man. We can do nothing until seven o'clock. At that hour we shall be with you, and it will not be long before we solve the mystery."

We were as good as our word, for it was just seven when we reached the Copper Beeches, having put up our trap at a wayside public-house. The group of trees, with their dark leaves shining like burnished metal in the light of the setting sun, were sufficient to mark the house even had Miss Hunter not been standing smiling on the door-step.

"Have you managed it?" asked Holmes.

A loud thudding noise came from somewhere downstairs. "That is Mrs. Toller in the cellar," said she. "Her husband lies snoring on the kitchen rug. Here are his keys, which are the duplicates of Mr. Rucastle's."

"You have done well indeed!" cried Holmes with enthusiasm. "Now lead the way, and we shall soon see the end of this black business."

We passed up the stair, unlocked the door, followed on down a passage, and found ourselves in front of the barricade which Miss Hunter had described. Holmes cut the cord and removed the transverse bar. Then he tried the various keys in the lock, but without success. No sound came from within, and at the silence Holmes's face clouded over.

"I trust that we are not too late," said he. "I think, Miss Hunter, that we had better go in without you. Now, Watson, put your shoulder to it, and we shall see whether we cannot make our way in."

It was an old rickety door and gave at once before our united strength. Together we rushed into the room. It was empty. There was no furniture save a little pallet bed, a small table, and a basketful of linen. The skylight above was open, and the prisoner gone.

"There has been some villainy here," said Holmes; "this beauty has guessed Miss Hunter's intentions and has carried his victim off."

"But how?"

"Through the skylight. We shall soon see how he managed it." He swung himself up onto the roof. "Ah, yes," he cried, "here's the end of a long light ladder against the eaves. That is how he did it."

"But it is impossible," said Miss Hunter; "the ladder was not there when the Rucastles went away."

"He has come back and done it. I tell you that he is a clever and dangerous man. I should not be very much surprised if this were he whose step I hear now upon the stair. I think, Watson, that it would be as well for you to have your pistol ready."

The words were hardly out of his mouth before a man appeared at the door of the room, a very fat and burly man, with a heavy stick in his hand. Miss Hunter screamed and shrunk against the wall at the sight of him, but Sherlock Holmes sprang forward and confronted him.

"You villain!" said he, "where's your daughter?"

The fat man cast his eyes round, and then up at the open skylight.

"It is for me to ask you that," he shrieked, "you thieves! Spies and thieves! I have caught you, have I? You are in my power. I'll serve you!" He turned and clattered down the stairs as hard as he could go.

"He's gone for the dog!" cried Miss Hunter.

"I have my revolver," said I.

"Better close the front door," cried Holmes, and we all rushed down the stairs together. We had hardly reached the hall when we heard the baying of a hound, and then a scream of agony, with a horrible worrying sound which it was dreadful to listen to. An elderly man with a red face and shaking limbs came staggering out at a side door.

"My God!" he cried. "Someone has loosed the dog. It's not been fed for two days. Quick, quick, or it'll be too late!"

Holmes and I rushed out and round the angle of the house, with Toller hurrying behind us. There was the huge famished brute, its black muzzle buried in Rucastle's throat, while he writhed and screamed upon the ground. Running up, I blew its brains out, and it fell over with its keen white teeth still meeting in the great creases of his neck. With much labour we separated them and carried him, living but horribly mangled, into the house. We laid him upon the drawing-room sofa, and having dispatched the sobered Toller to bear the news to his wife, I did what I could to relieve his pain. We were all assembled round him when the door opened, and a tall, gaunt woman entered the room.

"Mrs. Toller!" cried Miss Hunter.

"Yes, miss. Mr. Rucastle let me out when he came back before he went up to you. Ah, miss, it is a pity you didn't let me know what you were planning, for I would have told you that your pains were wasted."

"Ha!" said Holmes, looking keenly at her. "It is clear that Mrs. Toller knows more about this matter than anyone else."

"Yes, sir, I do, and I am ready enough to tell what I know."

"Then, pray, sit down, and let us hear it, for there are several points on which I must confess that I am still in the dark."

"I will soon make it clear to you," said she; "and I'd have done so before now if I could ha' got out from the cellar. If there's police-court business over this, you'll remember that I was the one that stood your friend, and that I was Miss Alice's friend too.

"She was never happy at home, Miss Alice wasn't, from the time that her father married again. She was slighted like and had no say in anything, but it never really became bad for her until after she met Mr. Fowler at a friend's house. As well as I could learn, Miss Alice had rights of her own by will, but she was so quiet and patient, she was, that she never said a word about them, but just left everything in Mr. Rucastle's hands. He knew he was safe with her; but when there was a chance of a husband coming forward, who would ask for all that the law would give him, then her father thought it time to put a stop on it. He wanted her to sign a paper, so that whether she married or not, he could use her money. When she wouldn't do it, he kept on worrying her until she got brain-fever, and for six weeks was at death's door. Then she got better at last, all worn to a shadow, and with her beautiful hair cut off; but that didn't make no change in her young man, and he stuck to her as true as man could be."

"Ah," said Holmes, "I think that what you have been good enough to tell us makes the matter fairly clear, and that I can deduce all that remains. Mr. Rucastle then, I presume, took to this system of imprisonment?"

"Yes, sir."

"And brought Miss Hunter down from London in order to get rid of the disagreeable persistence of Mr. Fowler."

"That was it, sir."

"But Mr. Fowler being a persevering man, as a good seaman should be, blockaded the house, and having met you succeeded by certain arguments, metallic or otherwise, in convincing you that your interests were the same as his."

"Mr. Fowler was a very kind-spoken, free-handed gentleman," said Mrs. Toller serenely.

"And in this way he managed that your good man should have no want of drink, and that a ladder should be ready at the moment when your master had gone out."

"You have it, sir, just as it happened."

"I am sure we owe you an apology, Mrs. Toller," said Holmes, "for you have certainly cleared up everything which puzzled us. And here comes the country surgeon and Mrs. Rucastle, so I think, Watson, that we had best escort Miss Hunter back to Winchester, as it seems to me that our *locus standi* now is rather a questionable one."

And thus was solved the mystery of the sinister house with the copper beeches in front of the door. Mr. Rucastle survived, but was always a broken man, kept alive solely through the care of his devoted wife. They still live with their old servants, who probably know so much of Rucastle's past life that he finds it difficult to part from them. Mr. Fowler and Miss Rucastle were married, by special license, in Southampton the day after their flight, and he is now the holder of a government appointment in the island of Mauritius. As to Miss Violet Hunter, my friend Holmes, rather to my disappointment, manifested no further interest in her when once she had ceased to be the centre of one of his problems, and she is now the head of a private school at Walsall, where I believe that she has met with considerable success.

Arthur Morrison

(1863–1945)

ARTHUR MORRISON created Martin Hewitt, the most important of Sherlock Holmes's immediate successors, because of the Strand's need to find a fictional detective to replace Doyle's great character. (Doyle had tired of Holmes, and tried to end his cases by sending him and his archenemy, Professor Moriarty, to their deaths at Reichenbach Falls.) Arthur Morrison depicted Hewitt as a contrast to Holmes: Instead of being tall and thin, with a hawk-like face, Hewitt was "a stoutish, clean-shaven man, of middle height, and of a cheerful, round countenance." Hewitt ascribed his success to the "judicious use of ordinary faculties," though the admiring narrator, a journalist named Brett, in true Watsonian fashion thinks that the detective's faculties are "very extra-ordinary indeed."

When the cases of Martin Hewitt began appearing, Morrison's most important work, *Tales of Mean Streets*, had just been published. That book and the novel *The Hole in the Wall* made him one of the era's most important chroniclers of slum life. He was also an expert on Chinese and Japanese art, writing several books on those subjects. Though he ceased writing detective fiction early in this century, he became a member of the Detection Club, made up of the most important writers of the 1930s, on its founding in 1930.

Morrison wrote four volumes of stories about Martin Hewitt, as well as *The Dorrington Deed-Box*, an innovative, though flawed, book about a detective who takes on cases so that he may commit crimes himself. The following story, taken from the second Hewitt volume, *Chronicles of Martin Hewitt* (1895), shows Morrison's understated approach to what turns out to be a sensational crime.

24

The Case of the Lost Foreigner

I HAVE ALREADY SAID in more than one place that Hewitt's personal relations with the members of the London police force were of a cordial character. In the course of his work it has frequently been Hewitt's hap to learn of matters on which the police were glad of information, and that information was always passed on at once; and so long as no infringement of regulations or damage to public service were involved, Hewitt could always rely on a return in kind.

It was with a message of a useful sort that Hewitt one day dropped into Vine Street police-station and asked for a particular inspector, who was not in. Hewitt sat and wrote a note, and by way of making conversation said to the inspector on duty, "Anything very startling this way to-day?"

"Nothing *very* startling, perhaps, as yet," the inspector replied. "But one of our chaps picked up rather an odd customer a little while ago. Lunatic of some sort, I should think—in fact, I've sent for the doctor to see him. He's a foreigner—a Frenchman, I believe. He seemed horribly weak and faint; but the oddest thing occurred when one of the men, thinking he might be hungry, brought in some bread. He went into fits of terror at the sight of it, and wouldn't be pacified till they took it away again."

"That was strange."

"Odd, wasn't it? And he *was* hungry too. They brought him some more a little while after, and he didn't funk it a bit,—pitched into it, in fact, like anything, and ate it all with some cold beef. It's the way with some lunatics—never the same five minutes together. He keeps crying like a baby, and saying things we can't understand. As it happens, there's nobody in just now who speaks French."

"I speak French," Hewitt replied. "Shall I try him?"

"Certainly, if you will. He's in the men's room below. They've been making him as comfortable as possible by the fire until the doctor comes. He's a long time. I expect he's got a case on."

Hewitt found his way to the large mess-room, where three or four policemen in their shirt-sleeves were curiously regarding a young man of very disordered appearance who sat on a chair by the fire. He was pale, and exhibited marks of bruises on his face, while over one eye was a scarcely healed cut. His figure was small and slight, his coat was torn, and he sat with a certain indefinite air of shivering suffering. He started and looked round apprehensively as Hewitt entered. Hewitt bowed smilingly, wished him good-day, speaking in French, and asked him if he spoke the language.

The man looked up with a dull expression, and after an effort or two, as of one who stutters, burst out with, "*Je le nie!*"

"That's strange," Hewitt observed to the men. "I ask him if he speaks French, and he says he denies it—speaking *in* French."

"He's been saying that very often, sir," one of the men answered, "as well as other things we can't make anything of."

Hewitt placed his hand kindly on the man's shoulder and asked his name. The reply was for a little while an inarticulate gurgle, presently merging into a meaningless medley of words and syllables—"*Qu'est ce qu'—il n'a*—Leystar Squarr—*sacré nom*—not spik it—*quel chemin*—sank you ver' mosh—*je le nie! je le nie!*' He paused, stared, and then, as though realizing his helplessness, he burst into tears.

"He's been a-cryin' two or three times," said the man who had spoken before. "He was a-cryin' when we found him."

Several more attempts Hewitt made to communicate with the man, but though he seemed to comprehend what was meant, he replied with nothing but meaningless gibber, and finally gave up the attempt, and, leaning against the side of the fireplace, buried his head in the bend of his arm.

Then the doctor arrived and made *his* examination. While it was in progress Hewitt took aside the policeman who had been speaking before and questioned him further. He had himself found the Frenchman in a dull back street by Golden Square, where the man was standing helpless and trembling, apparently quite bewildered and very weak. He had brought him in, without having been able to learn anything about him. One or two shopkeepers in the street where he was found were asked, but knew nothing of him—indeed, had never seen him before.

"But the curiousest thing," the policeman proceeded, "was in this 'ere room, when I brought him a loaf to give him a bit of a snack, seein' he looked so weak an' 'ungry. You'd 'a thought we was a-goin' to poison 'im. He fair screamed at the very sight o' the bread, an' he scrouged his-self up in that corner an' put his hands in front of his face. I couldn't make out what was up at first—didn't tumble to it's bein' the bread he was frightened of, seein' as he looked like a man as 'ud be frightened at anything else afore *that*. But the nearer I came with it the more he yelled, so I took it away an' left it outside, an' then he calmed down. An' s'elp me, when I cut some bits off that there very loaf an' brought 'em in, with a bit o' beef, he just went for 'em like one o'clock. *He* wasn't frightened o' no bread then, you bet. Rum thing, how the fancies takes 'em when they're a bit touched, ain't it? All one way one minute, all the other the next."

"Yes, it is. By the way, have you another uncut loaf in the place?"

"Yes, sir. Half a dozen if you like."

"One will be enough. I am going over to speak to the doctor. Wait awhile until he seems very quiet and fairly comfortable; then bring a loaf in quietly and put it on the table, not far from his elbow. Don't attract his attention to what you are doing."

The doctor stood looking thoughtfully down on the Frenchman, who, for his part, stared gloomily, but tranquilly, at the fire-place. Hewitt stepped quietly over to the doctor and, without disturbing the man by the fire, said interrogatively, "Aphasia?"

The doctor tightened his lips, frowned, and nodded significantly. "Motor," he murmured, just loudly enough for Hewitt to hear; "and there's a general nervous break-down as well, I should say. By the way, perhaps there's no agraphia. Have you tried him with pen and paper?"

Pen and paper were brought and set before the man. He was told, slowly and distinctly, that he was among friends, whose only object was to restore him to his proper health. Would he write his name and address, and any other information he might care to give about himself, on the paper before him?

The Frenchman took the pen and stared at the paper; then slowly, and with much hesitation, he traced these marks:—

The man paused after the last of these futile characters, and his pen stabbed into the paper with a blot, as he dazedly regarded his work. Then with a groan he dropped it, and his face sank again into the bend of his arm.

The doctor took the paper and handed it to Hewitt. "Complete agraphia, you see," he said. "He can't write a word. He begins to write 'Monsieur' from sheer habit in beginning letters thus; but the word tails off into a scrawl. Then his attempts become mere scribble, with just a trace of some familiar word here and there—but quite meaningless all."

Although he had never before chanced to come across a case of aphasia (happily a rare disease), Hewitt was acquainted with its general nature. He knew that it might arise either from some physical injury to the brain, or from a break-down consequent on some terrible nervous strain. He knew that in the case of motor aphasia the sufferer, though fully conscious of all that goes on about him, and though quite under-standing what is said to him is entirely powerless to put his own thoughts into spoken words—has lost, in fact, the connection between words and their spoken symbols. Also that in most bad cases agraphia—the loss of ability to write words with any reference to their meaning—is commonly an accompaniment.

"You will have him taken to the infirmary, I suppose?" Hewitt asked.

"Yes," the doctor replied. "I shall go and see about it at once."

The man looked up again as they spoke. The policeman had, in accordance with Hewitt's request, placed a loaf of bread on the table near him, and now as he looked up he caught sight of it. He started vis-ibly and paled, but gave no such signs of abject terror as the policeman had previously observed. He appeared nervous and uneasy, however, and presently reached stealthily toward the loaf. Hewitt continued to talk to the doctor, while closely watching the Frenchman's behaviour from the corner of his eye.

The loaf was what is called a "plain cottage," of solid and regular shape. The man reached it and immediately turned it bottom up on the table. Then he sank back in his chair with a more contented expres-sion, though his gaze was still directed toward the loaf. The policeman grinned silently at this curious manœuvre.

The doctor left, and Hewitt accompanied him to the door of the room. "He will not be moved just yet, I take it?" Hewitt asked as they parted.

"It may take an hour or two," the doctor replied. "Are you anxious to keep him here?"

"Not for long; but I think there's a curious inside to the case, and I may perhaps learn something of it by a little watching. But I can't spare very long."

At a sign from Hewitt the loaf was removed. Then Hewitt pulled the small table closer to the Frenchman and pushed the pen and sheets of paper toward him. The manœuvre had its result. The man looked up and down the room vacantly once or twice and then began to turn the papers over. From that he went to dipping the pen in the inkpot, and presently he was scribbling at random on the loose sheets. Hewitt affected to leave him entirely alone, and seemed to be absorbed in a contemplation of a photograph of a police-division brass band that hung on the wall, but he saw every scratch the man made.

At first there was nothing but meaningless scrawls and attempted words. Then rough sketches appeared, of a man's head, a chair or what not. On the mantelpiece stood a small clock—apparently a sort of humble presentation piece, the body of the clock being set in a horse-shoe frame, with crossed whips behind it. After a time the Frenchman's eyes fell on this, and he began a crude sketch of it. That he relin-

quished, and went on with other random sketches and scribblings on the same piece of paper, sketching and scribbling over the sketches in a half-mechanical sort of way, as of one who trifles with a pen during a brown study. Beginning at the top left-hand corner of the paper, he travelled all round it till he arrived at the left-hand bottom corner. Then dashing his pen hastily across his last sketch he dropped it, and with a great shudder turned away again and hid his face by the fireplace.

Hewitt turned at once and seized the papers on the table. He stuffed them all into his coat-pocket, with the exception of the last which the man had been engaged on, and this, a facsimile of which is subjoined, he studied earnestly for several minutes.

Hewitt wished the men good-day, and made his way to the inspector.

"Well," the inspector said, "not much to be got out of him, is there? The doctor will be sending for him presently."

"I fancy," said Hewitt, "that this may turn out a very important case. Possibly—quite possibly—I may not have guessed correctly, and so I won't tell you anything of it till I know a little more. But what I want now is a messenger. Can I send somebody at once in a cab to my friend Brett at his chambers?"

"Certainly. I'll find somebody. Want to write a note?"

Hewitt wrote and despatched a note, which reached me in less than ten minutes. Then he asked the inspector, "Have you searched the Frenchman?"

"Oh, yes. We went all over him, when we found he couldn't explain himself, to see if we could trace his friends or his address. He didn't seem to mind. But there wasn't a single thing in his pocket—not a single thing, barring a rag of a pocket-handkerchief with no marking on it."

"You noticed that somebody had stolen his watch, I suppose?"

"Well, he hadn't got one."

"But he had one of those little vertical buttonholes in his waistcoat, used to fasten a watchguard to, and it was much worn and frayed, so that he must be in the habit of carrying a watch; and it is gone."

"Yes, and everything else too, eh? Looks like robbery. He's had a knock or two in the face—notice that?"

"I saw the bruises and the cut, of course; and his collar has been broken away, with the back button; somebody has taken him by the collar or throat. Was he wearing a hat when he was found?"

"No."

"That would imply that he had only just left a house. What street was he found in?"

"Henry Street—a little off Golden Square. Low street, you know."

"Did the constable notice a door open near by?"

The inspector shook his head. "Half the doors in the street are open," he said, "pretty nearly all day."

"Ah, then there's nothing in that. I don't think he lives there, by the bye. I fancy he comes from more in the Seven Dials or Drury Lane direction. Did you notice anything about the man that gave you a clue to his occupation—or at any rate to his habits?"

"Can't say I did."

"Well, just take a look at the back of his coat before he goes away—just over the loins. Good-day."

As I have said, Hewitt's messenger was quick. I happened to be in—having lately returned from a latish lunch—when he arrived with this note:—

"MY DEAR B.,—

I meant to have lunched with you to-day, but have been kept. I expect you are idle this afternoon, and I have a case that will interest you—perhaps be useful to you from a journalistic point of view. If you care to see anything of it, cab away *at once* to Fitzroy Square, south side, where I'll meet you. I will wait no later than 3.30.

Yours,
M. H."

I had scarce a quarter of an hour, so I seized my hat and left my chambers at once. As it happened, my cab and Hewitt's burst into Fitzroy Square from opposite sides almost at the same moment, so that we lost no time.

"Come," said Hewitt, taking my arm and marching me off, "we are going to look for some stabling. Try to feel as though you'd just set up a brougham and had come out to look for a place to put it in. I fear we may have to delude some person with that belief presently."

"Why—what do you want stables for? And why make me your excuse?"

"As to what I want the stables for—really I'm not altogether sure myself. As to making you an excuse—well, even the humblest excuse is better than none. But come, here are some stables. Not good enough, though, even if any of them were empty. Come on."

We had stopped for an instant at the entrance to a small alley of rather dirty stables, and Hewitt, paying apparently but small attention to the stables themselves, had looked sharply about him with his gaze in the air.

"I know this part of London pretty well," Hewitt observed, "and I can only remember one other range of stabling near by; we must try that. As a matter of fact, I'm coming here on little more than conjecture, though I shall be surprised if there isn't something in it. Do you know anything of aphasia?"

"I have heard of it, of course, though I can't say I remember ever knowing a case."

"I've seen one to-day—very curious case. The man's a Frenchman discovered helpless in the street by a policeman. The only thing he can say that has any meaning in it at all is '*je le nie*,' and that he says mechanically, without in the least knowing what he is saying. And he can't write. But he got sketching and scrawling various things on some paper, and his scrawls—together with another thing or two—have given me an idea. We're following it up now. When we are less busy, and in a quiet place, I'll show you the sketches and explain things generally; there's no time now, and I *may* want your help for a bit, in which case ignorance may prevent you spoiling things, you clumsy ruffian. Hullo! here we are, I think!"

We had stopped at the end of another stable-yard, rather dirtier than the first. The stables were sound but inelegant sheds, and one or two appeared to be devoted to other purposes, having low chimneys, on one of which an old basket was rakishly set by way of cowl. Beside the entrance a worn-out old board was nailed, with the legend, "Stabling to Let," in letters formerly white on a ground formerly black.

"Come," said Hewitt, "we'll explore."

We picked our way over the greasy cobble-stones and looked about us. On the left was the wall enclosing certain back-yards, and on the right the stables. Two doors in the middle of these were open, and a butcher's young man, who with his shiny bullet head would have been known for a butcher's young man anywhere, was wiping over the new-washed wheel of a smart butcher's cart.

"Good-day," Hewitt said pleasantly to the young man. "I notice there's some stabling to let here. Now, where should I inquire about it?"

"Jones, Whitfield Street," the young man answered, giving the wheel a final spin. "But there's only one little place to let now, I think, and it ain't very grand."

"Oh, which is that?"

"Next but one to the street there. A chap 'ad it for wood-choppin', but 'e chucked it. There ain't room for more'n a donkey an' a barrow."

"Ah, that's a pity. We're not particular, but want something big enough, and we don't mind paying a fair price. Perhaps we might make an arrangement with somebody here who has a stable?"

The young man shook his head.

"I shouldn't think so," he said doubtfully; "they're mostly shop-people as wants all the room theirselves. My guv'nor couldn't do nothink, I know. These 'ere two stables ain't scarcely enough for all 'e wants as it is. Then there's Barkett the greengrocer 'ere next door. *That* ain't no good. Then, next to that, there's the little place as is to let, and at the end there's Griffith's at the butter-shop."

"And those the other way?"

"Well, this 'ere first one's Curtis's, Euston Road—that's a butter-shop, too, an' 'e 'as the next after that. The last one, up at the end—I dunno quite whose that is. It ain't been long took, but I b'lieve it's some foreign baker's. I ain't ever see anythink come out of it, though; but there's a 'orse there, I know—I seen the feed took in."

Hewitt turned thoughtfully away.

"Thanks," he said. "I suppose we can't manage it, then. Good-day."

We walked to the street as the butcher's young man wheeled in his cart and flung away his pail of water.

"Will you just hang about here, Brett," he asked, "while I hurry round to the nearest iron-monger's? I shan't be gone long. We're going to work a little burglary. Take note if anybody comes to that stable at the farther end."

He hurried away and I waited. In a few moments the butcher's young man shut his doors and went whistling down the street, and in a few moments more Hewitt appeared.

"Come," he said, "there's nobody about now; we'll lose no time. I've bought a pair of pliers and a few nails."

We re-entered the yard at the door of the last stable. Hewitt stooped and examined the padlock. Taking a nail in his pliers he bent it carefully against the brick wall. Then using the nail as a key, still held by the pliers, and working the padlock gently in his left hand, in an astonishingly few seconds he had released the hasp and taken off the padlock. "I'm not altogether a bad burglar," he remarked. "Not so bad, really."

The padlock fastened a bar which, when removed, allowed the door to be opened. Opening it, Hewitt immediately seized a candle stuck in a bottle which stood on a shelf, pulled me in, and closed the door behind us.

"We'll do this by candle-light," he said, as he struck a match. "If the door were left open it would be seen from the street. Keep your ears open in case anybody comes down the yard."

The part of the shed that we stood in was used as a coach-house, and was occupied by a rather shabby tradesman's cart, the shafts of which rested on the ground. From the stall adjoining came the sound of the shuffling and trampling of an impatient horse.

We turned to the cart. On the name-board at the side were painted in worn letters the words, "Schuyler, Baker." The address, which had been below, was painted out.

Hewitt took out the pins and let down the tail-board. Within the cart was a new bed-mattress which covered the whole surface at the bottom. I felt it, pressed it from the top, and saw that it was an ordinary spring mattress—perhaps rather unusually soft in the springs. It seemed a curious thing to keep in a baker's cart.

Hewitt, who had set the candle on a convenient shelf, plunged his arm into the farthermost recesses of the cart and brought forth a very long French loaf, and then another. Diving again he produced certain loaves of the sort known as the "plain cottage"—two sets of four each, each set baked together in a row. "Feel this bread," said Hewitt, and I felt it. It was stale—almost as hard as wood.

Hewitt produced a large pocket-knife, and with what seemed to me to be superfluous care and elaboration, cut into the top of one of the cottage loaves. Then he inserted his fingers in the gap he had made and firmly but slowly tore the hard bread into two pieces. He pulled away the crumb from within till there was nothing left but a rather thick outer shell.

"No," he said, rather to himself than to me, "there's nothing in *that*." He lifted one of the very long French loaves and measured it against the interior of the cart. It had before been propped diagonally, and now it was noticeable that it was just a shade longer than the inside of the cart was wide. Jammed in, in fact, it held firmly. Hewitt produced his knife again, and divided this long loaf in the centre; there was nothing but bread in *that*. The horse in the stall fidgeted more than ever.

"That horse hasn't been fed lately, I fancy," Hewitt said. "We'll give the poor chap a bit of this hay in the corner."

"But," I said, "what about this bread? What did you expect to find in it? I can't see what you're driving at."

"I'll tell you," Hewitt replied, "I'm driving after something I expect to find, and close at hand here, too. How are your nerves to-day—pretty steady? The thing may try them."

Before I could reply there was a sound of footsteps in the yard outside, approaching. Hewitt lifted his finger instantly for silence and whispered hurriedly, "There's only one. If he comes *here*, we grab him."

The steps came nearer and stopped outside the door. There was a pause, and then a slight drawing in of breath, as of a person suddenly surprised. At that moment the door was slightly shifted ajar and an eye peeped in.

"Catch him!" said Hewitt aloud, as we sprang to the door. "He mustn't get away!"

I had been nearer the doorway, and was first through it. The stranger ran down the yard at his best, but my legs were the longer, and half-way to the street I caught him by the shoulder and swung him round. Like lightning he whipped out a knife, and I flung in my left instantly on the chance of flooring him. It barely checked him, however, and the knife swung short of my chest by no more than two inches; but Hewitt had him by the wrist and tripped him forward on his face. He struggled like a wild beast, and Hewitt had to stand on his forearm and force up his wrist till the bones were near breaking before he dropped his knife. But throughout the struggle the man never shouted, called for help, nor, indeed, made the slightest sound, and we on our part were equally silent. It was quickly over, of course, for he was on his face, and we were two. We dragged our prisoner into the stable and closed the door behind us. So far as we had seen, nobody had witnessed the capture from the street, though, of course, we had been too busy to be certain.

"There's a set of harness hanging over at the back," said Hewitt; "I think we'll tie him up with the traces and reins—nothing like leather. We don't need a gag; I know he won't shout."

While I got the straps Hewitt held the prisoner by a peculiar neck-and-wrist grip that forbade him to move except at the peril of a snapped arm. He had probably never been a person of pleasant aspect, being short, strongly and squatly built, large and ugly of feature, and wild and dirty of hair and beard. And now, his face flushed with struggling and smeared with mud from the stable-yard, his nose bleeding and his forehead exhibiting a growing bump, he looked particularly repellent. We strapped his elbows together behind, and as he sullenly ignored a demand for the contents of his pockets Hewitt unceremoniously turned them out. Helpless as he was, the man struggled to prevent this, though, of course, ineffectually. There were papers, tobacco, a bunch of keys, and various odds and ends. Hewitt was glancing hastily at the papers when, suddenly dropping them, he caught the prisoner by the shoulder and pulled him away from a partly-consumed hay-truss which stood in a corner, and toward which he had quietly sidled.

"Keep him still," said Hewitt; "we haven't examined this place yet." And he commenced to pull away the hay from the corner.

Presently a large piece of sackcloth was revealed, and this being lifted left visible below it another batch of loaves of the same sort as we had seen in the cart. There were a dozen of them in one square batch, and the only thing about them that differed them from those in the cart was their position, for the batch lay bottom side up.

"That's enough, I think," Hewitt said. "Don't touch them, for Heaven's sake!" He picked up the papers he had dropped. "That has saved us a little search," he continued. "See here, Brett; I was in the act of telling you my suspicions when this little affair interrupted me. If you care to look at one or two of these letters you'll see what I should have told you. It's Anarchism and bombs, of course. I'm about as certain as I can be that there's a reversible dynamite bomb inside each of those innocent loaves, though I assure you I don't mean meddling with them now. But see here. Will you go and bring in a four-wheeler? Bring it right down the yard. There's more to do, and we mustn't attract attention."

I hurried away and found the cab. The meaning of the loaves, the cart, and the spring-mattress was now plain. There was an Anarchist plot to carry out a number of explosions probably simultaneously, in different parts of the city. I had, of course, heard much of the terrible "reversing" bombs—those bombs which, containing a tube of acid plugged by wadding, required no fuse, and only needed to be inverted to be set going to explode in a few minutes. The loaves containing these bombs would form an effectual "blind," and they were to be distributed, probably in broad daylight, in the most natural manner possible, in a baker's cart. A man would be waiting near the scene of each contemplated explosion. He would be given a loaf taken from the inverted batch. He would take it—perhaps wrapped in paper, but still inverted, and apparently the most innocent object possible—to the spot selected, deposit it, right side up—which would reverse the inner tube and set up the action—in some quiet corner, behind a door or what not, and make his own escape, while the explosion tore down walls and—if the experiment were lucky—scattered the flesh and bones of unsuspecting people.

The infernal loaves were made and kept reversed, to begin with, in order to stand more firmly, and—if observed—more naturally, when turned over to explode. Even if a child picked up the loaf and carried it off, that child at least would be blown to atoms, which at any rate would have been something for the conspirators to congratulate themselves upon. The spring-mattress, of course, was to ease the jolting to the bombs, and obviate any random jerking loose of the acid, which might have had the deplorable result of sacrificing the valuable life of the conspirator who drove the cart. The other loaves, too, with no explosive contents, had their use. The two long ones, which fitted across the inside of the cart, would be jammed across so as to hold the bombs in the centre, and the others would be used to pack the batch on the other sides and prevent any dangerous slipping about. The thing seemed pretty plain, except that as yet I had no idea of how Hewitt learned anything of the business.

I brought the four-wheeler up to the door of the stable and we thrust the man into it, and Hewitt locked the stable door with its proper key. Then we drove off to Tottenham Court Road police-station, and, by Hewitt's order, straight into the yard.

In less than ten minutes from our departure from the stable our prisoner was finally secured, and Hewitt was deep in consultation with police officials. Messengers were sent and telegrams despatched, and presently Hewitt came to me with information.

"The name of the helpless Frenchman the police found this morning," he said, "appears to be Gérard—at least I am almost certain of it. Among the papers found on the prisoner—whose full name doesn't appear, but who seems to be spoken of as Luigi (he is Italian)—among the papers, I say, is a sort of notice convening a meeting for this evening to decide as to the 'final punishment' to be awarded the 'traitor Gérard, now in charge of comrade Pingard.'

"The place of meeting is not mentioned, but it seems more than probable that it will be at the Bakunin Club, not five minutes' walk from this place. The police have all these places under quiet observation, of course, and that is the club at which apparently important Anarchist meetings have been held lately. It is the only club that has never been raided as yet, and, it would seem, the only one they would feel at all safe in using for anything important.

"Moreover, Luigi just now simply declined to open his mouth when asked where the meeting was to be, and said nothing when the names of several other places were suggested, but suddenly found his tongue at the mention of the Bakunin Club, and denied vehemently that the meeting was to be there—it was the only thing he uttered. So that it seems pretty safe to assume that it *is* to be there. Now, of course, the matter's very serious. Men have been despatched to take charge of the

stable very quietly, and the club is to be taken possession of at once—
also very quietly. It must be done without a moment's delay, and as
there is a chance that the only detective officers within reach at the
moment may be known by sight, I have undertaken to get in first.
Perhaps you'll come? We may have to take the door with a rush."

Of course I meant to miss nothing if I could help it, and said so.

"Very well," replied Hewitt, "we'll get ourselves up a bit." He began
taking off his collar and tie. "It is getting dusk," he proceeded, "and we
shan't want old clothes to make ourselves look sufficiently shabby.
We're both wearing bowler hats, which is lucky. Make a dent in
yours—if you can do so without permanently damaging it."

We got rid of our collars and made chokers of our ties. We turned our
coat-collars up at one side only, and then, with dented hats worn raff-
ishly, and our hands in our pockets, we looked disreputable enough for
all practical purposes in twilight. A cordon of plain-clothes police had
already been forming round the club, we were told, and so we sallied
forth. We turned into Windmill Street, crossed Whitfield Street, and in
a turning or two we came to the Bakunin Club. I could see no sign of
anything like a ring of policemen, and said so. Hewitt chuckled. "Of
course not," he said; "they don't go about a job of this sort with drums
beating and flags flying. But they are all there, and some are watching
us. There is the house. I'll negotiate."

The house was one of the very shabby *passé* sort that abound in that
quarter. The very narrow area was railed over, and almost choked with
rubbish. Visible above it were three floors, the lowest indicated by the
door and one window, and the other two by two windows each—mean
and dirty all. A faint light appeared in the top floor, and another from
somewhere behind the refuse-heaped area. Everywhere else was in
darkness. Hewitt looked intently into the area, but it was impossible to
discern anything behind the sole grimy patch of window that was visible. Then we stepped lightly up the three or four steps to the door and
rang the bell.

We could hear slippered feet mounting a stair and approaching. A
latch was shifted, a door opened six inches, an indistinct face appeared,
and a female voice asked, "*Qui est là?*"

"*Deux camarades*," Hewitt grunted testily. "*Ouvrez vite.*"

I had noticed that the door was kept from opening further by a short
chain. This chain the woman unhooked from the door, but still kept
the latter merely ajar, as though intending to assure herself still further.
But Hewitt immediately pushed the door back, planted his foot against
it, and entered, asking carelessly as he did so, "*Où se trouve Luigi?*"

I followed on his heels, and in the dark could just distinguish that Hewitt pushed the woman instantly against the wall and clapped his hand to her mouth. At the same moment a file of quiet men were suddenly visible ascending the steps at my heels. They were the police.

The door was closed behind us almost noiselessly, and a match was struck. Two men stood at the bottom of the stairs, and the others searched the house. Only two men were found—both in a top room. They were secured and brought down.

The woman was now ungagged, and she used her tongue at a great rate. One of the men was a small, meek-looking slip of a fellow, and he appeared to be the woman's husband. "Eh, messieurs le police," she exclaimed vehemently, "it ees not of 'im, mon pauvre Pierre, zat you sall rrun in. 'Im and me—we are not of the clob—we work only—we housekeep."

Hewitt whispered to an officer, and the two men were taken below. Then Hewitt spoke to the woman, whose protests had not ceased. "You say you are not of the club," he said, "but what is there to prove that? If you are but housekeepers, as you say, you have nothing to fear. But you can only prove it by giving the police information. For instance, now, about Gérard. What have they done with him?"

"Jean Pingard—'im you 'ave take downstairs—'e 'ave lose 'im. Jean Pingard get last night all a-boosa—all dronk like zis"—she rolled her head and shoulders to express intoxication—"and he sleep too much to-day, when Émile go out, and Gérard, he go too, and nobody know. I will tell you anysing. We are not of the clob—we housekeep, me and Pierre."

"But what did they do to Gérard before he went away?"

The woman was ready and anxious to tell anything. Gérard had been selected to do something—what it was exactly she did not know, but there was a horse and cart, and he was to drive it. Where the horse and cart was also she did not know, but Gérard had driven a cart before in his work for a baker, and he was to drive one in connection with some scheme among the members of the club. But *le pauvre Gérard* at the last minute disliked to drive the cart; he had fear. He did not say he had fear, but he prepared a letter—a letter that was not signed. The letter was to be sent to the police, and it told them the whereabouts of the horse and cart, so that the police might seize these things, and then there would be nothing for Gérard, who had fear, to do in the way of driving. No, he did not betray the names of the comrades, but he told the place of the horse and the cart.

Nevertheless, the letter was never sent. There was suspicion, and the letter was found in a pocket and read. Then there was a meeting, and Gérard was confronted with his letter. He could say nothing but "*Je le nie!*"—found no explanation but that. There was much noise, and she had observed from a staircase, from which one might see through a ventilating hole, Gérard had much fear—very much fear. His face was white, and it moved; he prayed for mercy, and they talked of killing him. It was discussed how he should be killed, and the poor Gérard was more terrified. He was made to take off his collar, and a razor was drawn across his throat, though without cutting him, till he fainted.

Then water was flung over him, and he was struck in the face till he revived. He again repeated, "*Je le nie! je le nie!*" and nothing more. Then one struck him with a bottle, and another with a stick; the point of a knife was put against his throat and held there, but this time he did not faint, but cried softly, as a man who is drunk, "*Je le nie! je le nie!*" So they tied a handkerchief about his neck, and twisted it till his face grew purple and black, and his eyes were round and terrible, and then they struck his face, and he fainted again. But they took away the handkerchief, having fear that they could not easily get rid of the body if he were killed, for there was no preparation. So they decided to meet again and discuss when there would be preparation. Wherefore they took him away to the rooms of Jean Pingard—of Jean and Émile Pingard—in Henry Street, Golden Square. But Émile Pingard had gone out, and Jean was drunk and slept, and they lost him. Jean Pingard was he downstairs—the taller of the two; the other was but *le pauvre Pierre*, who, with herself, was not of the club. They worked only; they were the keepers of the house. There was nothing for which they should be arrested, and she would give the police any information they might ask.

"As I thought, you see," Hewitt said to me, "the man's nerves have broken down under the terror and the strain, and aphasia is the result. I think I told you that the only articulate thing he could say was '*Je le nie!*' and now we know how those words were impressed on him till he now pronounces them mechanically, with no idea of their meaning. Come, we can do no more here now. But wait a moment."

There were footsteps outside. The light was removed, and a policeman went to the door and opened it as soon as the bell rang. Three men stepped in one after another, and the door was immediately shut behind them—they were prisoners.

We left quietly, and although we, of course, expected it, it was not till the next morning that we learned absolutely that the largest arrest of

Anarchists ever made in this country was made at the Bakunin Club
that night. Each man as he came was admitted—and collared.

⁂   ⁂   ⁂

We made our way to Luzatti's, and it was over our dinner that Hewitt
put me in full possession of the earlier facts of this case, which I have
set down as impersonal narrative in their proper place at the beginning.

"But," I said, "what of that aimless scribble you spoke of that Gérard
made in the police-station? Can I see it?"

Hewitt turned to where his coat hung behind him and took a handful of papers from his pocket.

"Most of these," he said, "mean nothing at all. *That* is what he wrote
at first," and he handed me the first of the two papers which were presented in facsimile in the earlier part of this narrative.

"You see," he said, "he has begun mechanically from long use to
write 'monsieur'—the usual beginning of a letter. But he scarcely
makes three letters before tailing off into sheer scribble. He tries again
and again, and although once there is something very like 'que,' and
once something like a word preceded by a negative 'n,' the whole thing
is meaningless.

"This" (he handed me the other paper which has been printed in
facsimile) "*does* mean something, though Gérard never intended it.
Can you spot the meaning? Really, I think it's pretty plain—especially
now that you know as much as I about the day's adventures. The thing
at the top left-hand corner, I may tell you, Gérard intended for a sketch
of a clock on the mantelpiece in the police-station."

I stared hard at the paper, but could make nothing whatever of it. "I
only see the horse-shoe clock," I said, "and a sort of second, unsuccessful attempt to draw it again. Then there is a horse-shoe dotted, but
scribbled over, and then a sort of kite or balloon on a string, a
Highlander, and—well, I don't understand it, I confess. Tell me."

"I'll explain what I learned from that," Hewitt said, "and also what
led me to look for it. From what the inspector told me, I judged the
man to be in a very curious state, and I took a fancy to see him. Most I
was curious to know why he should have a terror of bread at one
moment and eat it ravenously at another. When I saw him I felt pretty
sure that he was not mad, in the common sense of the term. As far as I
could judge it seemed to be a case of aphasia.

"Then when the doctor came I had a chat (as I have already told
you) with the policeman who found the man. He told me about the
incident of the bread with rather more detail than I had had from the
inspector. Thus it was plain that the man was terrified at the bread only

when it was in the form of a loaf, and ate it eagerly when it was cut into pieces. That was *one* thing to bear in mind. He was not afraid of *bread*, but only of a *loaf*.

"Very well. I asked the policeman to find another uncut loaf, and to put it near the man when his attention was diverted. Meantime the doctor reported that my suspicion as to aphasia was right. The man grew more comfortable, and was assured that he was among friends and had nothing to fear, so that when at length he found the loaf near his elbow he was not so violently terrified, only very uneasy. I watched him and saw him turn it bottom up—a very curious thing to do; he immediately became less uneasy—the turning over of the loaf seemed to have set his mind at rest in some way. This was more curious still. I thought for some little while before accepting the bomb theory as the most probable.

"The doctor left, and I determined to give the man another chance with pen and paper. I felt pretty certain that if he were allowed to scribble and sketch as he pleased, sooner or later he would do something that would give me some sort of a hint. I left him entirely alone and let him do as he pleased, but I watched.

"After all the futile scribble which you have seen, he began to sketch, first a man's head, then a chair—just what he might happen to see in the room. Presently he took to the piece of paper you have before you. He observed that clock and began to sketch it, then went on to other things, such as you see, scribbling idly over most of them when finished. When he had made the last of the sketches he made a hasty scrawl of his pen over it and broke down. It had brought his terror to his mind again somehow.

"I seized the paper and examined it closely. Now just see. Ignore the clock, which was merely a sketch of a thing before him, and look at the three things following. What are they? A horse-shoe, a captive balloon, and a Highlander. Now, can't you think of something those three things in that order suggest?"

I could think of nothing whatever, and I confessed as much.

"Think, now. Tottenham Court Road!"

I started. "Of course," I said. "That never struck me. There's the Horse-shoe Hotel, with the sign outside, there's the large toy and fancy shop half-way up, where they have a captive balloon moored to the roof as an advertisement, and there's the tobacco and snuff shop on the left, toward the other end, where they have a life-size wooden Highlander at the door—an uncommon thing, indeed, nowadays."

"You are right. The curious conjunction struck me at once. There they are, all three, and just in the order in which one meets them going up from Oxford Street. Also, as if to confirm the conjecture, note the *dotted* horse-shoe. Don't you remember that at night the Horse-shoe Hotel sign is illuminated by two rows of gas lights?

"Now here was my clue at last. Plainly, this man, in his mechanical sketching, was following a regular train of thought, and unconsciously illustrating it as he went along. Many people in perfect health and mental soundness do the same thing if a pen and a piece of waste paper be near. The man's train of thought led him, in memory, up Tottenham Court Road, and further, to where some disagreeable recollection upset him. It was my business to trace this train of thought. Do you remember the feat of Dupin in Poe's story, 'The Murders in the Rue Morgue'—how he walks by his friend's side in silence for some distance, and then suddenly breaks out with a divination of his thoughts, having silently traced them from a fruiterer with a basket, through paving-stones, Epicurus, Dr. Nichols, the constellation Orion, and a Latin poem, to a cobbler lately turned actor?

"Well, it was some such task as this (but infinitely simpler, as a matter of fact) that was set me. This man begins by drawing the horse-shoe clock. Having done with that, and with the horse-shoe still in his mind, he starts to draw a horse-shoe simply. It is a failure, and he scribbles it out. His mind at once turns to the Horse-shoe Hotel, which he knows from frequently passing it, and its sign of gas-jets. He sketches *that*, making dots for the gas lights. Once started in Tottenham Court Road, his mind naturally follows his usual route along it. He remembers the advertising captive balloon half-way up, and down *that* goes on his paper. In imagination he crosses the road, and keeps on till he comes to the very noticeable Highlander outside the tobacconist's. *That* is sketched. Thus it is plain that a familiar route with him was from New Oxford Street up Tottenham Court Road.

"At the police-station I ventured to guess from this that he lived somewhere near Seven Dials. Perhaps before long we shall know if this was right. But to return to the sketches. After the Highlander there is something at first not very distinct. A little examination, however, shows it to be intended for a chimney-pot partly covered with a basket. Now an old basket, stuck sideways on a chimney by way of cowl, is not an uncommon thing in parts of the country, but it is very unusual in London. Probably, then, it would be in some by-street or alley. Next and last, there is a horse's head, and it was at this that the man's trouble returned to him.

"Now, when one goes to a place and finds a horse there, that place is not uncommonly a stable; and, as a matter of fact, the basket-cowl would be much more likely to be found in use in a range of back stabling than anywhere else. Suppose, then, that after taking the direction indicated in the sketches—the direction of Fitzroy Square, in fact—one were to find a range of stabling with a basket-cowl visible about it? I know my London pretty well, as you are aware, and I could remember but two likely stable-yards in that particular part—the two we looked at, in the second of which you may possibly have noticed just such a basket-cowl as I have been speaking of.

"Well, what we did you know, and that we found confirmation of my conjecture about the loaves you also know. It was the recollection of the horse and cart, and what they were to transport, and what the end of it all had been, that upset Gérard as he drew the horse's head. You will notice that the sketches have not been done in separate rows, left to right—they have simply followed one another all round the paper, which means preoccupation and unconsciousness on the part of the man who made them."

"But," I asked, "supposing those loaves to contain bombs, how were the bombs put there? Baking the bread round them would have been risky, wouldn't it?"

"Certainly. What they did was to cut the loaves, each row, down the centre. Then most of the crumb was scooped out, the explosive inserted, and the sides joined up and glued. I thought you had spotted the joins, though they certainly were neat."

"No, I didn't examine closely. Luigi, of course, had been told off for a daily visit to feed the horse, and that is how we caught him."

"One supposes so. They hadn't rearranged their plans as to going on with the outrages after Gérard's defection. By the way, I noticed that he was accustomed to driving when I first saw him. There was an unmistakable mark on his coat, just at the small of the back, that drivers get who lean against a rail in a cart."

The loaves were examined by official experts, and, as everybody now knows, were found to contain, as Hewitt had supposed, large charges of dynamite. What became of some half-dozen of the men captured is also well known: their sentences were exemplary.

Catherine L. Pirkis

(1839–1910)

FOR THE VICTORIANS, detecting was predominantly a male business, even in fiction, although a few women detectives showed up in the popular "yellowbacks" produced for sale primarily at railway bookstalls. After much debate, it is now certain that the earliest in the short-story form was Mrs. Paschal in *The Lady Detective* (1860 or 1861), reprinted as *Revelations of a Lady Detective* and *Experiences of a Lady Detective* "by the Author of 'Anonyma'." She was followed by the anonymous sleuth in Andrew Forrester's *The Female Detective* (1864) and possibly by the heroine of Mrs. George Corbett's *Adventures of a Lady Detective* (1890)—though no one of my acquaintance has ever seen a copy of this book, and I fear that it was never published.

These books are only of historical interest, but the same cannot be said for the finely crafted stories in Catherine L. Pirkis's *The Experiences of Loveday Brooke, Lady Detective* (1894). Brooke works for Ebenezer Dyer's detective agency as "the shrewdest and most clear-headed of our female detectives." She was "not tall, she was not short; she was not dark, she was not fair; she was neither handsome nor ugly." Dyer explains that Brooke "has the faculty—so rare among women—of carrying out orders to the very letter; . . . she has a clear, shrewd brain, unhampered by any hard-and-fast theories; . . . she has so much common sense that it amounts to genius."

What little is known about the creator of the first important female detective was unearthed by Michele Slung for her introduction to the Dover edition of Brooke's cases (now out of print). Pirkis was active in antivivisection and humanitarian causes, and the author of many melodramatic romances; I've read one of them and it has nothing to recommend it. But if she had written nothing more than the cases of Loveday Brooke, she would still have an honored place in the development of detective fiction.

The Ghost of Fountain Lane

WILL YOU be good enough to tell me how you procured my address?" said Miss Brooke, a little irritably. "I left strict orders that it was to be given to no one."

"I only obtained it with great difficulty from Mr. Dyer; had, in fact, to telegraph three times before I could get it," answered Mr. Clampe, the individual thus addressed. "I'm sure I'm awfully sorry to break into your holiday in this fashion, but—but pardon me if I say that it seems to be one in little more than name." Here he glanced meaningly at the newspapers, memoranda and books of reference with which the table at which Loveday sat was strewn.

She gave a little sigh.

"I suppose you are right," she answered; "it is a holiday in little more than name. I verily believe that we hard workers, after a time, lose our capacity for holiday-keeping. I thought I was pining for a week of perfect laziness and sea-breezes, and so I locked up my desk and fled. No sooner, however, do I find myself in full view of that magnificent sea-and-sky picture than I shut my eyes to it, fasten them instead on the daily papers and set my brains to work, *con amore*, on a ridiculous case that is never likely to come into my hands."

That "magnificent sea-and-sky picture" was one framed by the windows of a room on the fifth floor of the Métropole, at Brighton, whither Loveday, overtaxed in mind and body, had fled for a brief respite from hard work. Here Inspector Clampe, of the Local District Constabulary, had found her out, in order to press the claims of what seemed to him an important case upon her. He was a neat, dapper-looking man, of about fifty, with a manner less brusque and business-like than that of most men in his profession.

"Oh pray drop the ridiculous case," he said earnestly, "and set to work, 'con amore,' upon another far from ridiculous, and most interesting."

"I'm not sure that it would interest me one quarter so much as the ridiculous one."

"Don't be sure till you've heard the particulars. Listen to this." Here the inspector took a newspaper-cutting from his pocket-book and read aloud as follows:

"'A cheque, the property of the Rev. Charles Turner, Vicar of East Downes, has been stolen under somewhat peculiar circumstances. It appears that the Rev. gentleman was suddenly called from home by the death of a relative, and thinking he might possibly be away some little time, he left with his wife four blank cheques, signed, for her to fill in as required. They were made payable to self or bearer, and were drawn on the West Sussex Bank. Mrs. Turner, when first questioned on the matter, stated that as soon as her husband had departed, she locked up these cheques in her writing desk. She subsequently, however, corrected this statement, and admitted having left them on the table while she went into the garden to cut some flowers. In all, she was absent, she says, about ten minutes. When she came in from cutting her flowers, she immediately put the cheques away. She had not counted them on receiving them from her husband, and when, as she put them into her Davenport, she saw there were only three, she concluded that that was the number he had left with her. The loss of the cheque was not discovered until her husband's return, about a week later on. As soon as he was aware of the fact, he telegraphed to the West Sussex Bank to stop payment, only, however, to make the unpleasant discovery that the cheque, filled in to the amount of six hundred pounds, had been presented and cashed (in gold) two days previously. The clerk who cashed it took no particular notice of the person presenting it, except that he was of gentlemanly appearance, and declares himself to be quite incapable of identifying him. The largeness of the amount raised no suspicion in the mind of the clerk, as Mr. Turner is a man of good means, and since his marriage, about six months back, has been refurnishing the Vicarage, and paying away large sums for old oak furniture and for pictures.'"

"There, Miss Brooke," said the inspector as he finished reading, "if, in addition to these particulars, I tell you that one or two circumstances that have arisen seem to point suspicion in the direction of the young wife, I feel sure you will admit that a more interesting case, and one more worthy of your talents, is not to be found."

Loveday's answer was to take up a newspaper that lay beside her on the table. "So much for your interesting case," she said; "now listen to my ridiculous one." Then she read aloud as follows:—

"'Authentic Ghost Story.—The inhabitants of Fountain Lane, a small turning leading off Ship Street, have been greatly disturbed by the sudden appearance of a ghost in their midst. Last Tuesday night, between ten and eleven o'clock, a little girl named Martha Watts, who lives as a help to a shoemaker and his wife at No. 5 in the lane, ran out into the streets in her night-clothes in a great state of terror, saying that a ghost had come to her bedside. The child refused to return to the house to sleep, and was accordingly taken in by some neighbours. The shoemaker and his wife, Freer by name, when questioned by the neighbours on the matter, admitted, with great reluctance, that they, too, had seen the apparition, which they described as being a soldier-like individual, with a broad, white forehead and having his arms folded on his breast. This description is, in all respects, confirmed by the child, Martha Watts, who asserts that the ghost she saw reminded her of pictures she had seen of the great Napoleon. The Freers state that it first appeared in the course of a prayer-meeting held at their house on the previous night, when it was distinctly seen by Mr. Freer. Subsequently, the wife, awakening suddenly in the middle of the night, saw the apparition standing at the foot of the bed. They are quite at a loss for an explanation of the matter. The affair has caused quite a sensation in the district, and at the time of going to press, the lane is so thronged and crowded by would-be ghost-seers that the inhabitants have great difficulty in going to and from their houses.'"

"A scare—a vulgar scare, nothing more," said the inspector as Loveday laid aside the paper. "Now, Miss Brooke, I ask you seriously, supposing you get to the bottom of such a stupid, commonplace fraud as that, will you in any way add to your reputation?"

"And supposing I get to the bottom of such a stupid, commonplace fraud as a stolen cheque, how much, I should like to know, do I add to my reputation?"

"Well, put it on other grounds and allow Christian charity to have some claims. Think of the misery in that gentleman's house unless suspicion can be lifted from the young wife and directed to the proper quarter."

"Think of the misery of the landlord of the Fountain Lane houses if all his tenants decamp in a body, as they no doubt will, unless the ghost mystery is solved."

The inspector sighed. "Well, I suppose I must take it for granted that you will have nothing to do with the case," he said. "I brought the cheque with me, thinking you might like to see it."

"I suppose it's very much like other cheques?" said Loveday indifferently, and turning over her memoranda as if she meant to go back to her ghost again.

"Ye—es," said Mr. Clampe, taking the cheque from his pocket-book and glancing down at it. "I suppose the cheque is very much like other cheques. This little scribble of figures in pencil at the back—144,000— can scarcely be called a distinguishing mark."

"What's that, Mr. Clampe?" asked Loveday, pushing her memoranda on one side. "144,000 did you say?"

Her whole manner had suddenly changed from apathy to that of keenest interest.

Mr. Clampe, delighted, rose and spread the cheque before her on the table.

"The writing of the words 'six hundred pounds,'" he said, "bears so close a resemblance to Mr. Turner's signature, that the gentleman himself told me he would have thought it was his own writing if he had not known that he had not drawn a cheque for that amount on the given date. You see it is that round, school-boy's hand, so easy to imitate, I could write it myself with half-an-hour's practice; no flourishes, nothing distinctive about it."

Loveday made no reply. She had turned the cheque, and was now closely scrutinizing the pencilled figures at the back.

"Of course," continued the inspector, "those figures were not written by the person who wrote the figures on the face of the cheque. That, however, matters but little. I really do not think they are of the slightest importance in the case. They might have been scribbled by someone making a calculation as to the number of pennies in six hundred pounds—there are, as no doubt you know, exactly 144,000."

"Who has engaged your services in this case, the Bank or Mr. Turner?"

"Mr. Turner. When the loss of the cheque was first discovered, he was very excited and irate, and when he came to me the day before yesterday, I had much difficulty in persuading him that there was no need to telegraph to London for half-a-dozen detectives, as we could do the work quite as well as the London men. When, however, I went over to East Downes yesterday to look round and ask a few questions, I found things had altogether changed. He was exceedingly reluctant to answer any questions, lost his temper when I pressed them, and as good as told me that he wished he had not moved in the matter at all. It was this sudden change of demeanour that turned my thoughts in the direction of Mrs. Turner. A man must have a very strong reason for wishing to sit idle under a loss of six hundred pounds, for, of course, under the circumstances, the Bank will not bear the brunt of it."

"Some other motives may be at work in his mind, consideration for old servants, the wish to avoid a scandal in the house."

"Quite so. The fact, taken by itself, would give no ground for suspicion, but certainly looks ugly if taken in connection with another fact which I have since ascertained, namely, that during her husband's absence from home, Mrs. Turner paid off certain debts contracted by her in Brighton before her marriage, and amounting to nearly £500. Paid them off, too, in gold. I think I mentioned to you that the gentleman who presented the stolen cheque at the Bank preferred payment in gold."

"You are supposing not only a confederate, but also a vast amount of cunning as well as of simplicity on the lady's part."

"Quite so. Three parts cunning to one of simplicity is precisely what lady criminals are composed of. And it is, as a rule, that one part of simplicity that betrays them and leads to their detection."

"What sort of woman is Mrs. Turner in other respects?"

"She is young, handsome and of good birth, but is scarcely suited for the position of vicar's wife in a country parish. She has lived a good deal in society and is fond of gaiety, and, in addition, is a Roman Catholic, and, I am told, utterly ignores her husband's church and drives every Sunday to Brighton to attend mass."

"What about the servants in the house? Do they seem steady-going and respectable?"

"There was nothing on the surface to excite suspicion against any one of them. But it is precisely in that quarter that your services would be invaluable. It will, however, be impossible to get you inside the vicarage walls. Mr. Turner, I am confident, would never open his doors to you."

"What do you suggest?"

"I can suggest nothing better than the house of the village schoolmistress, or, rather, of the village schoolmistress's mother, Mrs. Brown. It is only a stone's throw from the vicarage; in fact, its windows overlook the vicarage grounds. It is a four-roomed cottage, and Mrs. Brown, who is a very respectable person, turns over a little money in the summer by receiving lady lodgers desirous of a breath of country air. There would be no difficulty in getting you in there; her spare bedroom is empty now."

"I should have preferred being at the vicarage, but if it cannot be, I must make the most of my stay at Mrs. Brown's. How do we get there?"

"I drove from East Downes here in a trap I hired at the village inn where I put up last night, and where I shall stay to-night. I will drive you, if you will allow me; it is only seven miles off. It's a lovely day for a drive; breezy and not too much dust. Could you be ready in about half-an-hour's time, say?"

But this, Loveday said, would be an impossibility. She had a special engagement that afternoon; there was a religious service in the town that she particularly wished to attend. It would not be over until three o'clock, and, consequently, not until half-past three would she be ready for the drive to East Downes.

Although Mr. Clampe looked in unutterable astonishment at the claims of a religious service being set before those of professional duty, he made no demur to the arrangement, and accordingly half-past three saw Loveday and the inspector in a high-wheeled dog-cart rattling along the Marina in the direction of East Downes.

Loveday made no further allusion to her ghost story, so Mr. Clampe, out of politeness, felt compelled to refer to it.

"I heard all about the Fountain Lane ghost yesterday, before I started for East Downes," he said; "and it seemed to me, with all defer-ence to you, Miss Brooke, an every-day sort of affair, the sort of thing to be explained by a heavy supper or an extra glass of beer."

"There are a few points in this ghost story that separate it from the every-day ghost story," answered Loveday. "For instance, you would expect that such emotionally religious people, as I have since found the Freers to be, would have seen a vision of angels, or at least a solitary saint. Instead, they see a soldier! A soldier, too, in the likeness of a man who is anathema maranatha to every religious mind—the great Napoleon."

"To what denomination do the Freers belong?"

"To the Wesleyan. Their fathers and mothers before them were Wesleyans; their relatives and friends are Wesleyans, one and all, they say; and, most important item of all, the man's boot and shoe connec-tion lies exclusively among Wesleyan ministers. This, he told me, is the most paying connection that a small boot-maker can have. Half-a-dozen Wesleyan ministers pay better than three times the number of Church clergy, for whereas the Wesleyan minister is always on the tramp among his people, the clergyman generally contrives in the country to keep a horse, or else turns student, and shuts himself up in his study."

"Ha, ha! Capital," laughed Mr. Clampe; "tell that to the Church Defence Society in Wales. Isn't this a first-rate little horse? In another ten minutes we shall be in sight of East Downes."

The long, dusty road down which they had driven, was ending now in a narrow, sloping lane, hedged in on either side with hawthorns and wild plum trees. Through these, the August sunshine was beginning to slant now, and from a distant wood there came a faint sound of fluting and piping, as if the blackbirds were thinking of tuning up for their evening carols.

A sudden, sharp curve in this lane brought them in sight of East Downes, a tiny hamlet of about thirty cottages, dominated by the steeple of a church of early English architecture. Adjoining the church was the vicarage, a goodly-sized house, with extensive grounds, and in a lane running alongside these grounds were situated the village schools and the schoolmistress's house. The latter was simply a four-roomed cottage, standing in a pretty garden, with cluster roses and honeysuckle, now in the fulness of their August glory, climbing upwards to its very roof.

Outside this cottage Mr. Clampe drew rein.

"If you'll give me five minutes' grace," he said, "I'll go in and tell the good woman that I have brought her, as a lodger, a friend of mine, who is anxious to get away for a time from the noise and glare of Brighton. Of course, the story of the stolen cheque is all over the place, but I don't think anyone has, at present, connected me with the affair. I am supposed to be a gentleman from Brighton, who is anxious to buy a horse the Vicar wishes to sell, and who can't quite arrange terms with him."

While Loveday waited outside in the cart, an open carriage drove past and then in through the vicarage gates. In the carriage were seated a gentleman and lady whom, from the respectful greetings they received from the village children, she conjectured to be the Rev. Charles and Mrs. Turner. Mr. Turner was sanguine-complexioned, red-haired, and wore a distinctly troubled expression of countenance. With Mrs. Turner's appearance Loveday was not favourably impressed. Although a decidedly handsome woman, she was hard-featured and had a scornful curl to her upper lip. She was dressed in the extreme of London fashion.

They threw a look of enquiry at Loveday as they passed, and she felt sure that enquiries as to the latest addition to Mrs. Brown's ménage would soon be afloat in the village.

Mr. Clampe speedily returned, saying that Mrs. Brown was only too delighted to get her spare-room occupied. He whispered a hint as they made their way up to the cottage door between borders thickly planted with stocks and mignonette.

It was:

"Don't ask her any questions, or she'll draw herself up as straight as a ramrod, and say she never listens to gossip of any sort. But just let her alone, and she'll run on like a mill-stream, and tell you as much as you'll want to know about everyone and everything. She and the village postmistress are great friends, and between them they contrive to know pretty much what goes on inside every house in the place."

Mrs. Brown was a stout, rosy-cheeked woman of about fifty, neatly dressed in a dark stuff gown with a big white cap and apron. She welcomed Loveday respectfully, and introduced, evidently with a little pride, her daughter, the village schoolmistress, a well-spoken young woman of about eight-and-twenty.

Mr. Clampe departed with his dog-cart to the village inn, announcing his intention of calling on Loveday at the cottage on the following morning before he returned to Brighton.

Miss Brown also departed, saying she would prepare tea. Left alone with Loveday, Mrs. Brown speedily unloosed her tongue. She had a dozen questions to ask respecting Mr. Clampe and his business in the village. Now, was it true that he had come to East Downes for the whole and sole purpose of buying one of the Vicar's horses? She had heard it whispered that he had been sent by the police to watch the servants at the vicarage. She hoped it was not true, for a more respectable set of servants were not to be met with in any house, far or near. Had Miss Brooke heard about that lost cheque? Such a terrible affair! She had been told that the story of it had reached London. Now, had Miss Brooke seen an account of it in any of the London papers?

Here a reply from Loveday in the negative formed a sufficient excuse for relating with elaborate detail the story of the stolen cheque. Except in its elaborateness of detail, it differed but little from the one Loveday had already heard.

She listened patiently, bearing in mind Mr. Clampe's hint, and asking no questions. And when, in about a quarter of an hour's time, Miss Brown came in with the tea-tray in her hand, Loveday could have passed an examination in the events of the daily family life at the vicarage. She could have answered questions as to the ill-assortedness of the newly-married couple; she knew that they wrangled from morning till night; that the chief subjects of their disagreement were religion and money matters; that the Vicar was hot-tempered, and said whatever came to the tip of his tongue; that the beautiful young wife, though slower of speech, was scathing and sarcastic, and that, in addition, she was wildly extravagant and threw money away in all directions.

In addition to these interesting facts, Loveday could have undertaken to supply information respecting the number of servants at the vicarage, together with their names, ages and respective duties.

During tea, conversation flagged somewhat; Miss Brown's presence evidently acted repressively on her mother, and it was not until the meal was over and Loveday was being shown to her room by Mrs. Brown that opportunity to continue the talk was found.

Loveday opened the ball by remarking on the fact that no Dissenting chapel was to be found in the village.

"Generally, wherever there is a handful of cottages, we find a church at one end and a chapel at the other," she said; "but here, willy-nilly, one must go to church."

"Do you belong to chapel, ma'am?" was Mrs. Brown's reply. "Old Mrs. Turner, the Vicar's mother, who died over a year ago, was so 'low' she was almost chapel, and used often to drive over to Brighton to attend the Countess of Huntingdon's church. People used to say that was bad enough in the Vicar's mother; but what was it compared with what goes on now—the Vicar's wife driving regularly every Sunday into Brighton to a Catholic Church to say her prayers to candles and images? I'm glad you like the room, ma'am. Feather bolster, feather pillows, do you see, ma'am? I've nothing in the way of flock or wool on either of my beds to make people's heads ache." Here Mrs. Brown, by way of emphasis, patted and pinched the fat pillows and bolster showing above the spotless white counterpane.

Loveday stood at the cottage window drinking in the sweetness of the country air, laden now with the heavy evening scents of carnation and jessamine. Across the road, from the vicarage, came the loud clanging of a dinner-gong, and almost simultaneously the church clock chimed the hour—seven o'clock.

"Who is that person coming up the lane?" asked Loveday, her attention suddenly attracted by a tall, thin figure, dressed in shabby black, with a large, dowdyish bonnet, and carrying a basket in her hand as if she were returning from some errand. Mrs. Brown peeped over Loveday's shoulder.

"Ah, that's the peculiar young woman I was telling you about, ma'am—Maria Lisle, who used to be old Mrs. Turner's maid. Not that she is over young now; she's five-and-thirty if she's a day. The Vicar kept her on to be his wife's maid after the old lady died, but young Mrs. Turner will have nothing to do with her, she's not good enough for her; so Mr. Turner is just paying her £30 a-year for doing nothing. And what Maria does with all that money it would be hard to say. She doesn't spend it on dress, that's certain, and she hasn't kith nor kin, not a soul belonging to her to give a penny to."

"Perhaps she gives it to charities in Brighton. There are plenty of outlets for money there."

"She may," said Mrs. Brown dubiously; "she is always going to Brighton whenever she gets a chance. She used to be a Wesleyan in old Mrs. Turner's time, and went regularly to all the revival meetings for miles round; what she is now, it would be hard to say. Where she goes to church in Brighton, no one knows. She drives over with Mrs. Turner every Sunday, but everyone knows nothing would induce her to go near the candles and images. Thomas—that's the coachman—says he puts her down at the corner of a dirty little street in mid-Brighton, and there he picks her up again after he has fetched Mrs. Turner from her church. No, there's something very queer in her ways."

Maria passed in through the lodge gates of the vicarage. She walked with her head bent, her eyes cast down to the ground.

"Something very queer in her ways," repeated Mrs. Brown. "She never speaks to a soul unless they speak first to her, and gets by herself on every possible opportunity. Do you see that old summer-house over there in the vicarage grounds—it stands between the orchard and kitchen garden—well, every evening at sunset, out comes Maria and disappears into it, and there she stays for over an hour at a time. And what she does there goodness only knows!"

"Perhaps she keeps books there, and studies."

"Studies! My daughter showed her some new books that had come down for the fifth standard the other day, and Maria turned upon her and said quite sharply that there was only one book in the whole world that people ought to study, and that book was the Bible."

"How pretty those vicarage gardens are," said Loveday, a little abruptly. "Does the Vicar ever allow people to see them?"

"Oh, yes, miss; he doesn't at all mind people taking a walk round them. Only yesterday he said to me, 'Mrs. Brown, if ever you feel yourself circumscribed'—yes, 'circumscribed' was the word—'just walk out of your garden-gate and in at mine and enjoy yourself at your leisure among my fruit-trees.' Not that I would like to take advantage of his kindness and make too free; but if you'd care, ma'am, to go for a walk through the grounds, I'll go with you with pleasure. There's a wonderful old cedar hard by the pond people have come ever so far to see."

"It's that old summer-house and little bit of orchard that fascinate me," said Loveday, putting on her hat.

"We shall frighten Maria to death if she sees us so near her haunt," said Mrs. Brown as she led the way downstairs. "This way, if you please, ma'am, the kitchen-garden leads straight into the orchard."

Twilight was deepening rapidly into night now. Bird notes had ceased, the whirr of insects, the croaking of a distant frog were the only sounds that broke the evening stillness.

As Mrs. Brown swung back the gate that divided the kitchen-garden from the orchard, the gaunt, black figure of Maria Lisle was seen approaching in an opposite direction.

"Well, really, I don't see why she should expect to have the orchard all to herself every evening," said Mrs. Brown, with a little toss of her head. "Mind the gooseberry bushes, ma'am, they do catch at your clothes so. My word! what a fine show of fruit the Vicar has this year! I never saw pear trees more laden!"

They were now in the "bit of orchard" to be seen from the cottage windows. As they rounded the corner of the path in which the old summer-house stood, Maria Lisle turned its corner at the farther end, and suddenly found herself almost face to face with them. If her eyes had not been so persistently fastened on the ground, she would have noted the approach of the intruders as quickly as they had noted hers. Now, as she saw them for the first time, she gave a sudden start, paused for a moment irresolutely, and then turned sharply and walked rapidly away in an opposite direction.

"Maria, Maria!" called Mrs. Brown, "don't run away; we sha'n't stay here for more than a minute or so."

Her words met with no response. The woman did not so much as turn her head.

Loveday stood at the entrance of the old summer-house. It was considerably out of repair, and most probably was never entered by anyone save Maria Lisle, its unswept, undusted condition suggesting colonies of spiders and other creeping things within.

Loveday braved them all and took her seat on the bench that ran round the little place in a semi-circle.

"Do try and overtake the girl, and tell her we shall be gone in a minute," she said, addressing Mrs. Brown. "I will wait here meanwhile. I am so sorry to have frightened her away in that fashion."

Mrs. Brown, under protest, and with a little grumble at the ridiculousness of "people who couldn't look other people in the face," set off in pursuit of Maria.

It was getting dim inside the summer-house now. There was, however, sufficient light to enable Loveday to discover a small pocket of books lying in a corner of the bench on which she sat.

One by one she took them in her hand and closely scrutinized them. The first was a much read and pencil-marked Bible; the others were respectively, a "congregational hymn-book," a book in a paper cover, on which was printed a flaming picture of a red and yellow angel, pouring blood and fire from out a big black bottle, and entitled "The End of the Age," and a smaller book, also in a paper cover, on which was depicted a huge black horse, snorting fire and brimstone into ochre-coloured clouds. This book was entitled "The Year Book of the Saints," and was simply a ruled diary with sensational mottoes for every day in the year. In parts, this diary was filled in with large and very untidy handwriting.

In these books seemed to lie the explanation of Maria Lisle's love of evening solitude and the lonely old summer-house.

Mrs. Brown pursued Maria to the servants' entrance to the house, but could not overtake her, the girl making good her retreat there.

She returned to Loveday a little hot, a little breathless and a little out of temper. It was all so absurd, she said; why couldn't the woman have stayed and had a chat with them? It wasn't as if she would get any harm out of the talk; she knew as well as everyone else in the village that she (Mrs. Brown) was no idle gossip, tittle-tattling over other people's affairs.

But here Loveday, a little sharply, cut short her meanderings.

"Mrs. Brown," she said, and to Mrs. Brown's fancy her voice and manner had entirely changed from that of the pleasant, chatty lady of half-an-hour ago, "I'm sorry to say it will be impossible for me to stay even one night in your pleasant home. I have just recollected some important business that I must transact in Brighton to-night. I haven't unpacked my porte-manteau, so if you'll kindly have it taken to your garden-gate, I'll call for it as we drive past—I am going now, at once, to the inn, to see if Mr. Clampe can drive me back into Brighton to-night."

Mrs. Brown had no words ready wherewith to express her astonishment, and Loveday assuredly gave her no time to hunt for them. Ten minutes later saw her rousing Mr. Clampe from a comfortable supper, to which he had just settled himself, with the surprising announcement that she must get back to Brighton with as little delay as possible; now, would he be good enough to drive her there?

"We'll have a pair if they are to be had," she added. "The road is good; it will be moonlight in a quarter of an hour; we ought to do it in less than half the time we took coming."

While a phaeton and pair were being got ready, Loveday had time for a few words of explanation.

Maria Lisle's diary in the old summer-house had given her the last of the links in her chain of evidence that was to bring the theft of the cheque home to the criminal.

"It will be best to drive straight to the police station," she said; "they must take out three warrants, one for Maria Lisle, and two others respectively for Richard Steele, late Wesleyan minister of a chapel in Gordon Street, Brighton, and John Rogers, formerly elder of the same chapel. And let me tell you," she added with a little smile, "that these three worthies would most likely have been left at large to carry on their depredations for some little time to come if it had not been for that ridiculous ghost in Fountain Lane."

More than this there was not time to add, and when, a few minutes later, the two were rattling along the road to Brighton, the presence of the man, whom they were forced to take with them in order to bring back the horses to East Downes, prevented any but the most jerky and fragmentary of additions to this brief explanation.

"I very much fear that John Rogers has bolted," once Loveday whispered under her breath.

And again, a little later, when a smooth bit of road admitted of low-voiced talk, she said:

"We can't wait for the warrant for Steele; they must follow us with it to 15, Draycott Street."

"But I want to know about the ghost," said Mr. Clampe; "I am deeply interested in that 'ridiculous ghost.'"

"Wait till we get to 15, Draycott Street," was Loveday's reply; "when you've been there, I feel sure you will understand everything."

Church clocks were chiming a quarter to nine as they drove through Kemp Town at a pace that made the passers-by imagine they must be bound on an errand of life and death.

Loveday did not alight at the police station, and five minutes' talk with the inspector in charge there was all that Mr. Clampe required to put things en train for the arrest of the three criminals.

It had evidently been an "excursionists' day" at Brighton. The streets leading to the railway station were thronged, and their progress along the bystreets was impeded by the overflow of traffic from the main road.

"We shall get along better on foot; Draycott Street is only a stone's throw from here," said Loveday; "there's a turning on the north side of Western Road that will bring us straight into it."

So they dismissed their trap, and Loveday, acting as cicerone still, led the way through narrow turnings into the district, half town, half country, that skirts the road leading to the Dyke.

Draycott Street was not difficult to find. It consisted of two rows of newly-built houses of the eight-roomed, lodging-letting order. A dim light shone from the first-floor windows of number fifteen, but the lower window was dark and uncurtained, and a board hanging from its balcony rails proclaimed that it was "to let unfurnished." The door of the house stood slightly ajar, and pushing it open, Loveday led the way up a flight of stairs—lighted halfway up with a paraffin lamp—to the first floor.

"I know the way. I was here this afternoon," she whispered to her companion. "This is the last lecture he will give before he starts for Judæa; or, in other words, bolts with the money he has managed to conjure from other people's purses into his own."

The door of the room for which they were making, on the first floor, stood open, possibly on account of the heat. It laid bare to view a double row of forms, on which were seated some eight or ten persons in the attitude of all-absorbed listeners. Their faces were upturned, as if fixed on a preacher at the farther end of the room, and wore that expression of rapt, painful interest that is sometimes seen on the faces of a congregation of revivalists before the smouldering excitement bursts into flame.

As Loveday and her companion mounted the last of the flight of stairs the voice of the preacher—full, arrestive, resonant—fell upon their ear; and, standing on the small outside landing, it was possible to catch a glimpse of that preacher through the crack of the half-opened door.

He was a tall, dignified-looking man, of about five-and-forty, with a close crop of white hair, black eye-brows and remarkably luminous and expressive eyes. Altogether his appearance matched his voice: it was emphatically that of a man born to sway, lead, govern the multitude.

A boy came out of an adjoining room and asked Loveday respectfully if she would not like to go in and hear the lecture. She shook her head.

"I could not stand the heat," she said. "Kindly bring us chairs here."

The lecture was evidently drawing to a close now, and Loveday and Mr. Clampe, as they sat outside listening, could not resist an occasional thrill of admiration at the skilful manner in which the preacher led his hearers from one figure of rhetoric to another, until the oratorical climax was reached.

"That man is a born orator," whispered Loveday; "and in addition to the power of the voice has the power of the eye. That audience is as completely hypnotised by him as if they had surrendered themselves to a professional mesmerist."

To judge from the portion of the discourse that fell upon their ear, the preacher was a member of one of the many sects known under the generic name, "Millenarian." His topic was Apollyon and the great battle of Armageddon. This he described as vividly as if it were being fought out under his very eye, and it would scarcely be an exaggeration to say that he made the cannon roar in the ears of his listeners and the tortured cries of the wounded wail in them. He drew an appalling picture of the carnage of that battlefield, of the blood flowing like a river across the plain, of the mangled men and horses, with the birds of prey swooping down from all quarters, and the stealthy tigers and leopards creeping out from their mountain lairs. "And all this time," he said, suddenly raising his voice from a whisper to a full, thrilling tone, "gazing calmly down upon the field of slaughter, with bent brows and folded arms, stands the imperial Apollyon. Apollyon did I say? No, I will give him his right name, the name in which he will stand revealed in that dread day, Napoleon! A Napoleon it will be who, in that day, will stand as the embodiment of Satanic majesty. Out of the mists suddenly he will walk, a tall, dark figure, with frowning brows and firm-set lips, a man to rule, a man to drive, a man to kill! Apollyon the mighty, Napoleon the imperial, they are one and the same——"

Here a sob and a choking cry from one of the women in the front seats interrupted the discourse and sent the small boy who acted as verger into the room with a glass of water.

"That sermon has been preached before," said Loveday. "Now can you not understand the origin of the ghost in Fountain Lane?"

"Hysterics are catching, there's another woman off now," said Mr. Clampe; "it's high time this sort of thing was put a stop to. Pearson ought to be here in another minute with his warrant."

The words had scarcely passed his lips before heavy steps mounting the stairs announced that Pearson and his warrant were at hand.

"I don't think I can be of any further use," said Loveday, rising to depart. "If you like to come to me to-morrow morning at my hotel at ten o'clock I will tell you, step by step, how I came to connect a stolen cheque with a 'ridiculous ghost.'"

"We had a tussle—he showed fight at first," said Mr. Clampe, when, precisely at ten o'clock the next morning, he called upon Miss Brooke at the Métropole. "If he had had time to get his wits together and had called some of the men in that room to the rescue, I verily believe we should have been roughly handled and he might have slipped through our fingers after all. It's wonderful what power these 'born orators,' as you call them, have over minds of a certain order."

"Ah, yes," answered Loveday thoughtfully; "we talk glibly enough about 'magnetic influence,' but scarcely realise how literally true the phrase is. It is my firm opinion that the 'leaders of men,' as they are called, have as absolute and genuine hypnotic power as any modern French expert, although perhaps it may be less consciously exercised. Now tell me about Rogers and Maria Lisle."

"Rogers had bolted, as you expected he would have done, with the six hundred pounds he had been good enough to cash for his reverend colleague. Ostensibly he had started for Judæa to collect the elect, as he phrased it, under one banner. In reality, he has sailed for New York, where, thanks to the cable, he will be arrested on his arrival and sent back by return packet. Maria Lisle was arrested this morning on a charge of having stolen the cheque from Mrs. Turner. By the way, Miss Brooke, I think it is almost a pity you didn't take possession of her diary when you had the chance. It would have been invaluable evidence against her and her rascally colleagues."

"I did not see the slightest necessity for so doing. Remember, she is not one of the criminal classes, but a religious enthusiast, and when put upon her defence will at once confess and plead religious conviction as an extenuating circumstance — at least, if she is well advised she will do so. I never read anything that laid bare more frankly than did this diary the mischief that the sensational teaching of these millenarians is doing at the present moment. But I must not take up your time with moralising. I know you are anxious to learn what, in the first instance, led me to identify a millenarian preacher with a receiver of stolen property."

"Yes, that's it; I want to know about the ghost: that's the point that interests me."

"Very well. As I told you yesterday afternoon, the first thing that struck me as remarkable in this ghost story was the soldierly character of the ghost. One expects emotionally religious people like Freer and his wife to see visions, but one also expects those visions to partake of the nature of those emotions, and to be somewhat shadowy and ecstatic. It seemed to me certain that this Napoleonic ghost must have some sort of religious significance to these people. This conviction it was that set my thoughts running in the direction of the millenarians, who have attached a religious significance (although not a polite one) to the name of Napoleon by embodying the evil Apollyon in the person of a descendant of the great Emperor, and endowing him with all the qualities of his illustrious ancestor. I called upon the Freers, ordered a pair of boots, and while the man was taking my measure, I asked him a few very pointed questions on these millenarian notions. The man prevaricated a good deal at first, but at length was driven to admit that he and his wife were millenarians at heart, that, in fact, the prayer meeting at which the Napoleonic ghost had made its first appearance was a millenarian one, held by a man who had at one time been a Wesleyan preacher in the chapel in Gordon Street, but who had been dismissed from his charge there because his teaching had been held to be unsound. Freer further stated that this man had been so much liked that many members of the congregation seized every opportunity that presented itself of attending his ministrations, some openly, others, like himself and his wife, secretly, lest they might give offence to the elders and ministers of their chapel."

"And the bootmaking connection suffer proportionately," laughed Mr. Clampe.

"Precisely. A visit to the Wesleyan chapel in Gordon Street and a talk with the chapel attendant enabled me to complete the history of this inhibited preacher, the Rev. Richard Steele. From this attendant I ascertained that a certain elder of their chapel, John Rogers by name, had seceded from their communion, thrown in his lot with Richard Steele, and that the two together were now going about the country preaching that the world would come to an end on Thursday, April 11th, 1901, and that five years before this event, viz., on the 5th of March, 1896, one hundred and forty-four thousand living saints would be caught up to heaven. They furthermore announced that this translation would take place in the land of Judæa, that, shortly, saints from all parts of the world would be hastening thither, and that in view of this event a society had been formed to provide homes—a series, I suppose—for the multitudes who would otherwise be homeless. Also (a very vital point this), that subscriptions to this society would be gladly received by either gentleman. I had arrived so far in my ghost enquiry when you came to me, bringing the stolen cheque with its pencilled figures, 144,000."

"Ah, I begin to see!" murmured Mr. Clampe.

"It immediately occurred to me that the man who could make persons see an embodiment of his thought at will, would have very little difficulty in influencing other equally receptive minds to a breach of the ten commandments. The world, it seems to me, abounds in people who are little more than blank sheets of paper, on which a strong hand may transcribe what it will—hysteric subjects, the doctors would call them; hypnotic subjects others would say; really the line that divides the hysteric condition from the hypnotic is a very hazy one. So now, when I saw your stolen cheque, I said to myself, 'there is a sheet of blank paper somewhere in that country vicarage, the thing is to find it out.'"

"Ah, good Mrs. Brown's gossip made your work easy to you there."

"It did. She not only gave me a complete summary of the history of the people within the vicarage walls, but she put so many graphic touches to that history that they lived and moved before me. For instance, she told me that Maria Lisle was in the habit of speaking of Mrs. Turner as a 'Child of the Scarlet Woman,' a 'Daughter of Babylon,' and gave me various other minute particulars, which enabled me, so to speak, to see Maria Lisle going about her daily duties, rendering her mistress reluctant service, hating her in her heart as a member of a corrupt faith, and thinking she was doing God service by despoiling her of some of her wealth, in order to devote it to what seemed to her a holy cause. I would like here to read to you two entries which I copied from her diary under dates respectively, August 3rd (the day the cheque was lost), and August 7th (the following Sunday), when Maria no doubt found opportunity to meet Steele at some prayer-meeting in Brighton."

Here Loveday produced her note-book and read from it as follows:

"'To-day I have spoiled the Egyptians! Taken from a Daughter of Babylon that which would go to increase the power of the Beast!'

"And again, under date August 7th, she writes:

"'I have handed to-day to my beloved pastor that of which I despoiled a Daughter of Babylon. It was blank, but he told me he would fill it in so that 144,000 of the elect would be each the richer by one penny. Blessed thought! this is the doing of my most unworthy hand.'

"A wonderful farrago, that diary of distorted Scriptural phraseology — wild eulogies on the beloved pastor, and morbid ecstatics, such as one would think could be the outcome only of a diseased brain. It seems to me that Portland or Broadmoor, and the ministrations of a sober-minded chaplain, may be about the happiest thing that could befall Maria Lisle at this period of her career. I think I ought to mention in this connection that when at the religious service yesterday afternoon (to attend which I slightly postponed my drive to East Downes), I heard Steele pronounce a fervid eulogy on those who had strengthened his hands for the fight which he knew it would shortly fall to his lot to wage against Apollyon, I did not wonder at weak-minded persons like Maria Lisle, swayed by such eloquence, setting up new standards of right and wrong for themselves."

"Miss Brooke, another question or two. Can you in any way account for the sudden payment of Mrs. Turner's debts—a circumstance that led me a little astray in the first instance?"

"Mrs. Brown explained the matter easily enough. She said that a day or two back, when she was walking on the other side of the vicarage hedge, and the husband and wife in the garden were squabbling as usual over money-matters, she heard Mr. Turner say indignantly, 'only a week or two ago I gave you nearly £500 to pay your debts in Brighton, and now there comes another bill.'"

"Ah, that makes it plain enough. One more question and I have done. I have no doubt there's something in your theory of the hypnotic power (unconsciously exercised) of such men as Richard Steele, although, at the same time, it seems to me a trifle far-fetched and fanciful. But even admitting it, I don't see how you account for the girl, Martha Watts, seeing the ghost. She was not present at the prayer-meeting which called the ghost into being, nor does she appear in any way to have come into contact with the Rev. Richard Steele."

"Don't you think that ghost-seeing is quite as catching as scarlet-fever or measles?" answered Loveday, with a little smile. "Let one member of a family see a much individualized and easily described ghost, such as the one these good people saw, and ten to one others in the same house will see it before the week is over. We are all in the habit of asserting that 'seeing is believing.' Don't you think the converse of the saying is true also, and that 'believing is seeing?'"

Rudyard Kipling

(1865–1936)

JOSEPH RUDYARD KIPLING, the chronicler from the British viewpoint of the pageant of India, the creator of *Just So Stories*, the balladeer who wrote about the "better man than I am, Gunga Din," and one of the most popular writers of his age, was born in Bombay in 1865. The son of a Methodist minister, he was educated in England but returned to India in 1882, where he remained until 1889. Between 1892 and 1896, he lived in Vermont. In 1907, he received the Nobel Prize for Literature, and at his death he was honored with a burial at Westminster Abbey. It is odd to think that one of the most celebrated writers and one who is still well-known is no longer widely read, but tastes change, and Kipling's defense of the empire and his invention of the phrase "the white man's burden" have made his works uncomfortable to many contemporary readers. In fact, however, he was far more sympathetic to Indian culture than many of his contemporaries, and as the following story shows, he was a master of the short tale.

Kipling was interested in crime and, occasionally, in investigation. He wrote five stories about "E. Strickland of the Police," three of which have no detection (but one of those, "The Mark of the Beast," is a splendid horror story). "The Return of Imray" was first published in Kipling's collection *Life's Handicaps: Stories of Mine Own People* in 1891. Kipling also wrote "The House Surgeon" (1909), an occult detective story about investigating a ghost, and, fairly late in his life, a full-fledged detective story called "Fairy-Kist" (1927).

65

The Return of Imray

The doors were wide, the story saith,
Out of the night came the patient wraith,
He might not speak, and he could not stir
A hair of the Baron's minniver—
Speechless and strengthless, a shadow thin,
He roved the castle to seek his kin.
And oh, 'twas a piteous thing to see
The dumb ghost follow his enemy!
                                    The Baron

IMRAY ACHIEVED the impossible. Without warning, for no conceivable motive, in his youth, at the threshold of his career he chose to disappear from the world—which is to say, the little Indian station where he lived.

Upon a day he was alive, well, happy, and in great evidence among the billiard-tables at his Club. Upon a morning, he was not, and no manner of search could make sure where he might be. He had stepped out of his place; he had not appeared at his office at the proper time, and his dogcart was not upon the public roads. For these reasons, and because he was hampering, in a microscopical degree, the administration of the Indian Empire, that Empire paused for one microscopical moment to make inquiry into the fate of Imray. Ponds were dragged, wells were plumbed, telegrams were despatched down the lines of railways and to the nearest seaport town—twelve hundred miles away; but Imray was not at the end of the drag-ropes nor the telegraph wires. He was gone, and his place knew him no more. Then the work of the great Indian Empire swept forward, because it could not be delayed, and Imray from being a man became a mystery—such a thing as men talk over at their tables in the Club for a month, and then forget utterly. His guns, horses, and carts were sold to the highest bidder.

His superior officer wrote an altogether absurd letter to his mother, saying that Imray had unaccountably disappeared, and his bungalow stood
empty.

After three or four months of the scorching hot weather had gone by,
my friend Strickland, of the Police, saw fit to rent the bungalow from
the native landlord. This was before he was engaged to Miss Youghal—
an affair which has been described in another place—and while he was
pursuing his investigations into native life. His own life was sufficiently
peculiar, and men complained of his manners and customs. There was
always food in his house, but there were no regular times for meals. He
ate, standing up and walking about, whatever he might find at the side-
board, and this is not good for human beings. His domestic equipment
was limited to six rifles, three shot-guns, five saddles, and a collection
of stiff-jointed mahseer-rods, bigger and stronger than the largest
salmon-rods. These occupied one-half of his bungalow, and the other
half was given up to Strickland and his dog Tietjens—an enormous
Rampur slut who devoured daily the rations of two men. She spoke to
Strickland in a language of her own; and whenever, walking abroad,
she saw things calculated to destroy the peace of Her Majesty the
Queen-Empress, she returned to her master and laid information.
Strickland would take steps at once, and the end of his labours was
trouble and fine and imprisonment for other people. The natives
believed that Tietjens was a familiar spirit, and treated her with the
great reverence that is born of hate and fear. One room in the bungalow was set apart for her special use. She owned a bedstead, a blanket,
and a drinking-trough, and if any one came into Strickland's room at
night her custom was to knock down the invader and give tongue till
some one came with a light. Strickland owed his life to her, when he
was on the Frontier, in search of a local murderer, who came in the
gray dawn to send Strickland much farther than the Andaman Islands.
Tietjens caught the man as he was crawling into Strickland's tent with
a dagger between his teeth; and after his record of iniquity was established in the eyes of the law he was hanged. From that date Tietjens
wore a collar of rough silver, and employed a monogram on her night-
blanket; and the blanket was of double woven Kashmir cloth, for she
was a delicate dog.

Under no circumstances would she be separated from Strickland;
and once, when he was ill with fever, made great trouble for the doctors, because she did not know how to help her master and would not
allow another creature to attempt aid. Macarnaght, of the Indian
Medical Service, beat her over her head with a gun-butt before she

could understand that she must give room for those who could give quinine.

A short time after Strickland had taken Imray's bungalow, my business took me through that Station, and naturally, the Club quarters being full, I quartered myself upon Strickland. It was a desirable bungalow, eight-roomed and heavily thatched against any chance of leakage from rain. Under the pitch of the roof ran a ceiling-cloth which looked just as neat as a white-washed ceiling. The landlord had repainted it when Strickland took the bungalow. Unless you knew how Indian bungalows were built you would never have suspected that above the cloth lay the dark three-cornered cavern of the roof, where the beams and the underside of the thatch harboured all manner of rats, bats, ants, and foul things.

Tietjens met me in the verandah with a bay like the boom of the bell of St. Paul's, putting her paws on my shoulder to show she was glad to see me. Strickland had contrived to claw together a sort of meal which he called lunch, and immediately after it was finished went out about his business. I was left alone with Tietjens and my own affairs. The heat of the summer had broken up and turned to the warm damp of the rains. There was no motion in the heated air, but the rain fell like ramrods on the earth, and flung up a blue mist when it splashed back. The bamboos, and the custard-apples, the poinsettias, and the mango-trees in the garden stood still while the warm water lashed through them, and the frogs began to sing among the aloe hedges. A little before the light failed, and when the rain was at its worst, I sat in the back verandah and heard the water roar from the eaves, and scratched myself because I was covered with the thing called prickly-heat. Tietjens came out with me and put her head in my lap and was very sorrowful; so I gave her biscuits when tea was ready, and I took tea in the back verandah on account of the little coolness found there. The rooms of the house were dark behind me. I could smell Strickland's saddlery and the oil on his guns, and I had no desire to sit among these things. My own servant came to me in the twilight, the muslin of his clothes clinging tightly to his drenched body, and told me that a gentleman had called and wished to see some one. Very much against my will, but only because of the darkness of the rooms, I went into the naked drawing-room, telling my man to bring the lights. There might or might not have been a caller waiting—it seemed to me that I saw a figure by one of the windows—but when the lights came there was nothing save the spikes of the rain without, and the smell of the drinking earth in my nostrils. I explained to my servant that he was no wiser than he ought to be, and went back to the verandah to talk to Tietjens. She had gone out into the wet, and I could hardly coax her back to me; even with biscuits with sugar tops. Strickland came home, dripping wet, just before dinner, and the first thing he said was,

"Has any one called?"

I explained, with apologies, that my servant had summoned me into the drawing-room on a false alarm; or that some loafer had tried to call on Strickland, and thinking better of it had fled after giving his name. Strickland ordered dinner, without comment, and since it was a real dinner with a white tablecloth attached, we sat down.

At nine o'clock Strickland wanted to go to bed, and I was tired too. Tietjens, who had been lying underneath the table, rose up, and swung into the least exposed verandah as soon as her master moved to his own room, which was next to the stately chamber set apart for Tietjens. If a mere wife had wished to sleep out of doors in that pelting rain it would not have mattered; but Tietjens was a dog, and therefore the better animal. I looked at Strickland, expecting to see him flay her with a whip. He smiled queerly, as a man would smile after telling some unpleasant domestic tragedy. "She has done this ever since I moved in here," said he. "Let her go."

The dog was Strickland's dog, so I said nothing, but I felt all that Strickland felt in being thus made light of. Tietjens encamped outside my bedroom window, and storm after storm came up, thundered on the thatch, and died away. The lightning spattered the sky as a thrown egg spatters a barn-door, but the light was pale blue, not yellow; and, looking through my split bamboo blinds, I could see the great dog standing, not sleeping, in the verandah, the hackles alift on her back and her feet anchored as tensely as the drawn wire-rope of a suspension bridge. In the very short pauses of the thunder I tried to sleep, but it seemed that some one wanted me very urgently. He, whoever he was, was trying to call me by name, but his voice was no more than a husky whisper. The thunder ceased, and Tietjens went into the garden and howled at the low moon. Somebody tried to open my door, walked about and about through the house and stood breathing heavily in the verandahs, and just when I was falling asleep I fancied that I heard a wild hammering and clamouring above my head or on the door.

I ran into Strickland's room and asked him whether he was ill, and had been calling for me. He was lying on his bed half dressed, a pipe in his mouth. "I thought you'd come," he said. "Have I been walking round the house recently?"

I explained that he had been tramping in the dining-room and the smoking-room and two or three other places; and he laughed and told me to go back to bed. I went back to bed and slept till the morning, but through all my mixed dreams I was sure I was doing some one an injustice in not attending to his wants. What those wants were I could not tell; but a fluttering, whispering, bolt-fumbling, lurking, loitering Someone was reproaching me for my slackness, and, half awake, I heard the howling of Tietjens in the garden and the threshing of the rain.

I lived in that house for two days. Strickland went to his office daily, leaving me alone for eight rotten hours with Tietjens for my only companion. As long as the full light lasted I was comfortable, and so was Tietjens; but in the twilight she and I moved into the back verandah and cuddled each other for company. We were alone in the house, but none the less it was much too fully occupied by a tenant with whom I did not wish to interfere. I never saw him, but I could see the curtains between the rooms quivering where he had just passed through; I could hear the chairs creaking as the bamboos sprung under a weight that had just quitted them; and I could feel when I went to get a book from the dining-room that somebody was waiting in the shadows of the front verandah till I should have gone away. Tietjens made the twilight more interesting by glaring into the darkened rooms with every hair erect, and following the motions of something that I could not see. She never entered the rooms, but her eyes moved interestedly: that was quite sufficient. Only when my servant came to trim the lamps and make all light and habitable she would come in with me and spend her time sitting on her haunches, watching an invisible extra man as he moved about behind my shoulder. Dogs are cheerful companions.

I explained to Strickland, gently as might be, that I would go over to the Club and find for myself quarters there. I admired his hospitality, was pleased with his guns and rods, but I did not much care for his house and its atmosphere. He heard me out to the end, and then smiled very wearily, but without contempt, for he is a man who understands things. "Stay on," he said, "and see what this thing means. All you have talked about I have known since I took the bungalow. Stay on and wait. Tietjens has left me. Are you going too?"

I had seen him through one little affair, connected with a heathen idol, that had brought me to the doors of a lunatic asylum, and I had no desire to help him through further experiences. He was a man to whom unpleasantnesses arrived as do dinners to ordinary people.

Therefore I explained more clearly than ever that I liked him immensely, and would be happy to see him in the daytime; but that I

did not care to sleep under his roof. This was after dinner, when
Tietjens had gone out to lie in the verandah.

"'Pon my soul, I don't wonder," said Strickland, with his eyes on the
ceiling-cloth. "Look at that!"

The tails of two brown snakes were hanging between the cloth and
the cornice of the wall. They threw long shadows in the lamplight.

"If you are afraid of snakes of course——" said Strickland.

I hate and fear snakes, because if you look into the eyes of any
snake you will see that it knows all and more of the mystery of man's
fall, and that it feels all the contempt that the Devil felt when Adam
was evicted from Eden. Besides which its bite is generally fatal, and it
twists up trouser legs.

"You ought to get your thatch overhauled," I said. "Give me a
mahseer-rod, and we'll poke 'em down."

"They'll hide among the roof-beams," said Strickland. "I can't stand
snakes overhead. I'm going up into the roof. If I shake 'em down, stand
by with a cleaning-rod and break their backs."

I was not anxious to assist Strickland in his work, but I took the
cleaning-rod and waited in the dining-room, while Strickland brought
a gardener's ladder from the verandah, and set it against the side of the
room. The snake-tails drew themselves up and disappeared. We could
hear the dry rushing scuttle of long bodies running over the baggy
ceiling-cloth. Strickland took a lamp with him, while I tried to make
clear to him the danger of hunting roof-snakes between a ceiling-cloth
and a thatch, apart from the deterioration of property caused by ripping
out ceiling-cloths.

"Nonsense!" said Strickland. "They're sure to hide near the walls by
the cloth. The bricks are too cold for 'em, and the heat of the room is
just what they like." He put his hand to the corner of the stuff and
ripped it from the cornice. It gave with a great sound of tearing, and
Strickland put his head through the opening into the dark of the angle
of the roof-beams. I set my teeth and lifted the rod, for I had not the
least knowledge of what might descend.

"H'm!" said Strickland, and his voice rolled and rumbled in the roof.
"There's room for another set of rooms up here, and, by Jove, some one
is occupying 'em!"

"Snakes?" I said from below.

"No. It's a buffalo. Hand me up the two last joints of a mahseer-rod,
and I'll prod it. It's lying on the main roof-beam."

I handed up the rod.

"What a nest for owls and serpents! No wonder the snakes live here," said Strickland, climbing farther into the roof. I could see his elbow thrusting with the rod. "Come out of that, whoever you are! Heads below there! It's falling."

I saw the ceiling cloth nearly in the centre of the room bag with a shape that was pressing it downwards and downwards towards the lighted lamp on the table. I snatched the lamp out of danger and stood back. Then the cloth ripped out from the walls, tore, split, swayed, and shot down upon the table something that I dared not look at, till Strickland had slid down the ladder and was standing by my side.

He did not say much, being a man of few words; but he picked up the loose end of the tablecloth and threw it over the remnants on the table.

"It strikes me," said he, putting down the lamp, "our friend Imray has come back. Oh! you would, would you?"

There was a movement under the cloth, and a little snake wriggled out, to be back-broken by the butt of the mahseer-rod. I was sufficiently sick to make no remarks worth recording.

Strickland meditated, and helped himself to drinks. The arrangement under the cloth made no more signs of life.

"Is it Imray?" I said.

Strickland turned back the cloth for a moment, and looked.

"It is Imray," he said; "and his throat is cut from ear to ear."

Then we spoke, both together and to ourselves: "That's why he whispered about the house."

Tietjens, in the garden, began to bay furiously. A little later her great nose heaved open the dining-room door.

She snuffed and was still. The tattered ceiling-cloth hung down almost to the level of the table, and there was hardly room to move away from the discovery.

Tietjens came in and sat down; her teeth bared under her lip and her forepaws planted. She looked at Strickland.

"It's a bad business, old lady," said he. "Men don't climb up into the roofs of their bungalows to die, and they don't fasten up the ceiling cloth behind 'em. Let's think it out."

"Let's think it out somewhere else," I said.

"Excellent idea! Turn the lamps out. We'll get into my room."

I did not turn the lamps out. I went into Strickland's room first, and allowed him to make the darkness. Then he followed me, and we lit tobacco and thought. Strickland thought. I smoked furiously, because I was afraid.

"Imray is back," said Strickland. "The question is—who killed

Imray? Don't talk, I've a notion of my own. When I took this bungalow I took over most of Imray's servants. Imray was guileless and inoffensive, wasn't he?"

I agreed; though the heap under the cloth had looked neither one thing nor the other.

"If I call in all the servants they will stand fast in a crowd and lie like Aryans. What do you suggest?"

"Call 'em in one by one," I said.

"They'll run away and give the news to all their fellows," said Strickland. "We must segregate 'em. Do you suppose your servant knows anything about it?"

"He may, for aught I know; but I don't think it's likely. He has only been here two or three days," I answered. "What's your notion?"

"I can't quite tell. How the dickens did the man get the wrong side of the ceiling-cloth?"

There was a heavy coughing outside Strickland's bedroom door. This showed that Bahadur Khan, his body-servant, had waked from sleep and wished to put Strickland to bed.

"Come in," said Strickland. "It's a very warm night, isn't it?"

Bahadur Khan, a great, green-turbaned, six-foot Mahomedan, said that it was a very warm night; but that there was more rain pending, which, by his Honour's favour, would bring relief to the country.

"It will be so, if God pleases," said Strickland, tugging off his boots. "It is in my mind, Bahadur Khan, that I have worked thee remorselessly for many days—ever since that time when thou first camest into my service. What time was that?"

"Has the Heaven-born forgotten? It was when Imray Sahib went secretly to Europe without warning given; and I—even I—came into the honoured service of the protector of the poor."

"And Imray Sahib went to Europe?"

"It is so said among those who were his servants."

"And thou wilt take service with him when he returns?"

"Assuredly, Sahib. He was a good master, and cherished his dependants."

"That is true. I am very tired, but I go buck-shooting to-morrow. Give me the little sharp rifle that I use for black-buck; it is in the case yonder."

The man stooped over the case; handed barrels, stock, and fore-end to Strickland, who fitted all together, yawning dolefully. Then he reached down to the gun-case, took a solid-drawn cartridge, and slipped it into the breech of the .360 Express.

"And Imray Sahib has gone to Europe secretly! That is very strange, Bahadur Khan, is it not?"

"What do I know of the ways of the white man, Heaven-born?"

"Very little, truly. But thou shalt know more anon. It has reached me that Imray Sahib has returned from his so long journeyings, and that even now he lies in the next room, waiting his servant."

"Sahib!"

The lamplight slid along the barrels of the rifle as they levelled themselves at Bahadur Khan's broad breast.

"Go and look!" said Strickland. "Take a lamp. Thy master is tired, and he waits thee. Go!"

The man picked up a lamp, and went into the dining-room, Strickland following, and almost pushing him with the muzzle of the rifle. He looked for a moment at the black depths behind the ceiling-cloth; at the writhing snake under foot; and last, a gray glaze settling on his face, at the thing under the tablecloth.

"Hast thou seen?" said Strickland after a pause.

"I have seen. I am clay in the white man's hands. What does the Presence do?"

"Hang thee within the month. What else?"

"For killing him? Nay, Sahib, consider. Walking among us, his servants, he cast his eyes upon my child, who was four years old. Him he bewitched, and in ten days he died of the fever—my child!"

"What said Imray Sahib?"

"He said he was a handsome child, and patted him on the head; wherefore my child died. Wherefore I killed Imray Sahib in the twilight, when he had come back from office, and was sleeping. Wherefore I dragged him up into the roof-beams and made all fast behind him. The Heaven-born knows all things. I am the servant of the Heaven-born."

Strickland looked at me above the rifle, and said, in the vernacular, "Thou art witness to this saying? He has killed."

Bahadur Khan stood ashen gray in the light of the one lamp. The need for justification came upon him very swiftly. "I am trapped," he said, "but the offence was that man's. He cast an evil eye upon my child, and I killed and hid him. Only such as are served by devils," he glared at Tietjens, couched stolidly before him, "only such could know what I did."

"It was clever. But thou shouldst have lashed him to the beam with a rope. Now, thou thyself wilt hang by a rope. Orderly!"

A drowsy policeman answered Strickland's call. He was followed by another, and Tietjens sat wondrous still.

"Take him to the police-station," said Strickland. "There is a case toward."

"Do I hang, then?" said Bahadur Khan, making no attempt to escape, and keeping his eyes on the ground.

"If the sun shines or the water runs—yes!" said Strickland.

Bahadur Khan stepped back one long pace, quivered, and stood still. The two policemen waited further orders.

"Go!" said Strickland.

"Nay; but I go very swiftly," said Bahadur Khan. "Look! I am even now a dead man."

He lifted his foot, and to the little toe there clung the head of the half-killed snake, firm fixed in the agony of death.

"I come of land-holding stock," said Bahadur Khan, rocking where he stood. "It were a disgrace to me to go to the public scaffold: therefore I take this way. Be it remembered that the Sahib's shirts are correctly enumerated, and that there is an extra piece of soap in his washbasin. My child was bewitched, and I slew the wizard. Why should you seek to slay me with the rope? My honour is saved, and—and—I die."

At the end of an hour he died, as they die who are bitten by the little brown *karait*, and the policemen bore him and the thing under the tablecloth to their appointed places. All were needed to make clear the disappearance of Imray.

"This," said Strickland, very calmly, as he climbed into bed, "is called the nineteenth century. Did you hear what that man said?"

"I heard," I answered. "Imray made a mistake."

"Simply and solely through not knowing the nature of the Oriental, and the coincidence of a little seasonal fever. Bahadur Khan had been with him for four years."

I shuddered. My own servant had been with me for exactly that length of time. When I went over to my own room I found my man waiting, impassive as the copper head on a penny, to pull off my boots.

"What has befallen Bahadur Khan?" said I.

"He was bitten by a snake and died. The rest the Sahib knows," was the answer.

"And how much of this matter hast thou known?"

"As much as might be gathered from One coming in in the twilight to seek satisfaction. Gently, Sahib. Let me pull off those boots."

I had just settled to the sleep of exhaustion when I heard Strickland shouting from his side of the house—

"Tietjens has come back to her place!"

And so she had. The great deerhound was couched statelily on her own bedstead on her own blanket, while, in the next room, the idle, empty, ceiling-cloth waggled as it trailed on the table.

Headon Hill

(1857–1924)

"HEADON HILL" (the pseudonym of Francis Edward Grainger) is one of the forgotten authors of detective fiction. The most complimentary thing that has been said about him is John Carter's comment that Hill "ill deserves his oblivion." Certainly among collectors, his short-story volumes remain well-known, but only because they are of legendary rarity: *Clues from a Detective's Camera* (1893), *Zambra, The Detective* (1894), *The Divinations of Kala Persad* (1895), *Coronation Mysteries* (1902), *Seaward for the Foe* (1903), and *Radford Shone* (1908). The rarest of all is *Cabinet Pictures* (or *Cabinet Secrets*); It was definitely published in a cheap paperback in 1893, but no copy is known to survive.

The stories about Sebastian Zambra in Hill's first two surviving volumes retain some interest, though too often they borrow plotlines from Sherlock Holmes. Of much more significance are the cases in *The Divination of Kala Persad*. In the first story, Mark Poignand goes to India and a wizened old native supplies the clue to solve a mystery. In the later stories, Poignand brings the old man to England with him, where his meditative techniques help resolve crimes.

The Divination of the Zagury Capsules

ON THE FIRST FLOOR of one of the handsome buildings that are rapidly replacing "Old London" in the streets running from the Strand to the Embankment was a suite of offices, bearing on the outer door the words "Confidential Advice," and below, in smaller letters, "Mark Poignand, Manager." The outer offices, providing accommodation for a couple of up-to-date clerks and a lady typist, were resplendent with brass-furnished counters and cathedral-glass partitions; and the private room in the rear, used by the manager, was fitted up in the quietly luxurious style of a club smoking-room. But even this latter did not form the innermost sanctum of all, for at its far corner a locked door led into a still more private chamber, which was never entered by any of the inferior staff, and but rarely by the manager himself. In this room—strange anomaly within earshot of the thronging traffic of the Strand—a little wizened old Hindoo mostly sat cross-legged, playing with a basket of cobras, and chewing betel-nut from morning to night. Now and again he would be called on to lay aside his occupations for a brief space, and these intervals were quickly becoming a factor to be reckoned with by those who desired to envelop their doings in darkness.

Mark Poignand, though the younger son of a good family, possessed only a modest capital, bringing him an income of under three hundred a year, and after his success in the matter of the Afghan Kukhri, he was taken with the idea of entering professionally on the field of "private investigation." He was shrewd enough to see that without Kala Persad's aid his journey to India would have ended in failure, and he determined to utilise the snake-charmer's instinctive faculty as the mainstay of the new undertaking. He had no difficulty in working upon the old man's sense of gratitude to induce him to go to England, and all that remained was to sell out a portion of his capital and establish himself in good style as a private investigator, with Kala Persad installed in the back room. A rumour had got about that he had successfully conducted a delicate mission to India, and this, in conjunction with the novelty of such a business being run by a young man not unknown in society, brought him clients from the start.

At first Mark felt some anxiety as to the outcome of his experiment, but by compelling himself with an effort to be true to the system he had drawn up, he found that his first few unimportant cases worked out with the best results. Briefly, his system was this:—When an inquiry was placed in his hands, he would lay the facts as presented to him before Kala Persad, and would then be guided in future operations by his follower's suspicions. On one or two occasions he had nearly failed through a tendency to prefer his own judgment to the snake-charmer's instinct, but he had been able to retrace his steps in time to prove the correctness of Kala Persad's original solution, and to save the credit of the office. It devolved upon himself entirely to procure evidence and discover how the mysteries were brought about, and in this he found ample scope for his ingenuity, for Kala Persad was profoundly ignorant of the methods adopted by those whom he suspected. It was more than half the battle, however, to start with the weird old man's finger pointed, so far unerringly, at the right person, and Mark Poignand recognised that without the oracle of the back room he would have been nowhere. Some of Kala Persad's indications pointed in directions into which his own wildest flights of fancy would never have led him.

It was not till Poignand had been in practice for nearly three months that a case was brought to him involving the capital charge—a case of such terrible interest to one of our oldest noble families that its unravelling sent clients thronging to the office, and assured the success of the enterprise. One murky, fog-laden morning in December he was sitting in the private room, going through the day's correspondence, when the clerk brought him a lady's visiting card, engraved with the name of "Miss Lascelles."

"What like is she?" asked Poignand.

"Well-dressed, young, and, as far as I can make out under her thick veil, good-looking," replied the clerk. "I should judge from her voice that she is anxious and agitated."

"Very well," replied Poignand; "show her in when I ring." And the other having retired, he rose and went to the back wall, where an oil painting, heavily framed, and tilted at a considerable angle, was hung.

Behind the picture was a sliding panel, which he shot back, leaving an opening about a foot square into the inner room.

"Ho! there, Kala Persad," he called through. "A lady is here with a secret; are you ready?"

As soon as a wheezy voice on the other side had chuckled "Ha, Sahib!" in reply, Poignand readjusted the picture, but left the aperture open. Settling himself in his chair, he touched a bell, and the next moment was rising to receive his client—a tall, graceful girl, clad in expensive mourning. Directly the clerk had left the room, she raised her veil, displaying a face winningly beautiful, but intensely pale, and marked with the traces of recent grief. Her nervousness was so painfully evident that Poignand hastened to reassure her.

"I hope you will try and treat me as though I were a private friend," he said. "If you can bring yourself to give me your entire confidence, I have no doubt that I can serve you, but it is necessary that you should state your case with the utmost fulness."

His soothing tones had the desired effect. "I have every confidence in you," was the reply, given in a low, sweet voice. "It is not that that troubles me, but the fearful peril threatening the honour, and perhaps the life, of one very dear to me. I was tempted to come to you, Mr. Poignand, because of the marvellous insight which enabled you to recover the Duchess of Gainsborough's jewel-case the other day. It seemed almost as though you could read the minds of persons you have not even seen, and, Heaven knows, there is a secret in some dark mind somewhere that I must uncover."

"Let me have the details as concisely as possible, please," said Poignand, pushing his own chair back a little, so as to bring the sound of her voice more in line with the hidden opening.

"You must know then," Miss Lascelles began, "that I live with my father, who is a retired general of the Indian army, at The Briary—a house on the outskirts of Beechfield, in Buckinghamshire. I am engaged to be married to the second son of Lord Bradstock—the Honble. Harry Furnival, as he is called by courtesy. The matter which I want you to investigate is the death of Lord Bradstock's eldest son, Leonard Furnival, which took place last week."

"Indeed!" exclaimed Poignand; "I saw the death announced in the paper, but there was no hint of anything wrong. I gathered that the death arose from natural causes."

"So it was believed at the time," replied Miss Lascelles, "but owing to circumstances that have since occurred, the body was exhumed on the day after the funeral. As the result of an autopsy held yesterday,

Leonard's death is now attributed to poison, and an inquest has been ordered for to-morrow. In the meanwhile, by some cruel combination of chances, Harry is suspected of having given the poison to the brother whom he loved so well, in order to clear the way for his own succession; and the terrible part of it all is that his father, and others who ought to stand by him in his need, share in that suspicion. He has not the slightest wish to go away or to shirk inquiry, but he believes that he is already watched by the police, and that he will certainly be arrested after the inquest to-morrow.

"I must go back a little, so as to make you understand exactly what is known to have happened, and also what is supposed to have happened at Bradstock Hall, which is a large mansion, standing about a mile and a half from the small country town of Beechfield. For the last twelve months of his life, or, to speak more correctly, for the last ten months but two, Leonard was given up as in a hopeless consumption, from which he could not possibly recover. At the commencement of his illness, which arose from a chill caught while out shooting, he was attended by Dr. Youle, of Beechfield. Almost from the first the doctor gave Lord Bradstock to understand that his eldest son's lungs were seriously affected, and that his recovery was very doubtful. As time went on, Dr. Youle became confirmed in his view, and, despite the most constant attention, the invalid gradually declined till, about two months ago, Lord Bradstock determined to have a second medical opinion. Though Dr. Youle was very confident that he had diagnosed and treated the case correctly, he consented to meet Dr. Lucas, the other Beechfield medical man, in consultation. After a careful examination Dr. Lucas entirely disagreed with Dr. Youle as to the nature of the disease, being of the opinion that the trouble arose from pneumonia, which should yield to the proper treatment for that malady. This meant, of course, that if he was right there was still a prospect of the patient's recovery, and so buoyed up was Lord Bradstock with hope that he installed Dr. Lucas in the place of Dr. Youle, who was very angry at the doubt cast on his treatment. The new *regimen* worked well for some weeks, and Leonard began to gain ground, very slowly, but still so decidedly that Dr. Lucas was hopeful of getting him downstairs by the early spring.

"Imagine then the consternation of every one when, one morning last week, the valet, on going into the room, found the poor fellow so much worse that Dr. Lucas had to be hurriedly sent for, and only arrived in time to see his patient die. Death was immediately preceded by the spitting of blood and by violent paroxysms of coughing, and these being more or less symptoms of both the maladies that had been in turn treated, no one thought of foul play for an instant. Discussion of the case was confined to the fact that Dr. Youle was now proved to have been right and Dr. Lucas wrong.

"The first hint of anything irregular came from Dixon, the valet, on Monday last, the day of the funeral. After the ceremony, he was clearing away from the sick-room the last sad traces of Leonard's illness, when, among the medicine bottles and appliances, he came across a small box of gelatine capsules, which he remembered to have seen Mr. Harry Furnival give to his brother the day before the latter's death. Thinking that they had been furnished by Dr. Lucas, and there being a good many left in the box, he put them aside with a stethoscope and one or two things which the doctor had left, and later in the day took them over to his house at Beechfield. The moment Dr. Lucas saw the capsules he disclaimed having furnished them, or even having prescribed anything of the kind, and expressed surprise at Dixon's statement that he had seen Harry present the box to his brother. Recognising them as a freely advertised patent specific, he was curious to test their composition, and, having opened one with this purpose in view, he at once made the most dreadful discovery. Instead of its original filling—probably harmless, whatever it may have been—the capsule contained a substance which he believed to be a fatal dose of a vegetable poison—little known in this country, but in common use among the natives of Madagascar—called tanghin. Turning again to one of the entire capsules, he found slight traces of the gelatine case having been melted and re-sealed.

"I cannot blame him for the course he took. It was his duty to report the discovery, and apart from this he was naturally anxious to follow up a theory which would prove his own opinion, and not Dr. Youle's, to have been right. For if Leonard Furnival had really died by poison, it was still likely that, given a fair chance, he might have verified his, Dr. Lucas', prediction of recovery. The necessary steps were taken, and the examination of the body, conducted by the Home Office authorities, proved Dr. Lucas to be right in both points. Not only was it shown that Leonard Furnival undoubtedly died from the effects of the poison, but it was clearly demonstrated that he was recovering from the pneumonia for which Dr. Lucas was treating him."

"You have stated the case admirably, Miss Lascelles," said Poignand. "There is yet one important point left, though. How does Mr. Harry Furnival account for his having provided the deceased with these capsules?"

"He admits that he procured them for his brother at his request, and he indignantly denies that he tampered with them," was the reply. "It seems that Leonard was attracted some months ago by the advertisement of a patent medicine known as the 'Zagury Capsules,' which profess to be a sleep-producing tonic. Not liking to incur the professional ridicule of his medical man, he induced his brother to procure them for him. This first occurred when Dr. Youle was in attendance, and being under the impression that they did him some good, he continued to take them while in Dr. Lucas' care. Harry was in the habit of purchasing them quite openly at the chemist's in Beechfield as though for himself, but he says that before humouring his brother he took the precaution of asking Dr. Youle if the capsules were harmless, and received an affirmative reply. Unfortunately Dr. Youle, though naturally anxious to refute the poison theory, has forgotten the circumstance, both he and Dr. Lucas having been successively ignorant of the use of the capsules."

"You say that Lord Bradstock believes in his son's guilt?" asked Poignand.

"He has not said so in so many words," replied Miss Lascelles, "but he refuses to see him till the matter is cleared up. Lord Bradstock is a very stern man, and Leonard was always his favourite. My dear father and I are the only ones to refuse to listen to the rumours against Harry that are flying about Beechfield. We know that Harry could no more have committed a crime than Lord Bradstock himself, and papa would have come with me here to-day were he not laid up with gout. And now, Mr. Poignand, can you help us? It is almost too much to expect you to do anything in time to prevent an arrest, but—but will you try?"

The circumstances demanded a guarded answer. "Indeed I will," said Poignand. "It is not my custom to give a definite opinion till I have had an opportunity to look into a case, but I shall go down to Beechfield presently—it is only an hour's run, I think—and I will call upon you later in the day. I trust by then to be able to report progress."

At his request, Miss Lascelles added a few particulars about the persons living at Bradstock Hall on the day of the death—besides Lord Bradstock and his two sons, there were only the servants—and took her leave, being anxious to catch the next train home. Poignand waited till her cab wheels sounded in the street below, then rose hastily, and, having first closed the sliding panel, passed into the room beyond. He looked thoughtful and worried, for he could not, rack his brains as he would, see any other solution to the puzzle than the one he was called upon to refute. It was true that the details of which he was so far in possession were of the broadest, but every one of them pointed to Harry Furnival—the admittedly secret purchaser of the capsule—as the only person who could have given them their deadly attributes. And then, to back up that admission, there loomed up, in the way of a successful issue, the damning supplement of a powerful motive. The tenant of the back room, he fully expected, would confirm his own impression—that they were called on to champion a lost cause.

There was nothing at first sight as he entered the plainly furnished apartment either to reassure or to dash his hopes. Kala Persad despised the two chairs that had been provided for his accommodation, and spent most of his time squatting or reclining on the Indian *charpoy* which had been unearthed for him from some East-end opium den. He was sitting on the edge of it now, with his skinny brown hands stretched out to the warmth of a glowing fire, for Miss Lascelles' story had kept him at the panel long enough to induce shivering; and if there was one thing that made him repent his bargain, it was the cold of an English winter. At his feet, like-minded with their owner, the cobras squirmed and twisted in the basket which had first excited Poignand's curiosity on the midnight solitudes of the Sholapur road.

"Well?" said Poignand; "do you know enough English by this time to have understood what the lady said, or must I repeat it?"

The old man raised his filmy eyes, and regarded the other with a puckering of the leathery brows that might have meant anything from contempt to deep reverence.

"Words—seprit words—tell Kala Persad nothing, Sahib," he said. "All words together—what you call one burra jumble—help Kala Persad to pick kernel from the nut. Mem Sahib ishpoke many things no use, but I understand enough to read secret. Why!"—with infinite scorn—"the secret read itself."

Poignand's heart sank within him.

"I was afraid it was rather too clear a case for us to be of any use," he said.

The snake-charmer, as though he had not heard, went on to recapitulate the heads of the story in little snappy jerks. "One old burra Lord Sahib, big estates; two son, one very sick. First one *hakim* (doctor) try to cure—no use. Then other *hakim*; no use too—sick man die. Other son bring physic, poison physic, give him brother. Servant man find poison after dead. Old lord angry, says his son common *budmash* murderer; but missee Mem Sahib, betrothed of Harry, she say no, and come buy wisdom of Kala Persad. You not think that plain enough, sahib?"

"Uncommonly so," said Poignand dejectedly. "It is pretty clear that the Mem Sahib, as you call her, wants us to undertake a job not exactly in our line of business. If we are to satisfy her, we shall have to prove that a guilty man is innocent."

"Yah! Yah-ah-ah-ah!" Kala Persad drawled, hugging himself, and rocking to and fro in delight. And before Poignand could divine his intention, he had leaped from the *charpoy* to hiss with his betel-stained lips an emphatic sentence into the ear of his employer, who first started back in astonishment, then listened gravely. Having thus unburdened himself, Kala Persad returned to the warmth of the fire, nodding and mouthing and muttering, much as when his wizened face had peered from among the bushes in Major Merwood's garden. The old man was excited; the jungle-instinct of pursuit was strong upon him, and he began to croon weird noises to his cobras.

Poignand looked at the red-turbaned, huddled figure almost in awe; then went slowly back into his own room.

"It is marvellous," he muttered to himself. "As usual! the solution is the very last thing one would have thought of, and yet when once presented in shape is distinctly possible. It is on the cards that he may be wrong, but I will fight it out on that line."

*   *   *

Early in the afternoon of the same day there was some commotion at the Beechfield railway station, on the arrival of a London train, through the station-master being called to a first-class compartment in which a gentleman had been taken suddenly ill. The passenger, who was booked through to the North, was, at his own request, removed from the train to the adjacent Railway Hotel, where he was deposited, weak and shivering all over with ague, in the landlord's private room at the back of the bar. The administration of some very potent brown brandy caused him to recover sufficiently to give some account of himself, and to inquire if medical skill was within the capabilities of Beechfield. He was an officer in the army, it appeared—Captain Hawke, of the 24th Lancers—and was home on sick leave from India, where he had contracted the intermittent fever that was his present trouble.

"I ought to have known better than to travel on one of the days when this infernal scourge was due," he said; "but having done so, I must make the best of it. Are there any doctors in the place who are not absolute duffers?"

The landlord, anxious for the medical credit of Beechfield, informed his guest that there was a choice of two qualified practitioners. "Dr. Youle is the old-established man, sir, and accounted clever by some.

Dr. Lucas is younger, and lately set up, though he is getting on better since his lordship took him up at the Hall."

"I don't care who took him up," replied Captain Hawke irascibly. "Which was the last to lose a patient? that will be as good a test as anything."

"Well, sir, I suppose, in a manner of speaking, Dr. Lucas was," said the landlord, "seeing that the Honourable Leonard died under his care; but people are saying that Mr. Harry——"

"That will do," interposed the invalid, with military testiness; "don't worry me with your Toms and Harrys. Send for the other man—Youle, or whatever his name is."

The subservient landlord, much impressed with the captain's imperious petulance, which bespoke an ability and willingness to pay for the best, went out to execute the errand in person. The moment his broad back had disappeared into the outer regions, Captain Hawke, doubtless under the influence of the brown brandy, grew so much better that he sat up and looked about him. The bar-parlour in which he found himself was partly separated from the private bar by a glass partition, having a movable window that had been left open. The customers were thus both audible and visible to the belated traveller, who, strangely enough for a dapper young captain of Lancers, evinced a furtive interest in their personality and conversation. The first was chiefly of the country tradesman type, while the latter consisted of the "'E done it, sure enough" style of argument, usual in such places when rustic stolidity is startled by the commission of some serious crime.

"There was two 'tecs from Scotland Yard watching the Hall all night. 'Tain't no use his trying to bolt," said the local butcher.

"They do say as how the warrant's made out already," put in another; "only they won't lock him up till to-morrow, owing to wanting his evidence at the inquest. Terrible hard on his lordship, ain't it?"

"That be so," added a third worthy; "the old lord was always partial to Leonard—natural like, perhaps, seeing as he was the heir. But whatever ailed Master Harry to go and do such a thing licks me. He was always a nice-spoken lad, and open as the day, to my thinking."

"These rustics have got hold of a foregone conclusion, apparently," said the sufferer from ague to himself, as footsteps sounded in the passage, and he sank wearily down on the sofa again.

The next moment the landlord re-entered, accompanied by a stout and rather tall man, whom he introduced as Dr. Youle. The doctor's age might have been forty-five, and his figure, just tending to middle-aged stoutness, was encased in the regulation black frock-coat of his profession. There was nothing about him to suggest even a remote connection with the tragedy that was engrossing the town. In fact, the expression of his broad face, taken as a whole, was that of one on good terms with himself and with all the world; though it is a question whether the large, not to say "hungry" mouth, if studied separately, did not discount the value of its perpetual smile. He entered with the mingled air of importance and genial respect which the occasion demanded.

The captain's manner to the doctor differed from his manner to the landlord. Leaving medical skill out of the question, he recognised that he had a gentleman and a man of some local position to deal with, and he modified his petulance accordingly. The landlord had already told the doctor the history of his arrival, so that it only remained to describe his sensations and the nature of his ailment. The latter, indeed, was more or less apparent; for the shivering was still sufficiently violent to shake the horse-hair sofa on which he lay.

"The surgeon of my regiment used to give me some stuff that relieved this horrid trembling instantly," said the captain; "but I never could get him to part with the prescription. However, I daresay, doctor, that you know of something equally efficacious."

"Yes, I flatter myself that I can improve matters in that direction," was the reply. "My house is quite close, and I will run over and fetch you a draught. You are, of course, aware that the ague is of an intermittent character, recurring every other day till it subsides?"

"I know it only too well," replied Captain Hawke. "I shall be as fit as a fiddle to-morrow, probably only to relapse the next day into another of these attacks. I do not know how you are situated domestically, doctor; but I was wondering whether you could take me in, and look after me for a few days till I get over this bout. I am nervous about myself, and, without any disparagement to the hospitality of our friend here, I should feel happier under medical supervision."

Dr. Youle's hungry mouth showed by its eager twitching that the prospect of a resident patient, even for a day or two, was by no means distasteful to him. "I shall be only too pleased to look after you," he said. "I shall be much occupied to-morrow—rather unpleasantly employed as a witness at an inquest; but, as you say, you will most likely be feeling better then, and not so much in need of my services. If you really wish the arrangement, you had better have a closed fly and come over at once. I will run on ahead, and prepare a draught for you."

The landlord, not best pleased with the abstraction of his guest, went to order a carriage, and a quarter of an hour later Captain Hawke, with his luggage, was driven to the doctor's residence—a prim, red-brick house in the middle of the sleepy High Street. Dr. Youle was waiting on the doorstep to receive his patient, and at once conducted him to a small back room on the ground floor, evidently the surgery.

"Drink this," he said, handing the invalid a glass of foaming liquid, "and then if you will sit quietly in the easy chair while I see about your things, I don't doubt that I shall find you better. The effect is almost instantaneous."

But the doctor himself could hardly have foreseen with what rapidity his words were to be verified. He had no sooner closed the door than Captain Hawke sprang to his feet, all traces of shivering gone, and applied himself to the task of searching the room. One wall was fitted with shelves laden with bottles containing liquids, and these obtained the eccentric invalid's first attention. Rapidly scanning the labels, he passed along the shelves apparently without satisfying his quest, for he came to the end without putting his hand to bottle or jar. Pausing for a moment to listen to the doctor's voice in the distance directing the fly-man with the luggage, he recommenced his search by examining a range of drawers that formed a back to the mixing dresser, and which, also systematically labelled, were found to contain dry drugs. Here again nothing held his attention, and he was turning away with vexed impatience on his face, when, at the very end of the row, and lower than the others, he espied a drawer ticketted "Miscellaneous." Pulling it open, he saw that it was three parts filled with medicine corks, scarlet string, and sealing wax, all heaped together in such confusion that it was impossible to take in the details of the medley at a glance. Removing the string and sealing wax, the inquisitive captain ran his fingers lightly through the bulk of the corks, till they closed on some hard substance hidden from view. When he withdrew his hand it held a small package, which, after one flash of eager scrutiny, he transferred to his pocket.

Even now, however, though he drew a long breath of relief, it seemed that the search was not yet complete; for, after carefully rearranging and closing the drawer, he tried the door of a corner cupboard, only to find it locked. He had just drawn a bunch of peculiar-looking keys from his pocket, when the voice of the doctor bidding the flyman a cheery "Good-day!" caused him to glide quietly back to the armchair. The next moment his host entered, rubbing his hands, and smiling professionally.

"Your mixture has done wonders, doctor," the captain said. "I am another man already, and my experience tells me that I am safe for another forty-eight hours. By the way, I was so seedy when they hauled me out of the train that I don't even know where I am. What place is this?"

"This is Beechfield in Buckinghamshire, about an hour from town," said the doctor. "An old-fashioned country centre, you know."

"Beechfield, by Jove!" exclaimed Captain Hawke, with an air of mingled surprise and pleasure. "Well, that is a curious coincidence, for an old friend of my father's lives, or lived, somewhere about here, I believe—General Lascelles—do you know him?"

"Yes, I know the General," replied Dr. Youle, a little absently: then added, "He has a nice little place, called The Elms, a hundred yards or so beyond the top of the High Street."

"Well, I feel so much better that I will stroll out and see the General," said Hawke. "I will take care to be back in time to have the pleasure of dining with you—at half-past seven, I think you said?"

"Yes, that is the hour," replied the doctor thoughtfully; "but are you sure you are wise in venturing out? Besides, you will find the General and his daughter in some distress. They are interested——"

"All the more reason that I go and cheer them up. What is wrong with them?" snapped the patient.

"They are interested in the inquest on poor young Furnival, which I told you was to be held to-morrow. It is possible that you may hear me spoken of in connection with the case, though their view of it ought to be identical with mine—that death was due to natural causes. I believe the whole thing is a cock-and-bull story, got up by an impudent young practitioner here to account for his losing his patient, as I knew he would from the first. The wonder is that the Home Office analysts should back him up in pretending to discern a poison about which hardly anything is known."

The captain had risen, his face wearing a look of infinite boredom. "My dear doctor," he said, "you can't expect me to concern myself with the matter; I've quite enough to do to worry about my own ailments. I only want to see the General to chat about old times, not about local inquests. Will you kindly show me your front door, and point out the direction I should take to reach The Elms?"

Dr. Youle smiled, with perhaps a shade of relief at the invalid's self-absorption, and led the way out of the room. The captain followed him into the passage for a few paces, then, with an exclamation about a forgotten handkerchief, darted back into the surgery, and, quick as lightning, undid the catch that fastened the window, being at his host's heels again almost before the latter had noticed his absence. In another minute, duly instructed in the route, he started walking swiftly through the shadows of the early winter twilight towards the end of the town.

But apparently the immediate desire to visit his "father's old friend" had passed away. Taking the first by-way that ran at right angles to the High Street, he passed thence into a lane that brought him to the back of Dr. Youle's house, where he disappeared among the foliage of the garden. It was a long three-quarters of an hour before he crept cautiously into the lane again, and even then The Elms was not his first destination. Not till he had paid two other rather lengthy visits—one of them to the Beechfield chemist—did he find himself ushered into the presence of General and Miss Lascelles. A distinguished-looking young man, dressed, like father and daughter, in deep mourning, was with them in the fire-lit library, and evinced an equal agitation on the entrance of Dr. Youle's resident patient. The conversation, however, did not turn on bygone associations and mutual reminiscences. Miss Lascelles sprang forward with outstretched hands and glistening eyes,—

"Oh, Mr. Poignand!" she cried; "I can see that you have news for us—good news, too, I think?"

"Yes," was the reply; "I hold the real murderer of Leonard Furnival in the hollow of my hand, which means, of course, that the other absurd charge is demolished."

*　　*　　*

Dr. Youle, who was a bachelor, had ordered his cook to prepare a dainty little repast in honour of the guest, and as the dinner hour approached, and "the captain" had not returned, he began to get anxious about the fish. On the stroke of seven, however, the front door bell rang, and the laggard was admitted, looking so flushed and heated that, when they were seated in the cosy dining-room, the doctor ventured on a remonstrance.

"I have been interested," was the explanation, "very deeply interested, by what I heard at the Lascelles' about this poisoning case—so much so that I was obliged to stay and hear it out. It seems that the stuff employed was tanghin, the poison which the natives of Madagascar use in their trials by ordeal. Have you ever seen a trial by ordeal, doctor?"

It was the host's turn now to be bored by the subject. He shook his head absently, and passed the sherry decanter.

"It is an admirable institution for keeping down the population," persisted the other. "Whenever a man is suspected of a crime, he has to eat half a dozen of these berries, on the supposition that if he is innocent they will do him no harm. Needless to say, the poison fails to discriminate between the stomachs of good and bad men, and the accused is always proved guilty. It must be a terrible thing to be proved guilty when you are innocent, Dr. Youle."

Some change of tone caused the doctor to look up and catch his guest's eye. The two men stared steadily at each other for the space of ten seconds, then the doctor winced a little and said,—

"What have I to do with Madagascar poisons and innocent men? Tanghin is hardly known in this country, and cannot be procured at the wholesale druggists. I have never even seen it."

The sound of a bell ringing somewhere in the kitchen premises reached them, and Poignand pushed his chair back from the table as he replied,—

"Not even seen it, eh? Strange, then, that a supply of the berries, and a tincture distilled from them, should have been discovered in that corner cupboard in your surgery. Strange, too, that a box of the Zagury capsules, in which vehicle the poison was administered to Leonard Furnival, should have been found among your medicine corks, stamped with the rubber stamp of Hollings, the Beechfield chemist, though he swears he never supplied you with any capsules. Stranger still that Hollings should remember—now that it has been called to his mind—your apparently aimless lingering in his shop on the day before the death, and the fidgety movements now revealed as the legerdemain by which you substituted your poisoned packet for the one the chemist had lying ready on the counter against Mr. Harry Furnival's call. It is no use, Dr. Youle; you would have been wiser to have destroyed such fatal evidences. Your wicked sacrifice of a valuable life, in order to prove your mistaken treatment right at the expense of your successful rival, is as clear as noonday. Ah! here is the inspector."

As he spoke, two or three men entered the room, and one of them— the detective who had been detailed to watch Harry Furnival—quietly effected the arrest. The wretched culprit, broken down completely by Mark Poignand's unofficial "bluff," blustered a little at first, but quickly weakened, and saved further trouble by a full admission, almost on the exact lines of the accusation. Knowing, by his previous observations, and from the question asked him by Harry, that Leonard Furnival was in the habit of taking the patent capsules, he had bought a box in London, and, after replacing the original contents with poison, had watched his chance to change the boxes. His motive was to injure, and put in the wrong, the rising young practitioner who had supplanted him, and whose toxicological knowledge, by a curious irony of fate, was the first link in the chain of detection. The tanghin berries he had procured from a firm of Madagascar merchants, by passing himself off as the representative of a well-known wholesale druggist, who, at the trial, disclaimed all knowledge of him and all dealings in the fatal drug.

Poignand's working out of the case was regarded as masterly; but he knew very well that unless he had started on the presupposition of Youle's guilt, he should never have come upon the truth. When he got back to the office, he went straight through to the inner room, where the shrunken, red-turbaned figure was playing with the cobras by the fire.

"Now tell me, how did you suspect the doctor?" asked Poignand, after outlining the events which had led to a successful issue.

"Sahib," said Kala Persad gravely, "what else was there of hatred, of injury, of revenge in the story the pretty Missee Mem Sahib told? Where there is a wound on the black heart of man, there is the place to look for crime."

Baroness Orczy

(1865–1947)

EMMA MAGDALENA ROSALIA MARIE JOSEPHA BARBARA, Baroness Orczy, was born in Hungary, educated in Paris and Brussels, and at the age of fifteen moved to London. In 1899 her first novel, *The Emperor's Candlesticks*, was published, and in 1902 she created her most enduring character, Sir Percy Blakeney. (Blakeney, known as the Scarlet Pimpernel, rescues aristocrats from the guillotine during the French Revolution.) After the First World War she moved to Monte Carlo, returning occasionally to London, where she died shortly after the Second World War.

Orczy's first stories about the Old Man in the Corner (who in one story receives the incongruous name of Bill Owen) were published in the 1901 volume of *The Royal Magazine*. In the final story of the first series, the Old Man is revealed as a murderer himself, but Orczy blithely ignored that problem and wrote a second series, each story set in a major British town. The third series, under the title *The Case of Miss Elliott* (1905), was actually published in book form before the first and second series, which were collected as *The Old Man in the Corner** four years later. Perhaps making the Old Man a murderer did not sit well with the publisher, for when the first series was finally collected in book form, Orczy omitted the section positively incriminating the Old Man.

Besides their constant variety and cleverness, the Old Man in the Corner stories are notable for offering the first example of the armchair detective. True, the Old Man does occasionally visit the crime scenes and take photographs, and sometimes he attends trials, but mostly he solves the mysteries brought him by a reporter named Polly Burton while sitting in a small restaurant, drinking milk, eating cheesecake, and tying endless knots in a piece of string.

---

*"The York Mystery" is comprised of three consecutive chapters from that volume: "The York Mystery," "The Capital Charge," and "A Broken-Hearted Woman."

The York Mystery

THE MAN in the corner looked quite cheerful that morning; he had had two glasses of milk and had even gone to the extravagance of an extra cheese-cake. Polly knew that he was itching to talk police and murders, for he cast furtive glances at her from time to time, produced a bit of string, tied and untied it into scores of complicated knots, and finally, bringing out his pocket-book, he placed two or three photographs before her.

"Do you know who that is?" he asked, pointing to one of these.

The girl looked at the face on the picture. It was that of a woman, not exactly pretty, but very gentle and childlike, with a strange pathetic look in the large eyes which was wonderfully appealing.

"That was Lady Arthur Skelmerton," he said, and in a flash there flitted before Polly's mind the weird and tragic history which had broken this loving woman's heart. Lady Arthur Skelmerton! That name recalled one of the most bewildering, most mysterious passages in the annals of undiscovered crimes.

"Yes. It was sad, wasn't it?" he commented, in answer to Polly's thoughts. "Another case which but for idiotic blunders on the part of the police must have stood clear as daylight before the public and satisfied general anxiety. Would you object to my recapitulating its preliminary details?"

She said nothing, so he continued without waiting further for a reply.

"It all occurred during the York racing week, a time which brings to the quiet cathedral city its quota of shady characters, who congregate wherever money and wits happen to fly away from their owners. Lord Arthur Skelmerton, a very well-known figure in London society and in racing circles, had rented one of the fine houses which overlook the

94

racecourse. He had entered Peppercorn, by St. Armand–Notre Dame, for the Great Ebor Handicap. Peppercorn was the winner of the New-market, and his chances for the Ebor were considered a practical certainty.

"If you have ever been to York you will have noticed the fine houses which have their drive and front entrances in the road called 'The Mount,' and the gardens of which extend as far as the racecourse, commanding a lovely view over the entire track. It was one of these houses, called 'The Elms,' which Lord Arthur Skelmerton had rented for the summer.

"Lady Arthur came down some little time before the racing week with her servants—she had no children; but she had many relatives and friends in York, since she was the daughter of old Sir John Etty, the cocoa manufacturer, a rigid Quaker, who, it was generally said, kept the tightest possible hold on his own purse-strings and looked with marked disfavour upon his aristocratic son-in-law's fondness for gaming tables and betting books.

"As a matter of fact, Maud Etty had married the handsome young lieutenant in the —— th Hussars, quite against her father's wishes. But she was an only child, and after a good deal of demur and grumbling, Sir John, who idolized his daughter, gave way to her whim, and a reluctant consent to the marriage was wrung from him.

"But, as a Yorkshireman, he was far too shrewd a man of the world not to know that love played but a very small part in persuading a Duke's son to marry the daughter of a cocoa manufacturer, and as long as he lived he determined that since his daughter was being wed because of her wealth, that wealth should at least secure her own happiness. He refused to give Lady Arthur any capital, which, in spite of the most carefully worded settlements, would inevitably, sooner or later, have found its way into the pockets of Lord Arthur's racing friends. But he made his daughter a very handsome allowance, amounting to over £3000 a year, which enabled her to keep up an establishment befitting her new rank.

"A great many of these facts, intimate enough as they are, leaked out, you see, during that period of intense excitement which followed the murder of Charles Lavender, and when the public eye was fixed searchingly upon Lord Arthur Skelmerton, probing all the inner details of his idle, useless life.

"It soon became a matter of common gossip that poor little Lady Arthur continued to worship her handsome husband in spite of his obvious neglect, and not having as yet presented him with an heir, she settled herself down into a life of humble apology for her plebeian existence, atoning for it by condoning all his faults and forgiving all his vices, even to the extent of cloaking them before the prying eyes of Sir John, who was persuaded to look upon his son-in-law as a paragon of all the domestic virtues and a perfect model of a husband.

"Among Lord Arthur Skelmerton's many expensive tastes there was certainly that for horse-flesh and cards. After some successful betting at the beginning of his married life, he had started a racing-stable which it was generally believed—as he was very lucky—was a regular source of income to him.

"Peppercorn, however, after his brilliant performances at Newmarket did not continue to fulfil his master's expectations. His collapse at York was attributed to the hardness of the course and to various other causes, but its immediate effect was to put Lord Arthur Skelmerton in what is popularly called a tight place, for he had backed his horse for all he was worth, and must have stood to lose considerably over £5000 on that one day.

"The collapse of the favourite and the grand victory of King Cole, a rank outsider, on the other hand, had proved a golden harvest for the bookmakers, and all the York hotels were busy with dinners and suppers given by the confraternity of the Turf to celebrate the happy occasion. The next day was Friday, one of few important racing events, after which the brilliant and the shady throng which had flocked into the venerable city for the week would fly to more congenial climes, and leave it, with its fine old Minster and its ancient walls, as sleepy, as quiet as before.

"Lord Arthur Skelmerton also intended to leave York on the Saturday, and on the Friday night he gave a farewell bachelor dinner party at 'The Elms,' at which Lady Arthur did not appear. After dinner the gentlemen settled down to bridge, with pretty stiff points, you may be sure. It had just struck eleven at the Minster Tower, when constables McNaught and Murphy, who were patrolling the racecourse, were startled by loud cries of 'murder' and 'police.'

"Quickly ascertaining whence these cries proceeded, they hurried on at a gallop, and came up—quite close to the boundary of Lord Arthur Skelmerton's grounds—upon a group of three men, two of whom seemed to be wrestling vigorously with one another, whilst the third was lying face downwards on the ground. As soon as the constables drew near, one of the wrestlers shouted more vigorously, and with a certain tone of authority:

"'Here, you fellows, hurry up, sharp; the brute is giving me the slip!'

"But the brute did not seem inclined to do anything of the sort; he certainly extricated himself with a violent jerk from his assailant's grasp, but made no attempt to run away. The constables had quickly dismounted, whilst he who had shouted for help originally added more quietly:

"'My name is Skelmerton. This is the boundary of my property. I was smoking a cigar at the pavilion over there with a friend when I heard loud voices, followed by a cry and a groan. I hurried down the steps, and saw this poor fellow lying on the ground, with a knife sticking between his shoulder-blades, and his murderer,' he added, pointing to the man who stood quietly by with Constable McNaught's firm grip upon his shoulder, 'still stooping over the body of his victim. I was too late, I fear, to save the latter, but just in time to grapple with the assassin——"

"'It's a lie!' here interrupted the man hoarsely. 'I didn't do it, constable; I swear I didn't do it. I saw him fall—I was coming along a couple of hundred yards away, and I tried to see if the poor fellow was dead. I swear I didn't do it."

"'You'll have to explain that to the inspector presently, my man,' was Constable McNaught's quiet comment, and, still vigorously protesting his innocence, the accused allowed himself to be led away, and the body was conveyed to the station, pending fuller identification.

"The next morning the papers were full of the tragedy; a column and a half of the *York Herald* was devoted to an account of Lord Arthur Skelmerton's plucky capture of the assassin. The latter had continued to declare his innocence, but had remarked, it appears, with grim humour, that he quite saw he was in a tight place, out of which, however, he would find it easy to extricate himself. He had stated to the police that the deceased's name was Charles Lavender, a well-known bookmaker, which fact was soon verified, for many of the murdered man's 'pals' were still in the city.

"So far the most pushing of newspaper reporters had been unable to glean further information from the police; no one doubted, however, but that the man in charge, who gave his name as George Higgins, had killed the bookmaker for purposes of robbery. The inquest had been fixed for the Tuesday after the murder.

"Lord Arthur had been obliged to stay in York a few days, as his evidence would be needed. That fact gave the case, perhaps, a certain amount of interest as far as York and London 'society' were concerned. Charles Lavender, moreover, was well known on the turf; but no bombshell exploding beneath the walls of the ancient cathedral city could more have astonished its inhabitants than the news which, at about five in the afternoon on the day of the inquest, spread like wildfire throughout the town. That news was that the inquest had concluded at three o'clock with a verdict of 'Wilful murder against some person or persons unknown,' and that two hours later the police had arrested Lord Arthur Skelmerton at his private residence, 'The Elms,' and charged him on a warrant with the murder of Charles Lavender, the bookmaker."

The Capital Charge

"The police, it appears, instinctively feeling that some mystery lurked round the death of the bookmaker and his supposed murderer's quiet protestations of innocence, had taken a very considerable amount of trouble in collecting all the evidence they could for the inquest which might throw some light upon Charles Lavender's life, previous to his tragic end. Thus it was that a very large array of witnesses was brought before the coroner, chief among whom was, of course, Lord Arthur Skelmerton.

"The first witnesses called were the two constables, who deposed that, just as the church clocks in the neighbourhood were striking eleven, they had heard the cries for help, had ridden to the spot whence the sounds proceeded, and had found the prisoner in the tight grasp of Lord Arthur Skelmerton, who at once accused the man of murder, and gave him in charge. Both constables gave the same version of the incident, and both were positive as to the time when it occurred.

"Medical evidence went to prove that the deceased had been stabbed from behind between the shoulder-blades whilst he was walking, that the wound was inflicted by a large hunting knife, which was produced, and which had been left sticking in the wound.

"Lord Arthur Skelmerton was then called and substantially repeated what he had already told the constables. He stated, namely, that on the night in question he had some gentlemen friends to dinner, and afterwards bridge was played. He himself was not playing much, and at a few minutes before eleven he strolled out with a cigar as far as the pavilion at the end of his garden; he then heard the voices, the cry and the groan previously described by him, and managed to hold the murderer down until the arrival of the constables.

"At this point the police proposed to call a witness, James Terry by name and a bookmaker by profession, who had been chiefly instrumental in identifying the deceased, a 'pal' of his. It was his evidence which first introduced that element of sensation into the case which culminated in the wildly exciting arrest of a Duke's son upon a capital charge.

"It appears that on the evening after the Ebor, Terry and Lavender were in the bar of the Black Swan Hotel having drinks.

"'I had done pretty well over Peppercorn's fiasco,' he explained, 'but poor old Lavender was very much down in the dumps; he had held only a few very small bets against the favourite, and the rest of the day had been a poor one with him. I asked him if he had any bets with the owner of Peppercorn, and he told me that he only held one for less than £500.

"'I laughed and said that if he held one for £5000 it would make no difference, as from what I had heard from the other fellows, Lord Arthur Skelmerton must be about stumped. Lavender seemed terribly put out at this, and swore he would get that £500 out of Lord Arthur, if no one else got another penny from him.

"'It's the only money I've made to-day,' he says to me. 'I mean to get it.'

"'You won't,' I says.

"'I will,' he says.

"'You will have to look pretty sharp about it then,' I says, 'for every one will be wanting to get something, and first come first served.'

"'Oh! He'll serve me right enough, never you mind!' says Lavender to me with a laugh. 'If he don't pay up willingly, I've got that in my pocket which will make him sit up and open my lady's eyes and Sir John Etty's too about their precious noble lord.'

"'Then he seemed to think he had gone too far, and wouldn't say anything more to me about that affair. I saw him on the course the next day. I asked him if he had got his £500. He said: "No, but I shall get it to-day."'

"Lord Arthur Skelmerton, after having given his own evidence, had left the court; it was therefore impossible to know how he would take this account, which threw so serious a light upon an association with the dead man, of which he himself had said nothing.

"Nothing could shake James Terry's account of the facts he had placed before the jury, and when the police informed the coroner that they proposed to place George Higgins himself in the witness-box, as his evidence would prove, as it were, a complement and corollary of that of Terry, the jury very eagerly assented.

"If James Terry, the bookmaker, loud, florid, vulgar, was an unprepossessing individual, certainly George Higgins, who was still under the accusation of murder, was ten thousand times more so.

"None too clean, slouchy, obsequious yet insolent, he was the very personification of the cad who haunts the racecourse and who lives not so much by his own wits as by the lack of them in others. He described himself as a turf commission agent, whatever that may be.

"He stated that at about six o'clock on the Friday afternoon, when the racecourse was still full of people, all hurrying after the day's excitements, he himself happened to be standing close to the hedge which marks the boundary of Lord Arthur Skelmerton's grounds. There is a pavilion there at the end of the garden, he explained, on slightly elevated ground, and he could hear and see a group of ladies and gentlemen having tea. Some steps lead down a little to the left of the garden on to the course, and presently he noticed at the bottom of these steps Lord Arthur Skelmerton and Charles Lavender standing talking together. He knew both gentlemen by sight, but he could not see them very well as they were both partly hidden by the hedge. He was quite sure that the gentlemen had not seen him, and he could not help overhearing some of their conversation.

"'That's my last word, Lavender,' Lord Arthur was saying very quietly. 'I haven't got the money and I can't pay you now. You'll have to wait.'

"'Wait? I can't wait,' said old Lavender in reply. 'I've got my engagements to meet, same as you. I'm not going to risk being posted up as a defaulter while you hold £500 of my money. You'd better give it me now or——'

"But Lord Arthur interrupted him very quietly, and said:

"'Yes, my good man. . . . or?'

"'Or I'll let Sir John have a good look at that little bill I had of yours a couple of years ago. If you'll remember, my lord, it has got at the bottom of it Sir John's signature in *your* handwriting. Perhaps Sir John, or perhaps my lady, would pay me something for that little bill. If not, the police can have a squint at it. I've held my tongue long enough, and——'

"'Look here, Lavender,' said Lord Arthur, 'do you know what this little game of yours is called in law?'

"'Yes, and I don't care' says Lavender. 'If I don't have that £500 I am a ruined man. If you ruin me I'll do for you, and we shall be quits. That's my last word.'

"He was talking very loudly, and I thought some of Lord Arthur's friends up in the pavilion must have heard. He thought so, too, I think, for he said quickly:

"'If you don't hold your confounded tongue, I'll give you in charge for blackmail this instant.'

"'You wouldn't dare,' says Lavender, and he began to laugh. But just then a lady from the top of the steps said: 'Your tea is getting cold,' and Lord Arthur turned to go; but just before he went Lavender says to him: 'I'll come back to-night. You'll have the money then.'

"George Higgins, it appears, after he had heard this interesting conversation, pondered as to whether he could not turn what he knew into some sort of profit. Being a gentleman who lives entirely by his wits, this type of knowledge forms his chief source of income. As a preliminary to future moves, he decided not to lose sight of Lavender for the rest of the day.

"'Lavender went and had dinner at The Black Swan,' explained Mr. George Higgins, 'and I, after I had had a bite myself, waited outside till I saw him come out. At about ten o'clock I was rewarded for my trouble. He told the hall porter to get him a fly and he jumped into it. I could not hear what direction he gave the driver, but the fly certainly drove off towards the racecourse.

"'Now, I was interested in this little affair,' continued the witness, 'and I couldn't afford a fly. I started to run. Of course, I couldn't keep up with it, but I thought I knew which way my gentleman had gone. I made straight for the racecourse, and for the hedge at the bottom of Lord Arthur Skelmerton's grounds.

"'It was rather a dark night and there was a slight drizzle. I couldn't see more than about a hundred yards before me. All at once it seemed to me as if I heard Lavender's voice talking loudly in the distance. I hurried forward, and suddenly saw a group of two figures—mere blurs in the darkness—for one instant, at a distance of about fifty yards from where I was.

"'The next moment one figure had fallen forward and the other had disappeared. I ran to the spot, only to find the body of the murdered man lying on the ground. I stooped to see if I could be of any use to him, and immediately I was collared from behind by Lord Arthur himself.'

"You may imagine," said the man in the corner, "how keen was the excitement of that moment in court. Coroner and jury alike literally hung breathless on every word that shabby, vulgar individual uttered. You see, by itself his evidence would have been worth very little, but coming on the top of that given by James Terry, its significance—more, its truth—had become glaringly apparent. Closely cross-examined, he adhered strictly to his statement; and having finished his evidence, George Higgins remained in charge of the constables, and the next witness of importance was called up.

"This was Mr. Chipps, the senior footman in the employment of Lord Arthur Skelmerton. He deposed that at about 10.30 on the Friday evening a 'party' drove up to 'The Elms' in a fly, and asked to see Lord Arthur. On being told that his lordship had company he seemed terribly put out.

"'I hasked the party to give me 'is card,' continued Mr. Chipps, 'as I didn't know, perhaps, that 'is lordship might wish to see 'im, but I kept 'im standing at the 'all door, as I didn't altogether like his looks. I took the card in. His lordship and the gentlemen was playin' cards in the smoking-room, and as soon as I could do so without disturbing 'is lordship, I give him the party's card.'

"'What name was there on the card?' here interrupted the coroner.

"'I couldn't say now, sir,' replied Mr. Chipps; 'I don't really remember. It was a name I had never seen before. But I see so many visiting cards one way and the other in 'is lordship's 'all that I can't remember all the names.'

"'Then, after a few minutes' waiting, you gave his lordship the card? What happened then?'

"''Is lordship didn't seem at all pleased,' said Mr. Chipps with much guarded dignity; 'but finally he said: "Show him into the library, Chipps, I'll see him," and he got up from the card table, saying to the gentlemen: "Go on without me; I'll be back in a minute or two."

"'I was about to open the door for 'is lordship when my lady came into the room, and then his lordship suddenly changed his mind like, and said to me: "Tell that man I'm busy and can't see him," and 'e sat down again at the card table. I went back to the 'all, and told the party 'is lordship wouldn't see 'im. 'E said: "Oh! it doesn't matter," and went away quite quiet like.'

"'Do you recollect at all at what time that was?' asked one of the jury.

"'Yes, sir, while I was waiting to speak to 'is lordship I looked at the clock, sir; it was twenty past ten, sir.'

"There was one more significant fact in connection with the case, which tended still more to excite the curiosity of the public at the time, and still further to bewilder the police later on, and that fact was mentioned by Chipps in his evidence. The knife, namely, with which Charles Lavender had been stabbed, and which, remember, had been left in the wound, was now produced in court. After a little hesitation Chipps identified it as the property of his master, Lord Arthur Skelmerton.

"Can you wonder, then, that the jury absolutely refused to bring in a verdict against George Higgins? There was really, beyond Lord Arthur Skelmerton's testimony, not one particle of evidence against him, whilst, as the day wore on and witness after witness was called up, suspicion ripened in the minds of all those present that the murderer could be no other than Lord Arthur Skelmerton himself.

"The knife was, of course, the strongest piece of circumstantial evidence, and no doubt the police hoped to collect a great deal more now that they held a clue in their hands. Directly after the verdict, therefore, which was guardedly directed against some person unknown, the police obtained a warrant and later on arrested Lord Arthur in his own house."

"The sensation, of course, was tremendous. Hours before he was brought up before the magistrate the approach to the court was thronged. His friends, mostly ladies, were all eager, you see, to watch the dashing society man in so terrible a position. There was universal sympathy for Lady Arthur, who was in a very precarious state of health. Her worship of her worthless husband was well known; small wonder that his final and awful misdeed had practically broken her heart. The latest bulletin issued just after his arrest stated that her ladyship was not expected to live. She was then in a comatose condition, and all hope had perforce to be abandoned.

"At last the prisoner was brought in. He looked very pale, perhaps, but otherwise kept up the bearing of a high-bred gentleman. He was accompanied by his solicitor, Sir Marmaduke Ingersoll, who was evidently talking to him in quiet, reassuring tones.

"Mr. Buchanan prosecuted for the Treasury, and certainly his indictment was terrific. According to him but one decision could be arrived at, namely, that the accused in the dock had, in a moment of passion, and perhaps of fear, killed the blackmailer who threatened him with disclosures which might for ever have ruined him socially, and, having committed the deed and fearing its consequences, probably realizing that the patrolling constables might catch sight of his retreating figure, he had availed himself of George Higgins's presence on the spot to loudly accuse him of the murder.

"Having concluded his able speech, Mr. Buchanan called his witnesses, and the evidence, which on second hearing seemed more damning than ever, was all gone through again.

"Sir Marmaduke had no question to ask of the witnesses for the prosecution; he stared at them placidly through his gold-rimmed spectacles. Then he was ready to call his own for the defence. Colonel McIntosh, R.A., was the first. He was present at the bachelors' party given by Lord Arthur the night of the murder. His evidence tended at first to corroborate that of Chipps the footman with regard to Lord Arthur's orders to show the visitor into the library, and his counter-order as soon as his wife came into the room.

"'Did you not think it strange, Colonel?' asked Mr. Buchanan, 'that Lord Arthur should so suddenly have changed his mind about seeing his visitor?'

"'Well, not exactly strange,' said the Colonel, a fine, manly, soldierly figure who looked curiously out of his element in the witness-box. 'I don't think that it is a very rare occurrence for racing men to have certain acquaintances whom they would not wish their wives to know anything about.'

"'Then it did not strike you that Lord Arthur Skelmerton had some reason for not wishing his wife to know of that particular visitor's presence in his house?'

"'I don't think that I gave the matter the slightest serious consideration,' was the Colonel's guarded reply.

"Mr. Buchanan did not press the point, and allowed the witness to conclude his statements.

"'I had finished my turn at bridge,' he said, 'and went out into the garden to smoke a cigar. Lord Arthur Skelmerton joined me a few minutes later, and we were sitting in the pavilion when I heard a loud and, as I thought, threatening voice from the other side of the hedge.

"'I did not catch the words, but Lord Arthur said to me: "There seems to be a row down there. I'll go and have a look and see what it is." I tried to dissuade him, and certainly made no attempt to follow him, but not more than half a minute could have elapsed before I heard a cry and a groan, then Lord Arthur's footsteps hurrying down the wooden stairs which lead on to the racecourse.'

"You may imagine," said the man in the corner, "what severe cross-examination the gallant Colonel had to undergo in order that his assertions might in some way be shaken by the prosecution, but with military precision and frigid calm he repeated his important statements amidst a general silence, through which you could have heard the proverbial pin.

"He had heard the threatening voice *while* sitting with Lord Arthur Skelmerton; then came the cry and groan, and, *after that*, Lord Arthur's steps down the stairs. He himself thought of following to see what had happened, but it was a very dark night and he did not know the grounds very well. While trying to find his way to the garden steps he heard Lord Arthur's cry for help, the tramp of the patrolling constables' horses, and subsequently the whole scene between Lord Arthur, the man Higgins, and the constables. When he finally found his way to the stairs, Lord Arthur was returning in order to send a groom for police assistance.

"The witness stuck to his points as he had to his guns at Beckfontein a year ago; nothing could shake him, and Sir Marmaduke looked triumphantly across at his opposing colleague.

"With the gallant Colonel's statements the edifice of the prosecution certainly began to collapse. You see, there was not a particle of evidence to show that the accused had met and spoken to the deceased after the latter's visit at the front door of 'The Elms.' He told Chipps that he wouldn't see the visitor, and Chipps went into the hall directly and showed Lavender out the way he came. No assignation could have been made, no hint could have been given by the murdered man to Lord Arthur that he would go round to the back entrance and wished to see him there.

"Two other guests of Lord Arthur's swore positively that after Chipps had announced the visitor, their host stayed at the card-table until a quarter to eleven, when evidently he went out to join Colonel McIntosh in the garden. Sir Marmaduke's speech was clever in the extreme. Bit by bit he demolished that tower of strength, the case against the accused, basing his defence entirely upon the evidence of Lord Arthur Skelmerton's guests that night.

"Until 10.45 Lord Arthur was playing cards; a quarter of an hour later the police were on the scene, and the murder had been committed. In the meanwhile Colonel McIntosh's evidence proved conclusively that the accused had been sitting with him, smoking a cigar. It was obvious, therefore, clear as daylight, concluded the great lawyer, that his client was entitled to a full discharge; nay, more, he thought that the police should have been more careful before they harrowed up public feeling by arresting a high-born gentleman on such insufficient evidence as they had brought forward.

"The question of the knife remained certainly, but Sir Marmaduke passed over it with guarded eloquence, placing that strange question in the category of those inexplicable coincidences which tend to puzzle the ablest detectives, and cause them to commit such unpardonable blunders as the present one had been. After all, the footman may have been mistaken. The pattern of that knife was not an exclusive one, and he, on behalf of his client, flatly denied that it had ever belonged to him.

"Well," continued the man in the corner, with the chuckle peculiar to him in moments of excitement, "the noble prisoner was discharged. Perhaps it would be invidious to say that he left the court without a stain on his character, for I daresay you know from experience that the crime known as the York Mystery has never been satisfactorily cleared up.

"Many people shook their heads dubiously when they remembered that, after all, Charles Lavender was killed with a knife which one witness had sworn belonged to Lord Arthur; others, again, reverted to the original theory that George Higgins was the murderer, that he and James Terry had concocted the story of Lavender's attempt at blackmail on Lord Arthur, and that the murder had been committed for the sole purpose of robbery.

"Be that as it may, the police have not so far been able to collect sufficient evidence against Higgins or Terry, and the crime has been classed by press and public alike in the category of so-called impenetrable mysteries."

A Broken-Hearted Woman

The man in the corner called for another glass of milk, and drank it down slowly before he resumed:

"Now Lord Arthur lives mostly abroad," he said. "His poor, suffering wife died the day after he was liberated by the magistrate. She never recovered consciousness even sufficiently to hear the joyful news that the man she loved so well was innocent after all.

"Mystery!" he added as if in answer to Polly's own thoughts. "The murder of that man was never a mystery to me. I cannot understand how the police could have been so blind when every one of the witnesses, both for the prosecution and defence, practically pointed all the time to the one guilty person. What do you think of it all yourself?"

"I think the whole case so bewildering," she replied, "that I do not see one single clear point in it."

"You don't?" he said excitedly, while the bony fingers fidgeted again with that inevitable bit of string. "You don't see that there is one point clear which to me was the key of the whole thing?

"Lavender was murdered, wasn't he? Lord Arthur did not kill him. He had, at least, in Colonel McIntosh an unimpeachable witness to prove that he could not have committed that murder—and yet," he added with slow, excited emphasis, marking each sentence with a knot, "and yet he deliberately tries to throw the guilt upon a man who obviously was also innocent. Now why?"

"He may have thought him guilty."

"Or wished to shield or cover the retreat of *one he knew to be guilty*."

"I don't understand."

"Think of someone," he said excitedly, "someone whose desire would be as great as that of Lord Arthur to silence a scandal round that gentleman's name. Someone who, unknown perhaps to Lord Arthur, had overheard the same conversation which George Higgins related to the police and the magistrate, someone who, whilst Chipps was taking Lavender's card in to his master, had a few minutes' time wherein to make an assignation with Lavender, promising him money, no doubt, in exchange for the compromising bills."

"Surely you don't mean——" gasped Polly.

"Point number one," he interrupted quietly, "utterly missed by the police. George Higgins in his deposition stated that at the most animated stage of Lavender's conversation with Lord Arthur, and when the bookmaker's tone of voice became loud and threatening, a voice from the top of the steps interrupted that conversation, saying: 'Your tea is getting cold.'"

"Yes—but——" she argued.

"Wait a moment, for there is point number two. That voice was a lady's voice. Now, I did exactly what the police should have done, but did not do. I went to have a look from the racecourse side at those garden steps which to my mind are such important factors in the discovery of this crime. I found only about a dozen rather low steps; anyone standing on the top must have heard every word Charles Lavender uttered the moment he raised his voice."

"Even then——"

"Very well, you grant that," he said excitedly. "Then there was the great, the all-important point which, oddly enough, the prosecution never for a moment took into consideration. When Chipps, the footman, first told Lavender that Lord Arthur could not see him the bookmaker was terribly put out; Chipps then goes to speak to his master; a few minutes elapse, and when the footman once again tells Lavender that his lordship won't see him, the latter says 'Very well,' and seems to treat the matter with complete indifference.

"Obviously, therefore, something must have happened in between to alter the bookmaker's frame of mind. Well! What had happened? Think over all the evidence, and you will see that one thing only had occurred in the interval, namely, Lady Arthur's advent into the room.

"In order to go into the smoking-room she must have crossed the hall; she must have seen Lavender. In that brief interval she must have realized that the man was persistent, and therefore a living danger to her husband. Remember, women have done strange things; they are a far greater puzzle to the student of human nature than the sterner, less complex sex has ever been. As I argued before—as the police should have argued all along—why did Lord Arthur deliberately accuse an innocent man of murder if not to shield the guilty one?

"Remember, Lady Arthur may have been discovered; the man, George Higgins, may have caught sight of her before she had time to make good her retreat. His attention, as well as that of the constables, had to be diverted. Lord Arthur acted on the blind impulse of saving his wife at any cost."

"She may have been met by Colonel McIntosh," argued Polly.

"Perhaps she was," he said. "Who knows? The gallant colonel had to swear to his friend's innocence. He could do that in all conscience— after that his duty was accomplished. No innocent man was suffering for the guilty. The knife which had belonged to Lord Arthur would always save George Higgins. For a time it had pointed to the husband; fortunately never to the wife. Poor thing, she died probably of a broken heart, but women when they love, think only of one object on earth— the one who is beloved.

"To me the whole thing was clear from the very first. When I read the account of the murder—the knife! stabbing!—bah! Don't I know enough of *English* crime not to be certain at once that no English*man*, be he ruffian from the gutter or be he Duke's son, ever stabs his victim in the back. Italians, French, Spaniards do it, if you will, and women of most nations. An Englishman's instinct is to strike and not to stab. George Higgins or Lord Arthur Skelmerton would have knocked their victim down; the woman only would lie in wait till the enemy's back was turned. She knows her weakness, and she does not mean to miss.

"Think it over. There is not one flaw in my argument, but the police never thought the matter out—perhaps in this case it was as well."

He had gone and left Miss Polly Burton still staring at the photograph of a pretty, gentle-looking woman, with a decided, wilful curve round the mouth, and a strange, unaccountable look in the large pathetic eyes; and the little journalist felt quite thankful that in this case the murder of Charles Lavender the bookmaker—cowardly, wicked as it was—had remained a mystery to the police and the public.

George R. Sims

(1847–1922)

GEORGE R. SIMS was a London journalist, novelist, and short-story writer, many of whose works sympathize with the conditions of London's poor, though perhaps not quite as consistently as Arthur Morrison's *Tales of Mean Streets. The Devil in London* (1908), for example, has Satan show up in Edwardian London and comment on all its social problems. Besides his detective stories, Sims is best remembered for editing three huge volumes entitled *Living London* (1902), containing elaborately illustrated essays about all aspects of that capital city at the turn of the century. The volumes were recently reprinted in England under the title *Edwardian London*.

Beginning in 1889, most of Sims's short-story collections contain detective or crime stories, but his most important work was a series of tales, published in two volumes, called *Dorcas Dene, Detective: Her Adventures** (1897–1898). Except for having probably the least euphonious name in mystery fiction, Dorcas Dene is one of the most interesting sleuths of the period. Born Dorcas Lester, she became an actress, but retired from the stage to marry Paul Dene, an artist. After her husband became blind, she used her acting ability to become a professional detective. Like so many detective stories of this period, her cases are narrated by a friend (in this instance "an old-fashioned, humdrum family solicitor") for whom she can do no wrong.

---

*"The Haverstock Hill Murder" excerpts in their entirety two consecutive chapters from this work.

The Haverstock Hill Murder

THE BLINDS had been down at the house in Elm Tree Road and the house shut for nearly six weeks. I had received a note from Dorcas saying that she was engaged on a case which would take her away for some little time, and that as Paul had not been very well lately she had arranged that he and her mother should accompany her. She would advise me as soon as they returned. I called once at Elm Tree Road and found it was in charge of the two servants and Toddlekins, the bulldog. The housemaid informed me that Mrs. Dene had not written, so that she did not know where she was or when she would be back, but that letters which arrived for her were forwarded by her instructions to Mr. Jackson of Penton Street, King's Cross.

Mr. Jackson, I remembered, was the ex-police-sergeant who was generally employed by Dorcas when she wanted a house watched or certain inquiries made among tradespeople. I felt that it would be unfair to go to Jackson. Had Dorcas wanted me to know where she was she would have told me in her letter.

The departure had been a hurried one. I had gone to the North in connection with a business matter of my own on a Thursday evening, leaving Dorcas at Elm Tree Road, and when I returned on Monday afternoon I found Dorcas's letter at my chambers. It was written on the Saturday, and evidently on the eve of departure.

But something that Dorcas did not tell me I learned quite accidentally from my old friend Inspector Swanage, of Scotland Yard, whom I met one cold February afternoon at Kempton Park Steeplechases.

Inspector Swanage has a much greater acquaintance with the fraternity known as "the boys" than any other officer. He has attended race meetings for years, and the "boys" always greet him respectfully, though they wish him further. Many a prettily-planned coup of theirs has he nipped in the bud, and many an unsuspecting greenhorn has he saved from pillage by a timely whisper that the well-dressed young gentlemen who are putting their fivers on so merrily and coming out of the enclosure with their pockets stuffed full of bank-notes are men who get their living by clever swindling, and are far more dangerous than the ordinary vulgar pick-pocket.

On one occasion not many years ago I found a well-known publisher at a race meeting in earnest conversation with a beautifully-dressed, grey-haired sportsman. The publisher informed me that his new acquaintance was the owner of a horse which was certain to win the next race, and that it would start at ten to one. Only in order not to shorten the price nobody was to know the name of the horse, as the stable had three in the race. He had obligingly taken a fiver off the publisher to put on with his own money.

I told the publisher that he was the victim of a "tale-pitcher," and that he would never see his fiver again. At that moment Inspector Swanage came on the scene, and the owner of racehorses disappeared as if by magic. Swanage recognized the man instantly, and having heard my publisher's story said, "If I have the man taken will you prosecute?" The publisher shook his head. He didn't want to send his authors mad with delight at the idea that somebody had eventually succeeded in getting a fiver the best of him. So Inspector Swanage strolled away. Half an hour later he came to us in the enclosure and said, "Your friend's horse doesn't run, so he's given me that fiver back again for you." And with a broad grin he handed my friend a bank-note.

It was Inspector Swanage's skill and kindness on this occasion that made me always eager to have a chat with him when I saw him at a race meeting, for his conversation was always interesting.

The February afternoon had been a cold one, and soon after the commencement of racing there were signs of fog. Now a foggy afternoon is dear to the hearts of the "boys." It conceals their operations, and helps to cover their retreat. As the fog came up the Inspector began to look anxious, and I went up to him.

"You don't like the look of things?" I said.

"No, if this gets worse the band will begin to play—there are some very warm members of it here this afternoon. It was a day just like this last year that they held up a bookmaker going to the station, and eased him of over £500. Hullo?"

As he uttered the exclamation the Inspector pulled out his race card and seemed to be anxiously studying it.

But under his voice he said to me, "Do you see that tall man in a fur coat talking to a bookmaker? See, he's just handed him a bank-note?"

"Where?—I don't see him."

"Yonder. Do you see that old gipsy-looking woman with race cards? She has just thrust her hand through the railings and offered one to the man."

"Yes, yes—I see him now."

"That's Flash George. I've missed him lately, and I heard he was broke, but he's in funds again evidently by his get-up."

"One of the boys?"

"Has been—but he's been on another lay lately. He was mixed up in that big jewel case—£10,000 worth of diamonds stolen from a demi-mondaine. He got rid of some of the jewels for the thieves, but we could never bring it home to him. But he was watched for a long time afterwards and his game was stopped. The last we heard of him he was hard up and borrowing from some of his pals. He's gone now. I'll just go and ask the bookie what he's betting to."

The Inspector stepped across to the bookmaker and presently returned.

"He *is* in luck again," he said. "He's put a hundred ready on the favourite for this race. By the bye, how's your friend Mrs. Dene getting on with her case?"

I confessed my ignorance as to what Dorcas was doing at the present moment—all I knew was that she was away.

"Oh, I thought you'd have known all about it," said the Inspector. "She's on the Hannaford case."

"What, the murder?"

"Yes."

"But surely that was settled by the police? The husband was arrested immediately after the inquest."

"Yes, and the case against him was very strong, but we know that Dorcas Dene has been engaged by Mr. Hannaford's family, who have made up their minds that the police, firmly believing him guilty, won't look anywhere else for the murderer—of course they are convinced of his innocence. But you must excuse me—the fog looks like thickening, and may stop racing—I must go and put my men to work."

"One moment before you go—why did you suddenly ask me how Mrs. Dene was getting on? Was it anything to do with Flash George that put it in your head?"

The Inspector looked at me curiously.

"Yes," he said, "though I didn't expect you'd see the connection. It was a mere coincidence. On the night that Mrs. Hannaford was murdered, Flash George, who had been lost sight of for some time by our people, was reported to have been seen by the Inspector who was going his rounds in the neighbourhood. He was seen about half-past two o'clock in the morning looking rather dilapidated and seedy. When the report of the murder came in, the Inspector at once remembered that he had seen Flash George in Haverstock Hill. But there was nothing in it—as the house hadn't been broken into and there was nothing stolen. You understand now why seeing Flash George carried my train of thought on to the Hannaford murder and Dorcas Dene. Good-bye."

The Inspector hurried away and a few minutes afterwards the favourite came in alone for the second race on the card. The stewards immediately afterwards announced that racing would be abandoned on account of the fog increasing, and I made my way to the railway station and went home by the members' train.

Directly I reached home I turned eagerly to my newspaper file and read up the Hannaford murder. I knew the leading features, but every detail of it had now a special interest to me, seeing that Dorcas Dene had taken the case up.

These were the facts as reported in the Press:

Early in the morning of January 5 a maid-servant rushed out of the house, standing in its own grounds on Haverstock Hill, calling "Murder!" Several people who were passing instantly came to her and inquired what was the matter, but all she could gasp was, "Fetch a policeman." When the policeman arrived he followed the terrified girl into the house and was conducted to the drawing-room, where he found a lady lying in her nightdress in the centre of the room covered with blood, but still alive. He sent one of the servants for a doctor, and another to the police-station to inform the superintendent. The doctor came immediately and declared that the woman was dying. He did everything that could be done for her, and presently she partially regained consciousness. The superintendent had by this time arrived, and in the presence of the doctor asked her who had injured her.

She seemed anxious to say something, but the effort was too much for her, and presently she relapsed into unconsciousness. She died two hours later, without speaking.

The woman's injuries had been inflicted with some heavy instrument. On making a search of the room the poker was found lying between the fireplace and the body. The poker was found to have blood upon it, and some hair from the unfortunate lady's head.

The servants stated that their master and mistress, Mr. and Mrs. Hannaford, had retired to rest at their usual time, shortly before midnight. The housemaid had seen them go up together. She had been working at a dress which she wanted for next Sunday, and sat up late, using her sewing-machine in the kitchen. It was one o'clock in the morning when she passed her master and mistress's door, and she judged by what she heard that they were quarrelling. Mr. Hannaford was not in the house when the murder was discovered. The house was searched thoroughly in every direction, the first idea of the police being that he had committed suicide. The telegraph was then set to work, and at ten o'clock a man answering Mr. Hannaford's description was arrested at Paddington Station, where he was taking a ticket for Uxbridge.

Taken to the police-station and informed that he would be charged with murdering his wife, he appeared to be horrified, and for some time was a prey to the most violent emotion. When he had recovered himself and was made aware of the serious position in which he stood, he volunteered a statement. He was warned, but he insisted on making it. He declared that he and his wife had quarrelled violently after they had retired to rest. Their quarrel was about a purely domestic matter, but he was in an irritable, nervous condition, owing to his health, and at last he had worked himself up into such a state, that he had risen, dressed himself, and gone out into the street. That would be about two in the morning. He had wandered about in a state of nervous excitement until daybreak. At seven he had gone into a coffee-house and had breakfast, and had then gone into the park and sat on a seat and fallen asleep. When he woke up it was nine o'clock. He had taken a cab to Paddington, and had intended to go to Uxbridge to see his mother, who resided there. Quarrels between himself and his wife had been frequent of late, and he was ill and wanted to get away, and he thought perhaps if he went to his mother for a day or two he might get calmer and feel better. He had been very much worried lately over business matters. He was a stock-jobber, and the market in the securities in which he had been speculating was against him.

At the conclusion of the statement, which was made in a nervous, excited manner, he broke down so completely that it was deemed desirable to send for the doctor and keep him under close observation.

Police investigations of the premises failed to find any further clue. Everything pointed to the supposition that the result of the quarrel had been an attack by the husband—possibly in a sudden fit of homicidal mania—on the unfortunate woman. The police suggestion was that the lady, terrified by her husband's behaviour, had risen in the night and run down the stairs to the drawing-room, and that he had followed her there, picked up the poker, and furiously attacked her. When she fell, apparently lifeless, he had run back to his bedroom, dressed himself, and made his escape quietly from the house. There was nothing missing so far as could be ascertained—nothing to suggest in any way that any third party, a burglar from outside or some person inside, had had anything to do with the matter.

The coroner's jury brought in a verdict of wilful murder, and the husband was charged before a magistrate and committed for trial. But in the interval his reason gave way, and, the doctors certifying that he was undoubtedly insane, he was sent to Broadmoor.

Nobody had the slightest doubt of his guilt, and it was his mother who, broken-hearted, and absolutely refusing to believe in her son's guilt, had come to Dorcas Dene and requested her to take up the case privately and investigate it. The poor old lady declared that she was perfectly certain that her son could not have been guilty of such a deed, but the police were satisfied, and would make no further investigation.

This I learnt afterwards when I went to see Inspector Swanage. All I knew when I had finished reading up the case in the newspapers was that the husband of Mrs. Hannaford was in Broadmoor, practically condemned for the murder of his wife, and that Dorcas Dene had left home to try and prove his innocence.

The history of the Hannafords as given in the public Press was as follows: Mrs. Hannaford was a widow when Mr. Hannaford, a man of six-and-thirty, married her. Her first husband was a Mr. Charles Drayson, a financier, who had been among the victims of the disastrous fire in Paris. His wife was with him in the rue Jean Goujon that fatal night. When the fire broke out they both tried to escape together. They became separated in the crush. She was only slightly injured, and succeeded in getting out; he was less fortunate. His gold watch, a presentation one, with an inscription, was found among a mass of charred unrecognizable remains when the ruins were searched.

Three years after this tragedy the widow married Mr. Hannaford. The death of her first husband did not leave her well off. It was found that he was heavily in debt, and had he lived a serious charge of fraud would undoubtedly have been preferred against him. As it was, his partner, a Mr. Thomas Holmes, was arrested and sentenced to five years' penal servitude in connection with a joint fraudulent transaction.

The estate of Mr. Drayson went to satisfy the creditors, but Mrs. Drayson, the widow, retained the house at Haverstock Hill, which he had purchased and settled on her, with all the furniture and contents, some years previously. She wished to continue living in the house when she married again, and Mr. Hannaford consented, and they made it their home. Hannaford himself, though not a wealthy man, was a fairly successful stock-jobber, and until the crisis, which had brought on great anxiety and helped to break down his health, had had no financial worries. But the marriage, so it was alleged, had not been a very happy one and quarrels had been frequent. Old Mrs. Hannaford was against it from the first, and to her her son always turned in his later matrimonial troubles. Now that his life had probably been spared by this mental breakdown, and he had been sent to Broadmoor, she had but one object in life—to set her son free, some day restored to reason, and with his innocence proved to the world.

❊   ❊   ❊

It was about a fortnight after my interview with Inspector Swanage, and my study of the details of the Haverstock Hill murder, that one morning I opened a telegram and to my intense delight found that it was from Dorcas Dene. It was from London, and informed me that in the evening they would be very pleased to see me at Elm Tree Road.

In the evening I presented myself about eight o'clock. Paul was alone in the drawing-room when I entered, and his face and his voice when he greeted me showed me plainly that he had benefited greatly by the change.

"Where have you been, to look so well?" I asked. "The South of Europe, I suppose—Nice or Monte Carlo?"

"No," said Paul smiling, "we haven't been nearly so far as that. But I mustn't tell tales out of school. You must ask Dorcas."

At that moment Dorcas came in and gave me a cordial greeting.

"Well," I said, after the first conversational preliminaries, "who committed the Haverstock Hill murder?"

"Oh, so you know that I have taken that up, do you? I imagined it would get about through the Yard people. You see, Paul dear, how wise I was to give out that I had gone away."

"Give out!" I exclaimed. "*Haven't* you been away then?"

"No, Paul and mother have been staying at Hastings, and I have been down whenever I have been able to spare a day, but as a matter of fact I have been in London the greater part of the time."

"But I don't see the use of your pretending you were going away."

"I did it on purpose. I knew the fact that old Mrs. Hannaford had engaged me would get about in certain circles, and I wanted certain people to think that I had gone away to investigate some clue which I thought I had discovered. In order to baulk all possible inquirers I didn't even let the servants forward my letters. They went to Jackson, who sent them on to me."

"Then you were really investigating in London?"

"Now shall I tell you where you heard that I was on this case?"

"Yes."

"You heard it at Kempton Park Steeplechases, and your informant was Inspector Swanage."

"You have seen him and he has told you."

"No; I saw you there talking to him."

"*You* saw me? You were at Kempton Park? I never saw you."

"Yes, you did, for I caught you looking full at me. I was trying to sell some race cards just before the second race, and was holding them between the railings of the enclosure."

"What! You were that old gipsy woman? I'm certain Swanage didn't know you."

"I didn't want him to, or anybody else."

"It was an astonishing disguise. But come, aren't you going to tell me anything about the Hannaford case? I've been reading it up, but I fail entirely to see the slightest suspicion against any one but the husband. Everything points to his having committed the crime in a moment of madness. The fact that he has since gone completely out of his mind seems to me to show that conclusively."

"It is a good job he did go out of his mind—but for that I am afraid he would have suffered for the crime, and the poor broken-hearted old mother for whom I am working would soon have followed him to the grave."

"Then you don't share the general belief in his guilt?"

"I did at first, but I don't now."

"You have discovered the guilty party?"

"No—not yet—but I hope to."

"Tell me exactly all that has happened—there may still be a chance for your 'assistant.'"

"Yes, it is quite possible that now I may be able to avail myself of your services. You say you have studied the details of this case—let us just run through them together, and see what you think of my plan of campaign so far as it has gone. When old Mrs. Hannaford came to me, her son had already been declared insane and unable to plead, and had gone to Broadmoor. That was nearly a month after the commission of the crime, so that much valuable time had been lost. At first I declined to take the matter up—the police had so thoroughly investigated the affair. The case seemed so absolutely conclusive that I told her that it would be useless for her to incur the heavy expense of a private investigation. But she pleaded so earnestly—her faith in her son was so great—and she seemed such a sweet, dear old lady, that at last she conquered my scruples, and I consented to study the case, and see if there was the slightest alternative theory to go on. I had almost abandoned hope, for there was nothing in the published reports to encourage it, when I determined to go to the fountain-head, and see the Superintendent who had had the case in hand.

"He received me courteously, and told me everything. He was certain that the husband committed the murder. There was an entire absence of motive for any one else in the house to have done it, and the husband's flight from the house in the middle of the night was absolutely damning. I inquired if they had found any one who had seen the husband in the street—any one who could fix the time at which he had left the house. He replied that no such witness had been found. Then I asked if the policeman on duty that night had made any report of any suspicious characters being seen about. He said that the only person he had noticed at all was a man well known to the police—a man named Flash George. I asked what time Flash George had been seen and whereabouts, and I ascertained that it was at half-past two in the morning, and about a hundred yards below the scene of the crime, that when the policeman spoke to him he said he was coming from Hampstead, and was going to Covent Garden Market. He walked away in the direction of the Chalk Farm Road. I inquired what Flash George's record was, and ascertained that he was the associate of thieves and swindlers, and he was suspected of having disposed of some jewels, the proceeds of a robbery which had made a nine days' sensation. But the police had failed to bring the charge home to him, and the jewels had never been traced. He was also a gambler, a frequenter of racecourses and certain night-clubs of evil repute, and had not been seen about for some time previous to that evening."

"And didn't the police make any further investigations in that direction?"

"No. Why should they? There was nothing missing from the house—not the slightest sign of an attempted burglary. All their efforts were directed to proving the guilt of the unfortunate woman's husband."

"And you?"

"I had a different task—mine was to prove the husband's innocence. I determined to find out something more of Flash George. I shut the house up, gave out that I had gone away, and took, amongst other things, to selling cards and pencils on racecourses. The day that Flash George made his reappearance on the turf after a long absence was the day that he backed the winner of the second race at Kempton Park for a hundred pounds."

"But surely that proves that if he had been connected with any crime it must have been one in which money was obtained. No one has attempted to associate the murder of Mrs. Hannaford with robbery."

"No. But one thing is certain—that on the night of the crime Flash George was in the neighbourhood. Two days previously he had borrowed a few pounds of a pal because he was 'stony broke.' When he reappears as a racing man he has on a fur coat, is evidently in first-class circumstances, and he bets in hundred-pound notes. He is a considerably richer man after the murder of Mrs. Hannaford than he was before, and he was seen within a hundred yards of the house at half-past two o'clock on the night that the crime was committed."

"That might have been a mere accident. His sudden wealth may be the result of a lucky gamble, or a swindle of which you know nothing. I can't see that it can possibly have any bearing on the Hannaford crime, because nothing was taken from the house."

"Quite true. But here is a remarkable fact. When he went up to the betting man he went to one who was betting close to the rails. When he pulled out that hundred-pound note I was at the rails, and I pushed my cards in between and asked him to buy one. Flash George is a 'suspected character,' and quite capable on a foggy day of trying to swindle a bookmaker. The bookmaker took the precaution to open that note, it being for a hundred pounds, and examined it carefully. That enabled me to see the number. I had sharpened pencils to sell, and with one of them I hastily took down the number of that note——^2_x35421."

"That was clever. And you have traced it?"

"Yes."

"And has that furnished you with any clue?"

"It has placed me in possession of a most remarkable fact. The hundred-pound note which was in Flash George's possession on Kempton Park racecourse was one of a number which were paid over the counter of the Union Bank of London for a five-thousand-pound cheque over ten years ago. And that cheque was drawn by the murdered woman's husband."

"Mr. Hannaford!"

"No; her first husband—Mr. Charles Drayson."

The Brown Bear Lamp

When Dorcas Dene told me that the £100 note Flash George had handed to the bookmaker at Kempton Park was one which had some years previously been paid to Mr. Charles Drayson, the first husband of the murdered woman, Mrs. Hannaford, I had to sit still and think for a moment.

It was curious certainly, but after all much more remarkable coincidences than that occur daily. I could not see what practical value there was in Dorcas's extraordinary discovery, because Mr. Charles Drayson was dead, and it was hardly likely that his wife would have kept a £100 note of his for several years. And if she had, she had not been murdered for that, because there were no signs of the house having been broken into. The more I thought the business over the more confused I became in my attempt to establish a clue from it, and so after a minute's silence I frankly confessed to Dorcas that I didn't see where her discovery led to.

"I don't say that it leads very far by itself," said Dorcas. "But you must look at *all* the circumstances. During the night of January 5 a lady is murdered in her own drawing-room. Round about the time that the attack is supposed to have been made upon her a well-known bad character is seen close to the house. That person, who just previously has been ascertained to have been so hard up that he had been borrowing of his associates, reappears on the turf a few weeks later expensively dressed and in possession of money. He bets with a £100 note, and that £100 note I have traced to the previous possession of the murdered woman's first husband, who lost his life in the disastrous fire in Paris, while on a short visit to that capital."

"Yes, it certainly is curious, but——"

"Wait a minute—I haven't finished yet. Of the bank-notes—several of them for £100—which were paid some years ago to Mr. Charles Drayson, not one had come back to the bank *before* the murder."

"Indeed!"

"Since the murder *several* of them have come in. Now, is it not a remarkable circumstance that during all those years £5,000 worth of bank-notes should have remained out!"

"It is remarkable, but after all bank-notes circulate—they may pass through hundreds of hands before returning to the bank."

"Some may, undoubtedly, but it is highly improbable that *all* would under ordinary circumstances—especially notes for £100. These are sums which are not passed from pocket to pocket. As a rule they go to the bank of one of the early receivers of them, and from that bank into the Bank of England."

"You mean that it is an extraordinary fact that for many years not one of the notes paid to Mr. Charles Drayson by the Union Bank came back to the Bank of England."

"Yes, that *is* an extraordinary fact, but there is a fact which is more extraordinary still, and that is that soon after the murder of Mrs. Hannaford that state of things alters. It looks as though the murderer had placed the notes in circulation again."

"It does, certainly. Have you traced back any of the other notes that have come in?"

"Yes; but they have been cleverly worked. They have nearly all been circulated in the betting ring; those that have not have come in from money-changers in Paris and Rotterdam. My own belief is that before long the whole of those notes will come back to the bank."

"Then, my dear Dorcas, it seems to me that your course is plain, and you ought to go to the police and ask them to get the bank to circulate a list of the notes."

"Dorcas shook her head. "No, thank you," she said. "I'm going to carry this case through on my own account. The police are convinced that the murderer is Mr. Hannaford, who is at present in Broadmoor, and the bank has absolutely no reason to interfere. No question has been raised of the notes having been stolen. They were paid to the man who died over ten years ago, not to the woman who was murdered last January."

"But you have traced one note to Flash George, who is a bad lot, and he was near the house on the night of the tragedy. You suspect Flash George and——"

"I do not suspect Flash George of the actual murder," she said, "and I don't see how he is to be arrested for being in possession of a bank-note which forms no part of the police case, and which he might easily say he had received in the betting ring."

"Then what *are* you going to do?"

"Follow up the clue I have. I have been shadowing Flash George all the time I have been away. I know where he lives—I know who are his companions."

"And do you think the murderer is among them?"

"No. They are all a little astonished at his sudden good fortune. I have heard them 'chip' him, as they call it, on the subject. I have carried my investigations up to a certain point and there they stop short. I am going a step further to-morrow evening, and it is in that step that I want assistance."

"And you have come to me?" I said eagerly.

"Yes."

"What do you want me to do?"

"To-morrow morning I am going to make a thorough examination of the room in which the murder was committed. To-morrow evening I have to meet a gentleman of whom I know nothing but his career and his name. I want you to accompany me."

"Certainly; but if I am your assistant in the evening I shall expect to be your assistant in the morning—I should very much like to see the scene of the crime."

"I have no objection. The house on Haverstock Hill is at present shut up and in charge of a caretaker, but the solicitors who are managing the late Mrs. Hannaford's estate have given me permission to go over it and examine it."

The next day at eleven o'clock I met Dorcas outside Mrs. Hannaford's house, and the caretaker, who had received his instructions, admitted us. He was the gardener, and an old servant, and had been present during the police investigation.

The bedroom in which Mr. Hannaford and his wife slept on the fatal night was on the floor above. Dorcas told me to go upstairs, shut the door, lie down on the bed, and listen. Directly a noise in the room below attracted my attention, I was to jump up, open the door and call out.

I obeyed her instructions and listened intently, but lying on the bed I heard nothing for a long time. It must have been quite a quarter of an hour when suddenly I heard a sound as of a door opening with a cracking sound. I leapt up, ran to the balusters, and called over, "I heard that!"

"All right, then, come down," said Dorcas, who was standing in the hall with the caretaker.

She explained to me that she had been moving about the drawing-room with the man, and they had both made as much noise with their feet as they could. They had even opened and shut the drawing-room door, but nothing had attracted my attention. Then Dorcas had sent the man to open the front door. It had opened with the cracking sound that I had heard.

"Now," said Dorcas to the caretaker, "you were here when the police were coming and going—did the front door always make a sound like that?"

"Yes, madam. The door had swollen or warped, or something, and it was always difficult to open. Mrs. Hannaford spoke about it once and was going to have it eased."

"That's it, then," said Dorcas to me. "The probability is that it was the noise made by the opening of that front door which first attracted the attention of the murdered woman."

"That was Hannaford going out—if his story is correct."

"No; Hannaford went out in a range. He would pull the door open violently, and probably bang it to. That she would understand. It was when the door *opened again* with a sharp crack that she listened, thinking it was her husband come back."

"But she was murdered in the drawing-room!"

"Yes. My theory, therefore, is that after the opening of the front door she expected her husband to come upstairs. He didn't do so, and she concluded that he had gone into one of the rooms downstairs to spend the night, and she got up and came down to find him and ask him to get over his temper and come back to bed. She went into the drawing-room to see if he was there, and was struck down from behind before she had time to utter a cry. The servants heard nothing, remember."

"They said so at the inquest—yes."

"Now come into the drawing-room. This is where the caretaker tells me the body was found—here in the centre of the room—the poker with which the fatal blow had been struck was lying between the body and the fireplace. The absence of a cry and the position of the body show that when Mrs. Hannaford opened the door she *saw no one* (I am of course presuming that the murderer was *not* her husband) and she came in further. But there must have been some one in the room or she couldn't have been murdered in it."

"That is indisputable; but he might not have been in the room at the time—the person might have been hiding in the hall and followed her in."

"To suppose that we must presume that the murderer came into the room, took the poker from the fireplace, and went out again in order to come in again. That poker was secured, I am convinced, when the intruder heard footsteps coming down the stair. He picked up the poker and then concealed himself *here*."

"Then why, my dear Dorcas, shouldn't he have remained concealed until Mrs. Hannaford had gone out of the room again?"

"I think she was turning to go when he rushed out and struck her down. He probably thought that she had heard the noise of the door, and might go and alarm the servants."

"But just now you said she came in believing that her husband had returned and was in one of the rooms."

"The intruder could hardly be in possession of *her thoughts*."

"In the meantime he could have got out at the front door."

'Yes; but if his object was robbery he would have to go without the plunder. He struck the woman down in order to have time to get what he wanted."

"Then you think he left her here senseless while he searched the house?"

"Nobody got anything by searching the house, ma'am," broke in the caretaker. "The police satisfied themselves that nothing had been disturbed. Every door was locked, the plate was all complete, not a bit of jewellery or anything was missing. The servants were all examined about that, and the detectives went over every room and every cupboard to prove it wasn't no burglar broke in or anything of that sort. Besides, the windows were all fastened."

"What he says is quite true," said Dorcas to me, "but something alarmed Mrs. Hannaford in the night and brought her to the drawing-room in her nightdress. If it was, as I suspect, the opening of the front door, that is how the guilty person got in."

"The caretaker shook his head. "It was the poor master as did it, ma'am, right enough. He was out of his mind."

Dorcas shrugged her shoulders. "If he had done it, it would have been a furious attack, there would have been oaths and cries, and the poor lady would have received a rain of blows. The medical evidence shows that death resulted from *one* heavy blow on the *back* of the skull. But let us see where the murderer could have concealed himself ready armed with the poker here in the drawing-room."

In front of the drawing-room window were heavy curtains, and I at once suggested that curtains were the usual place of concealment on the stage and might be in real life.

As soon as I had asked the question Dorcas turned to the caretaker. "You are certain that every article of furniture is in its place exactly as it was that night?"

"Yes; the police prepared a plan of the room for the trial, and since then by the solicitors' orders we have not touched a thing."

"That settles the curtains then," continued Dorcas. "Look at the windows for yourself. In front of one, close by the curtains, is an ornamental table covered with china and glass and bric-à-brac; and in front of the other a large settee. No man could have come from behind those curtains without shifting that furniture out of his way. That would have immediately attracted Mrs. Hannaford's attention and given her time to scream and rush out of the room. No, we must find some other place for the assassin. Ah!—I wonder if——"

Dorcas's eyes were fixed on a large brown bear which stood nearly against the wall by the fireplace. The bear, a very fine, big specimen, was supported in its upright position by an ornamental iron pole, at the top of which was fixed an oil lamp covered with a yellow silk shade.

"That's a fine bear lamp," exclaimed Dorcas.

"Yes," said the caretaker, "it's been here ever since I've been in the family's service. It was bought by the poor mistress's first husband, Mr. Drayson, and he thought a lot of it. But," he added, looking at it curiously, "I always thought it stood closer to the wall than that. It used to— right against it."

"Ah," exclaimed Dorcas, "that's interesting. Pull the curtains right back and give me all the light you can."

As the man obeyed her directions she went down on her hands and knees and examined the carpet carefully.

"You are right," she said. "This has been moved a little forward, and not so very long ago—the carpet for a square of some inches is a different colour to the rest. The brown bear stands on a square mahogany stand, and the exact square now shows in the colour of the carpet that has been hidden by it. Only here is a discoloured portion and the bear does not now stand on it."

The evidence of the bear having been moved forward from a position it had long occupied was indisputable. Dorcas got up and went to the door of the drawing-room.

"Go and stand behind that bear," she said. "Stand as compact as you can, as though you were endeavouring to conceal yourself."

"I obeyed, and Dorcas, standing in the drawing-room doorway, declared that I was completely hidden.

"Now," she said, coming to the centre of the room and turning her back to me, "reach down from where you are and see if you can pick up the shovel from the fire-place without making a noise."

I reached out carefully and had the shovel in my hand without making a sound.

"I have it," I said.

"That's right. The poker would have been on the same side as the shovel, and much easier to pick up quietly. Now, while my back is turned, grasp the shovel by the handle, leap out at me, and raise the shovel as if to hit me—but don't get excited and do it, because I don't want to realize the scene *too* completely."

I obeyed. My footsteps were scarcely heard on the heavy-pile drawing-room carpet. When Dorcas turned round the shovel was above her head ready to strike.

"Thank you for letting me off," she said, with a smile. Then her face becoming serious again, she exclaimed: "The murderer of Mrs. Hannaford concealed himself behind that brown bear lamp, and attacked her in exactly the way I have indicated. But why had he moved the bear two or three inches forward?"

"To conceal himself behind it."

"Nonsense! His concealment was a sudden act. That bear is heavy—the glass chimney of the lamp would have rattled if it had been done violently and hurriedly while Mrs. Hannaford was coming down-stairs—that would have attracted her attention and she would have called out, 'Who's there?' at the doorway, and not have come in look-ing about for her husband."

Dorcas looked the animal over carefully, prodded it with her fingers, and then went behind it.

After a minute or two's close examination, she uttered a little cry and called me to her side.

She had found in the back of the bear a small straight slit. This was quite invisible. She had only discovered it by an accidentally violent thrust of her fingers into the animal's fur. Into this slit she thrust her hand, and the aperture yielded sufficiently for her to thrust her arm in. The interior of the bear was hollow, but Dorcas's hand as it went down struck against a wooden bottom. Then she withdrew her arm and the aperture closed up. It had evidently been specially prepared as a place of concealment, and only the most careful examination would have revealed it.

"Now," exclaimed Dorcas, triumphantly, "I think we are on a straight road! This, I believe, is where those missing bank-notes lay concealed for years. They were probably placed there by Mr. Drayson with the idea that some day his frauds might be discovered or he might be made a bankrupt. This was his little nest-egg, and his death in Paris before his fraud was discovered prevented him making use of them. Mrs. Hannaford evidently knew nothing of the hidden treasure, or she would speedily have removed it. But *some one* knew, and that some one put his knowledge to practical use the night that Mrs. Hannaford was murdered. The man who got in at the front door that night, got in to relieve the bear of its valuable stuffing; he moved the bear to get at the aperture, and was behind it when Mrs. Hannaford came in. The rest is easy to understand."

"But how did he get in at the front door?"

"That's what I have to find out. I am sure now that Flash George was in it. He was seen outside, and some of the notes that were concealed in the brown bear lamp have been traced to him. Who was Flash George's accomplice we may discover to-night. I think I have an idea, and if that is correct we shall have the solution of the whole mystery before dawn to-morrow morning."

"Why do you think you will learn so much to-night?"

"Because Flash George met a man two nights ago outside the Criterion. I was selling wax matches, and followed them up, pestering them. I heard George say to his companion, whom I had never seen with him before, 'Tell him Hungerford Bridge, midnight, Wednesday. Tell him to bring the lot and I'll cash up for them!'"

"And you think the 'him'——?"

"Is the man who rifled the brown bear and killed Mrs. Hannaford."

* * *

At eleven o'clock that evening I met Dorcas Dene in Villiers Street. I knew what she would be like, otherwise her disguise would have completely baffled me. She was dressed as an Italian street musician, and was with a man who looked like an Italian organ-grinder.

Dorcas took my breath away by her first words.

"Allow me to introduce you," she said, "to Mr. Thomas Holmes. This is the gentleman who was Charles Drayson's partner, and was sentenced to five years' penal servitude over the partnership frauds."

"Yes," replied the organ-grinder in excellent English. "I suppose I deserved it for being a fool, but the villain was Drayson—he had all my money, and involved me in a fraud at the finish."

"I have told Mr. Holmes the story of our discovery," said Dorcas. "I have been in communication with him ever since I discovered the notes were in circulation. He knew Drayson's affairs, and he has given me some valuable information. He is with us to-night because he knew Mr. Drayson's former associates, and he may be able to identify the man who knew the secret of the house at Haverstock Hill."

"You think that is the man Flash George is to meet?"

"I do. What else can 'Tell him to bring the lot and I'll cash up' mean but the rest of the bank-notes?"

Shortly before twelve we got on to Hungerford Bridge—the narrow footway that runs across the Thames by the side of the railway.

I was to walk ahead and keep clear of the Italians until I heard a signal.

We crossed the bridge after that once or twice, I coming from one end and the Italians from the other, and passing each other about the centre.

At five minutes to midnight I saw Flash George come slowly along from the Middlesex side. The Italians were not far behind. A minute later an old man with a grey beard, and wearing an old Inverness cape, passed me, coming from the Surrey side. When he met Flash George the two stopped and leant over the parapet, apparently interested in the river. Suddenly I heard Dorcas's signal. She began to sing the Italian song, "Santa Lucia."

I had my instructions. I jostled up against the two men and begged their pardon.

Flash George turned fiercely round. At the same moment I seized the old man and shouted for help. The Italians came hastily up. Several foot passengers rushed to the scene and inquired what was the matter.

"He was going to commit suicide," I cried. "He was just going to jump into the water."

The old man was struggling in my grasp. The crowd were keeping back Flash George. They believed the old man was struggling to get free to throw himself into the water.

The Italian rushed up to me.

"Ah, poor old man!" he said. "Don't let him get away!"

He gave a violent tug to the grey beard. It came off in his hands. Then with an oath he seized the supposed would-be suicide by the throat.

"You infernal villain!" he said.

"Who is he?" asked Dorcas.

"Who is he!" exclaimed Thomas Holmes, "why, the villain who brought me to ruin—*my precious partner—Charles Drayson!*"

As the words escaped from the supposed Italian's lips, Charles Drayson gave a cry of terror, and leaping on to the parapet, plunged into the river.

Flash George turned to run, but was stopped by a policeman who had just come up.

Dorcas whispered something in the man's ear, and the officer, thrusting his hand in the rascal's pocket, drew out a bundle of bank-notes.

A few minutes later the would-be suicide was brought ashore. He was still alive, but had injured himself terribly in his fall, and was taken to the hospital.

Before he died he was induced to confess that he had taken advantage of the Paris fire to disappear. He had flung his watch down in order that it might be found as evidence of his death. He had, previously to visiting the rue Jean Goujon, received a letter at his hotel which told him pretty plainly the game was up, and he knew that at any moment a warrant might be issued against him. After reading his name amongst the victims, he lived as best he could abroad, but after some years, being in desperate straits, he determined to do a bold thing, return to London and endeavour to get into his house and obtain possession of the money which was lying unsuspected in the interior of the brown bear lamp. He had concealed it, well knowing that at any time the crash might come, and everything belonging to him be seized. The hiding-place he had selected was one which neither his creditors nor his relatives would suspect.

On the night he entered the house, Flash George, whose acquaintance he had made in London, kept watch for him *while he let himself in with his latch-key*, which he had carefully preserved. Mr. Hannaford's leaving the house was one of those pieces of good fortune which occasionally favour the wicked.

With his dying breath Charles Drayson declared that he had no intention of killing his wife. He feared that, having heard a noise, she had come to see what it was, and might alarm the house in her terror, and as she turned to go out of the drawing-room he struck her, intending only to render her senseless until he had secured the booty.

*   *   *

Mr. Hannaford, completely recovered and in his right mind, was in due time released from Broadmoor. The letter from his mother to Dorcas Dene, thanking her for clearing her son's character and proving his innocence of the terrible crime for which he had been practically condemned, brought tears to my eyes as Dorcas read it aloud to Paul and myself. It was touching and beautiful to a degree.

As she folded it up and put it away, I saw that Dorcas herself was deeply moved.

"These are the *rewards* of my profession," she said. "They compensate for everything."

R. Austin Freeman

(1862–1943)

RICHARD AUSTIN FREEMAN was one of the most important writers of detective fiction. He created Dr. John Thorndyke, the first genuine scientific detective (Holmes talked about science but seldom used it in his cases), and he invented the "inverted detective story," in which the reader sees the crime committed, and the interest is in how the detective links the crime with its perpetrator. (Readers may be familiar with this structure through the *Columbo* television series.) After obtaining his medical degree, Freeman became Assistant Colonial Surgeon on the Gold Coast, West Africa, in 1887. In 1892, having become ill with a parasitic disease, he returned to England. As his health did not allow him to practice medicine regularly, Freeman turned to writing for his livelihood. His first book, *Travels and Life in Ashanti and Jaman*, appeared in 1898, as did his early short stories for *Cassell's Magazine*.

His first works in the crime field were crook stories featuring Rodney Pringle, written in collaboration with a friend, Dr. J. J. Pitcairn, and published under the pseudonym "Clifford Ashdown." In 1907, Freeman published *The Red Thumb Mark*, basing the character of the medico-legal detective, Dr. Thorndyke, on Professor Alfred Swaine Taylor. Freeman prefaced *John Thorndyke's Cases* (1909) with the note that "the experiments described have in all cases been performed by me," and he illustrated the book with photographs of the specimens examined through a microscope. *The Singing Bone* (1912) contains the first inverted detective stories, and the tale that follows, "The Dead Hand," is in that sub-sub-genre. The story appeared in two issues of *Pearson's Magazine*, October and November 1912, and some fourteen years later Freeman expanded it into a novel called *The Shadow of the Wolf*. As far as I have been able to determine, the original story has never previously been published in America.

The Dead Hand

I. How It Happened

ABOUT HALF-PAST EIGHT on a fine, sunny June morning, a small yacht crept out of Sennen Cove, near the Land's End, and headed for the open sea. On the shelving beach of the cove two women and a man, evidently visitors (or "foreigners," to use the local term), stood watching her departure with valedictory waving of cap or handkerchief, and the boatman who had put the crew on board, aided by two of his comrades, was hauling his boat up above the tide-mark.

A light, northerly breeze filled the yacht's sails and drew her gradually seaward. The figures of her crew dwindled to the size of dolls, shrank with the increasing distance to the magnitude of insects, and at last, losing all individuality, became mere specks merged in the form of the fabric that bore them.

On board the receding craft two men sat in the little cockpit. They formed the entire crew, for the *Sandhopper* was only a ship's lifeboat, timbered and decked, of light draught and, in the matter of spars and canvas, what the art critics would call "reticent."

Both men, despite the fineness of the weather, wore yellow oilskins and sou'westers, and that was about all they had in common. In other respects they made a curious contrast—the one small, slender, sharp-featured, dark almost to swarthiness, and restless and quick in his movements; the other large, massive, red-faced, blue-eyed, with the rounded outlines suggestive of ponderous strength; a great ox of a man, heavy, stolid, but much less unwieldy than he looked.

The conversation incidental to getting the yacht under way had ceased, and silence had fallen on the occupants of the cockpit. The big man grasped the tiller and looked sulky, which was probably his usual aspect, and the small man watched him furtively.

The land was nearly two miles distant when the latter broke the silence.

"Joan Haygarth has come on wonderfully the last few months; getting quite a fine-looking girl. Don't you think so, Purcell?"

"Yes," answered Purcell, "and so does Phil Rodney."

"You're right," agreed the other. "She isn't a patch on her sister, though, and never will be. I was looking at Maggie as we came down the beach this morning and thinking what a handsome girl she is. Don't you agree with me?"

Purcell stooped to look under the boom, and answered without turning his head:

"Yes, she's all right."

"All right!" exclaimed the other. "Is that the way——"

"Look here, Varney," interrupted Purcell. "I don't want to discuss my wife's looks with you or any other man. She'll do for me or I shouldn't have married her."

A deep, coppery flush stole into Varney's cheeks. But he had brought the rather brutal snub on himself and apparently had the fairness to recognise the fact, for he mumbled an apology and relapsed into silence.

When next he spoke he did so with a manner diffident and uneasy, as though approaching a disagreeable or difficult subject.

"There's a little matter, Dan, that I've been wanting to speak to you about when we got a chance of a private talk."

He glanced rather anxiously at his stolid companion, who grunted, and then, without removing his gaze from the horizon ahead, replied: "You've a pretty fair chance now, seeing that we shall be bottled up together for another five or six hours. And it's fairly private unless you bawl loud enough to be heard at the Longships."

It was not a gracious invitation. But if Varney resented the rebuff he showed no sign of annoyance, for reasons which appeared when he opened his subject.

"What I wanted to say," he resumed, "was this. We're both doing pretty well now on the square. You must be positively piling up the shekels, and I can earn a decent living, which is all I want. Why shouldn't we drop this flash note business?"

Purcell kept his blue eye fixed on the horizon and appeared to ignore the question; but after an interval and without moving a muscle he said gruffly: "Go on," and Varney continued:

"The lay isn't what it was, you know. At first it was all plain sailing. The notes were 1st-class copies and not a soul suspected anything until they were presented at the bank. Then the murder was out, and the next little trip that I made was a very different affair. Two or three of the notes were queried quite soon after I had changed them, and I had to be precious fly, I can tell you, to avoid complications. And now that the second batch has come in to the Bank, the planting of fresh specimens is going to be harder still. There isn't a money-changer on the Continent of Europe that isn't keeping his weather eyeball peeled, to say nothing of the detectives that the Bank people have sent abroad."

He paused and looked appealingly at his companion. But Purcell, still minding his helm, only growled "Well?"

"Well, I want to chuck it, Dan. When you've had a run of luck and pocketed your winnings it is time to stop play."

"You've come into some money, then, I take it?" said Purcell.

"No, I haven't. But I can make a living now by safe and respectable means, and I'm sick of all this scheming and dodging with the gaol everlastingly under my lee."

"The reason I asked," said Purcell, "is that there is a trifle outstanding. You hadn't forgotten that, I suppose?"

"No, I hadn't forgotten it, but I thought that perhaps you might be willing to let me down a bit easily."

The other man pursed up his thick lips and continued to gaze stonily over the bow.

"Oh, that's what you thought?" he said; and then, after a pause: "I fancy you must have lost sight of some of the facts when you thought that. Let me just remind you how the case stands. To begin with, you start your career with a little playful embezzlement, you blue the proceeds and you are mug enough to be found out. Then I come in. I compound the affair with old Marston for a couple of thousand, and practically clean myself out of every penny I possess, and he consents to regard your temporary absence in the light of a holiday.

"Now, why do I do this? Am I a philanthropist? Devil a bit. I'm a man of business. Before I ladle out that two thousand, I make a business contract with you. I have discovered how to make a passable imitation of the Bank of England paper; you are a skilled engraver and a plausible scamp. I am to supply you with paper blanks, you are to engrave plates, print the notes, and get them changed. I am to take two-thirds of the proceeds; and, although I have done the most difficult part of the work, I agree to regard my share of the profits as constituting repayment of the loan.

"Our contract amounts to this: I lend you two thousand without security—with an infernal amount of insecurity, in fact—you 'promise, covenant, and agree,' as the lawyers say, to hand me back ten thousand in instalments, being the products of our joint industry. It is a verbal contract which I have no means of enforcing, but I trust you to keep your word, and up to the present you have kept it. You have paid me a little over four thousand. Now you want to cry off and leave the balance unpaid. Isn't that the position?"

"Not exactly," said Varney. "I'm not crying off the debt; I only want time. Look here, Dan; I'm making about three fifty a year now. That isn't much, but I'll manage to let you have a hundred a year out of it. What do you say to that?"

Purcell laughed scornfully. "A hundred a year to pay off six thousand! That'll take just sixty years: and as I'm now forty-three, I shall be exactly a hundred and three years of age when the last instalment is paid. I think, Varney, you'll admit that a man of a hundred and three is getting past his prime."

"Well, I'll pay you something down to start. I've saved about eighteen hundred pounds out of the note business. You can have that now, and I'll pay off as much I can at a time until I'm clear. Remember, that if I should happen to get clapped in chokee for twenty years or so, you won't get anything. And, I tell you, it's getting a risky business."

"I'm willing to take the risk," said Purcell.

"I daresay you are," Varney retorted passionately, "because it's my risk. If I am grabbed, it's my racket. You sit out. It's I who passed the notes, and I'm known to be a skilled engraver. That'll be good enough for them. They won't trouble about who made the paper."

"I hope not," said Purcell.

"Of course they wouldn't; and you know I shouldn't give you away."

"Naturally. Why should you? Wouldn't do you any good."

"Well, give me a chance, Dan," Varney pleaded. "This business is getting on my nerves. I want to be quit of it. You've had four thousand; that's a hundred per cent. You haven't done so badly."

"I didn't expect to do badly. I took a big risk. I gambled two thousand for ten."

"Yes; and you got me out of the way while you put the screw on poor old Haygarth to make his daughter marry you."

It was an indiscreet thing to say, but Purcell's stolid indifference to his danger and distress had ruffled Varney's temper.

Purcell, however, was unmoved. "I don't know," he said, "what you mean by getting you out of the way. You were never in the way. You were always hankering after Maggie, but I could never see that she wanted you."

"Well, she certainly didn't want *you*," Varney retorted. "And, for that matter, I don't much think she wants you now."

For the first time Purcell withdrew his eye from the horizon to turn it on his companion. And an evil eye it was, set in the great, sensual face, now purple with anger.

"What the devil do you mean?" he exclaimed furiously; "you infernal, sallow-faced, little whipper-snapper! If you mention my wife's name again I'll knock you on the head and pitch you overboard."

Varney's face flushed darkly, and for a moment he was inclined to try the wager a battle. But the odds were impossible, and if Varney was not a coward, neither was he a fool. But the discussion was at an end. Nothing was to be hoped for now. These indiscreet words had rendered further pleading impossible.

The silence that settled down in the yacht and the aloofness that encompassed the two men were conducive to reflection. Each ignored the presence of the other. When the course was altered southerly, Purcell slacked out the sheets with his own hand as he put up the helm. He might have been sailing singlehanded. And Varney watched him askance, but made no move; sitting hunched up on the locker, nursing a slowly-matured hatred and thinking his thoughts.

Very queer thoughts they were. He was following out the train of events that might have happened, pursuing them to their possible consequences. Supposing Purcell had carried out his threat? Well, there would have been a pretty tough struggle, for Varney was no weakling. But a struggle with that solid fifteen stone of flesh could end only one way. No, there was no doubt; he would have gone overboard.

And what then? Would Purcell have gone back to Sennen Cove, or sailed alone into Penzance? In either case, he would have had to make up some sort of story; and no one could have contradicted him whether the story was believed or not. But it would have been awkward for Purcell.

Then there was the body. That would have been washed up sooner or later, as much of it as the lobsters had left. Well, lobsters don't eat clothes or bones, and a dent in the skull might take some accounting for. Very awkward this—for Purcell. He would probably have had to clear out; to make a bolt for it, in short.

The mental picture of this great bully fleeing in terror from the vengeance of the law gave Varney appreciable pleasure. Most of his life he had been borne down by the moral and physical weight of this domineering brute. At school, Purcell had fagged him; he had even bullied him up at Cambridge; and now he had fastened on for ever, like the Old

Man of the Sea. And Purcell always got the best of it. When he, Varney, had come back from Italy after that unfortunate little affair, behold! the girl whom they had both wanted (and who had wanted neither of them) had changed from Maggie Haygarth into Maggie Purcell. And so it was even unto this day. Purcell, a prosperous stockjobber now, spent a part of his secret leisure making, in absolute safety, these accursed paper blanks; which he, Varney, must risk his liberty to change into money. Yes, it was quite pleasant to think of Purcell sneaking from town to town, from country to country, with the police at his heels.

But in these days of telegraphs and extradition there isn't much chance for a fugitive. Purcell would have been caught to a certainty; and he would have been hanged; no doubt of it. The imagined picture of the execution gave him quite a lengthy entertainment. Then his errant thoughts began to spread out in search of other possibilities. For, after all, it was not an absolute certainty that Purcell could have got him overboard. There was just the chance that Purcell might have gone overboard himself. That would have been a very different affair.

Varney settled himself composedly to consider the new and interesting train of consequences that would thus have been set going. They were more agreeable to contemplate than the others, because they did not include his own demise. The execution scene made no appearance in this version. The salient fact was that his oppressor would have vanished; that the intolerable burden of his servitude would have been lifted for ever; that he would have been free.

It was mere idle speculation to while away a dull hour with an uncongenial companion, and he let his thoughts ramble at large. One moment he was dreamily wondering whether Maggie would ever have listened to him, ever have come to care for him; the next, he was back in the yacht's cabin, where hung from a hook on the bulkhead the revolver that the Rodneys used to practise at floating bottles. It was usually loaded, he knew, but, if not, there was a canvas bag full of cartridges in the starboard locker. Again, he found himself dreaming of the home that he would have had, a home very different from the cheerless lodgings in which he moped at present; and then his thoughts had flitted back to the yacht's hold, and were busying themselves with the row of half-hundredweights that rested on the timbers on either side of the kelson.

When Varney had thus brought his mental picture, so to speak, to a finish, its completeness surprised him. It was so simple, so secure. He had actually planned out the scheme of a murder, and he found himself wondering whether many murders passed undetected. They well might if murders were as easy and as safe as this—a dangerous reflection for an injured and angry man. And at this critical point his meditations were interrupted by Purcell, continuing the conversation as if there had been no pause:

"So you can take it from me, Varney, that I expect you to stick to your bargain. I paid down my money, and I'm going to have my pound of flesh."

It was a brutal thing to say, and it was brutally said. But more than that, it was inopportune—or opportune, as you will; for it came as a sort of infernal doxology to the devil's anthem that had been, all unknown, ringing in Varney's soul.

Purcell had spoken without looking round. That was his unpleasant habit. Had he looked at his companion, he might have been startled. A change in Varney's face might have given him pause; a warm flush, a sparkle of the eye, a look of elation, of settled purpose, deadly, inexorable—the look of a man who has made a fateful resolution.

It was so simple, so secure! That was the burden of the song that echoed in Varney's brain.

He glanced over the sea. They had opened the south coast now, and he could see, afar off, a fleet of black-sailed luggers heading east. They wouldn't be in his way. Nor would the big four-master that was creeping away to the west, for she was hull down already, and other ships there were none.

There was one hindrance, though. Dead ahead the Wolf Rock Lighthouse rose from the blue water, its red-and-white ringed tower looking like some gaudily painted toy. The keepers of lonely lighthouses have a natural habit of watching the passing shipping through their glasses, and it was possible that one of their telescopes might be pointed at the yacht at this very moment. That was a complication.

Suddenly there came down the wind a sharp report like the firing of a gun, quickly followed by a second. It was the explosive signal from the Longships Lighthouse; but when they looked round there was no lighthouse to be seen—the dark-blue, heaving water faded away at the foot of an advancing wall of vapour.

Purcell cursed fluently. A pretty place, this, to be caught in, in a fog! And then, as his eye lighted on his companion, he demanded angrily: "What the devil are you grinning at?"

For Varney, drunk with suppressed excitement, snapped his fingers at rocks and shoals; he was thinking only of the lighthouse keeper's telescope and of the revolver that hung on the bulkhead. He must make some excuse presently to go below and secure that revolver.

But no excuse was necessary. The opportunity came of itself. After a hasty glance at the vanishing land and another at the compass, Purcell put up the helm to gybe the yacht round on to an easterly course.

As she came round, the single headsail that she carried in place of jib and foresail shivered for a few seconds, and then filled suddenly on the opposite tack. And at this moment the halyards parted with a loud snap; the end of the rope flew through the blocks, and, in an instant, the sail was down and its upper half trailing in the water alongside.

Purcell swore volubly, but kept an eye to business. "Run below, Varney," said he, "and fetch up that coil of new rope out of the starboard locker while I had the sail on board. And look alive. We don't want to drift down on to the Wolf."

Varney obeyed with silent alacrity and a curious feeling of elation. It was going to be even easier and safer than he had thought. He slipped through the hatch into the cabin, quietly took the revolver from its hook, and examined the chambers.

Finding them all loaded, he cocked the hammer and slipped the weapon carefully into the inside breast pocket of his oilskin coat. Then he took the coil of rope from the locker and went on deck.

As he emerged from the hatch, he perceived that the yacht was already enveloped in fog, which drifted past in steamy clouds, and that she had come up head to wind. Purcell was kneeling on the forecastle, tugging at the sail, which had caught under the forefoot, and punctuating his efforts with deep-voiced curses.

Varney stole silently along the deck, steadying himself by mast and shroud, softly laid down the coil of rope, and approached. Purcell was quite engrossed with his task; his back was towards Varney, his face over the side, intent on the entangled sail. It was a chance in a thousand.

With scarcely a moment's hesitation, Varney stooped forward, steadying himself with a hand on the little windlass, and softly drawing forth the revolver, pointed it at the back of Purcell's head at the spot where the back seam of his sou'wester met the brim.

The report rang out but weak and flat in that open space, and a cloud of smoke mingled with the fog; but it blew away immediately, and showed Purcell almost unchanged in posture, crouching on the sail, with his chin resting on the little rim of bulwark, while behind him his murderer, as if turned into bronze, still stood stooping forward, one hand grasping the windlass, the other still pointing the revolver.

Thus the two figures remained for some seconds motionless like some horrible waxworks, until the little yacht, lifting to the swell, gave a more than usually lively curvet; when Purcell rolled over on to his back, and Varney relaxed the rigidity of his posture like a golf-player who has watched his ball drop.

Purcell was dead. That was the salient fact. The head wagged to and fro as the yacht pitched and rolled, the limp arms and legs seemed to twitch, the limp body to writhe uneasily. But Varney was not disturbed. Lifeless things will move on an unsteady deck. He was only interested to notice how the passive movements produced the illusion of life. But it was only illusion. Purcell was dead. There was no doubt of that.

The double report from the Longships came down the wind, and then, as if in answer, a prolonged, deep bellow. That was the fog-horn of the lighthouse on the Wolf Rock, and it sounded surprisingly near. But, of course, these signals were meant to be heard at a distance. Then a stream of hot sunshine, pouring down on deck, startled him, and made him hurry. The body must be got overboard before the fog lifted.

With an uneasy glance at the clear sky overhead, he hastily cast off the broken halyard from its cleat and cut off a couple of fathoms. Then he hurried below, and, lifting the trap in the cabin floor, hoisted out one of the iron half-hundredweights with which the yacht was ballasted.

As he stepped on deck with the weight in his hand, the sun was shining overhead; but the fog was still thick below, and the horn sounded once more from the Wolf. And again it struck him as surprisingly near.

He passed the length of rope that he had cut off twice round Purcell's body, hauled it tight, and secured it with a knot. Then he made the ends fast to the handle of the iron weight.

Not much fear of Purcell drifting ashore now. That weight would hold him as long as there was anything to hold. But it had taken some time to do, and the warning bellow from the Wolf seemed to draw nearer and nearer. He was about to heave the body over when his eye fell on the dead man's sou'wester, which had fallen off when the body rolled over.

That hat must be got rid of, for Purcell's name was worked in silk on the lining and there was an unmistakeable bullet-hole through the back. It must be destroyed, or, which would be simpler and quicker, lashed securely on the dead man's head.

Hurriedly, Varney ran aft and descended to the cabin. He had noticed a new ball of spunyarn in the locker when he had fetched the rope. This would be the very thing.

He was back again in a few moments with the ball in his hand, unwinding it as he came, and without wasting time he knelt down by the body and fell to work.

And every half minute the deep-voiced growl of the Wolf came to him out of the fog, and each time it sounded nearer and yet nearer.

By the time he had made the sou'wester secure the dead man's face and chin were encased in a web of spunyarn that made him look like some old-time, grotesque-vizored Samurai warrior.

Varney rose to his feet. But his task was not finished yet. There was Purcell's suitcase. That must be sunk, too, and there was something in it that had figured in the detailed picture that his imagination had drawn. He ran to the cockpit where the suit-case lay, and having tried its fastenings and found it unlocked, he opened it and took out a letter that lay on top of the other contents. This he tossed through the hatch into the cabin, and, having closed and fastened the suit-case, he carried it forward and made it fast to the iron weight with half a dozen turns of spunyarn.

That was really all, and indeed it was time. As he rose once more to his feet the growl of the foghorn burst out, as it seemed, right over the stern of the yacht, and she was drifting stern foremost, who could say how fast. Now, too, he caught a more ominous sound, which he might have heard sooner had he listened — the wash of water, the boom of breakers bursting on a rock.

A sudden revulsion came over him. He burst into a wild, sardonic laugh. And had it come to this, after all? Had he schemed and laboured only to leave himself alone on an unmanageable craft drifting down to shipwreck and certain death? Had he taken all this thought and care to secure Purcell's body, when his own might be resting beside it on the sea-bottom within an hour?

But the reverie was brief. Suddenly, from the white void over his very head, as it seemed, there issued a stunning, thunderous roar that shook the deck under his feet. The water around him boiled into a foamy chaos, the din of bursting waves was in his ears, the yacht plunged and wallowed amidst clouds of spray, and for an instant a dim, gigantic shadow loomed through the fog and was gone. In that moment his nerve had come back. Holding on with one hand to the windlass he dragged the body to the edge of the forecastle, hoisted the weight outboard, and then, taking advantage of a heavy lurch, gave the corpse a vigorous shove. There was a rattle and a hollow splash, and corpse and weight and suit-case had vanished into the seething water.

He clung to the swinging mast and waited. Breathlessly he told out the allotted seconds until once again the invisible Titan belched forth his thunderous warning. But this time the roar came over the yacht's bow. She had drifted past the rock then. The danger was over, and

Purcell would have to go down to Davy Jones' locker companionless after all.

Very soon the water around ceased to boil and tumble, and as the yacht's wild plunging settled down once more into the normal rise and fall on the long swell, Varney turned his attention to the refitting of the halyard. But what was this on the creamy, duck sail? A pool of blood and two gory imprints of his own left hand! That wouldn't do at all. He would have to clear that away before he could hoist the sail, which was annoying, as the yacht was helpless without her headsail, and was evidently drifting out to sea.

He fetched a bucket, a swab, and a scrubbing-brush, and set to work. The bulk of the large bloodstain cleared off pretty completely after he had drenched the sail with a bucketfull or two and given it a good scrubbing. But the edge of the stain where the heat of the deck had dried it remained like a painted boundary on a map, and the two hand-prints—which had also dried, though they faded to a pale buff—continued clearly visible.

Varney began to grow uneasy. If those stains would not come out—especially the hand-prints—it would be very awkward, they would take so much explaining. He decided to try the effect of marine soap, and fetched a cake from the cabin; but even this did not obliterate the stains completely, though it turned them a faint, greenish brown, very unlike the colour of blood. So he scrubbed on until at last the hand-prints faded away entirely, and the large stain was reduced to a faint green, wavy line, and that was the best he could do—and quite good enough, for if that faint line should ever be noticed no one would suspect its origin.

He put away the bucket and proceeded with the refitting. The sea had disengaged the sail from the forefoot, and he hauled it on board without difficulty. Then there was the reeving of the new halyard, a trouble-some business involving the necessity of his going aloft, where his weight—small man as he was—made the yacht roll most infernally, and set him swinging to and fro like the bob of a metronome. But he was a smart yachtsman and active, though not powerful, and a few minutes' strenuous exertion ended in his sliding down the shrouds with the new halyard running fairly through the upper block. A vigorous haul or two at the new, hairy rope sent the head of the dripping sail aloft, and the yacht was once more under control.

The rig of the *Sandhopper* was not smart, but it was handy. She carried a short bow-sprit to accommodate the single headsail and a relatively large mizzen, of which the advantage was, that by judicious management of the mizzen-sheet the yacht would sail with very little attention to the helm. Of this advantage Varney was keenly appreciative just now, for he had several things to do before entering port. He wanted refreshment, he wanted a wash, and the various traces of recent events had to be removed. Also, there was that letter to be attended to. So that it was convenient to be able to leave the helm in charge of a lashing for a minute now and again.

When he had washed, he put the kettle on the spirit stove, and while it was heating busied himself in cleaning the revolver, flinging the empty cartridge-case overboard, and replacing it with a cartridge from the bag in the locker. Then he picked up the letter that he had taken from Purcell's suit-case and examined it. It was addressed to "Joseph Penfield, Esq., George Yard, Lombard Street," and was unstamped, though the envelpe was fastened up. He affixed a stamp from his pocket-book, and when the kettle began to boil, he held the envelope in the steam that issued from the spout. Very soon the flap of the envelope loosened and curled back, when he laid it aside to mix himself a mug of hot grog, which, together with the letter and a biscuit-tin, he took out into the cockpit. The fog was still dense, and the hoot of a steamer's whistle from somewhere to the westward caused him to reach the foghorn out of the locker, and blow a long blast on it. As if in answer to his treble squeak came the deep bass note from the Wolf, and unconsciously he looked round. He turned automatically, as one does towards a sudden noise, not expecting to see anything but fog, and what he did see startled him not a little.

For there was the lighthouse—or half of it, rather—standing up above the fog-bank, clear, distinct, and hardly a mile away. The gilded vane, the sparkling lantern, the gallery, and the upper half of the red and white ringed tower, stood sharp against the pallid sky; but the lower half was invisible. It was a strange apparition—like half a lighthouse suspended in mid-air—and uncommonly disturbing, too. It raised a very awkward question. If he could see the lantern, the light-keepers could see him. But how long had the lantern been clear of the fog?

Thus he meditated as, with one hand on the tiller, he munched his biscuit and sipped his grog. Presently he picked up the stamped envelope and drew from it a letter and a folded document, both of which he tore into fragments and dropped overboard. Then, from his pocket-book, he took a similar but unaddressed envelope from which he drew out the contents, and very curious those contents were.

There was a letter, brief and laconic, which he read over thoughtfully. "These," it ran, "are all I have by me, but they will do for the present, and when you have planted them I will let you have a fresh supply." There was no date and no signature, but the rather peculiar hand-writing was similar to that on the envelope addressed to Joseph Penfield, Esq.

The other contents consisted of a dozen sheets of blank paper, each of the size of a Bank of England note. But they were not quite blank, for each bore an elaborate water-mark, identical with that of a twenty-pound banknote. They were, in fact, the "paper blanks" of which Purcell had spoken. The envelope with its contents had been slipped into his hand by Purcell, without remark, only three days ago.

Varney refolded the "blanks," enclosed them within the letter, and slipped letter and "blanks" together into the stamped envelope, the flap of which he licked and reclosed.

"I should like to see old Penfield's face when he opens that envelope," was his reflection as, with a grim smile, he put it away in his pocket-book. "And I wonder what he will do," he added, mentally; "however, I shall see before many days are over."

Varney looked at his watch. He was to meet Jack Rodney on Penzance Pier at a quarter to three. He would never do it at this rate, for when he opened Mount's Bay, Penzance would be right in the wind's eye. That would mean a long beat to windward. Then Rodney would be there first, waiting for him. Deuced awkward, this. He would have to account for his being alone on board; would have to invent some lie about having put Purcell ashore at Mousehole or Newlyn. But a lie is a very pernicious thing. Its effects are cumulative. You never know when you have done with it. Now, if he had reached Penzance before Rodney he need have said nothing about Purcell—for the present, at any rate, and that would have been so much safer.

When the yacht was about abreast of Lamorna Cove, though some seven miles to the south, the breeze began to draw ahead and the fog cleared off quite suddenly. The change of wind was unfavourable for the moment, but when it veered round yet a little more until it blew from east-north-east, Varney brightened up considerably. There was still a chance of reaching Penzance before Rodney arrived; for now, as soon as he had fairly opened Mount's Bay, he could head straight for his destination and make it on a single board.

Between two and three hours later the *Sandhopper* entered Penzance Harbour, and, threading her way among an assemblage of luggers and small coasters, brought up alongside the Albert Pier at the foot of a vacant ladder. Having made the yacht fast to a couple of rings, Varney divested himself of his oilskins, locked the cabin scuttle, and climbed the ladder. The change of wind had saved him after all, and, as he strode away along the pier, he glanced complacently at his watch. He still had nearly half an hour to the good.

He seemed to know the place well and to have a definite objective, for he struck out briskly from the foot of the pier into Market Jew Street, and from thence by a somewhat zig-zag route to a road which eventually brought him out about the middle of the Esplanade. Continuing westward, he entered the Newlyn Road along which he walked rapidly for about a third of a mile, when he drew up opposite a small letter-box which was let into a wall. Here he stopped to read the tablet on which was printed the hours of collection, and then, having glanced at his watch, he walked on again, but at a less rapid pace.

When he reached the outskirts of Newlyn he turned and began slowly to retrace his steps, looking at his watch from time to time with a certain air of impatience. Presently a quick step behind him caused him to look round. The newcomer was a postman, striding along, bag on shoulder, with the noisy tread of a heavily-shod man, and evidently collecting letters. Varney let him pass; watched him halt at the little letter-box, unlock the door, gather up the letters and stow them in his bag; heard the clang of the iron door, and finally saw the man set forth again on his pilgrimage. Then he brought forth his pocket-book and, drawing from it the letter addressed to Joseph Penfield, Esq., stepped up to the letter-box. The tablet now announced that the next collection would be at 8.30 p.m. Varney read the announcement with a faint smile, glanced again at his watch, which indicated two minutes past four, and dropped the letter into the box.

As he walked up the pier, with a large paper bag under his arm, he became aware of a tall man, who was doing sentry-go before a Gladstone bag, that stood on the coping opposite the ladder, and who, observing his approach, came forward to meet him.

"Here you are, then, Rodney," was Varney's rather unoriginal greeting.

"Yes," replied Rodney, "and here I've been for nearly half an hour. Purcell gone?"

"Bless you, yes; long ago," answered Varney.

"I didn't see him at the station. What train was he going by?"

"I don't know. He said something about taking Falmouth on the way; had some business or other there. But I expect he's gone to have a feed at one of the hotels. We got hung up in a fog—that's why I'm so late; I've been up to buy some prog."

"Well," said Rodney, "bring it on board. It's time we were under way.

As soon as we are outside, I'll take charge and you can go below and stoke up at your ease."

The two men descended the ladder and proceeded at once to hoist the sails and cast off the shore-ropes. A few strokes of an oar sent them clear of the lee of the pier, and in five minutes the yacht *Sandhopper* was once more outside, heading south with a steady breeze from east-north-east.

II. The Unravelling of the Mystery

Romance lurks in unsuspected places. We walk abroad amidst scenes made dull by familiarity, and let our thoughts ramble far away beyond the commonplace. In fancy we thread the ghostly aisles of some tropical forest; we linger on the white beach of some lonely coral island, where the cocoa-nut palms, shivering in the sea-breeze, patter a refrain to the song of the surf; we wander by moonlight through the narrow streets of some southern city, and hear the thrum of the guitar rise to the shrouded balcony; and behold! all the time Romance is at our very doors.

*   *   *

It was on a bright afternoon early in March, that I sat beside my friend Thorndyke on one of the lower benches of the lecture theatre of the Royal College of Surgeons. Not a likely place this to encounter Romance, and yet there it was, if we had only known it, lying unnoticed at present on the green baize cover of the lecturer's table. But, for the moment, we were thinking of nothing but the lecture.

The theatre was nearly full. It usually was when Professor D'Arcy lectured; for that genial *savant* had the magnetic gift of infusing his own enthusiasm into the lecture, and so into his audience, even when, as on this occasion, his subject lay on the outside edge of medical science. To-day he was lecturing on marine worms, standing before the great blackboard with a bunch of coloured chalks in either hand, talking with easy eloquence—mostly over his shoulder—while he covered the black surface with those delightful drawings that added so much to the charm of his lectures.

I watched his flying fingers with fascination, dividing my attention between him and a young man on the bench below me, who was frantically copying the diagrams in a large note-book, assisted by an older friend, who sat by him and handed him the coloured pencils as he needed them.

The latter part of the lecture dealt with those beautiful sea-worms that build themselves tubes to live in; worms like the *Serpula*, that make their shelly or stony tubes by secretion from their own bodies; or, like the *Sabella* or *Terbella*, build them up with sand-grains, little stones, or fragments of shell.

When the lecture came to an end, we trooped down into the arena to look at the exhibits and exchange a few words with the genial professor. Thorndyke knew him very well, and was welcomed with a warm handshake and a facetious question.

"What are you doing here, Thorndyke?" asked Professor D'Arcy. "Is it possible that there are medico-legal possibilities even in a marine worm?"

"Oh, come!" protested Thorndyke, "don't make me such a hidebound specialist. May I have no rational interest in life? Must I live for ever in the witness-box, like a marine worm in its tube?"

"I suspect you don't get very far out of your tube," said the professor, with a smile at my colleague. "And that reminds me that I have something in your line. What do you make of this? Let us hear you extract its history."

Here, with a mischievous twinkle, he handed Thorndyke a small, round object, which my friend inspected curiously as it lay in the palm of his hand.

"In the first place," said he, "it is a cork; the cork of a small jar."

"Right," said the professor—"full marks. What else?"

"The cork has been saturated with paraffin wax."

"Right again."

"Then some Robinson Crusoe seems to have used it as a button, judging by the two holes in it, and an end of what looks like cat-gut."

"Yes."

"Finally, a marine worm of some kind—a *Terebella*, I think—has built a tube on it."

"Quite right. And now tell us the history of the cork or button."

"I should like to know something more about the worm first," said Thorndyke.

"The worm," said Professor D'Arcy, "is *Terebella Rufescens*. It lives, unlike most other species, on a rocky bottom, and in a depth of water of not less than ten fathoms."

It was at this point that Romance stepped in. The young man whom I had noticed working so strenuously at his notes had edged up alongside, and was staring at the object in Thorndyke's hand, not with mere interest or curiosity, but with the utmost amazement and horror. His expression was so remarkable that we all, with one accord, dropped our conversation to look at him.

"Might I be allowed to examine that specimen?" he asked; and when Thorndyke handed it to him, he held it close to his eyes, scrutinising it with frowning astonishment, turned it over and over, and felt the frayed ends of cat-gut between his fingers. Finally, he beckoned to his friend, and the two whispered together for a while, and watching them I saw the second man's eyebrows lift, and the same expression of horrified surprise appear on his face. Then the younger man addressed the professor.

"Would you mind telling me where you got this specimen, sir?"

The professor was quite interested. "It was sent to me," he said, "by a friend, who picked it up on the beach at Morte Hoe, on the coast of North Cornwall."

The two young men looked significantly at one another, and, after a brief pause, the older one asked: "Is this specimen of much value, sir?"

"No," replied the professor; "it is only a curiosity. There are several specimens of the worm in our collection. But why do you ask?"

"Because I should like to acquire it. I can't give you particulars—I am a lawyer, I may explain—but, from what my brother tells me it appears that this object has a bearing on—er—on a case in which we are both interested. A very important bearing, I may add, on a very important case."

The professor was delighted. "There, now, Thorndyke," he chuckled. "What did I tell you? The medico-legal worm has arrived. I told you in was something in your line, and now you've been forestalled. Of course," he added, turning to the lawyer, "you are very welcome to this specimen. I'll give you a box to carry it in, with some cotton wool."

The specimen was duly packed in its box, and the latter deposited in the lawyer's pocket; but the two brothers did not immediately leave the theatre. They stood apart, talking earnestly together, until Thorndyke and I had taken our leave of the professor, when the lawyer advanced and addressed my colleague.

"I don't suppose you remember me, Dr. Thorndyke," he began; but my friend interrupted him.

"Yes, I do. You are Mr. Rodney. You were junior to Brooke in *Jelks* v. *Partington*. Can I be of any assistance to you?"

"If you would be so kind," replied Rodney. "My brother and I have been talking this over, and we think we should like to have your opinion on the case. The fact is, we both jumped to a conclusion at once, and now we've got what the Yankees call 'cold feet.' We think that we may have jumped too soon. Let me introduce my brother, Dr. Philip Rodney."

We shook hands, and, making our way out of the theatre, presently emerged from the big portico into Lincoln's Inn Fields.

"If you will come and take a cup of tea at my chambers in Old Buildings," said Rodney, "we can give you the necessary particulars. There isn't so very much to tell, after all. My brother identifies the cork or button, and that seems to be the only plain fact that we have. Tell Dr. Thorndyke how you identified it, Phil."

"It is a simple matter," said Philip Rodney. "I went out in a boat to do some dredging with a friend named Purcell. We both wore our oil-skins as the sea was choppy and there was a good deal of spray blowing about; but Purcell had lost the top button of his, so that the collar kept blowing open and letting the spray down his neck. We had no spare buttons or needles or thread on board, but it occurred to me that I could rig up a jury button with a cork from one of my little collecting jars; so I took one out, bored a couple of holes through it with a pipe-cleaner, and threaded a piece of cat-gut through the holes."

"Why cat-gut?" asked Thorndyke.

"Because I happened to have it. I play the fiddle, and I generally have a bit of a broken string in my pocket; usually an E string—the E strings are always breaking, you know. Well, I had the end of an E string in my pocket then, so I fastened the button on with it. I bored two holes in the coat, passed the ends of the string through, and tied a reef-knot. It was as strong as a house."

"You have no doubt that it is the same cork?"

"None at all. First there is the size, which I know from having ordered the corks separately from the jars. Then I paraffined them myself after sticking on the blank labels. The label is there still, protected by the wax. And lastly there is the cat-gut; the bit that is left is obviously part of an E string."

"Yes," said Thorndyke, "the identification seems to be unimpeachable. Now let us have the story."

"We'll have some tea first," said Rodney. "This is my burrow." As he spoke, he dived into the dark entry of one of the ancient buildings on the south side of the little square, and we followed him up the crabbed, time-worn stairs, so different from our own lordly staircase in King's Bench Walk. He let us into his chambers, and, having offered us each an armchair, said: "My brother will spin you the yarn while I make the tea. When you have heard him you can begin the examination-in-chief. You understand that this is a confidential matter and that we are dealing with it professionally?"

"Certainly," replied Thorndyke, "we quite understand that." And thereupon Philip Rodney began his story.

"One morning last June two men started from Sennen Cove, on the west coast of Cornwall, to sail to Penzance in a little yacht that belongs to my brother and me. One of them was Purcell, of whom I spoke just now, and the other was a man named Varney. When they started, Purcell was wearing the oilskin coat with this button on it. The yacht arrived at Penzance at about four in the afternoon. Purcell went ashore alone to take the train to London or Falmouth, and was never seen again dead or alive. The following day Purcell's solicitor, a Mr. Penfield, received a letter from him bearing the Penzance postmark and the hour 8.45 p.m. The letter was evidently sent by mistake—put into the wrong envelope—and it appears to have been a highly compromising document. Penfield refuses to give any particulars, but thinks that the letter fully accounts for Purcell's disappearance—thinks, in fact, that Purcell has bolted.

"It was understood that Purcell was going to London from Penzance, but he seems to have told Varney that he intended to call in at Falmouth. Whether or not he went to Falmouth we don't know. Varney saw him go up the ladder on to the pier, and there all traces of him vanished. Varney thinks he may have discovered the mistake about the letter and got on board some outward-bound ship at Falmouth; but that is only surmise. Still, it is highly probable; and when my brother and I saw that button at the museum, we remembered the suggestion and instantly jumped to the conclusion that poor Purcell had gone overboard."

"And then," said Rodney, handing us our tea-cups, "when we came to talk it over we rather tended to revise our conclusion."

"Why?" asked Thorndyke.

"Well, there are several other possibilities. Purcell may have found a proper button on the yacht and cut off the cork and thrown it overboard—we must ask Varney if he did—or the coat itself may have gone over or been lost or given away, and so on."

On this Thorndyke made no comment, stirring his tea slowly with an air of deep preoccupation. Presently he looked up and asked, "Who saw the yacht start?"

"I did," said Philip. "I and Mrs. Purcell and her sister and some fishermen on the beach. Purcell was steering, and he took the yacht right out to sea, outside the Longships. A sea fog came down soon after, and we were rather anxious, because the Wolf Rock lay right to leeward of the yacht."

"Did anyone besides Varney see Purcell at Penzance?"

"Apparently not. But we haven't asked. Varney's statement seemed to settle that question. He couldn't very well have been mistaken, you know," Philip added with a smile.

"Besides," said Rodney, "if there were any doubt, there is the letter. It was posted in Penzance after eight o'clock at night. Now I met Varney on the pier at a quarter-past four, and we sailed out of Penzance a few minutes later to return to Sennen."

"Had Varney been ashore?" asked Thorndyke.

"Yes, he had been up to the town buying some provisions."

"But you said Purcell went ashore alone."

"Yes, but there's nothing in that. Purcell was not a genial man. It was the sort of thing he would do."

"And that is all that you know of the matter?" Thorndyke asked, after a few moments' reflection.

"Yes. But we might see if Varney can remember anything more, and we might try if we can squeeze any more information out of old Penfield."

"You won't," said Thorndyke. "I know Penfield and I never trouble to ask him questions. Besides, there is nothing to ask at present. We have an item of evidence that we have not fully examined. I suggest that we exhaust that, and meanwhile keep our own counsel most completely."

Rodney looked dissatisfied. "If," said he, "the item of evidence that you refer to is the button, it seems to me that we have got all that we are likely to get out of it. We have identified it, and we know that it has been thrown up on the beach at Morte Hoe. What more can we learn from it?"

"That remains to be seen," replied Thorndyke. "We may learn nothing, but, on the other hand, we may be able to trace the course of its travels and learn its recent history. It may give us a hint as to where to start a fresh inquiry."

Rodney laughed sceptically. "You talk like a clairvoyant, as if you had the power to make this bit of cork break out into fluent discourse. Of course, you can look at the thing and speculate and guess, but surely the common sense of the matter is to ask a plain question of the man who probably knows. If it turns out that Varney saw Purcell throw the button overboard, or can tell us how it got into the sea, all your speculations will have been useless. I say, let us ask Varney first, and if he knows nothing, it will be time to start guessing."

But Thorndyke was calmly obdurate. "We are not going to guess, Rodney; we are going to investigate. Let me have the button for a couple of days. If I learn nothing from it, I will return it to you, and you can then refresh your legal soul with verbal testimony. But give scientific methods a chance first."

With evident reluctance Rodney handed him the little box. "I have asked your advice," he said rather ungraciously, "so I suppose I must take it; but your methods appeal more to the sporting than the business instincts."

"We shall see," said Thorndyke, rising with a satisfied air. "But, meanwhile, I stipulate that you make no communication to anybody."

"Very well," said Rodney; and we took leave of the two brothers.

"As walked down Chancery Lane, I looked at Thorndyke, and detected in him an air of purpose for which I could not quite account. Clearly, he had something in view.

"It seems to me," I said tentatively, "that there was something in what Rodney said. Why shouldn't the button just have been thrown overboard?"

He stopped and looked at me with humorous reproach. "Jervis!" he exclaimed, "I am ashamed of you. You are as bad as Rodney. You have utterly lost sight of the main fact, which is a most impressive one. Here is a cork button. Now an ordinary cork, if immersed long enough, will soak up water until it is water-logged, and then sink to the bottom. But this one is impregnated with paraffin wax. It can't get water-logged, and it can't sink. It would float for ever."

"Well?"

"But it *has* sunk. It has been lying at the bottom of the sea for months, long enough for a *Terebella* to build a tube on it. And we have D'Arcy's statement that it has been lying in not less than ten fathoms of water. Then, at last, it has broken loose and risen to the surface and drifted ashore. Now, I ask you, what has held it down at the bottom of the sea? Of course, it may have been only the coat, weighted by something in the pocket; but there is a much more probable suggestion."

"Yes, I see," said I.

"I suspect you don't—altogether," he rejoined, with a malicious smile. And in the end it turned out that he was right.

The air of purpose that I noted was not deceptive. No sooner had we reached our chambers, then he fell to work as if with a definite object. Standing by the window, he scrutinised the button, first with the naked eye, and then with a lens, and finally laying it on the stage of the micro-scope, examined the worm-tube by the light of a condenser with a two-inch objective. And the result seemed to please him amazingly.

His next proceeding was to detach, with a fine pair of forceps, the largest of the tiny fragments of stone of which the worm-tube was built. This fragment he cemented on a slide with Canada balsam; and, fetch-ing form the laboratory a slip of Turkey stone, he proceeded to grind the little fragment to a flat surface. Then he melted the balsam, turned the fragment over, and repeated the grinding process until the little fragment was ground down to a thin film or plate, when he applied fresh balsam and a cover-glass. The specimen was now ready for exam-ination; and it was at this point that I suddenly remembered I had an appointment at six o'clock.

It had struck half-past seven when I returned, and a glance round the room told me that the battle was over—and won. The table was littered with trays of mineralogical sections and open books of reference relat-ing to geology and petrology, and one end was occupied by an out-spread geological chart of the British Isles. Thorndyke sat in his arm-chair, smiling with a bland contentment, and smoking a Trichinopoly cheroot.

"Well," I said cheerfully, "what's the news?"

"He removed the cheroot, blew out a cloud of smoke, and replied in a single word:

"Phonolite."

"Thank you," I said. "Brevity is the soul of wit. But would you mind amplifying the joke to the dimensions of intelligibility?"

"Certainly," he replied gravely. "I will endeavour to temper the wind to the shorn lamb. You noticed, I suppose, that the fragments of rock of which that worm-tube was built are all alike?"

"All the same kind of rock? No, I did not."

"Well, they are, and I have spent a strenuous hour identifying that rock. It is the peculiar, resonant, volcanic rock known as phonolite or clink-stone."

"That is very interesting," said I. "And now I see the object of your researches. You hope to get a hint as to the locality where the button has been lying."

"I hoped, as you say, to get a hint, but I have succeeded beyond my expectations. I have been able to fix the locality exactly."

"Have you really?" I exclaimed. "How on earth did you manage that?"

"By a very singular chance," he replied. "It happens that phonolite occurs in two places only in the neighbourhood of the British Isles. One is inland and may be disregarded. The other is the Wolf Rock."

"The rock of which Philip Rodney was speaking?"

"Yes. He said, you remember, that he was afraid that the yacht might drift down on it in the fog. Well, this Wolf Rock is a very remarkable structure. It is what is called a 'volcanic neck,' that is, it is a mass of altered lava that once filled the funnel of a volcano. The volcano has disappeared, but this cast of the funnel remains standing up from the bottom of the sea like a great column. It is a single mass of phonolite, and thus entirely different in composition from the sea-bed around or anywhere near these islands. But, of course, immediately at its base, the sea-bottom must be covered with decomposed fragments which have fallen from its sides, and it is from these fragments that our *Terebella* has built its tube. So, you see, we can fix the exact locality in which that button has been lying all the months that the tube was building, and we now have a point of departure for fresh investigations."

"But," I said, "this is a very significant discovery, Thorndyke. Shall you tell Rodney?"

"Certainly I shall. But there are one or two questions that I shall ask him first. I have sent him a note inviting him to drop in to-night with his brother, so we had better run round to the club and get some dinner. I said nine o'clock."

It was a quarter to nine when we had finished dinner, and ten minutes later we were back in our chambers. Thorndyke made up the fire, placed the chairs hospitably round the hearth, and laid on the table the notes that he had taken at the late interview. Then the Treasury clock struck nine, and within less than a minute our two guests arrived.

"I should apologise," said Thorndyke, as we shook hands, "for my rather peremptory message, but I thought it best to waste no time."

"You certainly have wasted no time," said Rodney, "if you have already extracted its history from the button. Do you keep a tame medium on the premises, or are you a clairvoyant yourself?"

"There is our medium," replied Thorndyke, indicating the microscope standing on a side-table under its bell glass. "The man who uses it becomes to some extent a clairvoyant. But I should like to ask you one or two questions if I may."

Rodney made no secret of his disappointment. "We had hoped," said he, "to hear answers rather than questions. However, as you please."

"Then," said Thorndyke, quite unmoved by Rodney's manner, "I will proceed; and I will begin with the yacht in which Purcell and

Varney travelled from Sennen to Penzance. I understand that the yacht belongs to you and was lent by you to these two men?"

Rodney nodded, and Thorndyke then asked: "Has the yacht ever been out of your custody on any other occasion?"

"No," replied Rodney, "excepting on this occasion, one or both of us have always been on board."

Thorndyke made a note of the answer and proceeded: "When you resumed possession of the yacht, did you find her in all respects as you had left her?"

"My dear sir," Rodney exclaimed impatiently, "may I remind you that we are inquiring—if we are inquiring about anything—into the disappearance of a man who was seen to go ashore from this yacht and who certainly never came on board again? The yacht is out of it altogether."

"Nevertheless," said Thorndyke, "I should be glad if you would answer my question."

"Oh, very well," Rodney replied irritably. "Then we found her substantially as we had left her."

"Meaning by 'substantially'?——"

"Well, they had had to rig a new jib halyard. The old one had parted."

"Did you find the old one on board?"

"Yes; in two pieces, of course."

"Was the whole of it there?"

"I suppose so. We never measured the pieces. But really, sir, these questions seem extraordinarily irrelevant."

"They are not," said Thorndyke. "You will see that presently. I want to know if you missed any rope, cordage, or chain."

Here Philip interposed. "There was some spun-yarn missing. They opened a new ball and used up several yards. I meant to ask Varney what they used it for."

Thorndyke jotted down a note and asked: "Was there any of the iron-work missing? Any anchor, chain, or any other heavy object?"

Rodney shook his head impatiently, but again Philip broke in.

"You are forgetting the ballast-weight, Jack. You see," he continued, addressing Thorndyke, "the yacht is ballasted with half-hundred-weights, and, when we came to take out the ballast to lay her up for the winter, we found one of the weights missing. I have no idea when it disappeared, but there was certainly one short, and neither of us had taken it out."

"Can you," asked Thorndyke, "fix any date on which all the ballast-weights were in place?"

"Yes, I think I can. A few days before Purcell went to Penzance we beached the yacht—she is only a little boat—to give her a scrape. Of course, we had to take out the ballast, and when we launched her again I helped to put it back. I am certain all the weights were there then."

Here Jack Rodney, who had been listening with ill-concealed impatience, remarked:

"This is all very interesting, sir, but I cannot conceive what bearing it has on the movements of Purcell after he left the yacht."

"It has a most direct and important bearing," said Thorndyke. "Perhaps I had better explain before we go any further. Let me begin by pointing out that this button has been lying for many months at the bottom of the sea at a depth of not less than ten fathoms. That is proved by the worm-tube which has been built on it. Now, as this button is a waterproofed cork, it could not have sunk by itself; it has been sunk by some body to which it was attached, and there is evidence that that body was a very heavy one."

"What evidence is there of that?" asked Rodney.

"There is the fact that it has been lying continuously in one place. A body of moderate weight, as you know, moves about the sea-bottom impelled by currents and tide-streams, but this button has been lying unmoved in one place."

"Indeed," said Rodney with manifest scepticism. "Perhaps you can point out the spot where it has been lying."

"I can," Thorndyke replied. "That button, Mr. Rodney, has been lying all these months at the base of the Wolf Rock."

The two brothers started very perceptibly. They stared at Thorndyke, they looked at one another, and then the lawyer challenged the statement.

"You make this assertion very confidently," he said. "Can you give us any evidence to support it?"

Thorndyke's reply was to produce the button, the section, the test-specimens, the microscope, and the geological chart. In great detail, and with his incomparable lucidity, he assembled the facts, and explained their connection, evolving the unavoidable conclusion.

The different effect of the demonstration on the two men interested me greatly. To the lawyer, accustomed to dealing with verbal and documentary evidence, it manifestly appeared as a far-fetched, rather fantastic argument, ingenious, amusing, and entirely unconvincing. On Philip, the doctor, it made a profound impression. Accustomed to acting on inferences from facts of his own observing, he gave full weight to each item of evidence, and I could see that his mind was already stretching out to the, as yet unstated, corollaries.

The lawyer was the first to speak. "What inference," he asked, "do you wish us to draw from this very ingenious theory of yours?"

"The inference," Thorndyke replied impassively, "I leave to you; but perhaps it would help you if I recapitulate the facts."

"Perhaps it would," said Rodney.

"Then," said Thorndyke, "I will take them in order. This is the case of a man who was seen to start on a voyage for a given destination in company with one other person. His start out to sea was witnessed by a number of persons. From that moment he was never seen again by any person excepting his one companion. He is said to have reached his destination, but his arrival there rests upon the unsupported verbal testimony of one person, the said companion. Thereafter he vanished utterly, and since then has made no sign of being alive, although there are several persons with whom he could have safely communicated.

"Some eight months later a portion of this man's clothing is found. It bears evidence of having been lying at the bottom of the sea for many months, so that it must have sunk to its resting place within a very short time of the man's disappearance. The place where it has been lying is one over, or near, which the man must have sailed in the yacht. It has been moored to the bottom by some very heavy object; and a very heavy object has disappeared from the yacht. That heavy object had apparently not disappeared when the yacht started, and was not seen on the yacht afterwards. The evidence goes to show that the disappearance of that object coincided in time with the disappearance of the man; and a quantity of cordage disappeared, certainly, on that day. Those are the facts in our possession at present, Mr. Rodney, and I think the inference emerges automatically."

There was a brief silence, during which the two brothers cogitated profoundly and with very disturbed expressions. Then Rodney spoke.

"I am bound to admit, Dr. Thorndyke, that, as a scheme of circumstantial evidence, this is extremely ingenious and complete. It is impossible to mistake your meaning. But you would hardly expect us to charge a highly respectable gentleman of our acquaintance with having murdered his friend and made away with the body, on a—well—a rather far-fetched theory."

"Certainly not," replied Thorndyke. "But, on the other hand, with this body of circumstantial evidence before us, it is clearly imperative that some further investigations should be made before we speak of the matter to any human soul."

Rodney agreed somewhat grudgingly. "What do you suggest?" he asked.

"I suggest that we thoroughly overhaul the yacht in the first place. Where is she now?"

"Under a tarpaulin in a yard at Battersea. The gear and stores are in a disused workshop in the yard."

"When could we look over her?"

"To-morrow morning, if you like," said Rodney.

"Very well," said Thorndyke. "We will call for you at nine, if that will suit."

It suited perfectly, and the arrangement was accordingly made. A few minutes later the two brothers took their leave, but as they were shaking hands, Philip said suddenly:

"There is one little matter that occurs to me. I have only just remembered it, and I don't suppose it is of any consequence, but it is as well to mention everything. You remember my brother saying that one of the jib halyards broke that day?"

"Yes."

"Well, of course, the jib came down and went partly overboard. Now, the next time I hoisted the sail, I noticed a small stain on it; a greenish stain like that of mud, only it wouldn't wash out, and it is there still. I meant to ask Varney about it. Stains of that kind on the jib usually come from a bit of mud on the fluke of the anchor, but the anchor was quite clean when I examined it, and besides, it hadn't been down on that day. I thought I'd better tell you about it."

"I'm glad you did," said Thorndyke. "We will have a look at that stain to-morrow. Good-night." Once more he shook hands, and then, re-entering the room, stood for quite a long time with his back to the fire, thoughtfully examining the toes of his boots.

We started forth next morning for our rendezvous considerably earlier than seemed necessary. But I made no comment, for Thorndyke was in that state of extreme taciturnity which characterised him whenever he was engaged on an absorbing case with an insufficiency of evidence. I knew that he was turning over and over the facts that he had, and searching for new openings; but I had no clue to the trend of his thoughts until, passing the gateway of Lincoln's Inn, he walked briskly up Chancery Lane into Holborn, and finally halted outside a wholesale druggist's.

"I shan't be more than a few minutes," said he; "are you coming in?"

I was, most emphatically. Questions were forbidden at this stage, but there was no harm in keeping one's ears open; and when I heard his order I was the richer by a distinct clue to his next movements. Tincture of Guiacum and Ozonic Ether formed a familiar combination, and the size of the bottles indicated the field of investigation.

We found the brothers waiting for us at Lincoln's Inn. They both looked rather hard at the parcel that I was now carrying, and especially at Thorndyke's green canvas-covered research case; but they made no comment, and we set forth at once on the rather awkward cross-country journey to Battersea. Very little was said on the way, but I noticed that both men took our quest more seriously than I had expected, and I judged that they had been talking the case over.

Our journey terminated at a large wooden gate on which Rodney knocked loudly with his stick; whereupon a wicket was opened, and, after a few words of explanation, we passed through into a large yard. Crossing this, we came to a wharf, beyond which was a small stretch of unreclaimed shore, and here, drawn well above high-water mark, a small, double-ended yacht stood on chocks under a tarpaulin cover.

"This is the yacht," said Rodney. "The gear and loose fittings are stored in the workshop behind us. Which will you see first?"

"Let us look at the gear," said Thorndyke, and we turned to the disused workshop into which Rodney admitted us with a key from his pocket. I looked curiously about the long, narrow interior with its prosaic contents, so little suggestive of tragedy or romance. Overhead the yacht's spars rested on the tie-beams, from which hung bunches of blocks; on the floor a long row of neatly-painted half-hundredweights, a pile of chain-cable, two anchors, a stove, and other oddments such as water breakers, buckets, mops, etc., and on the long benches at the side, folded sails, locker cushions, side-light lanterns, the binnacle, the cabin lamp, and other more delicate fittings. Thorndyke, too, glanced round inquisitively, and, depositing his case on the bench, asked, "Have you still got the broken jib halyard of which you were telling me?"

"Yes," said Rodney, "it is here under the bench." He drew out a coil of rope, and flinging it on the floor, began to uncoil it, when it separated into two lengths.

"Which are the broken ends?" Thorndyke asked.

"It broke near the middle," said Rodney, "where it chafed on the cleat when the sail was hoisted. This is the one end, you see, frayed out like a brush in breaking, and the other——" He picked up the second half and, passing it rapidly through his hands, held up the end. He did not finish the sentence, but stood with a frown of surprise staring at the rope in his hands.

"This is queer," he said, after a pause, "The broken end has been cut off. Did you cut it off, Phil?"

"No," replied Philip. "It is just as I took it from the locker, where, I suppose, you or Varney stowed it."

"The question is," said Thorndyke, "how much has it been cut off? Do you know the original length of the rope?"

"Yes. Forty-two feet. It is not down in the inventory, but I remember working it out. Let us see how much there is here."

He laid the two lengths of rope along the floor and we measured them with Thorndyke's spring tape. The combined length was exactly thirty-one feet.

"So," said Thorndyke, "there are eleven feet missing, without allowing for the lengthening of the rope by stretching. That is a very important fact."

"What made you suspect that part of the halyard might be missing as well as the spunyarn?" Philip asked.

"I did not think," replied Thorndyke, "that a yachtsman would use spunyarn to lash a half-handredweight to a corpse. I suspected that the spunyarn was used for something else. By the way, I see you have a revolver there. Was that on board at the time?"

"Yes," said Rodney. "It was hanging on the cabin bulkhead. Be careful. I don't think it has been unloaded."

Thorndyke opened the breech of the revolver, and dropping the cartridges into his hand, peered down the barrel and into each chamber separately.

"It is quite clean inside," he remarked. Then, glancing at the ammunition in his hand, "I notice," said he, "that these cartridges are not all alike. There is one Curtis and Harvey, and five Eleys."

Philip looked with a distinctly startled expression at the little heap of cartridges in Thorndyke's hand, and picking out the odd one, examined it with knitted brows.

"When did you fire the revolver last, Jack?" he asked, looking up at his brother.

"On the day when we potted at those champagne bottles," was the reply.

Philip raised his eyebrows. "Then," said he, "this is a very remarkable affair. I distinctly remember on that occasion, when we had sunk all the bottles, reloading the revolver with Eleys, and that there were then three cartridges left over in the bag. When I had loaded I opened the new box of Curtis and Harvey's, upped them into the bag and threw the box overboard."

"Did you clean the revolver?" asked Thorndyke.

"No, I didn't. I mean to do it later, but forgot to."

"But," said Thorndyke, "it has undoubtedly been cleaned, and very thoroughly. Shall we check the cartridges in the bag? There ought to be forty-nine Curtis and Harvey's and three Eley's if what you tell us is correct."

Philip searched among the raffle on the bench and produced a small linen bag. Untying the string, he shot out on the bench a heap of cartridges which he counted one by one. There were fifty-two in all, and three of them were Eley's.

"Then," said Thorndyke, "it comes to this: since you used that revolver it has been used by someone else. That someone fired only a single shot, after which he carefully cleaned the barrel and reloaded. Incidentally, he seems to have known where the cartridge bag was kept, but did not know about the change in the make of the cartridges. You notice," he added, looking at Rodney, "that the circumstantial evidence accumulates."

"I do, indeed," Rodney replied gloomily. "Is there anything else that you wish to examine?"

"Yes. There is the sail. You spoke of a stain on the jib. Shall we see if we can make anything of that?"

"I don't think you will make much of it," said Philip. "It is very faint. However, you shall see it." He picked out one of the bundles of white duck, and, while he was unfolding it, Thorndyke dragged an empty bench into the middle of the floor under the skylight. Over this the sail was spread so that the mysterious mark was in the middle of the bench. It was very inconspicuous; just a faint, grey-green, wavy line like the representation of an island on a map. We all looked at it attentively for a few moments, and then Thorndyke said, "Would you mind if I made a further stain on the sail? I should like to apply some re-agents."

"Of course, you must do what is necessary," said Rodney. "The evidence is more important than the sail."

Accordingly Thorndyke unpacked our parcel, and as the two bottles emerged, Philip read the labels with evident surprise, remarking:

"I shouldn't have thought the Guiacum test would have been of any use after all these months."

"It will act, I think, if the pigment is there," said Thorndyke; and as he spoke he poured a quantity of the tincture—which he had ordered diluted to our usual working strength—on the middle of the stained area. The pool of liquid rapidly spread considerably beyond the limits of the stain, growing paler as it extended. Then Thorndyke cautiously dropped small quantities of the Ether at various points around the stained area and watched closely as the two liquids mingled in the fabric of the sail. Gradually the Ether spread towards the stain, and, first at one point and then at another, approached and finally crossed the wavy grey line, and at each point the same change occurred; first, the faint grey line turned into a strong blue line, and then the colour extended to the enclosed space, until the entire area of the stain stood out, a conspicuous blue patch.

Philip and Thorndyke looked at one another significantly, and the latter said, "You understand the meaning of this reaction, Mr. Rodney; this is a bloodstain, and a very carefully washed bloodstain."

"So I supposed," Rodney replied, and for a while we were all silent.

There was something very dramatic and solemn in the sudden appearance of this staring blue patch on the sail, with the sinister message that it brought. But what followed was more dramatic still. As we stood silently regarding the blue stain, the mingled liquids continued to spread: and suddenly, at the extreme edge of the wet area, we became aware of a new spot of blue. At first a mere speck, it grew slowly as the liquid spread over the canvas into a small oval, and then a second spot appeared by its side.

At this point Thorndyke poured out a fresh charge of the tincture, and when it had soaked into the cloth, cautiously applied a sprinkling of Ether. Instantly the blue spots began to elongate, fresh spots and patches appeared, and as they ran together there sprang out of the blank surface the clear impression of a hand—a left hand, complete in all its details excepting the third finger, which was represented by an oval spot at some two-thirds of its length.

The dreaded significance of this apparition and the uncanny and mysterious manner of its emergence from the white surface impressed us so that for a while none of us spoke. At length I ventured to remark on the absence of the impression of the third finger.

"I think," said Thorndyke, "that the impression is there. That spot looks like the mark of a finger-tip, and its position rather suggests a finger with a stiff joint."

As he made this statement, both brothers simultaneously uttered a smothered exclamation.

Thorndyke looked up at them sharply. "What is it?" he asked.

The two men looked at one another with an expression of awe. Then Rodney said in a hushed voice, hardly above a whisper, "Varney, the man who was with Purcell on the yacht—he has a stiff joint on the third finger of his left hand."

There was nothing more to say. The case was complete. The keystone had been laid in the edifice of circumstantial evidence. The investigation was at an end.

After an interval of silence, during which Thorndyke was busily writing up his notes, Rodney asked, "What is to be done now? Shall I swear an information?"

Thorndyke shook his head. No man was more expert in accumulating circumstantial evidence; none was more loth to rely on it.

"A murder charge," said he, "should be supported by proof of death and, if possible, by production of the body."

"But the body is at the bottom of the sea!"

"True. But we know its whereabouts. It is a small area, with the lighthouse as a landmark. If that area were systematically worked over with a trawl or dredge, or better still, with a creper, there should be a very good chance of recovering the body, or, at least, the clothing and the weight."

Rodney reflected for a few moments. "I think you are right," he said at length. "The thing is practicable, and it is our duty to do it. I suppose you couldn't come down and help us?"

"Not now. But in a few days the spring vacation will commence, and then Jervis and I could join you, if the weather were suitable." "Thank you both," replied Rodney. "We will make the arrangements, and let you know when we are ready."

*   *   *

It was quite early on a bright April morning when the two Rodneys, Thorndyke, and I steamed out of Penzance Harbour in a small open launch. The sea was very calm for the time of year, the sky was of a warm blue, and a gentle breeze stole out of the north-east. Over the launch's side hung a long spar, secured to a tow-rope by a bridle, and to the spar were attached a number of creepers—lengths of chain fitted with rows of hooks. The outfit further included a spirit compass, provided with sights, a sextant, and a hand-lead.

"It's lucky we didn't run up against Varney in the town," Philip remarked, as the harbour dwindled in the distance.

"Varney!" exclaimed Thorndyke. "Do you mean that he lives at Penzance?"

"He keeps rooms there, and spends most of his spare time down in this part. He was always keen on sea-fishing, and he's keener than ever now. He keeps a boat of his own, too. It's queer, isn't it, if what we think is true?"

"Very," said Thorndyke; and by his meditative manner I judge that circumstances afforded him matter for curious speculation.

As we passed abreast of the Land's End, and the solitary lighthouse rose ahead on the verge of the horizon, we began to overtake the scattered members of a fleet of luggers, home with lowered mainsails and hand-lines down, others with their black sails set, heading for a more distant fishing-ground. Threading our way among them, we suddenly became aware that one of the smaller luggers was heading so as to close in on us. Rodney, observing this, was putting over the helm to avoid her when a seafaring voice from the little craft hailed us.

"Launch ahoy there! Gentleman aboard wants to speak to you."

We looked at one another significantly and in some confusion; and meanwhile our solitary "hand"—seaman, engineer, and fireman combined—without waiting for orders, shut off steam. The lugger closed in rapidly and of a sudden there appeared, holding on by the mainstay, a small dark fellow who hailed us cheerfully: "Hullo, you fellows! Whither away? What's your game?"

"God!" exclaimed Philip. "It's Varney. Sheer off, Jack! Don't let him come alongside."

"But it was too late. The launch had lost way and failed to answer the helm. The lugger sheered in, sweeping abreast of us within a foot; and, as she crept past, Varney sprang lightly from her gunwale and dropped neatly on the side bench in our stern sheets.

"Where are you off to?" he asked. "You can't be going out to fish in this baked-potato can?"

"No," faltered Rodney, "we're not. We're going to do some dredging—or rather——"

Here Thorndyke came to his assistance. "Marine worms," said he, "are the occasion of this little voyage. There seem to be some very uncommon ones on the bottom at the base of the Wolf Rock. I have seen some in a collection, and I want to get a few more if I can."

It was a skillfully-worded explanation, and I could see that, for the time, Varney accepted it. But from the moment when the Wolf Rock was mentioned all his vivacity of manner died out. In an instant he had become grave, thoughtful, and a trifle uneasy.

The introductions over, he reverted to the subject. He questioned us closely, especially as to our proposed methods. And it was impossible to evade his questions. There were the creepers in full view; there was the compass and the sextant; and presently these appliances would have to be put in use. Gradually, as the nature of our operations dawned on him, his manner changed more and more. A horrible pallor overspread his face, and a terrible restlessness took possession of him.

Rodney, who was navigating, brought the launch to within a quarter of a mile of the rock, and then, taking cross-bearings on the lighthouse and a point of land, directed us to lower the creepers.

It was a most disagreeable experience for us all. Varney, pale and clammy, fidgeted about the boat, now silent and moody, now almost hysterically boisterous. Thorndyke watched him furtively and, I think, judged by his manner how near we were to the object of our search.

Calm as the day was, the sea was breaking heavily over the rock, and as we worked in closer the water around boiled and eddied in an unpleasant and even dangerous manner. The three keepers in the gallery of the lighthouse watched us through their glasses, and one of them bellowed to us through a megaphone to keep further away.

"What do you say?" asked Rodney. "It's a bit risky here, with the rock right under our lee. Shall we try another side?"

"Better try one more cast this side," said Thorndyke; and he spoke so definitely that we all, including Varney, looked at him curiously. But no one answered, and the creepers were dropped for a fresh cast still nearer the rock. We were then north of the lighthouse, and headed south so as to pass the rock on its east side. As we approached, the man with the megaphone bawled out fresh warnings, and continued to roar at us until we were abreast of the rock in a wild tumble of confused waves.

At this moment Philip, who held the towline with a single turn round a cleat, said that he felt a pull, but that it seemed as if the creepers had broken away. As soon, therefore, as we were out of the backwash into smooth water, we hauled in the linen to examine the creepers.

I looked over the side eagerly, for something new in Thorndyke's manner impressed me. Varney, too, who had hitherto taken little notice of the creepers, now knelt on the side bench, gazing earnestly into the clear water, when the tow-rope was rising.

At length the beam came in sight, and below it, on one of the creepers, a yellowish object, dimly seen through the wavering water.

"There's somethin' on this time," said the engineer, craning over the side. He shut off steam, and, with the rest of us, watched the incoming creeper. I looked at Varney, kneeling on the bench apart from us, not fidgeting now, but still rigid, pale as wax, and staring with dreadful fascination at the slowly-rising object.

Suddenly the engineer uttered an exclamation. "Why, 'tis a sou'wester, and all laced about wi' spuny'n. Surely 'tis——Hi! steady, sir! My God!"

There was a heavy splash, and as Rodney rushed forward for the boat-hook I saw Varney rapidly sinking head first through the clear, blue-green water, dragged down by the hand-lead that he had hitched to his waist. By the time Rodney was back he was far out of reach; but for a long time, as it seemed, we could see him sinking, sinking, growing paler, more shadowy, more shapeless, but always steadily following the lead sinker, until at last he faded from our sight into the darkness of the ocean.

Not until he had vanished did we haul on board the creeper with its dreadful burden. Indeed, we never hauled it on board; for as Philip, with an unsteady hand, unhooked the sou'wester hat from the creeper, the encircling coils of spunyarn slipped, and from inside the hat a skull dropped into the water and sank. We watched it grow green and pallid and small, until it vanished, as Varney had vanished. Then Philip turned and flung the hat down in the bottom of the boat. Thorndyke picked it up and unwound the spunyarn.

"Do you identify it?" he asked, and then, as he turned it over, he added, "But I see it identifies itself." He held it towards me, and I read in embroidered letters on the silk lining, "Dan Purcell."

L. T. Meade

(1854–1914)

and

Robert Eustace

(1868–1943)

ELIZABETH THOMASINA MEADE SMITH was one of the most successful writers of books for teenaged girls—until recently it was easy to find one of her more than two hundred fifty volumes at almost any used bookstore—as well as the creator of sensational sleuths and criminals. Madam Koluchy of *The Brotherhood of the Seven Kings* (1899) is one of the first female criminals to appear in a series of short stories, and Madame Sara in *The Sorceress of the Strand* (1903) is a serial murderer. Meade also created the first collection of medical mysteries published in England, *Stories from the Diary of a Doctor* (1894); the first collection of seemingly impossible crime detective stories, *The Master of Mysteries* (1898); and one of the earliest collections of secret-service stories, *The Lost Square* (1902). She even created a palmist detective in *The Oracle of Maddox Street* (1904).

It is generally agreed that her collaborators—Clifford Halifax in the earlier stories and Dr. Robert Eustace in the later ones—supplied the scientific, or pseudo-scientific, gimmicks while Meade did the actual writing. In one book Meade thanked Eustace, "to whose genius I owe the extraordinary and original ideas contained therein." In his only book without a collaborator, however, *The Human Bacillus* (1907), Eustace said that he was the true author of the stories. Whatever the exact method of collaboration, Eustace specialized in working with other authors, including Gertrude Warden and Dorothy L. Sayers. For many years, scholars debated whether Eustace was the pseudonym of Eustace Rawlins (1854–?) or of Dr. Robert Eustace Barton (1868–1943); the recent publication of *The Letters of Dorothy L. Sayers*, ed. Barbara Reynolds (1996), definitively identified him as Dr. Barton.

"Mr. Bovey's Unexpected Will" appeared in *The Harmsworth Magazine* in 1898. It is one of the few Meade stories never to appear in one of her books, and it is the first of a four-story series about Florence Kusack.

Mr. Bovey's Unexpected Will

AMONGST ALL MY PATIENTS there were none who excited my sense of curiosity like Miss Florence Cusack. I never thought of her without a sense of baffled inquiry taking possession of me, and I never visited her without the hope that some day I should get to the bottom of the mystery which surrounded her.

Miss Cusack was a young and handsome woman. She possessed to all appearance superabundant health, her energies were extraordinary, and her life completely out of the common. She lived alone in a large house in Kensington Court Gardens, kept a good staff of servants, and went much into society. Her beauty, her sprightliness, her wealth, and, above all, her extraordinary life, caused her to be much talked about. As one glanced at this handsome girl with her slender figure, her eyes of the darkest blue, her raven black hair and clear complexion, it was almost impossible to believe that she was a power in the police courts, and highly respected by every detective in Scotland Yard.

I shall never forget my first visit to Miss Cusack. I had been asked by a brother doctor to see her in his absence. Strong as she was, she was subject to periodical and very acute nervous attacks. When I entered her house she came up to me eagerly.

"Pray do not ask me too many questions or look too curious, Dr. Lonsdale," she said; "I know well that my whole condition is abnormal; but, believe me, I am forced to do what I do."

"What is that?" I inquired.

"You see before you," she continued, with emphasis, "the most acute and, I believe, successful lady detective in the whole of London."

"Why do you lead such an extraordinary life?" I asked.

"To me the life is fraught with the very deepest interest," she

168

answered. "In any case," and now the colour faded from her cheeks, and her eyes grew full of emotion, "I have no choice; I am under a promise, which I must fulfil. There are times, however, when I need help—such help as you, for instance, can give me. I have never seen you before, but I like your face. If the time should ever come, will you give me your assistance?"

I asked her a few more questions, and finally agreed to do what she wished.

From that hour Miss Cusack and I became the staunchest friends. She constantly invited me to her house, introduced me to her friends, and gave me her confidence to a marvellous extent.

On my first visit I noticed in her study two enormous brazen bull-dogs. They were splendidly cast, and made a striking feature in the arrangements of the room; but I did not pay them any special attention until she happened to mention that there was a story, and a strange one, in connection with them.

"But for these dogs," she said, "and the mystery attached to them, I should not be the woman I am, nor would my life be set apart for the performance of duties at once herculean and ghastly."

When she said these words her face once more turned pale, and her eyes flashed with an ominous fire.

On a certain afternoon in November 1894, I received a telegram from Miss Cusack, asking me to put aside all other work and go to her at once. Handing my patients over to the care of my partner, I started for her house. I found her in her study and alone. She came up to me holding a newspaper in her hand.

"Do you see this?" she asked. As she spoke she pointed to the agony column. The following words met my eyes:—

Send more sand and charcoal dust. Core and mould ready for casting.
JOSHUA LINKLATER.

I read those curious words slowly, then glanced at the eager face of the young girl.

"I have been waiting for this," she said, in a tone of triumph.

"But what can it mean?" I said. "Core and mould ready for casting?"

She folded up the paper, and laid it deliberately on the table.

"I thought that Joshua Linklater would say something of the kind," she continued. "I have been watching for a similar advertisement in all the dailies for the last three weeks. This may be of the utmost importance."

"Will you explain?" I said.

"I may never have to explain, or, on the other hand, I may," she answered. "I have not really sent for you to point out this advertisement, but in connection with another matter. Now, pray, come into the next room with me."

She led me into a prettily and luxuriously furnished boudoir on the same floor. Standing by the hearth was a slender fair-haired girl, looking very little more than a child.

"May I introduce you to my cousin, Letitia Ransom?" said Miss Cusack, eagerly. "Pray sit down, Letty," she continued, addressing the girl with a certain asperity, "Dr. Lonsdale is the man of all others we want. Now, doctor, will you give me your full attention, for I have an extraordinary story to relate."

At Miss Cusack's words Miss Random immediately seated herself. Miss Cusack favoured her with a quick glance, and then once more turned to me.

"You are much interested in queer mental phases, are you not?" she said.

"I certainly am," I replied.

"Well, I should like to ask your opinion with regard to such a will as this."

Once again she unfolded a newspaper, and, pointing to a paragraph, handed it to me. I read as follows:—

EXTRAORDINARY TERMS OF A MISER'S WILL.

Mr. Henry Bovey, who died last week at a small house at Kew, has left one of the most extraordinary wills on record. During his life his eccentricities and miserly habits were well known, but this eclipses them all, by the surprising method in which he has disposed of his property.

Mr. Bovey was unmarried, and, as far as can be proved, has no near relations in the world. The small balance at his banker's is to be used for defraying fees, duties, and sundry charges, also any existing debts, but the main bulk of his securities were recently realised, and the money in sovereigns is locked in a safe in his house.

A clause in the will states that there are three claimants to this property, and that the one whose net bodily weight is nearest to the weight of these sovereigns is to become the legatee. The safe containing the property is not to be opened till the three claimants are present; the competition is then to take place, and the winner is at once to remove his fortune.

Considerable excitement has been manifested over the affair, the amount of the fortune being unknown. The date of the competition is also kept a close secret for obvious reasons.

"Well," I said, laying the paper down, "whoever this Mr. Bovey was, there is little doubt that he must have been out of his mind. I never heard of a more crazy idea."

"Nevertheless it is to be carried out," replied Miss Cusack. "Now listen, please, Mr. Lonsdale. This paper is a fortnight old. It is now three weeks since the death of Mr. Bovey, his will has been proved, and the time has come for the carrying out of the competition. I happen to know two of the claimants well, and intend to be present at the ceremony."

I did not make any answer, and after a pause she continued—

"One of the gentlemen who is to be weighed against his own fortune is Edgar Wimburne. He is engaged to my cousin Letitia. If he turns out to be the successful claimant there is nothing to prevent their marrying at once; if otherwise—" here she turned and looked full at Miss Ransom, who stood up, the colour coming and going in her cheeks— "if otherwise, Mr. Campbell Graham has to be dealt with."

"Who is he?" I asked.

"Another claimant, a much older man than Edgar. Nay, I must tell you everything. He is a claimant in a double sense, being also a lover, and a very ardent one, of Letitia's.

"Letty must be saved," she said, looking at me, "and I believe I know how to do it."

"You spoke of three claimants," I interrupted; "who is the third?"

"Oh, he scarcely counts, unless indeed he carries off the prize. He is William Tyndall, Mr. Bovey's servant and retainer."

"And when, may I ask, is this momentous competition to take place?" I continued.

"To-morrow morning at half-past nine, at Mr. Bovey's house. Will you come with us to-morrow, Dr. Lonsdale, and be present at the weighing?"

"I certainly will," I answered, "it will be a novel experience."

"Very well; can you be at this house a little before half-past eight, and we will drive straight to Kew?"

I promised to do so, and soon after took my leave. The next day I was at Miss Cusack's house in good time. I found waiting for me Miss Cusack herself, Miss Ransom, and Edgar Wimburne.

A moment or two later we all found ourselves seated in a large landau, and in less than an hour had reached our destination. We drew up at a small dilapidated-looking house, standing in a row of prim suburban villas, and found that Mr. Graham, the lawyer, and the executors had already arrived.

The room into which we had been ushered was fitted up as a sort of study. The furniture was very poor and scanty, the carpet was old, and the only ornaments on the walls were a few tattered prints yellow with age.

As soon as ever we came in, Mr. Southby, the lawyer, came forward and spoke.

"We are met here to-day," he said, "as you are all of course aware, to carry out the clause of Mr. Bovey's last will and testament. What reasons prompted him to make these extraordinary conditions we do not know; we only know that we are bound to carry them out. In a safe in his bedroom there is, according to his own statement, a large sum of money in gold, which is to be the property of the one of these three gentlemen whose weight shall nearest approach to the weight of the gold. Messrs. Hutchinson and Co. have been kind enough to supply one of their latest weighing machines, which has been carefully checked, and now if you three gentlemen will kindly come with me into the next room we will begin the business at once. Perhaps you, Dr. Lonsdale, as a medical man, will be kind enough to accompany us."

Leaving Miss Cusack and Miss Ransom we then went into the old man's bedroom, where the three claimants undressed and were carefully weighed. I append their respective weights, which I noted down:—

Graham—13 stone 9 lbs. 6 oz.

Tyndall—11 stone 6 lbs. 3 oz.

Wimburne—12 stone 11 lbs.

Having resumed their attire, Miss Cusack and Miss Random were summoned, and the lawyer, drawing out a bunch of keys, went across to a large iron safe which had been built into the wall.

We all pressed round him, every one anxious to get the first glimpse of the old man's hoard. The lawyer turned the key, shot back the lock, and flung open the heavy doors. We found that the safe was literally packed with small canvas bags—indeed, so full was it that as the doors swung open two of the bags fell to the floor with a heavy crunching noise. Mr. Southby lifted them up, and then cutting the strings of one, opened it. It was full of bright sovereigns.

An exclamation burst from us all. If all those bags contained gold there was a fine fortune awaiting the successful candidate! The business was now begun in earnest. The lawyer rapidly extracted bag after bag, untied the string, and shot the contents with a crash into the great copper scale pan, while the attendant kept adding weights to the other side to balance it, calling out the amounts as he did so. No one spoke, but our eyes were fixed as if by some strange fascination on the pile of yellow metal that rose higher and higher each moment.

As the weight reached one hundred and fifty pounds, I heard the old servant behind me utter a smothered oath. I turned and glanced at him; he was staring at the gold with a fierce expression of disappointment and avarice. He at any rate was out of the reckoning, as at eleven stone six, or one hundred and sixty pounds, he could be nowhere near the weight of the sovereigns, there being still eight more bags to untie.

The competition, therefore, now lay between Wimburne and Graham. The latter's face bore strong marks of the agitation which consumed him: the veins stood out like cords on his forehead, and his lips trembled. It would evidently be a near thing, and the suspense was almost intolerable. The lawyer continued to deliberately add to the pile. As the last bag was shot into the scale, the attendant put four ten-pound weights into the other side. It was too much. The gold rose at once. He took one off, and then the two great pans swayed slowly up and down, finally coming to a dead stop.

"Exactly one hundred and eighty pounds, gentlemen," he cried, and a shout went up from us all. Wimburne at twelve stone eleven, or one hundred and seventy-nine pounds, had won.

I turned and shook him by the hand.

"I congratulate you most heartily," I cried. "Now let us calculate the amount of your fortune."

I took a piece of paper from my pocket and made a rough calculation. Taking £56 to the pound avoirdupois, there were at least ten thousand and eighty sovereigns in the scale before us.

"I can hardly believe it," cried Miss Ransom.

I saw her gazing down at the gold, then she looked up into her lover's face.

"Is it true?" she said, panting as she spoke.

"Yes, it is true," he answered. Then he dropped his voice. "It removes all difficulties," I heard him whisper to her.

Her eyes filled with tears, and she turned aside to conceal her emotion.

"There is no doubt whatever as to your ownership of this money, Mr. Wimburne," said the lawyer, "and now the next thing is to ensure its safe transport to the bank."

As soon as the amount of the gold had been made known, Graham, without bidding good-bye to anyone, abruptly left the room, and I assisted the rest of the men in shovelling the sovereigns into a stout canvas bag, which we then lifted and placed in a four-wheeled cab which had arrived for the purpose of conveying the gold to the city.

"Surely someone is going to accompany Mr. Wimburne?" said Miss Cusack at this juncture. "My dear Edgar," she continued, "you are not going to be so mad as to go alone?"

To my surprise, Wimburne coloured, and then gave a laugh of annoyance.

"What could possibly happen to me?" he said. "Nobody knows that I am carrying practically my own weight in gold into the city."

"If Mr. Wimburne wishes I will go with him," said Tyndall, now coming forward. The old man had to all appearance got over his disappointment, and spoke eagerly.

"The thing is fair and square," he added. "I am sorry I did not win, but I'd rather you had it, sir, than Mr. Graham. Yes, that I would, and I congratulate you, sir."

"Thank you, Tyndall," replied Wimburne, "and if you like to come with me I shall be very glad of your company."

The bag of sovereigns being placed in the cab, Wimburne bade us all a hasty good-bye, told Miss Ransom that he would call to see her at Miss Cusack's house that evening, and, accompanied by Tyndall, started off. As we watched the cab turn the corner I heard Miss Ransom utter a sigh.

"I do hope it will be all right," she said, looking at me. "Don't you think it is a risky thing to drive with so much gold through London?"

I laughed in order to reassure her.

"Oh, no, it is perfectly safe," I answered, "safer perhaps than if the gold were conveyed in a more pretentious vehicle. There is nothing to announce the fact that it is bearing ten thousand and eighty sovereigns to the bank."

A moment or two later I left the two ladies and returned to my interrupted duties. The affair of the weighing, the strange clause in the will, Miss Ransom's eager pathetic face, Wimburne's manifest anxiety, had all impressed me considerably, and I could scarcely get the affair off my mind. I hoped that the young couple would now be married quickly, and I could not help being heartily glad that Graham had lost, for I had by no means taken to his appearance.

My work occupied me during the greater part of the afternoon, and I did not get back again to my own house until about six o'clock. When I did so I was told to my utter amazement that Miss Cusack had arrived and was waiting to see me with great impatience. I went at once into my consulting room, where I found her pacing restlessly up and down.

"What is the matter?" I asked.

"Matter!" she cried; "have you not heard? Why, it has been cried in the streets already—the money is gone, was stolen on the way to London. There was a regular highway robbery in the Richmond Road, in broad daylight too. The facts are simply these: Two men in a dogcart met the cab, shot the driver, and after a desperate struggle, in which Edgar Wimburne was badly hurt, seized the gold and drove off. The thing was planned, of course—planned to a moment."

"But what about Tyndall?" I asked.

"He was probably in the plot. All we know is that he has escaped and has not been heard of since."

"But what a daring thing!" I cried. "They will be caught, of course; they cannot have gone far with the money."

"You do not understand their tricks, Dr. Lonsdale; but I do," was her quick answer, "and I venture to guarantee that if we do not get that money back before the morning, Edgar Wimburne has seen the last of his fortune. Now, I mean to follow up this business, all night if necessary."

I did not reply. Her dark, bright eyes were blazing with excitement, and she began to pace up and down.

"You must come with me," she continued, "you promised to help me if the necessity should arise."

"And I will keep my word," I answered.

"That is an immense relief." She gave a deep sigh as she spoke.

"What about Miss Ransom?" I asked.

"Oh, I have left Letty at home. She is too excited to be of the slightest use."

"One other question," I interrupted, "and then I am completely at your service. You mentioned that Wimburne was hurt."

"Yes, but I believe not seriously. He has been taken to the hospital. He has already given evidence, but it amounts to very little. The robbery took place in a lonely part of the road, and just for the moment there was no one in sight."

"Well," I said, as she paused, "you have some scheme in your head, have you not?"

"I have," she answered. "The fact is this: from the very first I feared some such catastrophe as has really taken place. I have known Mr. Graham for a long time, and—distrusted him. He has passed for a man of position and means, but I believe him to be a mere adventurer. There is little doubt that all his future depended on his getting this fortune. I saw his face when the scales declared in Edgar Wimburne's favour—but there! I must ask you to accompany me to Hammersmith immediately. On the way I will tell you more."

"We will go in my carriage," I said, "it happens to be at the door."

We started directly. As we had left the more noisy streets Miss Cusack continued—

"You remember the advertisement I showed you yesterday morning?"

I nodded.

"You naturally could make no sense of it, but to me it was fraught with much meaning. This is by no means the first advertisement which has appeared under the name of Joshua Linklater. I have observed similar advertisements, and all, strange to say, in connection with founder's work, appearing at intervals in the big dailies for the last four or five months, but my attention was never specially directed to them until a circumstance occurred of which I am about to tell you."

"What is that?" I asked.

"Three weeks ago a certain investigation took me to Hammersmith in order to trace a stolen necklace. It was necessary that I should go to a small pawnbroker's shop—the man's name was Higgins. In my queer work, Dr. Lonsdale, I employ many disguises. That night, dressed quietly as a domestic servant on her evening out, I entered the pawnbroker's. I wore a thick veil and a plainly trimmed hat. I entered one of the little boxes where one stands to pawn goods, and waited for the man to appear.

For the moment he was engaged, and looking through a small window in the door I saw to my astonishment that the pawnbroker was in earnest conversation with no less a person than Mr. Campbell Graham. This was the last place I should have expected to see Mr. Graham in, and I immediately used both my eyes and ears. I heard the pawnbroker address him as Linklater.

Immediately the memory of the advertisements under that name flashed through my brain. From the attitude of the two men there was little doubt that they were discussing a matter of the utmost importance, and as Mr. Graham, *alias* Linklater, was leaving the shop, I distinctly overheard the following words: 'In all probability Bovey will die to-night. I may or may not be successful, but in order to insure against loss we must be prepared. It is not safe for me to come here often—look out for advertisement—it will be in the agony column.'

"I naturally thought such words very strange, and when I heard of Mr. Bovey's death and read an account of the queer will, it seemed to me that I began to see daylight. It was also my business to look out for the advertisement, and when I saw it yesterday morning you may well imagine that my keenest suspicions were aroused. I immediately suspected foul play, but could do nothing except watch and await events. Directly I heard the details of the robbery I wired to the inspector at Hammersmith to have Higgins's house watched. You remember that Mr. Wimburne left Kew in the cab at ten o'clock; the robbery must therefore have taken place some time about ten-twenty. The news reached me shortly after eleven, and my wire was sent off about eleven-fifteen. I mention these hours, as much may turn upon them. Just before I came to you I received a wire from the police-station containing startling news that was sent on at five-thirty. Here, you had better read it."

As she spoke she took a telegram from her pocket and handed it to me. I glanced over the words it contained.

"Just heard that cart was seen at Higgins's this morning. Man and assistant arrested on suspicion. House searched. No gold there. Please come down at once."

"So they have bolted with it?" I said.

"That we shall see," was her reply.

Shortly afterwards we arrived at the police station. The inspector was waiting for us, and took us at once into a private room.

"I am glad you were able to come, Miss Cusack," he said, bowing with great respect to the handsome girl.

"Pray tell me what you have done," she answered, "there is not a moment to spare."

"When I received your wire," he said, "I immediately placed a man on duty to watch Higgins's shop, but evidently before I did this the cart must have arrived and gone—the news with regard to the cart being seen outside Higgins's shop did not reach me till four-thirty. On receiving it I immediately arrested both Higgins and his assistant, and we searched the house from attic to cellar, but have found no gold whatever. There is little doubt that the pawnbroker received the gold, and has already removed it to another quarter."

"Did you find a furnace in the basement?" suddenly asked Miss Cusack.

"We did," he replied, in some astonishment; "but why do you ask?"

To my surprise Miss Cusack took out of her pocket the advertisement which she had shown me that morning and handed it the inspector. The man read the queer words aloud in a slow and wondering voice:—

Send more sand and charcoal dust. Core and mould ready for casting.

JOSHUA LINKLATER.

"I can make nothing of it, miss," he said, glancing at Miss Cusack. "These words seem to me to have something to do with founder's work."

"I believe they have," was her eager reply. "It is also highly probable that they have something to do with the furnace in the basement of Higgins's shop."

"I do not know what you are talking about, miss, but you have something at the back of your head which does not appear."

"I have," she answered, "and in order to confirm certain suspicions I wish to search the house."

"But the place has just been searched by us," was the man's almost testy answer. "It is impossible that a mass of gold should be there and be overlooked; every square inch of space has been accounted for."

"Who is in the house now?"

"No one; the place is locked up, and one of our men is on duty."

"What size is the furnace?"

"Unusually large," was the inspector's answer.

Miss Cusack gave a smile which almost immediately vanished.

"We are wasting time," she said; "let us go there immediately."

"I must do so, of course, if nothing else will satisfy you, miss; but I assure you——"

"Oh, don't let us waste any more time in arguing," said Miss Cusack, her impatience now getting the better of her. "I have a reason for what I do, and must visit the pawnbroker's immediately."

The man hesitated no longer, but took a bunch of keys down from the wall. A blaze of light from a public-house guided us to the pawnbroker's, which bore the well-known sign, the three golden balls. These were just visible through the fog above us. The inspector nodded to the man on duty, and unlocking the door we entered a narrow passage into which the swing doors of several smaller compartments opened. The inspector struck a match, and lighting the lantern, looked at Miss Cusack, as much as to say, "What do you propose to do now?"

"Take me to the room where the furnace is," said the lady.

"Come this way," he replied.

We turned at once in the direction of the stairs which led to the basement, and entered a room on the right. At the further end was an open range which had evidently been enlarged in order to allow the consumption of a great quantity of fuel, and upon it now stood an iron vessel, shaped as a chemist's crucible. Considerable heat still radiated from it. Miss Cusack peered inside, then she slowly commenced raking out the ashes with an iron rod, examining them closely and turning them over and over. Two or three white fragments she examined with peculiar care.

"One thing at least is abundantly clear," she said at last; "gold has been melted here, and within a very short time; whether it was the sovereigns or not we have yet to discover."

"But surely, Miss Cusack," said the inspector, "no one would be rash enough to destroy sovereigns."

"I am thinking of Joshua Linklater's advertisement," she said. "'*Send more sand and charcoal dust.*' This," she continued, once more examining the white fragments, "is undoubtedly sand."

She said nothing further, but went back to the ground floor and now commenced a systematic search on her own account.

At last we reached the top floor, where the pawnbroker and his assistant had evidently slept. Here Miss Cusack walked at once to the window and flung it open. She gazed out for a minute, and then turned to face us. Her eyes looked brighter than ever, and a certain smile played about her face.

"Well, miss," said the police inspector, "we have now searched the whole house, and I hope you are satisfied."

"I am," she replied.

"The gold is not here, miss."

"We will see," she said. As she spoke she turned once more and bent slightly out, as if to look down through the murky air at the street below.

The inspector gave an impatient exclamation.

"If you have quite finished, miss, we must return to the station," he said. "I am expecting some men from Scotland Yard to go into this affair."

"I do not think they will have much to do," she answered, "except, indeed, to arrest the criminal." As she spoke she leant a little further out of the window, and then withdrawing her head said quietly, "Yes, we may as well go back now; I have quite finished. Things are exactly as I expected to find them; we can take the gold away with us."

Both the inspector and I stared at her in utter amazement.

"What do you mean, Miss Cusack?" I cried.

"What I say," she answered, and now she gave a light laugh; "the gold is here, close to us; we have only to take it away. Come," she added, "look out, both of you. Why, you are both gazing at it."

I glanced round in utter astonishment. My expression of face was reproduced in that of the inspector's.

"Look," she said, "what do you call that?" As she spoke she pointed to the sign that hung outside—the sign of the three balls.

"Lean out and feel that lower ball," she said to the inspector.

He stretched out his arm, and as his fingers touched it he started back.

"Why, it is hot," he said; "what in the world does it mean?"

"It means the lost gold," replied Miss Cusack; "it has been cast as that ball. I said that the advertisement would give me the necessary clue, and it has done so. Yes, the lost fortune is hanging outside the house. The gold was melted in the crucible downstairs, and cast as this ball between twelve o'clock and four-thirty to-day. Remember it was after four-thirty that you arrested the pawnbroker and his assistant."

To verify her extraordinary words was the work of a few moments. Owing to its great weight, the inspector and I had some difficulty in detaching the ball from its hook. At the same time we noticed that a very strong stay, in the shape of an iron-wire rope, had been attached to the iron frame from which the three balls hung.

"You will find, I am sure," said Miss Cusack, "that this ball is not of solid gold; if it were, it would not be the size of the other two balls. It has probably been cast round a centre of plaster of Paris to give it the same size as the others. This explains the advertisement with regard to the charcoal and sand. A ball of that size in pure gold would weigh nearly three hundred pounds, or twenty stone."

"Well," said the inspector, "of all the curious devices that I have ever seen or heard of, this beats the lot. But what did they do with the real ball? They must have put it somewhere."

"They burnt it in the furnace, of course," she answered; "these balls, as you know, are only wood covered with gold paint. Yes, it was a clever idea, worthy of the brain of Mr. Graham; and it might have hung there for weeks and been seen by thousands passing daily, till Mr. Higgins was released from imprisonment, as nothing whatever could be proved against him."

Owing to Miss Cusack's testimony, Graham was arrested that night, and, finding that circumstances were dead against him, he confessed the whole. For long years he was one of a gang of coiners, but managed to pass as a gentleman of position. He knew old Bovey well, and had heard him speak of the curious will he had made. Knowing of this, he determined, at any risk, to secure the fortune, intending, when he had obtained it, to immediately leave the country. He had discovered the exact amount of the money which he would leave behind him, and had gone carefully into the weight which such a number of sovereigns would make. He knew at once that Tyndall would be out of the reckoning, and that the competition would really be between himself and Wimburne. To provide against the contingency of Wimburne's being the lucky man, he had planned the robbery; the gold was to be melted, and made into a real golden ball, which was to hang over the pawnshop until suspicion had died away.

Silas K. Hocking

(1850–1935)

SILAS K. HOCKING, an ordained United Methodist minister, was at one time the best selling novelist in England, and his fifty novels were published and re-published in matching sets. In 1903, his publishers claimed that over one million of his books had been sold. His stories tended to be edifying, as were the periodicals he edited—*Family Circle* and *Temple Magazine*.

The short stories in *The Adventures of Latimer Field, Curate* (1903) are much more interesting to the modern taste. They are set in small towns, or in country houses, and occasionally they deal with hauntings and gypsy curses. More significantly, Latimer Field was probably the first clergyman to turn to fictional sleuthing, even though most of the time his religious and theological views don't play much of a role in the investigations. Still, as Field's first case shows, Hocking could put a twist in the tale.

A Perverted Genius

CONVERSATION THAT EVENING turned on the subject of burglary. Within the last fortnight there had been four cases of house-breaking of the most daring character, and not a single trace of the miscreants or their booty had been discovered. This, in a small town like Banfield, was exceptional and alarming.

Miss Pinskill, our landlady, who always sat at the head of the table, declared — not without hesitancy — that if she awoke in the middle of the night and found a burglar in her room, she should scream and scream, even if she were certain she would be shot for it, and would never stop screaming till either death or deliverance came.

"I'm certain I should do nothing of the kind," Miss Eliza, who sat at the opposite end of the table, remarked. "I should just hide my head in the clothes, and let him take everything in the room."

"I think that would be very foolish," said Mr. Ball, my fellow-lodger, a very clever and gentlemanly man, who occupied the drawing-room, and sat directly opposite me at dinner.

"And what would you do?" I questioned.

"I should show fight," he replied. "If I knew I should be killed, I should fight all the same. I admit I should stand no chance with a strong man; but, you see, I come from a race of fighters, and so the fighting instinct would leap to the top in spite of everything."

"You might feel differently if it came to the pinch, Mr. Ball," Miss Pinskill remarked.

"I don't think so," he answered quietly. "I don't like boasting; but I did tackle a burglar once."

"You don't say so!" cried Miss Eliza.

"I was only about nineteen at the time," went on Mr. Ball, "and a

183

burglar broke into my father's house. I woke up in the middle of the night, and found the rascal in my room. He had been in the other rooms before."

"And you went for him?" I questioned eagerly.

"I did. Before he knew it I had grabbed him by the collar. He tried to fling me from him, but I held on like grim death; and, finding I was determined, he just slipped out of his coat, leaving it in my hands, and before I could grip him again he had disappeared through the window."

"What a pity!" said Miss Pinskill.

"It was a pity; for three minutes later a policeman came on the scene, but, of course, too late. Now, what would you have done under the circumstances?" he said, turning to me.

"I—I don't know," I said, with some hesitation, at which he smiled, and went on with his dinner.

As a matter of fact, I felt pretty certain that if I found a burglar in my room in the dead of the night I should simply collapse, and let him work his will on me and on my property without the least resistance. I did not feel called upon, however, to say so. A man may be a coward, but he need not tell people. They generally find it out quite soon enough.

I was not at all sorry when the dinner ended, for the subject of burglary, having been introduced, was kept up, and such subjects always make me nervous. I am just as bad if people begin to tell ghost stories. I keep awake half the night after, fancying I hear all kinds of unaccountable noises.

Leaving the dining-room, I retired to my study, and lighted a cigarette to calm my nerves, first of all, however, making sure that my window was properly fastened.

I heard Mr. Ball walk slowly along the hall and up the stairs, and a few minutes later I heard him call, in an excited and most distressed tone of voice, "Miss Pinskill! Miss Pinskill!"

"Yes, Mr. Ball," she cried, running into the hall. "What is the matter?"

"Please come here at once," he said, "and ask the curate to come also."

Now, this was the one and only thing I disliked about my fellow-lodger. He always spoke of me to others as "the curate," and usually in a tone of voice that implied that, in his opinion, curates were something less than men. I knew, of course, that I had nothing to boast of in the way of physical strength, and, moreover, that I was frightfully nervous. These facts kept me from openly resenting his manner and tone.

There was nothing in his tone, however, to resent on the present occasion. Indeed, he spoke like one in mortal terror.

Instantly opening the door, I rushed up the stairs after Miss Pinskill. "What is it, Mr. Ball?" she kept asking, as she panted in front of me.

"Burglars!" he said. "Everything of value I possess has been stolen."

Miss Pinskill, true to her nature, sat down on the floor and began to shriek.

I followed Mr. Ball into his bedroom, and found the whole place in a litter. Nearly every drawer had been turned out on the floor, and—as he said, in a most lugubrious tone—all his valuables were missing.

"I hope *my* things are safe, at any rate," I said; and I made off to my own room, only to find that it was in as complete a state of upset as Mr. Ball's.

A minute later Miss Eliza—who had come to her sister's rescue—began to call out that their room had been entered also, and everything of value taken away.

The state of confusion that followed cannot be very well described. No one seemed to know what to do or what to say. I was in such a condition of nervous tremor that my legs almost gave way under me. I had not lost very much of value, it is true, for the simple reason that I possessed no valuables; but the shock had taken all the strength out of me, and left me absolutely helpless.

Mr. Ball suggested at length that the police should be sent for, and Mary, the housemaid, was quickly despatched for that purpose. Half an hour later the place was overrun with policemen.

They examined the windows and doors, they searched the garden for footmarks, they looked into the cellars and outbuildings, they questioned Mr. Ball and myself until we grew sick of answering their questions, they drew sketches of the various rooms in their notebooks, and finally took their departure.

The only discovery they made was that the drawing-room window was unfastened, for which Mary admitted she was to blame. The thief or thieves had evidently come in by that way while we were at dinner, and there the matter ended. As in the case of the other burglaries, not a trace of the robbers could be found.

On the following evening Mr. Ball and I went across to the vicarage, where we had accepted an invitation to dinner. Though Mr. Ball had been in Banfield not more than two months at the outside, he had established himself a general favourite with all who knew him. He was most agreeable in his manners, and was well informed on all questions of general interest, and practically sympathetic with all religious and philanthropic movements. He was clever, too, and knew how to say a commonplace thing in a striking way. And, though he could be very sarcastic at times, sarcasm was a weapon he very rarely used.

He was somewhat dull and silent as we walked across to the vicarage; but that was easily accounted for; he had not yet got over the loss of the previous night.

"I wish to my heart we could lay hands on the thief!" he said to me. "It is bad enough to be robbed, but to be so completely outwitted by a common burglar is humiliating."

Over the dinner he quite recovered his spirits, and for a while—much to my relief—nothing was said of the burglary of the previous night. He greatly admired the vicar's silver and glass, and went into raptures over a richly-chased antique cup that stood in the centre of the table. He spotted some valuable lace that Mrs. Ramsey wore, and admired it in such an adroit way that he quite won that good woman's heart. He discussed the paintings on the walls with keen insight and knowledge, and hinted to a fraction the value of some rare old china.

I quite envied him his knowledge, his easy grace, his rare conversational powers, his subtle diplomacy. I never knew him shine as he did that night, and my admiration of him very considerably increased.

The vicar became quite confidential, and showed him over the house, and gave him a sight of his treasures.

Mr. Ball suggested that, after our experience of the previous night, he ought to have his doors and windows well bolted. And, the inevitable subject having once started, there was no getting away from it for the rest of the evening.

We did not stay late, as Mr. Ball had to catch the early train to London next morning.

"Unfortunately, Mr. Ramsey, we business men, even when we come away for a few months' rest, cannot wholly escape," he said to the vicar as we were leaving. "I have to run up to town at least once a fortnight. But I feel infinitely better already for my sojourn here."

"I am glad to hear it. But Banfield is a wonderfully healthy and bracing place. What a pity that the good should be discounted by the robbery of last evening!"

"Yes, it is a very annoying affair. But I am not without hopes that I may yet recover some of the plunder. You know the old saying, that rogues are generally fools also."

"In the case of burglars that seems scarcely true," said the vicar. "I think of the fact that five houses have been broken into in Banfield, and not a single clue has been obtained."

"You will be saying soon that burglary must not be reckoned among the hazardous callings," was the laughing reply.

"Indeed, I shall."

And so we parted from our host, and made our way home through the dimly lighted streets.

He shook my hand cordially as we said good night in the hall.

"I shall not see you again for three days at least. But, all being well, I shall be back again on Saturday evening."

I never imagined that I should look for his return as eagerly as I did. I felt that we needed some one in our midst who was clever and resourceful and far seeing. The local police seemed utterly helpless, and the case was becoming desperate. The latest victim was the vicar. On the night following our little dinner his house was broken into, and literally stripped of every valuable thing that was at all portable.

When I told Mr. Ball, he fairly gasped, and sank into a chair, quite overcome.

"Good heavens!" he said. "You don't mean to say they've been mean enough to rob the vicarage?"

"They have indeed," I answered.

"And the fools of police have been foiled again?"

"Yes. It seems they had got a suspicion that a burglary had been planned quite the other side of the town."

"Just like them; they are always in the wrong place!" he said angrily.

"The vicar is inconsolable," I said.

"I don't wonder," he answered. "He had some lovely things. I must go across and condole with him."

"You must do more," I said. "You are a City man. You have courage and resource, and if you will only play the part of detective—and, mind you, I am willing to join you in it—if we don't catch the thieves, we may at least prevent further robberies."

"Not a bad idea," he said thoughtfully. "It will be a novelty, at any rate. But I am afraid, Mr. Field, you are too nervous for the task. You don't mind my saying so, do you?"

"Not in the least," I replied. "I own I'm nervous—ridiculously so. But something must be done, and done soon."

"You are right in that. After I have had a little refreshment, we will go across to the vicarage and see if we can find any clue to work upon."

The vicar received us with manifest relief, and entered into the scheme with enthusiasm.

Mr. Ball discovered a footprint outside the window that had been opened, of which he took careful measurements, and under a bundle of sticks in a corner of the garden I found an old pair of shoes, one of which tallied with the footprint. But most important of all, was a strip of tweed cloth in a thorn hedge which separated the vicarage grounds from an adjoining farm.

"If we can only find the jacket that this fits, we may soon find the wearer," Mr. Ball said exultingly. "I really think, Mr. Ramsey, we've got a clue at last."

"I hope so indeed!" said the vicar, warmly. "I would give almost anything if we could find the scoundrels!"

For nearly a month Mr. Ball and I exhausted all our energies, but without success. Mr. Ball even sacrificed his fortnightly visit to London, and gave up all his time to the work of tracking down the burglars. Every now and then we fancied we were on the right track, and followed up our supposed clue for days at a stretch, only to find that we were wasting our strength and energy on a wild-goose chase.

A month of keener disappointment than that I have rarely known. Nothing is more depressing than to have your hopes raised to the very highest pitch, and then suddenly to find yourself plunged headlong again into despair. This was our case time after time, till even Mr. Ball, with his seemingly inexhaustible patience and resource, began to lose heart.

One satisfaction, indeed, we had, and we made the most of it; and that was that, though we had not discovered the burglars, we had prevented any fresh burglaries.

"They evidently know we are on the war-path," Mr. Ball said to me, with a laugh, "and so, to all appearances, have withdrawn from the neighbourhood altogether. But it would have been a satisfaction to me if I could have tracked them before I said good-bye to Banfield."

"I feel dreadfully disappointed," I said. "Still, I think we have done some good."

Mr. Ball's three months in Banfield were now almost up, and he was returning to town quite recruited, notwithstanding all the work and worry of the last month.

I really felt sad when I saw his heavy luggage carted away to the station. As a fellow-lodger, he had been almost everything one could desire; and I felt certain that Miss Pinskill would never get any one to fill his place that in any way would compare with him.

We celebrated his last evening with us by a special little dinner; and in proposing his health I really think I excelled myself. Miss Eliza said it was the best after-dinner speech she had ever listened to, excepting the speech Mr. Ball made in reply. That speech I shall never forget, and for many reasons. He had a most winning manner with him, and once or twice while he was speaking quite a lump came into my throat. I have no gift of pathos myself; perhaps for that reason I appreciate it so much in others. Not that I like being made to cry, for in a man it looks weak.

Well, we all retired early that night, for the effort to appear cheerful when we did not feel it exhausted us somewhat.

I fell asleep quickly, notwithstanding the heaviness of my heart, and was in the depths of profound slumber, when I was startled by the violent ringing of the front-door bell. I waited for some time, leaning on my elbow, for some one to go down and open the door, but I heard no one stirring. So at length, as my window was directly over the front door, I went and raised it, and asked—

"Who is there?"

"Oh, is that you, Mr. Field?" came a female voice that I did not recognize. "Will you please come and baptize Mrs. Sandy's baby? They are afraid it is dying."

"I will come at once," I answered. "Go back, and say I am following as quickly as possible."

And I closed the window, turned up my gas, and began to dress. I felt thankful now that no one else in the house had been disturbed.

In less than ten minutes I was out of my room, and in passing Mr. Ball's door I was surprised to see it standing ajar. For a moment I stood and listened, but there was no sound within.

"I hope you have not been alarmed, Mr. Ball?" I said, standing close to the door.

But I waited in vain for a reply.

Now, I knew that Mr. Ball was a very light sleeper, and was therefore not a little surprised that he was not the first to awake.

I was impatient to get to Mrs. Sandy's child, and yet something detained me. Perhaps it was mere curiosity. I put my mouth to the opening of the door and spoke again, but still no reply.

Then I pushed the door wide open, and walked into the room. It was unoccupied. The bed had evidently not been slept in.

I was more concerned than I knew. A thousand vague suspicions seemed to rush through my mind in a moment, but I could not afford to lose any more time. Creeping gently downstairs, I took my hat from the stand in the hall, and proceeded to unbolt the door. It was unbolted already.

Could it be possible that Miss Pinskill had gone to bed and left it merely on the latch? No, it could not be that. Mr. Ball had evidently gone out before me. But why? That question haunted me as I hurried through the silent and deserted streets and lanes in the direction of the Sandys'.

Suddenly I halted, and drew into the shadow of the thorn hedge. I was near a large house that stood alone. I knew the house well, and was slightly acquainted with the people who lived in it, though not so well acquainted by any means as I desired.

I had heard a window creak, then I saw it slowly and almost noiselessly open, then the form of a man appeared.

"Another burglary," I reflected; "and, as usual, not a single policeman about."

How it was I did not cry out or faint I do not know to this day, but I did neither. I crept under the verandah with the tread of a cat. I knew the robber would descend by one of the pillars, and I got close up to it. Some trellis-work was carried along the ground from pillar to pillar. The thief would get his foot on this trellis-work, and then step lightly to the ground. All this passed through my mind as in a flash. I was surprised at myself. I never knew my brain act so readily before; and, stranger still, I was not for the moment conscious of any fear.

The foot of the thief came into sight, close to my face. Quickly it descended and rested on the trellis-work, as I had expected; another moment, and he had let loose with his hands. I seized the foot and gave it a jerk, and he fell with his head in a bank of flowers.

With a muttered oath, he tried to struggle to his feet; but I held the foot on the top of the trellis-work, and he could not rise. He was quick to see what had happened, and, with an awful curse, he hissed—

"Let go, you fool, or I'll blow your brains out!"

I almost let go then, for I recognized the voice of Mr. Ball, and the discovery for the moment seemed to unman me, but only for a moment.

"Mr. Ball!" I exclaimed. "Can it be possible?"

"What, the curate?" he said, in mocking tones. "Come, let go, for I don't want to hurt you."

"Never!" I replied.

And I began to shout, "Help! Murder! Police!" at the top of my voice.

"You fool!" he cried. "Another sound, and I shoot!"

"You think I'm a coward," I replied; "but I'll show you!"

And I began to shout louder than before, though I was almost dying with fright.

All this time he was struggling might and main to get away from me;

but I held on like grim death, and the more he struggled the more my strength seemed to increase.

Suddenly he ceased to struggle, and I heard the click of a revolver. I knew he was levelling it at me. I tried to get my head behind the pillar; but suddenly there was a blaze of light before my eyes, then a stinging sensation along the side of my head.

"I am not dead yet!" I cried; but I felt the warm blood running down my neck inside my collar.

The reply was another flash. I felt a hot spot burn suddenly in my right arm, my fingers relaxed their hold, a mist came up before my eyes, I heard a confused sound of voices and hurrying feet, then all the world grew dark and still.

When I recovered consciousness I found myself lying in bed in a strange room, with a doctor on one side of me, and a nurse on the other. They told me that I was at the "Cedars," the house that had been broken into, that Ball had been captured on the spot, where he fired at me, and that all the valuables that he had taken out of the house had been recovered.

Later in the day Mabel Rutherford (by common consent the sweetest girl in Banfield) came and sat by my side, and told me that I was a brave man, and that she hoped I would not die. I felt myself an awful hypocrite; but I was too weak to protest. I knew I was but a coward at best. Howbeit, her words were very sweet to me, and more than compensated me for all I suffered.

Well, I lay there many weeks, and so had ample time to reflect on the strange perversity of human nature. I never realized so vividly before how the best gifts of God might be turned to evil account, and the greatest and noblest talents prostituted to the most wicked ends. Here was a man whose gifts almost amounted to genius, a man who could shine in any company, and whose talents would win him success in any department of life, deliberately choosing to do evil, and turning Heaven's benedictions into a snare. Surely God is very merciful and infinitely patient with the most sinful of His children.

But to return. The morning after the burglary Ball was brought before the mayor and a full bench of magistrates. Of his guilt, there could, of course, be no doubt, for he had been caught red-handed in the act, as it were, with stolen goods upon him. But as there was a strong presumption that he was also the author of the other burglaries, the mayor, after animadverting very strongly upon his conduct, remanded him for a week, and he was conducted back to the cells. He appeared to be very crestfallen, and scarcely once lifted his eyes during the whole time he was in the dock.

The court, I was told, was crowded to excess, for the news of his capture had spread far and wide, and people were curious to see a man who had been able to act the part of honest man and thief with such success. That he had accomplices was taken for granted, and the hope was freely expressed that the rascals who had made themselves such a terror to the neighbourhood would soon be keeping him company. That night, the mayor—who was a very wealthy man—was about to retire to rest with his family, when there came a violent ring at the door-bell. As the servants had already gone to bed, the mayor went himself and unbolted the door and opened it, and was not a little surprised to see a policeman standing in front of him.

"Well, constable, what's up now?" the mayor inquired.

"I'm sorry to trouble your worship," was the answer, in a low voice; "but the truth is, Ball has confessed everything, and I think we are on the point of arresting the whole gang."

"That's good news, indeed!" said the mayor, rubbing his hands. "But come inside, and let me hear the details."

The policeman stepped inside, and the door was closed behind him.

"Please don't alarm the ladies," he said, in the same low tone. "But the truth is, there is to be an attempt to burgle your house to-night. But we shall be ready for them. Already there are police in hiding all round the place. May I suggest to you to put out all the lights, as though you had retired for the night, and remain quietly downstairs?"

"I will do so, most certainly," said the mayor, looking very white, and trembling visibly.

"They will seek an entrance at the back," the constable went on; "and, of course, we must let them get in before we arrest them."

"I suppose you could not arrest them before they got in?" the mayor asked nervously.

"If we did, I'm afraid we could prove nothing worse than trespass against them. No, no; we must bring the whole charge against them if possible."

"Quite right, quite right!" said the mayor, briskly. "I'll leave the matter entirely in your hands."

"Is your family in the drawing-room?"

"Yes; we were just about to retire for the night."

"Well, ask them to keep as still as possible, and if they hear any noise overhead, don't let them get alarmed. I will station myself against the staircase-window on the first landing, so that I may be able to signal to our men, and direct their movements. I hope before the clock strikes one the whole gang will be safe in our hands."

"I hope so, too. Let me get a chair for you to sit on while you wait; it will be better than standing all the time."

"Thank you; I shall be very much obliged if you will."

Five minutes later all the lights were put out. The mayor retired to the drawing-room with his family, and bolted the door, while the constable stationed himself at the staircase-window with his dark-lantern, and his truncheon ready to hand.

The time passed with painful slowness. Twelve o'clock came and went. Every one sat mute, intent, alert, listening for any sound that might break the oppressive stillness. Half-past twelve struck, then one, and still there was no movement in any part of the house.

"We may expect them at any moment now," whispered the mayor, his teeth chattering; but no one replied to him.

Half-past one struck, and finally two. What an age it had seemed! and still there was not the faintest sound in any part of the house.

The mayor got uneasy, and went to the keyhole and listened. Then he opened the door and looked into the dark hall. Everything was as still as the grave. He walked to the foot of the stairs, and looked up. He could see the chair outlined against the window, but no one sat in it. What could have become of the constable?

Five minutes later lights were got, and a search instituted, and then the whole truth was revealed. Every bedroom in the house, except those occupied by the servants, had been ransacked, and all the valuables taken clean away.

"Good heavens!" cried the mayor; "what does it all mean?"

Then a horrible suspicion darted through his mind, and he rushed off in his slippers to the police-station.

But everything appeared to be quiet and in order—too quiet, in fact, for no one seemed to be about. It was lively enough, however, five minutes later.

In the cell that Ball was supposed to occupy a constable was found, minus his coat and helmet, lying on the hard bed, and apparently fast asleep. Indeed, it was a long time before he could be aroused to anything like a comprehension of the situation.

Next day he told an incoherent story of how the prisoner Ball complained that he had something in his eye which gave him great pain, and he asked his warder to bring his lantern and look into his eye through the bars of the door. The warder did so, and then—well, he never knew exactly what happened then. He believed he was mesmerized or hypnotized. He seemed to lose control of himself, and had an indistinct recollection of doing whatever the prisoner told him.

One thing, however, was clear: that Ball attired himself in the policeman's coat and helmet, and, taking his truncheon and lantern, went direct to the mayor's house, with such results as I have described.

There were those who believed that Ball simply bribed the constable; but that was never proved. In any case, he got clear away, and that was the last ever seen of him in Banfield.

G. K. Chesterton

(1874–1936)

G. K. CHESTERTON was one of the greatest men of letters of his age—poet, essayist, novelist, editor, and creator of the immortal Father Brown. He was a huge man, wearing a flapping hat, carrying a sword-stick, and of prodigious absent-mindedness; he once telegraphed his wife, "Am in Market Harborough; where ought I to be?" He saw the world as a place of wonder—the signs of God's creation were to be found everywhere. It was a fairy world, full of paradoxes, each of which ultimately showed the unity of God's plan.

Father Brown was perhaps the greatest paradox of all—a humble priest, clumsy and described by his creator as "innocent," and yet a person who finds solutions to mysteries much more clearly than professional detectives like his friend Flambeau. To Chesterton, the Father Brown stories were essays in theology, and Father Brown sees detection as a moral issue, an attempt to work out salvation—of both the victims and the criminals. Father Brown was based on Chesterton's friend Father O'Connor, but having been brought up in the Church of England, Chesterton waited more than ten years before he allowed Father Brown to convert him. In 1922, Father O'Connor received Chesterton into the Catholic church.

"The Eye of Apollo" is one of the stories in the first Father Brown book, *The Innocence of Father Brown* (1910).

The Eye of Apollo

THAT SINGULAR SMOKY SPARKLE, at once a confusion and a trans-
parency, which is the strange secret of the Thames, was changing more
and more from its grey to its glittering extreme as the sun climbed to
the zenith over Westminster, and two men crossed Westminster Bridge.
One man was very tall and the other very short; they might even have
been fantastically compared to the arrogant clocktower of Parliament
and the humbler humped shoulders of the Abbey, for the short man
was in clerical dress. The official description of the tall man was
M. Hercule Flambeau, private detective, and he was going to his new
offices in a new pile of flats facing the Abbey entrance. The official
description of the short man was the Rev. J. Brown, attached to St.
Francis Xavier's Church, Camberwell, and he was coming from a
Camberwell death-bed to see the new offices of his friend.

The building was American in its sky-scraping altitude, and
American also in the oiled elaboration of its machinery of telephones
and lifts. But it was barely finished and still understaffed; only three
tenants had moved in; the office just above Flambeau was occupied, as
also was the office just below him; the two floors above that and the
three floors below were entirely bare. But the first glance at the new
tower of flats caught something much more arresting. Save for a few
relics of scaffolding, the one glaring object was erected outside the
office just above Flambeau's. It was an enormous gilt effigy of the
human eye, surrounded with rays of gold, and taking up as much room
as two or three of the office windows.

"What on earth is that?" asked Father Brown, and stood still.

"Oh, a new religion," said Flambeau, laughing; "one of those new
religions that forgive your sins by saying you never had any. Rather like

196

Christian Science, I should think. The fact is that a fellow calling himself Kalon (I don't know what his name is, except that it can't be that) has taken the flat just above me. I have two lady typewriters underneath me, and this enthusiastic old humbug on top. He calls himself the New Priest of Apollo, and he worships the sun."

"Let him look out," said Father Brown. "The sun was the cruellest of all the gods. But what does that monstrous eye mean?"

"As I understand it, it is a theory of theirs," answered Flambeau, "that a man can endure anything if his mind is quite steady. Their two great symbols are the sun and the open eye; for they say that if a man were really healthy he could stare at the sun."

"If a man were really healthy," said Father Brown, "he would not bother to stare at it."

"Well, that's all I can tell you about the new religion," went on Flambeau carelessly. "It claims, of course, that it can cure all physical diseases."

"Can it cure the one spiritual disease?" asked Father Brown, with a serious curiosity.

"And what is the one spiritual disease?" asked Flambeau, smiling.

"Oh, thinking one is quite well," said his friend.

Flambeau was more interested in the quiet little office below him than in the flamboyant temple above. He was a lucid Southerner, incapable of conceiving himself as anything but a Catholic or an atheist; and new religions of a bright and pallid sort were not much in his line. But humanity was always in his line, especially when it was good-looking; moreover, the ladies downstairs were characters in their way. The office was kept by two sisters, both slight and dark, one of them tall and striking. She had a dark, eager and aquiline profile, and was one of those women whom one always thinks of in profile, as of the clean-cut edge of some weapon. She seemed to cleave her way through life. She had eyes of startling brilliancy, but it was the brilliancy of steel rather than of diamonds; and her straight, slim figure was a shade too stiff for its grace. Her younger sister was like her shortened shadow, a little greyer, paler, and more insignificant. They both wore a business-like black, with little masculine cuffs and collars. There are thousands of such curt, strenuous ladies in the offices of London, but the interest of these lay rather in their real than their apparent position.

For Pauline Stacey, the elder, was actually the heiress of a crest and half a county, as well as great wealth; she had been brought up in castles and gardens, before a frigid fierceness (peculiar to the modern woman) had driven her to what she considered a harsher and a higher existence. She had not, indeed, surrendered her money; in that there would have been a romantic or monkish abandon quite alien to her masterful utilitarianism. She held her wealth, she would say, for use upon practical social objects. Part of it she had put into her business, the nucleus of a model typewriting emporium; part of it was distributed in various leagues and causes for the advancement of such work among women. How far Joan, her sister and partner, shared this slightly prosaic idealism no one could be very sure. But she followed her leader with a dog-like affection which was somehow more attractive, with its touch of tragedy, than the hard, high spirits of the elder. For Pauline Stacey had nothing to say to tragedy; she was understood to deny its existence.

Her rigid rapidity and cold impatience had amused Flambeau very much on the first occasion of his entering the flats. He had lingered outside the lift in the entrance hall waiting for the lift-boy, who generally conducts strangers to the various floors. But this bright-eyed falcon of a girl had openly refused to endure such official delay. She said sharply that she knew all about the lift, and was not dependent on boys—or on men either. Though her flat was only three floors above, she managed in the few seconds of ascent to give Flambeau a great many of her fundamental views in an off-hand manner; they were to the general effect that she was a modern working woman and loved modern working machinery. Her bright black eyes blazed with abstract anger against those who rebuke mechanic science and ask for the return of romance. Everyone, she said, ought to be able to manage machines, just as she could manage the lift. She seemed almost to resent the fact of Flambeau opening the lift-door for her; and that gentleman went up to his own apartments smiling with somewhat mingled feelings at the memory of such spit-fire self-dependence.

She certainly had a temper, of a snappy, practical sort; the gestures of her thin, elegant hands were abrupt or even destructive. Once Flambeau entered her office on some typewriting business, and found she had just flung a pair of spectacles belonging to her sister into the middle of the floor and stamped on them. She was already in the rapids of an ethical tirade about the "sickly medical notions" and the morbid admission of weakness implied in such an apparatus. She dared her sister to bring such artificial, unhealthy rubbish into the place again. She asked if she was expected to wear wooden legs or false hair or glass eyes; and as she spoke her eyes sparkled like the terrible crystal.

Flambeau, quite bewildered with this fanaticism, could not refrain from asking Miss Pauline (with direct French logic) why a pair of spectacles was a more morbid sign of weakness than a lift, and why, if science might help us in the one effort, it might not help us in the other.

"That is *so* different," said Pauline Stacey, loftily. "Batteries and motors and all those things are marks of the force of man—yes, Mr. Flambeau, and the force of woman, too! We shall take our turn at these great engines that devour distance and defy time. That is high and splendid—that is really science. But these nasty props and plasters the doctors sell—why, they are just badges of poltroonery. Doctors stick on legs and arms as if we were born cripples and sick slaves. But I was free-born, Mr. Flambeau! People only think they need these things because they have been trained in fear instead of being trained in power and courage, just as the silly nurses tell children not to stare at the sun, and so they can't do it without blinking. But why among the stars should there be one star I may not see? The sun is not my master, and I will open my eyes and stare at him whenever I choose."

"Your eyes," said Flambeau, with a foreign bow, "will dazzle the sun." He took pleasure in complimenting this strange stiff beauty, partly because it threw her a little off her balance. But as he went upstairs to his floor he drew a deep breath and whistled, saying to himself: "So she has got into the hands of that conjurer upstairs with his golden eye." For, little as he knew or cared about the new religion of Kalon, he had heard of his special notion about sun-gazing.

He soon discovered that the spiritual bond between the floors above and below him was close and increasing. The man who called himself Kalon was a magnificent creature, worthy, in a physical sense, to be the pontiff of Apollo. He was nearly as tall even as Flambeau, and very much better looking, with a golden beard, strong blue eyes, and a mane flung back like a lion's. In structure he was the blonde beast of Nietzsche, but all this animal beauty was heightened, brightened and softened by genuine intellect and spirituality. If he looked like one of the great Saxon kings, he looked like one of the kings that were also saints. And this despite the cockney incongruity of his surroundings; the fact that he had an office half-way up a building in Victoria Street; that the clerk (a commonplace youth in cuffs and collars) sat in the outer room, between him and the corridor; that his name was on a brass plate, and the gilt emblem of his creed hung above his street, like the advertisement of an oculist. All this vulgarity could not take away from the man called Kalon the vivid oppression and inspiration that came from his soul and body. When all was said, a man in the presence of this quack did feel in the presence of a great man. Even in the loose jacket-suit of linen that he wore as a workshop dress in his office he was a fascinating and formidable figure; and when robed in the white vestments and crowned with the golden circlet, in which he daily saluted the sun, he really looked so splendid that the laughter of the street people sometimes died suddenly on their lips. For three times in the day the new sun-worshipper went out on his little balcony, in the face of all Westminster, to say some litany to his shining lord: once at daybreak, once at sunset, and once at the shock of noon. And it was while the shock of noon still shook faintly from the towers of Parliament and parish church that Father Brown, the friend of Flambeau, first looked up and saw the white priest of Apollo.

Flambeau had seen quite enough of these daily salutations of Phœbus, and plunged into the porch of the tall building without even looking for his clerical friend to follow. But Father Brown, whether from a professional interest in ritual or a strong individual interest in tomfoolery, stopped and stared up at the balcony of the sun-worshipper, just as he might have stopped and stared up at a Punch and Judy. Kalon the Prophet was already erect, with argent garments and uplifted hands, and the sound of his strangely penetrating voice could be heard all the way down the busy street uttering his solar litany. He was already in the middle of it; his eyes were fixed upon the flaming disc. It is doubtful if he saw anything or anyone on this earth; it is substantially certain that he did not see a stunted, round-faced priest who, in the crowd below, looked up at him with blinking eyes. That was perhaps the most startling difference between even these two far divided men. Father Brown could not look at anything without blinking; but the priest of Apollo could look on the blaze at noon without a quiver of the eyelid.

"O sun," cried the prophet, "O star that art too great to be allowed among the stars! O fountain that flowest quietly in that secret spot that is called space. White father of all white unwearied things, white flames and white flowers and white peaks. Father, who art more innocent than all thy most innocent and quiet children; primal purity, into the peace of which——"

A rush and crash like the reversed rush of a rocket was cloven with a strident and incessant yelling. Five people rushed into the gate of the mansions as three people rushed out, and for an instant they all deafened each other. The sense of some utterly abrupt horror seemed for a moment to fill half the street with bad news—bad news that was all the worse because no one knew what it was. Two figures remained still after the crash of commotion: the fair priest of Apollo on the balcony above, and the ugly priest of Christ below him.

At last the tall figure and titanic energy of Flambeau appeared in the doorway of the mansions and dominated the little mob. Talking at the top of his voice like a fog-horn, he told somebody or anybody to go for a surgeon; and as he turned back into the dark and thronged entrance his friend Father Brown slipped in insignificantly after him. Even as he ducked and dived through the crowd he could still hear the magnificent melody and monotony of the solar priest still calling on the happy god who is the friend of fountains and flowers.

Father Brown found Flambeau and some six other people standing round the enclosed space into which the lift commonly descended. But the lift had not descended. Something else had descended; something that ought to have come by a lift.

For the last four minutes Flambeau had looked down on it; had seen the brained and bleeding figure of that beautiful woman who denied the existence of tragedy. He had never had the slightest doubt that it was Pauline Stacey; and, though he had sent for a doctor, he had not the slightest doubt that she was dead.

He could not remember for certain whether he had liked her or disliked her; there was so much both to like and dislike. But she had been a person to him, and the unbearable pathos of details and habit stabbed him with all the small daggers of bereavement. He remembered her pretty face and priggish speeches with a sudden secret vividness which is all the bitterness of death. In an instant like a bolt from the blue, like a thunderbolt from nowhere, that beautiful and defiant body had been dashed down the open well of the lift to death at the bottom. Was it suicide? With so insolent an optimist it seemed impossible. Was it murder? But who was there in those hardly inhabited flats to murder anybody? In a rush of raucous words, which he meant to be strong and suddenly found weak, he asked where was that fellow Kalon. A voice, habitually heavy, quiet and full, assured him that Kalon for the last fifteen minutes had been away up on his balcony worshipping his god. When Flambeau heard the voice, and felt the hand of Father Brown, he turned his swarthy face and said abruptly:

"Then, if he has been up there all the time, who can have done it?"

"Perhaps," said the other, "we might go upstairs and find out. We have half an hour before the police will move."

Leaving the body of the slain heiress in charge of the surgeons, Flambeau dashed up the stairs to the typewriting office, found it utterly empty, and then dashed up to his own. Having entered that, he abruptly returned with a new and white face to his friend.

"Her sister," he said, with an unpleasant seriousness, "her sister seems to have gone out for a walk."

Father Brown nodded. "Or, she may have gone up to the office of that sun man," he said. "If I were you I should just verify that, and then let us all talk it over in your office. No," he added suddenly, as if remembering something, "shall I ever get over that stupidity of mine? Of course, in their office downstairs."

Flambeau stared; but he followed the little father downstairs to the empty flat of the Staceys, where that impenetrable pastor took a large red-leather chair in the very entrance, from which he could see the stairs and landings, and waited. He did not wait very long. In about four minutes three figures descended the stairs, alike only in their solemnity. The first was Joan Stacey, the sister of the dead woman— evidently she *had* been upstairs in the temporary temple of Apollo; the second was the priest of Apollo himself, his litany finished, sweeping down the empty stairs in utter magnificence—something in his white robes, beard and parted hair had the look of Doré's Christ leaving the Pretorium; the third was Flambeau, black browed and somewhat bewildered.

Miss Joan Stacey, dark, with a drawn face and hair prematurely touched with grey, walked straight to her own desk and set out her papers with a practical flap. The mere reaction rallied everyone else to sanity. If Miss Joan Stacey was a criminal, she was a cool one. Father Brown regarded her for some time with an odd little smile, and then, without taking his eyes off her, addressed himself to somebody else.

"Prophet," he said, presumably addressing Kalon, "I wish you would tell me a lot about your religion."

"I shall be proud to do it," said Kalon, inclining his still crowned head, "but I am not sure that I understand."

"Why, it's like this," said Father Brown, in his frankly doubtful way: "We are taught that if a man has really bad first principles, that must be partly his fault. But, for all that, we can make some difference between a man who insults his quite clear conscience and a man with a conscience more or less clouded with sophistries. Now, do you really think that murder is wrong at all?"

"Is this an accusation?" asked Kalon very quietly.

"No," answered Brown, equally gently, "it is the speech for the defence."

In the long and startled stillness of the room the prophet of Apollo slowly rose; and really it was like the rising of the sun. He filled that room with his light and life in such a manner that a man felt he could as easily have filled Salisbury Plain. His robed form seemed to hang the whole room with classic draperies; his epic gesture seemed to extend it into grander perspectives, till the little black figure of the modern cleric seemed to be a fault and an intrusion, a round, black blot upon some splendour of Hellas.

"We meet at last, Caiaphas," said the prophet. "Your church and mine are the only realities on this earth. I adore the sun, and you the darkening of the sun; you are the priest of the dying and I of the living God. Your present work of suspicion and slander is worthy of your coat and creed. All your church is but a black police; you are only spies and detectives seeking to tear from men confessions of guilt, whether by treachery or torture. You would convict men of crime, I would convict them of innocence. You would convince them of sin, I would convince them of virtue.

"Reader of the books of evil, one more word before I blow away your baseless nightmares for ever. Not even faintly could you understand how little I care whether you can convict me or no. The things you call disgrace and horrible hanging are to me no more than an ogre in a child's toy-book to a man once grown up. You said you were offering the speech for the defence. I care so little for the cloudland of this life that I will offer you the speech for the prosecution. There is but one thing that can be said against me in this matter, and I will say it myself. The woman that is dead was my love and my bride; not after such manner as your tin chapels call lawful, but by a law purer and sterner than you will ever understand. She and I walked another world from yours, and trod palaces of crystal while you were plodding through tunnels and corridors of brick. Well, I know that policemen, theological and otherwise, always fancy that where there has been love there must soon be hatred; so there you have the first point made for the prosecution. But the second point is stronger; I do not grudge it you. Not only is it true that Pauline loved me, but it is also true that this very morning, before she died, she wrote at that table a will leaving me and my new church half a million. Come, where are the handcuffs? Do you suppose I care what foolish things you do with me? Penal servitude will only be like waiting for her at a wayside station. The gallows will only be going to her in a headlong car."

He spoke with the brain-shaking authority of an orator, and Flambeau and Joan Stacey stared at him in amazed admiration. Father Brown's face seemed to express nothing but extreme distress; he looked at the ground with one wrinkle of pain across his forehead. The prophet of the sun leaned easily against the mantelpiece and resumed:

"In a few words I have put before you the whole case against me—the only possible case against me. In fewer words still I will blow it to pieces, so that not a trace of it remains. As to whether I have committed this crime, the truth is in one sentence: I could not have committed this crime. Pauline Stacey fell from this floor to the ground at five minutes past twelve. A hundred people will go into the witness-box and say that I was standing out upon the balcony of my own rooms above from just before the stroke of noon to a quarter-past—the usual period of my public prayers. My clerk (a respectable youth from Clapham, with no sort of connection with me) will swear that he sat in my outer office all the morning, and that no communication passed through. He will swear that I arrived a full ten minutes before the hour, fifteen minutes before any whisper of the accident, and that I did not leave the office or the balcony all that time. No one ever had so complete an alibi; I could subpœna half Westminster. I think you had better put the handcuffs away again. The case is at an end.

"But last of all, that no breath of this idiotic suspicion remain in the air, I will tell you all you want to know. I believe I do know how my unhappy friend came by her death. You can, if you choose, blame me for it, or my faith and philosophy at least; but you certainly cannot lock me up. It is well known to all students of the higher truths that certain adepts and *illuminati* have in history attained the power of levitation— that is, of being self-sustained upon the empty air. It is but a part of that general conquest of matter which is the main element in our occult wisdom. Poor Pauline was of an impulsive and ambitious temper. I think, to tell the truth, she thought herself somewhat deeper in the mysteries than she was; and she has often said to me, as we went down in the lift together, that if one's will were strong enough, one could float down as harmlessly as a feather. I solemnly believe that in some ecstasy of noble thoughts she attempted the miracle. Her will, or faith, must have failed her at the crucial instant, and the lower law of matter had its horrible revenge. There is the whole story, gentlemen, very sad and, as you think, very presumptuous and wicked, but certainly not criminal or in any way connected with me. In the short-hand of the police-courts, you had better call it suicide. I shall always call it heroic failure for the advance of science and the slow scaling of heaven."

It was the first time Flambeau had ever seen Father Brown vanquished. He still sat looking at the ground, with a painful and corrugated brow, as if in shame. It was impossible to avoid the feeling which the prophet's winged words had fanned, that here was a sullen, professional suspecter of men overwhelmed by a prouder and purer spirit of natural liberty and health. At last he said, blinking as if in bodily distress: "Well, if that is so, sir, you need do no more than take the testamentary paper you spoke of and go. I wonder where the poor lady left it."

"It will be over there on her desk by the door, I think," said Kalon, with that massive innocence of manner that seemed to acquit him wholly. "She told me specially she would write it this morning, and I actually saw her writing as I went up in the lift to my own room."

"Was her door open then?" asked the priest, with his eye on the corner of the matting.

"Yes," said Kalon calmly.

"Ah! it has been open ever since," said the other, and resumed his silent study of the mat.

"There is a paper over here," said the grim Miss Joan, in a somewhat singular voice. She had passed over to her sister's desk by the doorway, and was holding a sheet of blue foolscap in her hand. There was a sour smile on her face that seemed unfit for such a scene or occasion, and Flambeau looked at her with a darkening brow.

Kalon the prophet stood away from the paper with that loyal unconsciousness that had carried him through. But Flambeau took it out of the lady's hand, and read it with the utmost amazement. It did, indeed, begin in the formal manner of a will, but after the words "I give and bequeath all of which I die possessed" the writing abruptly stopped with a set of scratches, and there was no trace of the name of any legatee. Flambeau, in wonder, handed this truncated testament to his clerical friend, who glanced at it and silently gave it to the priest of the sun.

An instant afterwards that pontiff, in his splendid sweeping draperies, had crossed the room in two great strides, and was towering over Joan Stacey, his blue eyes standing from his head.

"What monkey tricks have you been playing here?" he cried. "That's not all Pauline wrote."

They were startled to hear him speak in quite a new voice, with a Yankee shrillness in it; all his grandeur and good English had fallen from him like a cloak.

"That is the only thing on her desk," said Joan, and confronted him steadily with the same smile of evil favour.

Of a sudden the man broke out into blasphemies and cataracts of incredulous words. There was something shocking about the dropping of his mask; it was like a man's real face falling off.

"See here!" he cried in broad American, when he was breathless with cursing, "I may be an adventurer, but I guess you're a murderess. Yes, gentlemen, here's your death explained, and without any levitation. The poor girl is writing a will in my favour; her cursed sister comes in, struggles for the pen, drags her to the well, and throws her down before she can finish it. Sakes! I reckon we want the handcuffs after all."

"As you have truly remarked," replied Joan, with ugly calm, "your clerk is a very respectable young man, who knows the nature of an oath; and he will swear in any court that I was up in your office arranging some typewriting work for five minutes before and five minutes after my sister fell. Mr. Flambeau will tell you that he found me there."

There was a silence.

"Why, then," cried Flambeau, "Pauline was alone when she fell, and it was suicide!"

"She was alone when she fell," said Father Brown, "but it was not suicide."

"Then how did she die?" asked Flambeau impatiently.

"She was murdered."

"But she was alone," objected the detective.

"She was murdered when she was all alone," answered the priest.

All the rest stared at him, but he remained sitting in the same old dejected attitude, with a wrinkle in his round forehead and an appearance of impersonal shame and sorrow; his voice was colourless and sad.

"What I want to know," cried Kalon, with an oath, "is when the police are coming for this bloody and wicked sister. She's killed her flesh and blood; she's robbed me of half a million that was just as sacredly mine as——"

"Come, come, prophet," interrupted Flambeau, with a kind of sneer; "remember that all this world is a cloudland."

The hierophant of the sun-god made an effort to climb back on his pedestal. "It is not the mere money," he cried, "though that would equip the cause throughout the world. It is also my beloved one's wishes. To Pauline all this was holy. In Pauline's eyes——"

Father Brown suddenly sprang erect, so that his chair fell over flat behind him. He was deathly pale, yet he seemed fired with a hope; his eyes shone.

"That's it!" he cried in a clear voice. "That's the way to begin. In Pauline's eyes——"

The tall prophet retreated before the tiny priest in an almost mad disorder. "What do you mean? How dare you?" he cried repeatedly.

"In Pauline's eyes," repeated the priest, his own shining more and more. "Go on—in God's name, go on. The foulest crime the fiends ever prompted feels lighter after confession; and I implore you to confess. Go on, go on—in Pauline's eyes——"

"Let me go, you devil!" thundered Kalon, struggling like a giant in bonds. "Who are you, you cursed spy, to weave your spiders' webs round me, and peep and peer? Let me go."

"Shall I stop him?" asked Flambeau, bounding towards the exit, for Kalon had already thrown the door wide open.

"No; let him pass," said Father Brown, with a strange deep sigh that seemed to come from the depths of the universe. "Let Cain pass by, for he belongs to God."

There was a long-drawn silence in the room when he had left it, which was to Flambeau's fierce wits one long agony of interrogation. Miss Joan Stacey very coolly tidied up the papers on her desk.

"Father," said Flambeau at last, "it is my duty, not my curiosity only—it is my duty to find out, if I can, who committed the crime."

"Which crime?" asked Father Brown.

"The one we are dealing with, of course," replied his impatient friend.

"We are dealing with two crimes," said Brown, "crimes of very different weight—and by very different criminals."

Miss Joan Stacey, having collected and put away her papers, proceeded to lock up her drawer. Father Brown went on, noticing her as little as she noticed him.

"The two crimes," he observed, "were committed against the same weakness of the same person, in a struggle for her money. The author of the larger crime found himself thwarted by the smaller crime; the author of the smaller crime got the money."

"Oh, don't go on like a lecturer," groaned Flambeau; "put it in a few words."

"I can put it in one word," answered his friend.

Miss Joan Stacey skewered her business-like black hat on to her head with a business-like black frown before a little mirror, and, as the conversation proceeded, took her handbag and umbrella in an unhurried style, and left the room.

"The truth is one word, and a short one," said Father Brown. "Pauline Stacey was blind."

"Blind!" repeated Flambeau, and rose slowly to his whole huge stature.

"She was subject to it by blood," Brown proceeded. "Her sister would have started eyeglasses if Pauline would have let her; but it was her special philosophy or fad that one must not encourage such diseases by yielding to them. She would not admit the cloud; or she tried to dispel it by will. So her eyes got worse and worse with straining; but the worst strain was to come. It came with this precious prophet, or whatever he calls himself, who taught her to stare at the hot sun with the naked eye. It was called accepting Apollo. Oh, if these new pagans would only be old pagans, they would be a little wiser! The old pagans knew that mere naked Nature-worship must have a cruel side. They knew that the eye of Apollo can blast and blind."

There was a pause, and the priest went on in a gentle and even broken voice. "Whether or no that devil deliberately made her blind, there is no doubt that he deliberately killed her through her blindness. The very simplicity of the crime is sickening. You know he and she went up and down in those lifts without official help; you know also how smoothly and silently the lifts slide. Kalon brought the lift to the girl's landing, and saw her, through the open door, writing in her slow, sightless way the will she had promised him. He called out to her cheerily that he had the lift ready for her, and she was to come out when she was ready. Then he pressed a button and shot soundlessly up to his own floor, walked through his own office, out on to his own balcony, and was safely praying before the crowded street when the poor girl, having finished her work, ran gaily out to where lover and lift were to receive her, and stepped——"

"Don't!" cried Flambeau.

"He ought to have got half a million by pressing that button," continued the little father, in the colourless voice in which he talked of such horrors. "But that went smash. It went smash because there happened to be another person who also wanted the money, and who also knew the secret about poor Pauline's sight. There was one thing about that will that I think nobody noticed: although it was unfinished and without signature, the other Miss Stacey and some servant of hers had already signed it as witnesses. Joan had signed first, saying Pauline could finish it later, with a typical feminine contempt for legal forms. Therefore, Joan wanted her sister to sign the will without real witnesses. Why? I thought of the blindness, and felt sure she had wanted Pauline to sign in solitude because she had wanted her not to sign at all.

"People like the Staceys always use fountain pens; but this was specially natural to Pauline. By habit and her strong will and memory she could still write almost as well as if she saw; but she could not tell when her pen needed dipping. Therefore, her fountain pens were carefully filled by her sister—all except this fountain pen. This was carefully *not* filled by her sister; the remains of the ink held out for a few lines and then failed altogether. And the prophet lost five hundred thousand pounds and committed one of the most brutal and brilliant murders in human history for nothing."

Flambeau went to the open door and heard the official police ascending the stairs. He turned and said: "You must have followed everything devilish close to have traced the crime to Kalon in ten minutes."

Father Brown gave a sort of start.

"Oh! to him," he said. "No; I had to follow rather close to find out about Miss Joan and the fountain pen. But I knew Kalon was the criminal before I came into the front door."

"You must be joking!" cried Flambeau.

"I'm quite serious," answered the priest. "I tell you I knew he had done it, even before I knew what he had done."

"But why?"

"These pagan stoics," said Brown reflectively, "always fail by their strength. There came a crash and a scream down the street, and the priest of Apollo did not start or look round. I did not know what it was. But I knew that he was expecting it."

Robert W. Chambers

(1865–1933)

BROOKLYN-BORN ROBERT W. CHAMBERS wrote light, frothy, forgettable (and, for the most part, forgotten) romances. With Charles Dana Gibson, he created the image of womanhood known both as "The Gibson Girl" and "The Chambers Girl." Typical of his work in the mystery field is *The Tracer of Lost Persons* (1906) in which Westrel Keen seeks lost loves for his clients.

More significant are Chambers' fantasy and supernatural writings. *The King in Yellow* (1895) is, according to E. F. Bleiler, "one of the basic documents in the history of fantastic fiction," and it directly influenced the works of H. P. Lovecraft. *Police!!!* (1915), despite its title, also contains fantasy rather than detective stories. But he did write one great tale of detection, "The Purple Emperor," the first story in *The Mystery of Choice* (1897), which may be the only (it's certainly the first) mystery surrounding butterfly collecting. The remainder of the book, told by the same narrator, is made up of fantasy and supernatural inventions, one story going so far as to feature a living dinosaur.

The Purple Emperor

Un souvenir heureux est peut-être, sur terre,
Plus vrai que le bonheur.

A. DE MUSSET

I.

THE PURPLE EMPEROR watched me in silence. I cast again, spinning out six feet more of water-proof silk, and, as the line hissed through the air far across the pool, I saw my three flies fall on the water like drifting thistledown. The Purple Emperor sneered.

"You see," he said, "I am right. There is not a trout in Brittany that will rise to a tailed fly."

"They do in America," I replied.

"Zut! for America!" observed the Purple Emperor.

"And trout take a tailed fly in England," I insisted sharply.

"Now do I care what things or people do in England?" demanded the Purple Emperor.

"You don't care for anything except yourself and your wriggling caterpillars," I said, more annoyed than I had yet been.

The Purple Emperor sniffed. His broad, hairless, sunburnt features bore that obstinate expression which always irritated me. Perhaps the manner in which he wore his hat intensified the irritation, for the flapping brim rested on both ears, and the two little velvet ribbons which hung from the silver buckle in front wiggled and fluttered with every trivial breeze. His cunning eyes and sharp-pointed nose were out of all keeping with his fat red face. When he met my eye, he chuckled.

211

"I know more about insects than any man in Morbihan—or Finistère either, for that matter," he said.

"The Red Admiral knows as much as you do," I retorted.

"He doesn't," replied the Purple Emperor angrily.

"And his collection of butterflies is twice as large as yours," I added, moving down the stream to a spot directly opposite him.

"It is, is it?" sneered the Purple Emperor. "Well, let me tell you, Monsieur Darrel, in all his collection he hasn't a specimen, a single specimen, of that magnificent butterfly, Apatura Iris, commonly known as the 'Purple Emperor.'"

"Everybody in Brittany knows that," I said, casting across the sparkling water; "but just because you happen to be the only man who ever captured a 'Purple Emperor' in Morbihan, it doesn't follow that you are an authority on sea-trout flies. Why do you say that a Breton sea-trout won't touch a tailed fly?"

"It's so," he replied.

"Why? There are plenty of May-flies about the stream."

"Let 'em fly!" snarled the Purple Emperor, "you won't see a trout touch 'em."

My arm was aching, but I grasped my split bamboo more firmly, and, half turning, waded out into the stream and began to whip the ripples at the head of the pool. A great green dragon-fly came drifting by on the summer breeze and hung a moment above the pool, glittering like an emerald.

"There's a chance! Where is your butterfly net?" I called across the stream.

"What for? That dragon-fly? I've got dozens—Anax Junius, Drury, characteristic, anal angle of posterior wings, in male, round; thorax marked with——"

"That will do," I said fiercely. "Can't I point out an insect in the air without this burst of erudition? Can you tell me, in simple everyday French, what this little fly is—this one, flitting over the eel grass here beside me? See, it has fallen on the water."

"Huh!" sneered the Purple Emperor, "that's a Linnobia annulus."

"What's that?" I demanded.

Before he could answer there came a heavy splash in the pool, and the fly disappeared.

"He! he! he!" tittered the Purple Emperor. "Didn't I tell you the fish knew their business? That was a sea-trout. I hope you don't get him."

He gathered up his butterfly net, collecting box, chloroform bottle, and cyanide jar. Then he rose, swung the box over his shoulder, stuffed the poison bottles into the pockets of his silver-buttoned velvet coat, and lighted his pipe. This latter operation was a demoralizing spectacle, for the Purple Emperor, like all Breton peasants, smoked one of those microscopical Breton pipes which requires ten minutes to find, ten minutes to fill, ten minutes to light, and ten seconds to finish. With true Breton stolidity he went through this solemn rite, blew three puffs of smoke into the air, scratched his pointed nose reflectively, and waddled away, calling back an ironical "Au revoir, and bad luck to all Yankees!"

I watched him out of sight, thinking sadly of the young girl whose life he made a hell upon earth—Lys Trevec, his niece. She never admitted it, but we all knew what the black-and-blue marks meant on her soft, round arm, and it made me sick to see the look of fear come into her eyes when the Purple Emperor waddled into the café of the Groix Inn.

It was commonly said that he half-starved her. This she denied. Marie Joseph and 'Fine Lelocard had seen him strike her the day after the Pardon of the Birds because she had liberated three bullfinches which he had limed the day before. I asked Lys if this were true, and she refused to speak to me for the rest of the week. There was nothing to do about it. If the Purple Emperor had not been avaricious, I should never have seen Lys at all, but he could not resist the thirty francs a week which I offered him; and Lys posed for me all day long, happy as a linnet in a pink thorn hedge. Nevertheless, the Purple Emperor hated me, and constantly threatened to send Lys back to her dreary flax-spinning. He was suspicious, too, and when he had gulped down the single glass of cider which proves fatal to the sobriety of most Bretons, he would pound the long, discoloured oaken table and roar curses on me, on Yves Terrec, and on the Red Admiral. We were the three objects in the world which he most hated: me, because I was a foreigner, and didn't care a rap for him and his butterflies; and the Red Admiral, because he was a rival entomologist.

He had other reasons for hating Terrec.

The Red Admiral, a little wizened wretch, with a badly adjusted glass eye and a passion for brandy, took his name from a butterfly which predominated in his collection. This butterfly, commonly known to amateurs as the "Red Admiral," and to entomologists as Vanessa Atalanta, had been the occasion of scandal among the entomologists of France and Brittany. For the Red Admiral had taken one of these common insects, dyed it a brilliant yellow by the aid of chemicals, and palmed it off on a credulous collector as a South African species, absolutely unique. The fifty francs which he gained by this rascality were, however, absorbed in a suit for damages brought by the outraged amateur a month later; and when he had sat in the Quimperlé jail for a month, he reappeared in the little village of St. Gildas soured, thirsty, and burning for revenge. Of course we named him the Red Admiral, and he accepted the name with suppressed fury.

The Purple Emperor, on the other hand, had gained his imperial title legitimately, for it was an undisputed fact that the only specimen of that beautiful butterfly, Apatura Iris, or the Purple Emperor, as it is called by amateurs—the only specimen that had ever been taken in Finistère or in Morbihan—was captured and brought home alive by Joseph Marie Gloanec, ever afterward to be known as the Purple Emperor.

When the capture of this rare butterfly became known the Red Admiral nearly went crazy. Every day for a week he trotted over to the Groix Inn, where the Purple Emperor lived with his niece, and brought his microscope to bear on the rare newly captured butterfly, in hopes of detecting a fraud. But this specimen was genuine, and he leered through his microscope in vain.

"No chemicals there, Admiral," grinned the Purple Emperor; and the Red Admiral chattered with rage.

To the scientific world of Brittany and France the capture of an Apatura Iris in Morbihan was of great importance. The Museum of Quimper offered to purchase the butterfly, but the Purple Emperor, though a hoarder of gold, was a monomaniac on butterflies, and he jeered at the Curator of the Museum. From all parts of Brittany and France letters of inquiry and congratulation poured in upon him. The French Academy of Sciences awarded him a prize, and the Paris Entomological Society made him an honorary member. Being a Breton peasant, and a more than commonly pig-headed one at that, these honours did not disturb his equanimity; but when the little hamlet of St. Gildas elected him mayor, and, as is the custom in Brittany under such circumstances, he left his thatched house to take up an official life in the little Groix Inn, his head became completely turned. To be mayor in a village of nearly one hundred and fifty people! It was an empire! So he became unbearable, drinking himself viciously drunk every night of his life, maltreating his niece, Lys Trevec, like the barbarous old wretch that he was, and driving the Red Admiral nearly frantic with his eternal harping on the capture of Apatura Iris. Of course he refused to tell where he had caught the butterfly. The Red Admiral stalked his footsteps, but in vain.

"He! he! he!" nagged the Purple Emperor, cuddling his chin over a glass of cider; "I saw you sneaking about the St. Gildas spinny yesterday morning. So you think you can find another Apatura Iris by running after me? It won't do, Admiral, it won't do, d'ye see?"

The Red Admiral turned yellow with mortification and envy, but the next day he actually took to his bed, for the Purple Emperor had brought home not a butterfly but a live chrysalis, which, if successfully hatched, would become a perfect specimen of the invaluable Apatura Iris. This was the last straw. The Red Admiral shut himself up in his little stone cottage, and for weeks now he had been invisible to everybody except 'Fine Lelocard who carried him a loaf of bread and a mullet or langouste every morning.

The withdrawal of the Red Admiral from the society of St. Gildas excited first the derision and finally the suspicion of the Purple Emperor. What deviltry could he be hatching? Was he experimenting with chemicals again, or was he engaged in some deeper plot, the object of which was to discredit the Purple Emperor? Roux, the postman, who carried the mail on foot once a day from Bannalec, a distance of fifteen miles each way, had brought several suspicious letters, bearing English stamps, to the Red Admiral, and the next day the Admiral had been observed at his window grinning up into the sky and rubbing his hands together. A night or two after this apparition the postman left two packages at the Groix Inn for a moment while he ran across the way to drink a glass of cider with me. The Purple Emperor, who was roaming about the café, snooping into everything that did not concern him, came upon the packages and examined the postmarks and addresses. One of the packages was square and heavy, and felt like a book. The other was also square, but very light, and felt like a pasteboard box. They were both addressed to the Red Admiral, and they bore English stamps.

When Roux, the postman, came back, the Purple Emperor tried to pump him, but the poor little postman knew nothing about the contents of the packages, and after he had taken them around the corner to the cottage of the Red Admiral the Purple Emperor ordered a glass of cider, and deliberately fuddled himself until Lys came in and tearfully supported him to his room. Here he became so abusive and brutal that Lys called to me, and I went and settled the trouble without wasting any words. This also the Purple Emperor remembered, and waited his chance to get even with me.

That had happened a week ago, and until to-day he had not deigned to speak to me.

Lys had posed for me all the week, and to-day being Saturday, and I lazy, we had decided to take a little relaxation, she to visit and gossip with her little black-eyed friend Yvette in the neighbouring hamlet of St. Julien, and I to try the appetites of the Breton trout with the contents of my American fly book.

I had thrashed the stream very conscientiously for three hours, but not a trout had risen to my cast, and I was piqued. I had begun to believe that there were no trout in the St. Gildas stream, and would probably have given up had I not seen the sea trout snap the little fly which the Purple Emperor had named so scientifically. That set me thinking. Probably the Purple Emperor was right, for he certainly was an expert in everything that crawled and wriggled in Brittany. So I matched, from my American fly book, the fly that the sea trout had snapped up, and withdrawing the cast of three, knotted a new leader to the silk and slipped a fly on the loop. It was a queer fly. It was one of those unnameable experiments which fascinate anglers in sporting stores and which generally prove utterly useless. Moreover, it was a tailed fly, but of course I easily remedied that with a stroke of my penknife. Then I was all ready, and I stepped out into the hurrying rapids and cast straight as an arrow to the spot where the sea trout had risen. Lightly as a plume the fly settled on the bosom of the pool; then came a startling splash, a gleam of silver, and the line tightened from the vibrating rod-tip to the shrieking reel. Almost instantly I checked the fish, and as he floundered for a moment, making the water boil along his glittering sides, I sprang to the bank again, for I saw that the fish was a heavy one and I should probably be in for a long run down the stream. The five-ounce rod swept in a splendid circle, quivering under the strain. "Oh, for a gaff-hook!" I cried aloud, for I was now firmly convinced that I had a salmon to deal with, and no sea trout at all.

Then as I stood, bringing every ounce to bear on the sulking fish, a lithe, slender girl came hurriedly along the opposite bank calling out to me by name.

"Why, Lys!" I said, glancing up for a second, "I thought you were at St. Julien with Yvette."

"Yvette has gone to Bannelec. I went home and found an awful fight going on at the Groix Inn, and I was so frightened that I came to tell you."

The fish dashed off at that moment, carrying all the line my reel held, and I was compelled to follow him at a jump. Lys, active and graceful as a young deer, in spite of her Pont-Aven sabots, followed along the opposite bank until the fish settled in a deep pool, shook the line savagely once or twice, and then relapsed into the sulks.

"Fight at the Groix Inn?" I called across the water. "What fight?"

"Not exactly fight," quavered Lys, "but the Red Admiral has come out of his house at last, and he and my uncle are drinking together and disputing about butterflies. I never saw my uncle so angry, and the Red Admiral is sneering and grinning. Oh, it is almost wicked to see such a face!"

"But Lys," I said, scarcely able to repress a smile, "your uncle and the Red Admiral are always quarrelling and drinking."

"I know—oh, dear me!—but this is different, Monsieur Darrel. The Red Admiral has grown old and fierce since he shut himself up three weeks ago, and—oh, dear! I never saw such a look in my uncle's eyes before. He seemed insane with fury. His eyes—I can't speak of it—and then Terrec came in."

"Oh," I said more gravely, "that was unfortunate. What did the Red Admiral say to his son?"

Lys sat down on a rock among the ferns, and gave me a mutinous glance from her blue eyes.

Yves Terrec, loafer, poacher, and son of Louis Jean Terrec, otherwise the Red Admiral, had been kicked out by his father, and had also been forbidden the village by the Purple Emperor, in his majestic capacity of mayor. Twice the young ruffian had returned: once to rifle the bedroom of the Purple Emperor—an unsuccessful enterprise—and another time to rob his own father. He succeeded in the latter attempt, but was never caught, although he was frequently seen roving about the forests and moors with his gun. He openly menaced the Purple Emperor; vowed that he would marry Lys in spite of all the gendarmes in Quimperlé; and these same gendarmes he led many a long chase through brier-filled swamps and over miles of yellow gorse.

What he did to the Purple Emperor—what he intended to do—disquieted me but little; but I worried over his threat concerning Lys. During the last three months this had bothered me a great deal; for when Lys came to St. Gildas from the convent the first thing she captured was my heart. For a long time I had refused to believe that any tie of blood linked this dainty blue-eyed creature with the Purple Emperor. Although she dressed in the velvet-laced bodice and blue petticoat of Finistère, and wore the bewitching white coiffe of St. Gildas, it seemed like a pretty masquerade. To me she was as sweet and as gently bred as many a maiden of the noble Faubourg who danced with her cousins at a Louis XV fête champêtre. So when Lys said that Yves

Terrec had returned openly to St. Gildas, I felt that I had better be there also.

"What did Terrec say, Lys?" I asked, watching the line vibrating above the placid pool.

The wild rose colour crept into her cheeks. "Oh," she answered, with a little toss of her chin, "you know what he always says."

"That he will carry you away?"

"Yes."

"In spite of the Purple Emperor, the Red Admiral, and the gendarmes?"

"Yes."

"And what do you say, Lys?"

"I? Oh, nothing."

"Then let me say it for you."

Lys looked at her delicate pointed sabots, the sabots from Pont-Aven, made to order. They fitted her little foot. They were her only luxury.

"Will you let me answer for you, Lys?" I asked.

"You, Monsieur Darrel?"

"Yes. Will you let me give him his answer?"

"Mon Dieu, why should you concern yourself, Monsieur Darrel?"

The fish lay very quiet, but the rod in my hand trembled.

"Because I love you, Lys."

The wild rose colour in her cheeks deepened; she gave a gentle gasp, then hid her curly head in her hands.

"I love you, Lys."

"Do you know what you say?" she stammered.

"Yes, I love you."

She raised her sweet face and looked at me across the pool.

"I love you," she said, while the tears stood like stars in her eyes. "Shall I come over the brook to you?"

II.

That night Yves Terrec left the village of St. Gildas vowing vengeance against his father, who refused him shelter.

I can see him now, standing in the road, his bare legs rising like pillars of bronze from his straw-stuffed sabots, his short velvet jacket torn and soiled by exposure and dissipation, and his eyes, fierce, roving, bloodshot—while the Red Admiral squeaked curses on him, and hobbled away into his little stone cottage.

"I will not forget you!" cried Yves Terrec, and stretched out his hand toward his father with a terrible gesture. Then he whipped his gun to his cheek and took a short step forward, but I caught him by the throat before he could fire, and a second later we were rolling in the dust of the Bannalec road. I had to hit him a heavy blow behind the ear before he would let go, and then, rising and shaking myself, I dashed his muzzle-loading fowling piece to bits against a wall, and threw his knife into the river. The Purple Emperor was looking on with a queer light in his eyes. It was plain that he was sorry Terrec had not choked me to death.

"He would have killed his father," I said, as I passed him, going toward the Groix Inn.

"That's his business," snarled the Purple Emperor. There was a deadly light in his eyes. For a moment I thought he was going to attack me; but he was merely viciously drunk, so I shoved him out of my way and went to bed, tired and disgusted.

The worst of it was I couldn't sleep, for I feared that the Purple Emperor might begin to abuse Lys. I lay restlessly tossing among the sheets until I could stay there no longer. I did not dress entirely; I merely slipped on a pair of chaussons and sabots, a pair of knickerbockers, a jersey, and a cap. Then, loosely tying a handkerchief about my throat, I went down the worm-eaten stairs and out into the moonlit road. There was a candle flaring in the Purple Emperor's window, but I could not see him.

"He's probably dead drunk," I thought, and looked up at the window where, three years before, I had first seen Lys.

"Asleep, thank Heaven!" I muttered, and wandered out along the road. Passing the small cottage of the Red Admiral, I saw that it was dark, but the door was open. I stepped inside the hedge to shut it, thinking, in case Yves Terrec should be roving about, his father would lose whatever he had left.

Then, after fastening the door with a stone, I wandered on through the dazzling Breton moonlight. A nightingale was singing in a willow swamp below, and from the edge of the mere, among the tall swamp grasses, myriads of frogs chanted a bass chorus.

When I returned, the eastern sky was beginning to lighten, and across the meadows on the cliffs, outlined against the paling horizon, I saw a seaweed gatherer going to his work among the curling breakers on the coast. His long rake was balanced on his shoulder, and the sea wind carried his song across the meadows to me:

> St. Gildas!
> St. Gildas!
> Pray for us,
> Shelter us,
> Us who toil in the sea.

Passing the shrine at the entrance of the village, I took off my cap and knelt in prayer to Our Lady of Faöuet; and if I neglected myself in that prayer, surely I believed Our Lady of Faöuet would be kinder to Lys. It is said that the shrine casts white shadows. I looked, but saw only the moonlight. Then very peacefully I went to bed again, and was only awakened by the clank of sabres and the trample of horses in the road below my window.

"Good gracious!" I thought, "it must be eleven o'clock, for there are the gendarmes from Quimperlé."

I looked at my watch; it was only half-past eight, and as the gendarmes made their rounds every Thursday at eleven, I wondered what had brought them out so early to St. Gildas.

"Of course," I grumbled, rubbing my eyes, "they are after Terrec," and I jumped into my limited bath.

Before I was completely dressed I heard a timid knock, and opening my door, razor in hand, stood astonished and silent. Lys, her blue eyes wide with terror, leaned on the threshold.

"My darling!" I cried, "what on earth is the matter?" But she only clung to me, panting like a wounded sea gull. At last, when I drew her into the room and raised her face to mine, she spoke in a heart-breaking voice:

"Oh, Dick! they are going to arrest you, but I will die before I believe one word of what they say. No, don't ask me," and she began to sob desperately.

When I found that something really serious was the matter, I flung on my coat and cap, and, slipping one arm about her waist, went down the stairs and out into the road. Four gendarmes sat on their horses in front of the café door; beyond them, the entire population of St. Gildas gaped, ten deep.

"Hello, Durand!" I said to the brigadier, "what the devil is this I hear about arresting me?"

"It's true, mon ami," replied Durand with sepulchral sympathy. I

looked him over from the tip of his spurred boots to his sulphur-yellow
sabre belt, then upward, button by button, to his disconcerted face.

"What for?" I said scornfully. "Don't try any cheap sleuth work on
me! Speak up, man, what's the trouble?"

The Purple Emperor, who sat in the doorway staring at me, started
to speak, but thought better of it and got up and went into the house.
The gendarmes rolled their eyes mysteriously and looked wise.

"Come, Durand," I said impatiently, "what's the charge?"

"Murder," he said in a faint voice.

"What!" I cried incredulously. "Nonsense! Do I look like a murderer? Get off your horse, you stupid, and tell me who's murdered."

Durand got down, looking very silly, and came up to me, offering his
hand with a propitiatory grin.

"It was the Purple Emperor who denounced you! See, they found
your handkerchief at his door——"

"Whose door, for Heaven's sake?" I cried.

"Why, the Red Admiral's!"

"The Red Admiral? What has he done?"

"Nothing—he's only been murdered."

I could scarcely believe my senses, although they took me over to the
little stone cottage and pointed out the blood-spattered room. But the
horror of the thing was that the corpse of the murdered man had disappeared, and there only remained a nauseating lake of blood on the
stone floor, in the centre of which lay a human hand. There was no
doubt as to whom the hand belonged, for everybody who had ever seen
the Red Admiral knew that the shrivelled bit of flesh which lay in the
thickening blood was the hand of the Red Admiral. To me it looked like
the severed claw of some gigantic bird.

"Well," I said, "there's been murder committed. Why don't you do
something?"

"What?" asked Durand.

"I don't know. Send for the Commissaire."

"He's at Quimperlé. I telegraphed."

"Then send for a doctor, and find out how long this blood has been
coagulating."

"The chemist from Quimperlé is here; he's a doctor."

"What does he say?"

"He says that he doesn't know."

"And who are you going to arrest?" I inquired, turning away from the
spectacle on the floor.

"I don't know," said the brigadier solemnly; "you are denounced by the Purple Emperor, because he found your handkerchief at the door when he went out this morning."

"Just like a pig-headed Breton!" I exclaimed, thoroughly angry. "Did he not mention Yves Terrec?"

"No."

"Of course not," I said. "He overlooked the fact that Terrec tried to shoot his father last night, and that I took away his gun. All that counts for nothing when he finds my handkerchief at the murdered man's door."

"Come into the café," said Durand, much disturbed, "we can talk it over, there. Of course, Monsieur Darrel, I have never had the faintest idea that you were the murderer!"

The four gendarmes and I walked across the road to the Groix Inn and entered the café. It was crowded with Britons, smoking, drinking, and jabbering in half a dozen dialects, all equally unsatisfactory to a civilized ear; and I pushed through the crowd to where little Max Fortin, the chemist of Quimperlé, stood smoking a vile cigar.

"This is a bad business," he said, shaking hands and offering me the mate to his cigar, which I politely declined.

"Now, Monsieur Fortin," I said, "it appears that the Purple Emperor found my handkerchief near the murdered man's door this morning, and so he concludes"—here I glared at the Purple Emperor—"that I am the assassin. I will now ask him a question," and turning on him suddenly, I shouted, "What were you doing at the Red Admiral's door?"

The Purple Emperor started and turned pale, and I pointed at him triumphantly.

"See what a sudden question will do. Look how embarrassed he is, and yet I do not charge him with murder; and I tell you, gentlemen, that man there knows as well as I do who was the murderer of the Red Admiral!"

"I don't!" bawled the Purple Emperor.

"You do," I said. "It was Yves Terrec."

"I don't believe it," he said obstinately, dropping his voice.

"Of course not, being pig-headed."

"I am not pig-headed," he roared again, "but I am mayor of St. Gildas, and I do not believe that Yves Terrec killed his father."

"You saw him try to kill him last night?"

The mayor grunted.

"And you saw what I did."

He grunted again.

"And," I went on, "you heard Yves Terrec threaten to kill his father.

You heard him curse the Red Admiral and swear to kill him. Now the father is murdered and his body is gone."

"And your handkerchief?" sneered the Purple Emperor.

"I dropped it, of course."

"And the seaweed gatherer who saw you last night lurking about the Red Admiral's cottage," grinned the Purple Emperor.

I was startled at the man's malice.

"That will do," I said. "It is perfectly true that I was walking on the Bannalec road last night, and that I stopped to close the Red Admiral's door, which was ajar, although his light was not burning. After that I went up the road to the Dinez Woods, and then walked over by St. Julien, whence I saw the seaweed gatherer on the cliffs. He was near enough for me to hear what he sang. What of that?"

"What did you do then?"

"Then I stopped at the shrine and said a prayer, and then I went to bed and slept until Brigadier Durand's gendarmes awoke me with their clatter."

"Now, Monsieur Darrel," said the Purple Emperor, lifting a fat finger and shooting a wicked glance at me, "Now, Monsieur Darrel, which did you wear last night on your midnight stroll—sabots or shoes?"

I thought a moment. "Shoes—no, sabots. I just slipped on my chaussons and went out in my sabots."

"Which was it, shoes or sabots?" snarled the Purple Emperor.

"Sabots, you fool."

"Are these your sabots?" he asked, lifting up a wooden shoe with my initials cut on the instep.

"Yes," I replied.

"Then how did this blood come on the other one?" he shouted, and held up a sabot, the mate to the first, on which a drop of blood had spattered.

"I haven't the least idea," I said calmly; but my heart was beating very fast and I was furiously angry.

"You blockhead!" I said, controlling my rage, "I'll make you pay for this when they catch Yves Terrec and convict him. Brigadier Durand, do your duty if you think I am under suspicion. Arrest me, but grant me one favour. Put me in the Red Admiral's cottage, and I'll see whether I can't find some clew that you have overlooked. Of course, I won't disturb anything until the Commissaire arrives. Bah! You all make me very ill."

"He's hardened," observed the Purple Emperor, wagging his head.

"What motive had I to kill the Red Admiral?" I asked them all scornfully. And they all cried:

"None! Yves Terrec is the man!"

Passing out of the door I swung around and shook my finger at the Purple Emperor.

"Oh, I'll make you dance for this, my friend," I said; and I followed Brigadier Durand across the street to the cottage of the murdered man.

III.

They took me at my word and placed a gendarme with a bared sabre at the gateway by the hedge.

"Give me your parole," said poor Durand, "and I will let you go where you wish." But I refused, and began prowling about the cottage looking for clews. I found lots of things that some people would have considered most important, such as ashes from the Red Admiral's pipe, footprints in a dusty vegetable bin, bottles smelling of Pouldu cider, and dust—oh, lots of dust!—but I was not an expert, only a stupid, everyday amateur; so I defaced the footprints with my thick shooting boots, and I declined to examine the pipe ashes through a microscope, although the Red Admiral's microscope stood on the table close at hand.

At last I found what I had been looking for, some long wisps of straw, curiously depressed and flattened in the middle, and I was certain I had found the evidence that would settle Yves Terrec for the rest of his life. It was plain as the nose on your face. The straws were sabot straws, flattened where the foot had pressed them, and sticking straight out where they projected beyond the sabot. Now nobody in St. Gildas used straw in sabots except a fisherman who lived near St. Julien, and the straw in his sabots was ordinary yellow wheat straw! This straw, or rather these straws, were from the stalks of the red wheat which only grows inland, and which, everybody in St. Gildas knew, Yves Terrec wore in his sabots. I was perfectly satisfied; and when, three hours later, a hoarse shouting from the Bannalec Road brought me to the window, I was not surprised to see Yves Terrec, bloody, dishevelled, hatless, with his strong arms bound behind him, walking with bent head between two mounted gendarmes. The crowd around him swelled every minute, crying: "Parricide! parricide! Death to the murderer!" As he passed my window

I saw great clots of mud on his dusty sabots, from the heels of which projected wisps of red wheat straw. Then I walked back into the Red Admiral's study, determined to find what the microscope would show on the wheat straws. I examined each one very carefully, and then, my eyes aching, I rested my chin on my hand and leaned back in the chair. I had not been as fortunate as some detectives, for there was no evidence that the straws had ever been used in a sabot at all. Furthermore, directly across the hallway stood a carved Breton chest, and now I noticed for the first time that, from beneath the closed lid, dozens of similar red wheat straws projected, bent exactly as mine were bent by the weight of the lid.

I yawned in disgust. It was apparent that I was not cut out for a detective, and I bitterly pondered over the difference between clews in real life and clews in a detective story. After a while I rose, walked over to the chest and opened the lid. The interior was wadded with the red wheat straws, and on this wadding lay two curious glass jars, two or three small vials, several empty bottles labelled chloroform, a collecting jar of cyanide of potassium, and a book. In a farther corner of the chest were some letters bearing English stamps, and also the torn coverings of two parcels, all from England, and all directed to the Red Admiral under his proper name of "Sieur Louis Jean Terrec, St. Gildas, par Moëlan, Finistère."

All these traps I carried over to the desk, shut the lid of the chest, and sat down to read the letters. They were written in commercial French, evidently by an Englishman.

Freely translated, the contents of the first letter were as follows:

"LONDON, *June 12, 1894.*

DEAR MONSIEUR *(sic)*:
Your kind favour of the 19th inst. received and contents noted. The latest work on the Lepidoptera of England is Blowzer's How to catch British Butterflies, with notes and tables, and an introduction by Sir Thomas Sniffer. The price of this work (in one volume, calf) is £5 or 125 francs of French money. A post-office order will receive our prompt attention. We beg to remain,

Yours, etc.,
FRADLEY & TOOMER,
470 Regent Square, London, S. W.

The next letter was even less interesting. It merely stated that the money had been received and the book would be forwarded. The third engaged my attention, and I shall quote it, the translation being a free one:

Dear Sir:

Your letter of the 1st of July was duly received, and we at once referred it to Mr. Fradley himself. Mr. Fradley being much interested in your question, sent your letter to Professor Schweineri, of the Berlin Entomological Society, whose note Blowzer refers to on page 630, in his How to catch British Butterflies. We have just received an answer from Professor Schweineri, which we translate into French—(see inclosed slip). Professor Schweineri begs to present to you two jars of cythyl, prepared under his own supervision. We forward the same to you. Trusting that you will find everything satisfactory, we remain,

Yours sincerely,
Fradley & Toomer.

The inclosed slip read as follows:

Messrs. Fradley & Toomer,
Gentlemen:

Cythaline, a complex hydrocarbon, was first used by Professor Schnoot, of Antwerp, a year ago. I discovered an analogous formula about the same time and named it cythyl. I have used it with great success everywhere. It is as certain as a magnet. I beg to present you three small jars, and would be pleased to have you forward two of them to your correspondent in St. Gildas with my compliments. Blowzer's quotation of me, on page 630 of his glorious work, How to catch British Butterflies, is correct.

Yours, etc.,
Heinrich Schweineri,
P. H. D., D. D., D. S., M. S.

When I had finished this letter I folded it up and put it into my pocket with the others. Then I opened Blowzer's valuable work, How to catch British Butterflies, and turned to page 630.

Now, although the Red Admiral could only have acquired the book very recently, and although all the other pages were perfectly clean, this particular page was thumbed black, and heavy pencil marks inclosed a paragraph at the bottom of the page. This is the paragraph:

Professor Schweineri says: 'Of the two old methods used by collectors for the capture of the swift-winged, high-flying Apatura Iris, or Purple Emperor, the first, which was using a long-handled net, proved successful once in a thousand times; and the second, the placing of bait upon the ground, such as decayed meat, dead cats, rats, etc., was not only disagreeable, even for an enthusiastic collector, but also very uncertain. Once in five hundred times would the splendid butterfly leave the tops of his favourite oak trees to circle about the fetid bait offered. I have found cythyl a perfectly sure bait to draw this beautiful butterfly to the ground, where it can be easily captured. An ounce of cythyl placed in a yellow saucer under an oak tree, will draw to it every Apatura Iris within a radius of twenty miles. So, if any collector who possesses a little cythyl, even though it be in a sealed bottle in his pocket—if such a collector does not find a single Apatura Iris fluttering close about him within an hour, let him be satisfied that the Apatura Iris does not inhabit his country.'

When I had finished reading this note I sat for a long while thinking hard. Then I examined the two jars. They were labelled "*Cythyl.*" One was full, the other *nearly full*. "The rest must be on the corpse of the Red Admiral," I thought, "no matter if it is in a corked bottle——"

I took all the things back to the chest, laid them carefully on the straw, and closed the lid. The gendarme sentinel at the gate saluted me respectfully as I crossed over to the Groix Inn. The Inn was surrounded by an excited crowd, and the hallway was choked with gendarmes and peasants. On every side they greeted me cordially, announcing that the real murderer was caught; but I pushed by them without a word and ran upstairs to find Lys. She opened her door when I knocked and threw both arms about my neck. I took her to my breast and kissed her. After a moment I asked her if she would obey me no matter what I commanded, and she said she would, with a proud humility that touched me.

"Then go at once to Yvette in St. Julien," I said. "Ask her to harness the dog-cart and drive you to the convent in Quimperlé. Wait for me there. Will you do this without questioning me, my darling?"

She raised her face to mine. "Kiss me," she said innocently; the next moment she had vanished.

I walked deliberately into the Purple Emperor's room and peered into the gauze-covered box which had held the chrysalis of Apatura Iris. It was as I expected. The chrysalis was empty and transparent, and a great crack ran down the middle of its back, but, on the netting inside the box, a magnificent butterfly slowly waved its burnished purple wings; for the chrysalis had given up its silent tenant, the butterfly symbol of immortality. Then a great fear fell upon me. I know now that it was the fear of the Black Priest, but neither then nor for years after did I know that the Black Priest had ever lived on earth. As I bent over the box I heard a confused murmur outside the house which ended in a furious shout of "Parricide!" and I heard the gendarmes ride away behind a wagon which rattled sharply on the flinty highway. I went to the window. In the wagon sat Yves Terrec, bound and wild-eyed, two gendarmes at either side of him, and all around the wagon rode mounted gendarmes whose bared sabres scarcely kept the crowd away.

"Parricide!" they howled. "Let him die!"

I stepped back and opened the gauze-covered box. Very gently but firmly I took the splendid butterfly by its closed fore wings and lifted it unharmed between my thumb and forefinger. Then, holding it concealed behind my back, I went down into the café.

Of all the crowd that had filled it, shouting for the death of Yves Terrec, only three persons remained seated in front of the huge empty fireplace. They were the Brigadier Durand, Max Fortin, the chemist of Quimperlé, and the Purple Emperor. The latter looked abashed when I entered, but I paid no attention to him and walked straight to the chemist.

"Monsieur Fortin," I said, "do you know much about hydrocarbons?"

"They are my specialty," he said astonished.

"Have you ever heard of such a thing as cythyl?"

"Schweineri's cythyl? Oh, yes! We use it in perfumery."

"Good!" I said. "Has it an odour?"

"No—and, yes. One is always aware of its presence, but really nobody can affirm it has an odour. It is curious," he continued, looking at me, "it is very curious you should have asked me that, for all day I have been imagining I detected the presence of cythyl."

"Do you imagine so now?" I asked.

"Yes, more than ever."

I sprang to the front door and tossed out the butterfly. The splendid creature beat the air for a moment, flitted uncertainly hither and thither, and then, to my astonishment, sailed majestically back into the café and alighted on the hearthstone. For a moment I was nonplussed, but when my eyes rested on the Purple Emperor I comprehended in a flash.

"Lift that hearthstone!" I cried to the Brigadier Durand; "pry it up with your scabbard!"

The Purple Emperor suddenly fell forward in his chair, his face ghastly white, his jaw loose with terror.

"What is cythyl?" I shouted, seizing him by the arm; but he plunged heavily from his chair, face downward on the floor, and at the same moment a cry from the chemist made me turn. There stood the Brigadier Durand, one hand supporting the hearthstone, one hand raised in horror. There stood Max Fortin, the chemist, rigid with excitement, and below, in the hollow bed where the hearthstone had rested, lay a crushed mass of bleeding human flesh, from the midst of which stared a cheap glass eye. I seized the Purple Emperor and dragged him to his feet.

"Look!" I cried; "look at your old friend, the Red Admiral!" but he only smiled in a vacant way, and rolled his head muttering; "Bait for butterflies! Cythyl! Oh, no, no, no! You can't do it, Admiral, d'ye see. I alone own the Purple Emperor! I alone am the Purple Emperor!"

And the same carriage that bore me to Quimperlé to claim my bride, carried him to Quimper, gagged and bound, a foaming, howling lunatic.

*   *   *

This, then, is the story of the Purple Emperor. I might tell you a pleasanter story if I chose; but concerning the fish that I had hold of, whether it was a salmon, a grilse, or a sea trout, I may not say, because I have promised Lys, and she has promised me, that no power on earth shall wring from our lips the mortifying confession that the fish escaped.

Jacques Futrelle

(1875–1912)

JACQUES FUTRELLE was born in Georgia, but he spent most of his working life as a newspaperman in Boston. His relatively short life ended when he was returning from Europe on the Titanic. He pushed his wife and child onto a life raft and went down with the ship.

In 1905, he created the most important detective character in American literature between the time of Poe's C. Auguste Dupin (1841) and Melville Davisson Post's Uncle Abner (1918). Professor S. F. X. Van Dusen, known as "The Thinking Machine," first appeared in "The Problem of Cell 13," in which he escapes from a locked and guarded jail cell. His cases are filled with bizarre and seemingly impossible events: an automobile which disappears from a road watched at both ends, a crystal ball which correctly prophesies a death, the total disappearance of a house, and so on. Some of the Thinking Machine stories were collected in *The Thinking Machine* (1907) and *The Thinking Machine on the Case* (1908), and others appeared in two Dover anthologies, collected by E. F. Bleiler: *Best "Thinking Machine" Detective Stories* and *Great Cases of the Thinking Machine* (both out of print). "The Tragedy of the Life Raft," however, has never appeared in a Futrelle collection. It is one of four Thinking Machine stories Futrelle left behind when he traveled to Europe. That it has to do with a shipwreck and even uses the word "titanic" must be put down to coincidence.

The Tragedy of the Life Raft

Twas a shabby picture altogether—old Peter Ordway in his office; the man shriveled, bent, cadaverous, aquiline of feature, with skin like parchment, and cunning, avaricious eyes; the room gaunt and curtainless, with smoke-grimed windows, dusty, cheerless walls, and threadbare carpet, worn through here and there to the rough flooring beneath. Peter Ordway sat in a swivel chair in front of an ancient rolltop desk. Opposite, at a typewriter upon a table of early vintage, was his secretary—one Walpole, almost a replica in middle age of his employer, seedy and servile, with lips curled sneeringly as a dog's.

Familiarly in the financial district, Peter Ordway was "The Usurer," a title which was at once a compliment to his merciless business sagacity and an expression of contempt for his methods. He was the money lender of the Street, holding in cash millions which no one dared to estimate. In the last big panic the richest man in America, the great John Morton in person, had spent hours in the shabby office, begging for the loan of the few millions in currency necessary to check the market. Peter Ordway didn't fail to take full advantage of his pressing need. Mr. Morton got the millions on collateral worth five times the sum borrowed, but Peter Ordway fixed the rate of interest, a staggering load.

Now we have the old man at the beginning of a day's work. After glancing through two or three letters which lay open on his desk, he picked up at last a white card, across the face of which was scribbled in pencil three words only:

One million dollars!

Ordinarily it was a phrase to bring a smile to his withered lips, a

231

morsel to roll under his wicked old tongue; but now he stared at it without comprehension. Finally he turned to his secretary, Walpole.

"What is this?" he demanded querulously, in his thin, rasping voice.

"I don't know, sir," was the reply, "I found it in the morning's mail, sir, addressed to you."

Peter Ordway tore the card across, and dropped it into the battered waste-basket beside him, after which he settled down to the ever-congenial occupation of making money.

On the following morning the card appeared again, with only three words, as before:

One million dollars!

Abruptly the aged millionaire wheeled around to face Walpole, who sat regarding him oddly.

"It came the same way, sir," the seedy little secretary explained hastily, "in a blank envelope. I saved the envelope, sir, if you would like to see it."

"Tear it up!" Peter Ordway directed sharply.

Reduced to fragments, the envelope found its way into the waste-basket. For many minutes Peter Ordway sat with dull, lusterless eyes, gazing through the window into the void of a leaden sky. Slowly, as he looked, the sky became a lashing, mist-covered sea, a titanic chaos of water; and upon its troubled bosom rode a life raft to which three persons were clinging. Now the frail craft was lifted up, up to the dizzy height of a giant wave; now it shot down sickeningly into the hissing trough beyond; again, for minutes it seemed altogether lost in the far-plunging spume. Peter Ordway shuddered and closed his eyes.

On the third morning the card, grown suddenly ominous, appeared again:

One million dollars!

Peter Ordway came to his feet with an exclamation that was almost a snarl, turning, twisting the white slip nervously in his talonlike fingers. Astonished, Walpole half arose, his yellow teeth bared defensively, and his eyes fixed upon the millionaire.

"Telephone Blake's Agency," the old man commanded, "and tell them to send a detective here at once."

Came in answer to the summons a suave, smooth-faced, indolent-appearing young man, Fragson by name, who sat down after having regarded with grave suspicion the rickety chair to which he was invited. He waited inquiringly.

"Find the person—man or woman—who sent me that!"

Peter Ordway flung the card and the envelope in which it had come upon a leaf of his desk. Fragson picked them up and scrutinized them leisurely. Obviously the handwriting was that of a man, an uneducated man, he would have said. The postmark on the envelope was Back Bay; the time of mailing seven p. m. on the night before. Both envelope and card were of a texture which might be purchased in a thousand shops.

"*One million dollars!*" Fragson read. "What does it mean?"

"I don't know," the millionaire answered.

"What do you think it means?"

"Nor do I know that, unless—unless it's some crank, or—or blackmailer. I've received three of them—one each morning for three days."

Fragson placed the card inside the envelope with irritating deliberation, and thrust it into his pocket, after which he lifted his eyes quite casually to those of the secretary, Walpole. Walpole, who had been staring at the two men tensely, averted his shifty gaze, and busied himself at his desk.

"Any idea who sent them?" Fragson was addressing Peter Ordway, but his eyes lingered lazily upon Walpole.

"No." The word came emphatically, after an almost imperceptible instant of hesitation.

"Why"—and the detective turned to the millionaire curiously—"why do you think it might be blackmail? Has any one any knowledge of any act of yours that——"

Some swift change crossed the parchmentlike face of the old man. For an instant he was silent; then his avaricious eyes leaped into flame; his fingers closed convulsively on the arms of his chair.

"Blackmail may be attempted without reason," he stormed suddenly. "Those cards must have some meaning. Find the person who sent them."

Fragson arose thoughtfully, and drew on his gloves.

"And then?" he queried.

"That's all!" curtly. "Find him, and let me know who he is."

"Do I understand that you don't want me to go into his motives? You merely want to locate the man?"

"That understanding is correct—yes."

. . . a lashing, mist-covered sea; a titanic chaos of water, and upon its troubled bosom rode a life raft to which three persons were clinging. . . .

Walpole's crafty eyes followed his millionaire employer's every movement as he entered his office on the morning of the fourth day. There
was nervous restlessness in Peter Ordway's manner; the parchment face
seemed more withered; the pale lips were tightly shut. For an instant he
hesitated, as if vaguely fearing to begin on the morning's mail. But no
fourth card had come! Walpole heard and understood the long breath
of relief which followed upon realization of this fact.

Just before ten o'clock a telegram was brought in. Peter Ordway
opened it:

> One million dollars!

Three hours later at his favorite table in the modest restaurant where
he always went for luncheon, Peter Ordway picked up his napkin, and
a white card fluttered to the floor:

> One million dollars!

Shortly after two o'clock a messenger boy entered his office,
whistling, and laid an evelope on the desk before him:

> One million dollars!

Instinctively he had known what was within.

At eight o'clock that night, in the shabby apartments where he lived
with his one servant, he answered an insistent ringing of the telephone
bell.

"What do you want?" he demanded abruptly.

"One million dollars!" The words came slowly, distinctly.

"Who are you?"

"One million dollars!" faintly, as an echo.

Again Fragson was summoned, and was ushered into the cheerless
room where the old millionaire sat cringing with fear, his face reflect-
ing some deadly terror which seemed to be consuming him.
Incoherently he related the events of the day. Fragson listened without
comment, and went out.

On the following morning—Sunday—he returned to report. He
found his client propped upon a sofa, haggard and worn, with eyes
feverishly aglitter.

"Nothing doing," the detective began crisply. "It looked as if we had

a clew which would at least give us a description of the man, but——"
He shook his head.

"But that telegram—some one filed it?" Peter Ordway questioned
huskily. "The message the boy brought——"

"The telegram was inclosed in an envelope with the money necessary to send it, and shoved through the mail slot of a telegraph office in
Cambridge," the detective informed him explicitly. "That was Friday
night. It was telegraphed to you on Saturday morning. The card
brought by the boy was handed in at a messenger agency by some street
urchin, paid for, and delivered to you. The telephone call was from an
automatic station in Brookline. A thousand persons use it every day."

For the first time in many years, Peter Ordway failed to appear at his
office Monday morning. Instead, he sent a note to his secretary:

Bring all important mail to my apartments to-night at eight o'clock. On your
way uptown buy a good revolver with cartridges to fit.

Twice that day a physician—Doctor Anderson—was hurriedly summoned to Peter Ordway's side. First there had been merely a fainting
spell; later in the afternoon came complete collapse. Doctor Anderson
diagnosed the case tersely.

"Nerves," he said. "Overwork, and no recreation."

"But, doctor, I have no time for recreation!" the old millionaire
whined. "My business——"

"Time!" Doctor Anderson growled indignantly. "You're seventy years
old, and you're worth fifty million dollars. The thing you must have if
you want to spend any of that money is an ocean trip—a good, long
ocean trip—around the world, if you like."

"No, no, no!" It was almost a shriek. Peter Ordway's evil countenance, already pallid, became ashen; abject terror was upon him. . . . a
lashing, mist-covered sea; a titanic chaos of water, and upon its troubled bosom rode a life raft to which three persons were clinging. . . .

"No, no, no!" he mumbled, his talon fingers clutching the physician's hand convulsively. "I'm afraid, afraid!"

The slender thread which held sordid soul to withered body was sev-
ered that night by a well-aimed bullet. Promptly at eight o'clock
Walpole had arrived, and gone straight to the room where Peter
Ordway sat propped up on a sofa. Nearly an hour later the old mil-
lionaire's one servant, Mrs. Robinson, answered the doorbell, admitting
Mr. Franklin Pingree, a well-known financier. He had barely stepped

into the hallway when there came a reverberating crash as of a revolver shot from the room where Peter Ordway and his secretary were.

Together Mr. Pingree and Mrs. Robinson ran to the door. Still propped upon the couch, Peter Ordway sat—dead. A bullet had penetrated his heart. His head was thrown back, his mouth was open, and his right hand dangled at his side. Leaning over the body was his secretary, Walpole. In one hand he held a revolver, still smoking. He didn't turn as they entered, but stood staring down upon the dead man blankly. Mr. Pingree disarmed him from behind.

Hereto I append a partial transcript of a statement made by Frederick Walpole immediately following his arrest on the charge of murdering his millionaire employer. This statement he repeated in substance at the trial:

I am forty-eight years old. I had been in Mr. Ordway's employ for twenty-two years. My salary was eight dollars a week. . . . I went to his apartments on the night of the murder in answer to a note. (Note produced.) I bought the revolver and gave it to him. He loaded it and thrust it under the covering beside him on the sofa. . . . He dictated four letters and was starting on another. I heard the door open behind me. I thought it was Mrs. Robinson, as I had not heard the front-door bell ring.

Mr. Ordway stopped dictating, and I looked at him. He was staring toward the door. He seemed to be frightened. I looked around. A man had come in. He seemed very old. He had a flowing white beard and long white hair. His face was ruddy, like a seaman's.

"Who are you?" Mr. Ordway asked.

"You know me all right," said the man. "We were together long enough on that craft." (Or "raft," prisoner was not positive.)

"I never saw you before," said Mr. Ordway. "I don't know what you mean."

"I have come for the reward," said the man.

"What reward?" Mr. Ordway asked.

"One million dollars!" said the man.

Nothing else was said. Mr. Ordway drew his revolver and fired. The other man must have fired at the same instant, for Mr. Ordway fell back dead. The man disappeared. I ran to Mr. Ordway and picked up the revolver. He had dropped it. Mr. Pingree and Mrs. Robinson came in. . . .

Reading of Peter Ordway's will disclosed the fact that he had bequeathed unconditionally the sum of one million dollars to his secretary, Walpole, for "loyal services." Despite Walpole's denial of any knowledge of this bequest, he was immediately placed under arrest. At his trial, the facts appeared as I have related them. The district attorney summed up briefly. The motive was obvious—Walpole's desire to get possession of one million dollars in cash. Mr. Pingree and Mrs. Robinson, entering the room directly after the shot had been fired, had met no one coming out, as they would have had there been another man—there was no other egress. Also, they had heard *only one shot*— and that shot had found Peter Ordway's heart. Also, the bullet which killed Peter Ordway had been positively identified by experts as of the same make and same caliber as those others in the revolver Walpole had bought. The jury was out twenty minutes. The verdict was guilty. Walpole was sentenced to death.

It was not until then that "The Thinking Machine"—otherwise Professor Augustus S. F. X. Van Dusen, Ph. D., F. R. S., M. D., LL. D., et cetera, et cetera, logician, analyst, master mind in the sciences— turned his crabbed genius upon the problem.

Five days before the date set for Walpole's execution, Hutchinson Hatch, newspaper reporter, intruded himself into The Thinking Machine's laboratory, bringing with him a small roll of newspapers. Incongruously enough, they were old friends, these two—on one hand, the man of science, absorbed in that profession of which he was already the master, small, almost grotesque in appearance, and living the life of a recluse; on the other, a young man of the world, worldly, enthusiastic, capable, indefatigable.

So it came about The Thinking Machine curled himself in a great chair, and sat for nearly two hours partially submerged in newspaper accounts of the murder and of the trial. The last paper finished, he dropped his enormous head back against his chair, turned his petulant, squinting eyes upward, and sat for minute after minute staring into nothingness.

"Why," he queried, at last, "do you think he is innocent?"

"I don't know that I do think it," Hatch replied. "It is simply that attention has been attracted to Walpole's story again because of a letter the governor received. Here is a copy of it."

The Thinking Machine read it:

You are about to allow the execution of an innocent man. Walpole's story on the witness stand was true. He didn't kill Peter Ordway. I killed him for a good and sufficient reason.

"Of course," the reporter explained, "the letter wasn't signed. However, three handwriting experts say it was written by the same hand that wrote the 'One million dollar' slips. Incidentally the prosecution made no attempt to connect Walpole's handwriting with those slips. They couldn't have done it, and it would have weakened their case."

"And what," inquired the diminutive scientist, "does the governor propose doing?"

"Nothing," was the reply. "To him it is merely one of a thousand crank letters."

"He knows the opinions of the experts?"

"He does. I told him."

"The governor," remarked The Thinking Machine gratuitously, "is a fool." Then: "It is sometimes interesting to assume the truth of the improbable. Suppose we assume Walpole's story to be true, assuming at the same time that this letter is true—what have we?"

Tiny, cobwebby lines of thought furrowed the domelike brow as Hatch watched; the slender fingers were brought precisely tip to tip; the pale-blue eyes narrowed still more.

"If," Hatch pointed out, "Walpole's attorney had been able to find a bullet mark anywhere in that room, or a single isolated drop of blood, it would have proven that Peter Ordway did fire as Walpole says he did, and——"

"If Walpole's story is true," The Thinking Machine went on serenely, heedless of the interruption, "we must believe that a man—say, Mr. X—entered a private apartment without ringing. Very well. Either the door was unlocked, he entered by a window, or he had a false key. We must believe that two shots were fired simultaneously, sounding as one. We must believe that Mr. X was either wounded or the bullet mark has been overlooked; we must believe Mr. X went out by the one door at the same instant Mr. Pingree and Mrs. Robinson entered. We must believe they either did not see him or they lied."

"That's what convicted Walpole," Hatch declared. "Of course, it's impossible——"

"Nothing is impossible, Mr. Hatch," stormed The Thinking Machine suddenly. "Don't say that. It annoys me exceedingly."

Hatch shrugged his shoulders, and was silent. Again minute after minute passed, and the scientist sat motionless, staring now at a plan of Peter Ordway's apartment he had found in a newspaper, the while his keen brain dissected the known facts.

"After all," he announced, at last, "there's only one vital question: Why Peter Ordway's deadly fear of water?"

The reporter shook his head blankly. He was never surprised any more at The Thinking Machine's manner of approaching a problem. Never by any chance did he take hold of it as any one else would have.

"Some personal eccentricity, perhaps," Hatch suggested hopefully. "Some people are afraid of cats, others of ——"

"Go to Peter Ordway's place," The Thinking Machine interrupted tartly, "and find if it has been necessary to replace a broken window-pane anywhere in the building since Mr. Ordway's death."

"You mean, perhaps, that Mr. X, as you call him, may have escaped——" the newspaper man began.

"Also find out if there was a curtain hanging over or near the door where Mr. X must have gone out."

"Right!"

"We'll assume that the room where Ordway died has been gone over inch by inch in the search for a stray shot," the scientist continued. "Let's go farther. If Ordway fired, it was probably toward the door where Mr. X entered. If Mr. X left the door open behind him, the shot may have gone into the private hall beyond, and may be buried in the door immediately opposite." He indicated on the plan as he talked. "This second door opens into a rear hall. If both doors chanced to be open——"

Hatch came to his feet with blazing eyes. He understood. It was a possibility no one had considered. Ordway's shot, if he had fired one, might have lodged a hundred feet away.

"Then, if we find a bullet mark——" he questioned tensely.

"Walpole will not go to the electric chair."

"And if we don't?"

"We will look farther," said The Thinking Machine. "We will look for a wounded man of perhaps sixty years, who is now, or has been, a sailor; who is either clean-shaven or else has a close-cropped beard, probably dyed—a man who may have a false key to the Ordway apartment—the man who wrote this note to the governor."

"You believe, then," Hatch demanded, "that Walpole is innocent?"

"I believe nothing of the sort," snapped the scientist. "He's probably guilty. If we find no bullet mark, I'm merely saying what sort of man we must look for."

"But—but how do you know so much about him—what he looks like?" asked the reporter, in bewilderment.

"How do I know?" repeated the crabbed little scientist. "How do I know that two and two make four, not *sometimes*, but *all* the time? By adding the units together. Logic, that's all—logic, logic!"

While Hatch was scrutinizing the shabby walls of the old building where Peter Ordway had lived his miserly life, The Thinking Machine called on Doctor Anderson, who had been Peter Ordway's physician for a score of years. Doctor Anderson couldn't explain the old millionaire's aversion to water, but perhaps if the scientist went farther back in his inquiries there was an old man, John Page, still living who had been Ordway's classmate in school. Doctor Anderson knew of him because he had once treated him at Peter Ordway's request. So The Thinking Machine came to discuss this curious trait of character with John Page. What the scientist learned didn't appear, but whatever it was it sent him to the public library, where he spent several hours pulling over the files of old newspapers.

All his enthusiasm gone, Hatch returned to report.

"Nothing," he said. "No trace of a bullet."

"Any windowpanes changed or broken?"

"Not one."

"There were curtains, of course, over the door through which Mr. X entered Ordway's room." It was not a question.

"There were. They're there yet."

"In that case," and The Thinking Machine raised his squinting eyes to the ceiling, "our sailorman was wounded."

"There is a sailorman, then?" Hatch questioned eagerly.

"I'm sure I don't know," was the astonishing reply. "If there is, he answers generally the description I gave. His name is Ben Holderby. His age is not sixty; it's fifty-eight."

The newspaper man took a long breath of amazement. Surely here was the logical faculty lifted to the nth power! The Thinking Machine was describing, naming, and giving the age of a man whose existence he didn't even venture to assert—a man who never had been in existence so far as the reporter knew! Hatch fanned himself weakly with his hat.

"Odd situation, isn't it?" asked The Thinking Machine. "It only proves that logic is inexorable—that it can only fail when the units fail; and no unit has failed yet. Meantime, I shall leave you to find Holderby. Begin with the sailors' lodging houses, and don't scare him off. I can add nothing to the description except that he is probably using another name."

Followed a feverish two days for Hatch—a hurried, nightmarish effort to find a man who might or might not exist, in order to prevent a legal murder. With half a dozen other clever men from his office, he finally achieved the impossible.

"I've found him!" he announced triumphantly over the telephone to The Thinking Machine. "He's stopping at Werner's, in the North End, under the name of Benjamin Goode. He is clean-shaven, his hair and brows are dyed black, and he is wounded in the left arm."

"Thanks," said The Thinking Machine simply. "Bring Detective Mallory, of the bureau of criminal investigation, and come here to-morrow at noon prepared to spend the day. You might go by and inform the governor, if you like, that Walpole will not be electrocuted Friday."

Detective Mallory came at Hatch's request—came with a mouthful of questions into the laboratory, where The Thinking Machine was at work.

"What's it all about?" he demanded.

"Precisely at five o'clock this afternoon a man will try to murder me," the scientist informed him placidly, without lifting his eyes. "I'd like to have you here to prevent it."

Mallory was much given to outbursts of amazement; he humored himself now:

"Who is the man? What's he going to try to kill you for? Why not arrest him now?"

"His name is Benjamin Holderby." The Thinking Machine answered the questions in order. "He'll try to kill me because I shall accuse him of murder. If he should be arrested now, he wouldn't talk. If I told you whom he murdered, you wouldn't believe it."

Detective Mallory stared without comprehension.

"If he isn't to try to kill you until five o'clock," he asked, "why send for me at noon?"

"Because he may know you, and if he watched and saw you enter he wouldn't come. At half past four you and Mr. Hatch will step into the adjoining room. When Holderby enters, he will face me. Come behind him, but don't lift a finger until he threatens me. If you have to shoot—kill! He'll be dangerous until he's dead."

It was just two minutes of five o'clock when the bell rang, and Martha ushered Benjamin Holderby into the laboratory. He was past middle age, powerful, with the deep-bronzed face and the keen eyes of the sea. His hair and brows were dyed—badly dyed; his left arm hung limply. He found The Thinking Machine alone.

"I got your letter, sir," he said respectfully. "If it's a yacht, I'm willing to ship as master; but I'm too old to do much——"

"Sit down, please," the little scientist invited courteously, dropping into a chair as he spoke. "There are one or two questions I should like to ask. First"—the petulant blue eyes were raised toward the ceiling; the slender fingers came together precisely, tip to tip—"first: Why did you kill Peter Ordway?"

Fell an instant's amazed silence. Benjamin Holderby's muscles flexed, the ruddy face was contorted suddenly with hideous anger, the sinewy right hand closed until great knots appeared in the tendons. Possibly The Thinking Machine had never been nearer death than in that moment when the sailorman towered above him—'twas giant and weakling. The tiger was about to spring. Then, suddenly as it had come, anger passed from Holderby's face; came instead curiosity, bewilderment, perplexity.

The silence was broken by the sinister click of a revolver. Holderby turned his head slowly, to face Detective Mallory, stared at him oddly, then drew his own revolver, and passed it over, butt foremost.

No word had been spoken. Not once had The Thinking Machine lowered his eyes.

"I killed Peter Ordway," Holderby explained distinctly, "for good and sufficient reasons."

"So you wrote the governor," the scientist observed. "Your motive was born thirty-two years ago?"

"Yes." The sailor seemed merely astonished.

"On a raft at sea?"

"Yes."

"There was murder done on that raft?"

"Yes."

"Instigated by Peter Ordway, who offered you——"

"One million dollars—yes."

"So Peter Ordway is the second man you have killed?"

"Yes."

With mouth agape, Hutchinson Hatch listened greedily; he had—they had—saved Walpole! Mallory's mind was a chaos. What sort of tommyrot was this? This man confessing to a murder for which Walpole was to be electrocuted! His line of thought was broken by the petulant voice of the Thinking Machine.

"Sit down, Mr. Holderby!" he was saying, "and tell us precisely what happened on that raft."

'Twas a dramatic story Benjamin Holderby told—a tragedy tale of the sea—a tale of starvation and thirst torture and madness, and cease-less battling for life—of crime and greed and the power of money even in that awful moment when death seemed the portion of all. The tale began with the foundering of the steamship *Neptune*, Liverpool to Boston, ninety-one passengers and crew, some thirty-two years ago. In mid-ocean she was smashed to bits by a gale, and went down. Of those aboard only nine persons reached shore alive.

Holderby told the story simply:

"God knows how any of us went through that storm; it raged for days.

There were ten of us on our raft when the ship settled, and by dusk of the second day there were only six—one woman, and one child, and four men. The waves would simply smash over us, and when we came to daylight again there was some one missing. There was little enough food and water aboard, anyway, so the people dropping off that way was really what saved—what saved two of us at the end. Peter Ordway was one, and I was the other.

"The first five days were bad enough—short rations, little or no water, no sleep, and all that; but what came after was hell! At the end of that fifth day there were only five of us—Ordway and me, the woman and child, and another man. I don't know whether I went to sleep or was just unconscious; anyway, when I came to there were only the three of us left. I asked Ordway where the woman and child was. He said they were washed off while I was asleep.

"'And a good thing,' he says.

"'Why?' I says.

"'Too many mouths to feed,' he says. 'And still too many.' He meant the other man. 'I've been looking at the rations and the water,' he says. 'There's enough to keep three people alive three days, but if there were only two people—me and you, for instance?' he says.

"'You mean throw him off?' I says.

"'You're a sailor,' says he. 'If you go, we all go. But we may not be picked up for days. We may starve or die of thirst first. If there were only two of us, we'd have a better chance. I'm worth millions of dollars,' he says. 'If you'll get rid of this other fellow, and we ever come out alive, I'll give you one million dollars!' I didn't say anything. 'If there were only two of us,' says he, 'we would increase our chances of being saved one-third. One million dollars!' says he. 'One million dollars!'

"I expect I was mad with hunger and thirst and sleeplessness and exhaustion. Perhaps he was, too. I know that, regardless of the money he offered, his argument appealed to me. Peter Ordway was a coward; he didn't have the nerve; so an hour later I threw the man overboard, with Peter Ordway looking on.

"Days passed somehow—God knows—and when I came to I had been picked up by a sailing vessel. I was in an asylum for months. When I came out, I asked Ordway for money. He threatened to have me arrested for murder. I pestered him a lot, I guess, for a little later I found myself shanghaied, on the high seas. I didn't come back for thirty years or so. I had almost forgotten the thing until I happened to see Peter Ordway's name in a paper. Then I wrote the slips and mailed them to him. He knew what they meant, and set a detective after me.

Then I began hating him all over again, worse than ever. Finally I thought I'd go to his house and make a holdup of it—one million dollars! I don't think I intended to kill him; I thought he'd give me money. I didn't know there was any one with him. I talked to him, and he shot me. I killed him."

Fell a long silence. The Thinking Machine broke it:

"You entered the apartment with a skeleton key?"

"Yes."

"And after the shot was fired, you started out, but dodged behind the curtain at the door when you heard Mr. Pingree and Mrs. Robinson coming in?"

"Yes."

Suddenly Hatch understood why The Thinking Machine had asked him to ascertain if there were curtains at that door. It was quite possible that in the excitement Mr. Pingree and Mrs. Robinson would not have noticed that the man who killed Peter Ordway actually passed them in the doorway.

"I think," said The Thinking Machine, "that that is all. You understand, Mr. Mallory, that this confession is to be presented to the governor immediately in order to save Walpole's life?" He turned to Holderby. "You don't want an innocent man to die for this crime?"

"Certainly not," was the reply. "That's why I wrote to the governor. Walpole's story was true. I was in court, and heard it." He glanced at Mallory curiously. "Now, if necessary, I'm willing to go to the chair."

"It won't be necessary," The Thinking Machine pointed out. "You didn't go to Peter Ordway's place to kill him—you went there for money you thought he owed you—he fired at you—you shot him. It's hardly self-defense, but it was not premeditated murder."

Detective Mallory whistled. It was the only satisfactory vent for the tangled mental condition which had befallen him. Shortly he went off with Holderby to the governor's office; and an hour later Walpole, deeply astonished, walked out of the death cell—a free man.

Meanwhile, Hutchinson Hatch had some questionsn to ask of The Thinking Machine.

"Logic, logic, Mr. Hatch!" the scientist answered, in that perpetual tone of irritation. "As an experiment, we assumed the truth of Walpole's story. Very well. Peter Ordway was afraid of water. Connect that with the one word 'raft' or 'craft' in Walpole's statement of what the intruder had said. Connect that with his description of that man—'ruddy, like a seaman.' Add them up, as you would a sum in arithmetic. You begin to get a glimmer of cause and effect, don't you? Peter Ordway was afraid of the water because of some tragedy there in which he had played a part. That was a tentative surmise. Walpole's description of the intruder said white hair and flowing white beard. It is a common failing of men who disguise themselves to go to the other extreme. I went to the other extreme in conjecturing Holderby's appearance—clean-shaven or else close-cropped beard and hair—dyed. Since no bullet mark was found in the building—remember, we are assuming Walpole's statement to be true—the man Ordway shot at carried the bullet away with him. Ergo, a seaman with a pistol wound. Seamen, as a rule, stop at the sailors' lodging houses. That's all."

"But—but you knew Holderby's name—his age!" the reporter stammered.

"I learned them in my effort to account for Ordway's fear of water," was the reply. "An old friend, John Page, whom I found through Doctor Anderson, informed me that he had seen some account in a newspaper thirty-two years before, at the time of the wreck of the *Neptune*, of Peter Ordway's rescue from a raft at sea. He and one other man were picked up. The old newspaper files in the libraries gave me Holderby's name as the other survivor, together with his age. You found Holderby. I wrote to him that I was about to put a yacht in commission, and he had been recommended to me—that is, Benjamin Goode had been recommended. He came in answer to the advertisement. You saw everything else that happened.

"And the so-called 'one million dollar' slips?"

"Had no bearing on the case *until* Holderby wrote to the governor," said The Thinking Machine. "In that note he confessed the killing; ergo I began to see that the 'One million dollar' slips probably indicated some enormous reward Ordway had offered Holderby. Walpole's statement, too, covers this point. What happened on the raft at sea? I didn't know. I followed an instinct, and guessed." The distinguished scientist arose. "And now," he said, "begone about your business. I must go to work."

Hatch started out, but turned at the door. "Why," he asked, "were you so anxious to know if any windowpane in the Ordway house had been replaced or was broken?"

"Because," the scientist didn't lift his head, "because a bullet might have smashed one, if it was not to be found in the woodwork. If it smashed one, our unknown Mr. X was not wounded."

Upon his own statement, Benjamin Holderby was sentenced to ten years in prison; at the end of three months he was transferred to an asylum after an examination by alienists.

E. and H. Heron

(Kate Prichard, ca. 1851–?; Hesketh Prichard, 1876–1922)

SHERLOCK HOLMES once remarked that at his agency "ghosts need not apply," and in general it is true that the detective story requires a rational, material explanation of the mystery. Occasionally, however, writers have used the investigatory techniques of the detective to confirm the supernatural. Probably the first series of such occult detective stories was "Real Ghost Stories," twelve tales by the mother-and-son team of Kate and Hesketh Prichard, published in *Pearson's Magazine* beginning in January 1898. Although the Prichards looked on the stories as pure fiction, the magazine claimed that they described genuine events investigated by "Flaxman Low—" the publisher explained, "under the thin disguise of which name many are sure to recognize one of the leading scientists of the day." Each story included a photograph of the supposedly haunted house. The stories were collected the next year under the title *Ghosts*.

Hesketh Prichard was also the author of *November Joe: The Detective of the Woods* (1913), stories set in the Canadian forests. With his mother, he wrote the once very popular series of rogue stories featuring Don Q, who in a movie starring Douglas Fairbanks was described as the "son of Zorro."

The Story of Baelbrow

IT IS A MATTER for regret that so many of Mr. Flaxman Low's reminiscences should deal with the darker episodes of his career. Yet this is almost unavoidable, as the more purely scientific and less strongly marked cases would not, perhaps, contain the same elements of interest for the general public, however valuable and instructive they might be to the expert student. It was also been considered better to choose the completer cases, those that ended in something like satisfactory proof, rather than the many instances where the thread broke off abruptly amongst surmisings, which it was never possible to subject to convincing tests.

North of a low-lying strip of country on the East Anglian coast, the promontory of Bael Ness thrusts out a blunt nose into the sea. On the Ness, backed by pinewoods, stands a square, comfortable stone mansion, known to the countryside as Baelbrow. It has faced the east winds for close upon three hundred years, and during the whole period has been the home of the Swaffam family, who were never in any wise put out of conceit of their ancestral dwelling by the fact that it had always been haunted. Indeed, the Swaffams were proud of the Baelbrow Ghost, which enjoyed a wide notoriety, and no one dreamt of complaining of its behaviour until Professor Jungvort, of Nuremburg, laid information against it, and sent an urgent appeal for help to Mr. Flaxman Low.

The Professor, who was well acquainted with Mr. Low, detailed the circumstances of his tenancy of Baelbrow, and the unpleasant events that had followed thereupon.

It appeared that Mr. Swaffam, senior, who spent a large portion of his time abroad, had offered to lend his house to the Professor for the summer season. When the Jungvorts arrived at Baelbrow, they were charmed with the place. The prospect, though not very varied, was at least extensive, and the air exhilarating. Also the Professor's daughter enjoyed frequent visits from her betrothed—Harold Swaffam—and the Professor was delightfully employed in overhauling the Swaffam library.

The Jungvorts had been duly told of the ghost, which lent distinction to the old house, but never in any way interfered with the comfort of the inmates. For some time they found this description to be strictly true, but with the beginning of October came a change. Up to this time and as far back as the Swaffam annals reached, the ghost had been a shadow, a rustle, a passing sigh—nothing definite or troublesome. But early in October strange things began to occur, and the terror culminated when a housemaid was found dead in a corridor three weeks later. Upon this the Professor felt that it was time to send for Flaxman Low.

Mr. Low arrived upon a chilly evening when the house was already beginning to blur in the purple twilight, and the resinous scent of the pine came sweetly on the land breeze. Jungvort welcomed him in the spacious, firelit hall. He was a stout German with a quantity of white hair, round eyes emphasised by spectacles, and a kindly, dreamy face. His life-study was philology, and his two relaxations chess and the smoking of a big Bismarck-bowled meerschaum.

"Now, Professor," said Mr. Low when they had settled themselves in the smoking-room, "how did it all begin?"

"I will tell you," replied Jungvort, thrusting out his chin, and tapping his broad chest, and speaking as if an unwarrantable liberty had been taken with him. "First of all, it has shown itself to me!"

Mr. Flaxman Low smiled and assured him that nothing could be more satisfactory.

"But not at all satisfactory!" exclaimed the Professor. "I was sitting here alone, it might have been midnight—when I hear something come creeping like a little dog with its nails, tick-tick, upon the oak flooring of the hall. I whistle, for I think it is the little 'Rags' of my daughter, and afterwards opened the door, and I saw"—he hesitated and looked hard at Low through his spectacles, "something that was just disappearing into the passage which connects the two wings of the house. It was a figure, not unlike the human figure, but narrow and straight. I fancied I saw a bunch of black hair, and a flutter of something detached, which may have been a handkerchief. I was overcome by a feeling of repulsion. I heard a few, clicking steps, then it stopped, as I thought, at the museum door. Come, I will show you the spot."

The Professor conducted Mr. Low into the hall. The main staircase, dark and massive, yawned above them, and directly behind it ran the passage referred to by the Professor. It was over twenty feet long, and about midway led past a deep arch containing a door reached by two steps. Jungvort explained that this door formed the entrance to a large room called the Museum, in which Mr. Swaffam, senior, who was something of a dilettante, stored the various curios he picked up during his excursions abroad. The Professor went on to say that he immediately followed the figure, which he believed had gone into the museum, but he found nothing there except the cases containing Swaffam's treasures.

"I mentioned my experience to no one. I concluded that I had seen the ghost. But two days after, one of the female servants coming through the passage in the dark, declared that a man leapt out at her from the embrasure of the Museum door, but she released herself and ran screaming into the servants' hall. We at once made a search but found nothing to substantiate her story.

"I took no notice of this, though it coincided pretty well with my own experience. The week after, my daughter Lena came down late one night for a book. As she was about to cross the hall, something leapt upon her from behind. Women are of little use in serious investigations—she fainted! Since then she has been ill and the doctor says 'Run down.'" Here the Professor spread out his hands. "So she leaves for a change to-morrow. Since then other members of the household have been attacked in much the same manner, with always the same result, they faint and are weak and useless when they recover.

"But, last Wednesday, the affair became a tragedy. By that time the servants had refused to come through the passage except in a crowd of three or four,—most of them preferring to go round by the terrace to reach this part of the house. But one maid, named Eliza Freeman, said she was not afraid of the Baelbrow Ghost, and undertook to put out the lights in the hall one night. When she had done so, and was returning through the passage past the Museum door, she appears to have been attacked, or at any rate frightened. In the grey of the morning they found her lying beside the steps dead. There was a little blood upon her sleeve but no mark upon her body except a small raised pustule under the ear. The doctor said the girl was extraordinarily anæmic, and that she probably died from fright, her heart being weak. I was surprised at this, for she had always seemed to be a particularly strong and active young woman."

"Can I see Miss Jungvort to-morrow before she goes?" asked Low, as the Professor signified he had nothing more to tell.

The Professor was rather unwilling that his daughter should be questioned, but he at last gave his permission, and next morning Low had a short talk with the girl before she left the house. He found her a very pretty girl, though listless and startlingly pale, and with a frightened stare in her light brown eyes. Mr. Low asked if she could describe her assailant.

"No," she answered, "I could not see him, for he was behind me. I only saw a dark, bony hand, with shining nails, and a bandaged arm pass just under my eyes before I fainted."

"Bandaged arm? I have heard nothing of this."

"Tut—tut, mere fancy!" put in the Professor impatiently.

"I saw the bandages on the arm," repeated the girl, turning her head wearily away, "and I smelt the antiseptics it was dressed with."

"You have hurt your neck," remarked Mr. Low, who noticed a small circular patch of pink under her ear.

She flushed and paled, raising her hand to her neck with a nervous jerk, as she said in a low voice:

"It has almost killed me. Before he touched me, I knew he was there! I felt it!"

When they left her the Professor apologised for the unreliability of her evidence, and pointed out the discrepancy between her statement and his own.

"She says she sees nothing but an arm, yet I tell you it had no arms! Preposterous! Conceive a wounded man entering this house to frighten the young women! I do not know what to make of it! Is it a man, or is it the Baelbrow Ghost?"

During the afternoon when Mr. Low and the Professor returned from a stroll on the shore, they found a dark-browed young man with a bull neck, and strongly marked features, standing sullenly before the hall fire. The Professor presented him to Mr. Low as Harold Swaffam.

Swaffam seemed to be about thirty, but was already known as a far-seeing and successful member of the Stock Exchange.

"I am pleased to meet you, Mr. Low," he began, with a keen glance, "though you don't look sufficiently high-strung for one of your profession."

Mr. Low merely bowed.

"Come, you don't defend your craft against my insinuations?" went

on Swaffam. "And so you have come to rout out our poor old ghost
from Baelbrow? You forget that he is an heirloom, a family possession!
What's this about his having turned rabid, eh, Professor?" he ended,
wheeling round upon Jungvort in his brusque way.

The Professor told the story over again. It was plain that he stood
rather in awe of his prospective son-in-law.

"I heard much the same from Lena, whom I met at the station," said
Swaffam. "It is my opinion that the women in this house are suffering
from an epidemic of hysteria. You agree with me, Mr. Low?"

"Possibly. Though hysteria could hardly account for Freeman's
death."

"I can't say as to that until I have looked further into the particulars.
I have not been idle since I arrived. I have examined the Museum. No
one has entered it from the outside, and there is no other way of
entrance except through the passage. The flooring is laid, I happen to
know, on a thick layer of concrete. And there the case for the ghost
stands at present." After a few moments of dogged reflection, he swung
round on Mr. Low, in a manner that seemed peculiar to him when
about to address any person. "What do you say to this plan, Mr. Low? I
propose to drive the Professor over to Ferryvale, to stop there for a day
or two at the hotel, and I will also dispose of the servants who still
remain in the house for, say, forty-eight hours. Meanwhile you and I
can try to go further into the secret of the ghost's new pranks?"

Flaxman Low replied that this scheme exactly met his views, but the
Professor protested against being sent away. Harold Swaffam however
was a man who liked to arrange things in his own fashion, and within
forty-five minutes he and Jungvort departed in the dogcart.

The evening was lowering, and Baelbrow, like all houses built in
exposed situations, was extremely susceptible to the changes of the
weather. Therefore, before many hours were over, the place was full of
creaking noises as the screaming gale battered at the shuttered windows, and the tree-branches tapped and groaned against the walls.

Harold Swaffam, on his way back, was caught in the storm and
drenched to the skin. It was, therefore, settled that after he had changed
his clothes he should have a couple of hours' rest on the smoking-room
sofa, while Mr. Low kept watch in the hall.

The early part of the night passed over uneventfully. A light burned
faintly in the great wainscotted hall, but the passage was dark. There
was nothing to be heard but the wild moan and whistle of the wind
coming in from the sea, and the squalls of rain dashing against the windows. As the hours advanced, Mr. Low lit a lantern that lay at hand,

and, carrying it along the passage, tried the Museum door. It yielded, and the wind came muttering through to meet him. He looked round at the shutters and behind the big cases which held Mr. Swaffam's treasures, to make sure that the room contained no living occupant but himself.

Suddenly he fancied he heard a scraping noise behind him, and turned round, but discovered nothing to account for it. Finally, he laid the lantern on a bench so that its light should fall through the door into the passage, and returned again to the hall, where he put out the lamp, and then once more took up his station by the closed door of the smoking-room.

A long hour passed, during which the wind continued to roar down the wide hall chimney, and the old boards creaked as if furtive footsteps were gathering from every corner of the house. But Flaxman Low heeded none of these; he was waiting for a certain sound.

After a while, he heard it—the cautious scraping of wood on wood. He leant forward to watch the Museum door. Click, click, came the curious dog-like tread upon the tiled floor of the Museum, till the thing, whatever it was, paused and listened behind the open door. The wind lulled at the moment, and Low listened also, but no further sound was to be heard, only slowly across the broad ray of light falling through the door grew a stealthy shadow.

Again the wind rose, and blew in heavy gusts about the house, till even the flame in the lantern flickered; but when it steadied once more, Flaxman Low saw that the silent form had passed through the door, and was now on the steps outside. He could just make out a dim shadow in the dark angle of the embrasure.

Presently, from the shapeless shadow came a sound Mr. Low was not prepared to hear. The thing sniffed the air with the strong, audible inspiration of a bear, or some large animal. At the same moment, carried on the draughts of the hall, a faint, unfamiliar odour reached his nostrils. Lena Jungvort's words flashed back upon him—this, then, was the creature with the bandaged arm!

Again, as the storm shrieked and shook the windows, a darkness passed across the light. The thing had sprung out from the angle of the door, and Flaxman Low knew that it was making its way towards him through the illusive blackness of the hall. He hesitated for a second; then he opened the smoking-room door.

Harold Swaffam sat up on the sofa, dazed with sleep.

"What has happened? Has it come?"

Low told him what he had just seen. Swaffam listened half-smilingly.

"What do you make of it now?" he said.

"I must ask you to defer that question for a little," replied Low.

"Then you mean me to suppose that you have a theory to fit all these incongruous items?"

"I have a theory, which may be modified by further knowledge," said Low. "Meantime, am I right in concluding from the name of this house that it was built on a barrow or burying-place?"

"You are right, though that has nothing to do with the latest freaks of our ghost," returned Swaffam decidedly.

"I also gather that Mr. Swaffam has lately sent home one of the many cases now lying in the Museum?" went on Mr. Low.

"He sent one, certainly, last September."

"And you have opened it," asserted Low.

"Yes; though I flattered myself I had left no trace of my handiwork."

"I have not examined the cases," said Low. "I inferred that you had done so from other facts."

"Now, one thing more," went on Swaffam, still smiling. "Do you imagine there is any danger—I mean to men like ourselves? Hysterical women cannot be taken into serious account."

"Certainly; the gravest danger to any person who moves about this part of the house alone after dark," replied Low.

Harold Swaffam leant back and crossed his legs.

"To go back to the beginning of our conversation, Mr. Low, may I remind you of the various conflicting particulars you will have to reconcile before you can present any decent theory to the world?"

"I am quite aware of that."

"First of all, our original ghost was a mere misty presence, rather guessed at from vague sounds and shadows—now we have a something that is tangible, and that can, as we have proof, kill with fright. Next Jungvort declares the thing was a narrow, long and distinctly armless object, while Miss Jungvort has not only seen the arm and hand of a human being, but saw them clearly enough to tell us that the nails were gleaming and the arm bandaged. She also felt its strength. Jungvort, on the other hand, maintained that it clicked along like a dog—you bear out this description with the additional information that it sniffs like a wild beast. Now what can this thing be? It is capable of being seen, smelt, and felt, yet it hides itself successfully in a room where there is no cavity or space sufficient to afford covert to a cat! You still tell me that you believe that you can explain?"

"Most certainly," replied Flaxman Low with conviction.

"I have not the slightest intention or desire to be rude, but as a mere

matter of common sense, I must express my opinion plainly. I believe
the whole thing to be the result of excited imaginations, and I am about
to prove it. Do you think there is any further danger to-night?"

"Very great danger to-night," replied Low.

"Very well; as I said, I am going to prove it. I will ask you to allow me
to lock you up in one of the distant rooms, where I can get no help from
you, and I will pass the remainder of the night walking about the passage and hall in the dark. That should give proof one way or the other."

"You can do so if you wish, but I must at least beg to be allowed to
look on. I will leave the house and watch what goes on from the window
in the passage, which I saw opposite the Museum door. You cannot, in
any fairness, refuse to let me be a witness."

"I cannot, of course," returned Swaffam. "Still, the night is too bad to
turn a dog out into, and I warn you that I shall lock you out."

"That will not matter. Lend me a macintosh, and leave the lantern lit
in the Museum, where I placed it."

Swaffam agreed to this. Mr. Low gives a graphic account of what followed. He left the house and was duly locked out, and, after groping his
way round the house, found himself at length outside the window of the
passage, which was almost opposite to the door of the Museum. The
door was still ajar and a thin band of light cut out into the gloom.
Further down the hall gaped black and void. Low, sheltering himself as
well as he could from the rain, waited for Swaffam's appearance. Was
the terrible yellow watcher balancing itself upon its lean legs in the dim
corner opposite, ready to spring out with its deadly strength upon the
passer-by?

Presently Low heard a door bang inside the house, and the next
moment Swaffam appeared with a candle in his hand, an isolated
spread of weak rays against the vast darkness behind. He advanced
steadily down the passage, his dark face grim and set, and as he came
Mr. Low experienced that tingling sensation, which is so often the fore-
runner of some strange experience. Swaffam passed on towards the
other end of the passage. There was a quick vibration of the Museum
door as a lean shape with a shrunken head leapt out into the passage
after him. Then all together came a hoarse shout, the noise of a fall and
utter darkness.

In an instant, Mr. Low had broken the glass, opened the window, and
swung himself into the passage. There he lit a match and as it flared he
saw by its dim light a picture painted for a second upon the obscurity
beyond.

Swaffam's big figure lay with outstretched arms, face downwards, and as Low looked a crouching shape extricated itself from the fallen man, raising a narrow vicious head from his shoulder.

The match spluttered feebly and went out, and Low heard a flying step click on the boards, before he could find the candle Swaffam had dropped. Lighting it, he stooped over Swaffam and turned him on his back. The man's strong colour had gone, and the wax-white face looked whiter still against the blackness of hair and brows, and upon his neck under the ear, was a little raised pustule, from which a thin line of blood was streaked up to the angle of his cheekbone.

Some instinctive feeling prompted Low to glance up at this moment. Half extended from the Museum doorway were a face and bony neck— a high-nosed, dull-eyed, malignant face, the eye-sockets hollow, and the darkened teeth showing. Low plunged his hand into his pocket, and a shot rang out in the echoing passage-way and hall. The wind sighed through the broken panes, a ribbon of stuff fluttered along the polished flooring, and that was all, as Flaxman Low half dragged, half carried Swaffam into the smoking-room.

It was some time before Swaffam recovered consciousness. He listened to Low's story of how he had found him with a red angry gleam in his sombre eyes.

"The ghost has scored off me," he said with an odd, sullen laugh, "but now I fancy it's my turn! But before we adjourn to the Museum to examine the place, I will ask you to let me hear your notion of things. You have been right in saying there was real danger. For myself I can only tell you that I felt something spring upon me, and I knew no more. Had this not happened I am afraid I should never have asked you a second time what your idea of the matter might be," he ended with a sort of sulky frankness.

"There are two main indications," replied Low. "This strip of yellow bandage; which I have just now picked up from the passage floor, and the mark on your neck."

"What's that you say?" Swaffam rose quickly and examined his neck in a small glass beside the mantel-shelf.

"Connect those two, and I think I can leave you to work it out for yourself," said Low.

"Pray let us have your theory in full," requested Swaffam shortly.

"Very well," answered Low good-humouredly—he thought Swaffam's annoyance natural under the circumstances—"The long, narrow figure which seemed to the Professor to be armless is developed on the next occasion. For Miss Jungvort sees a bandaged arm and a dark hand with gleaming—which means, of course, gilded—nails. The clicking sound of the footstep coincides with these particulars, for we know that sandals made of strips of leather are not uncommon in company with gilt nails and bandages. Old and dry leather would naturally click upon your polished floors."

"Bravo, Mr. Low! So you mean to say that this house is haunted by a mummy!"

"That is my idea, and all I have seen confirms me in my opinion."

"To do you justice, you held this theory before to-night—before, in fact, you had seen anything for yourself. You gathered that my father had sent home a mummy, and you went on to conclude that I had opened the case?"

"Yes. I imagine you took off most of, or rather all, the outer bandages, thus leaving the limbs free, wrapped only in the inner bandages which were swathed round each separate limb. I fancy this mummy was preserved on the Theban method with aromatic spices, which left the skin olive-coloured, dry and flexible, like tanned leather, and features remaining distinct, and the hair, teeth, and eyebrows perfect."

"So far, good," said Swaffam. "But now, how about the intermittent vitality? The pustule on the neck of those whom it attacks? And where is our old Baelbrow ghost to come in?"

Swaffam tried to speak in a rallying tone, but his excitement and lowering temper were visible enough, in spite of the attempts he made to suppress them.

"To begin at the beginning," said Flaxman Low, "everybody who, in a rational and honest manner, investigates the phenomena of spiritism will, sooner or later, meet in them some perplexing element, which is not to be explained by any of the ordinary theories. For reasons into which I need not now enter, this present case appears to me to be one of these. I am led to believe that the ghost which has for so many years given dim and vague manifestations of its existence in this house is a vampire."

Swaffam threw back his head with an incredulous gesture.

"We no longer live in the middle ages, Mr. Low! And besides, how could a vampire come here?" he said scoffingly.

"It is held by some authorities on these subjects that under certain conditions a vampire may be self-created. You tell me that this house is built upon an ancient barrow, in fact, on a spot where we might naturally expect to find such an elemental psychic germ. In those dead human systems were contained all the seeds for good and evil. The power which causes these psychic seeds or germs to grow is thought, and from being long dwelt on and indulged, a thought might finally gain a mysterious vitality, which could go on increasing more and more by attracting to itself suitable and appropriate elements from its environment. For a long period this germ remained a helpless intelligence, awaiting the opportunity to assume some material form, by means of which to carry out its desires. The invisible is the real; the material only subserves its manifestation. The impalpable reality already existed, when you provided for it a physical medium for action by unwrapping the mummy's form. Now, we can only judge of the nature of the germ by its manifestation through matter. Here we have every indication of a vampire intelligence touching into life and energy the dead human frame. Hence the mark on the neck of its victims, and their bloodless and anæmic condition. For a vampire, as you know, sucks blood."

Swaffam rose, and took up the lamp.

"Now, for proof," he said bluntly. "Wait a second, Mr. Low. You say you fired at this appearance?" And he took up the pistol which Low had laid down on the table.

"Yes, I aimed at a small portion of its foot which I saw on the step."

Without more words, and with the pistol still in his hand, Swaffam led the way to the Museum.

The wind howled round the house, and the darkness, which precedes the dawn, lay upon the world, when the two men looked upon one of the strangest sights it has ever been given to men to shudder at.

Half in and half out of an oblong wooden box in a corner of the great room, lay a lean shape in its rotten yellow bandages, the scraggy neck surmounted by a mop of frizzled hair. The toe strap of a sandal and a portion of the right foot had been shot away.

Swaffam, with a working face, gazed down at it, then seizing it by its tearing bandages, he flung it into the box, where it fell into a life-like posture, its wide, moist-lipped mouth gaping up at them.

For a moment Swaffam stood over the thing; then with a curse he raised the revolver and shot into the grinning face again and again with a deliberate vindictiveness. Finally he rammed the thing down into the box, and, clubbing the weapon, smashed the head into fragments with a vicious energy that coloured the whole horrible scene with a suggestion of murder done.

Then, turning to Low, he said:

"Help me to fasten the cover on it."

"Are you going to bury it?"

"No, we must rid the earth of it," he answered savagely. "I'll put it into the old canoe and burn it."

The rain had ceased when in the daybreak they carried the old canoe down to the shore. In it they placed the mummy case with its ghastly occupant, and piled faggots about it. The sail was raised and the pile lighted, and Low and Swaffam watched it creep out on the ebb-tide, at first a twinkling spark, then a flare of waving fire, until far out to sea the history of that dead thing ended 3000 years after the priests of Armen had laid it to rest in its appointed pyramid.

DOVER · THRIFT · EDITIONS

All books complete and unabridged. All 5³⁄₁₆ x 8¼, paperbound.
Just $1.00—$2.00 in U.S.A.

A selection of the more than 200 titles in the series.

DOVER · THRIFT · EDITIONS

All books complete and unabridged. All 5³⁄₁₆ x 8¹⁄₄, paperbound.
Just $1.00—$2.00 in U.S.A.

LYRIC POEMS, John Keats. 80pp. 26871-3 $1.00

THE BOOK OF PSALMS, King James Bible. 144pp. 27541-8 $1.00

THE MAN WHO WOULD BE KING AND OTHER STORIES, Rudyard Kipling. 128pp. 28051-9
$1.00

SELECTED SHORT STORIES, D. H. Lawrence. 128pp. 27794-1 $1.00

GREAT SPEECHES, Abraham Lincoln. 112pp. 26872-1 $1.00

THE CALL OF THE WILD, Jack London. 64pp. 26472-6 $1.00

FAVORITE POEMS, Henry Wadsworth Longfellow. 96pp. 27273-7 $1.00

THE PRINCE, Niccolò Machiavelli. 80pp. 27274-5 $1.00

DR. FAUSTUS, Christopher Marlowe. 64pp. 28208-2 $1.00

BARTLEBY AND BENITO CERENO, Herman Melville. 112pp. 26473-4 $1.00

THE MISANTHROPE, Molière. 64pp. 27065-3 $1.00

GREAT SONNETS, Paul Negri (ed.). 112pp. 28052-7 $1.00

THE EMPEROR JONES, Eugene O'Neill. 64pp. 29268-1 $1.50

SYMPOSIUM AND PHAEDRUS, Plato. 96pp. 27798-4 $1.00

THE TRIAL AND DEATH OF SOCRATES: FOUR DIALOGUES, Plato. 128pp. 27066-1 $1.00

THE GOLD-BUG AND OTHER TALES, Edgar Allan Poe. 128pp. 26875-6 $1.00

THE RAVEN AND OTHER FAVORITE POEMS, Edgar Allan Poe. 64pp. 26685-0 $1.00

ESSAY ON MAN AND OTHER POEMS, Alexander Pope. 128pp. 28053-5 $1.00

EARLY POEMS, Ezra Pound. 64pp. (Available in U.S. only) 28745-9 $1.00

GOBLIN MARKET AND OTHER POEMS, Christina Rossetti. 64pp. 28055-1 $1.00

CHICAGO POEMS, Carl Sandburg. 80pp. 28057-8 $1.00

COMPLETE SONNETS, William Shakespeare. 80pp. 26686-9 $1.00

HAMLET, William Shakespeare. 128pp. 27278-8 $1.00

KING LEAR, William Shakespeare. 112pp. 28058-6 $1.00

100 BEST-LOVED POEMS, Philip Smith (ed.). 96pp. 28553-7 $1.00

OEDIPUS REX, Sophocles. 64pp. 26877-2 $1.00

THREE LIVES, Gertrude Stein. 176pp. 28059-4 $2.00

THE STRANGE CASE OF DR. JEKYLL AND MR. HYDE, Robert Louis Stevenson. 64pp. 26688-5
$1.00

THE KREUTZER SONATA AND OTHER SHORT STORIES, Leo Tolstoy. 144pp. 27805-0 $1.00

ADVENTURES OF HUCKLEBERRY FINN, Mark Twain. 224pp. 28061-6 $2.00

ETHAN FROME, Edith Wharton. 96pp. 26690-7 $1.00

CANDIDE, Voltaire (François-Marie Arouet). 112pp. 26689-3 $1.00

GREAT LOVE POEMS, Shane Weller (ed.). 128pp. 27284-2 $1.00

SELECTED POEMS, Walt Whitman. 128pp. 26878-0 $1.00

THE IMPORTANCE OF BEING EARNEST, Oscar Wilde. 64pp. 26478-5 $1.00

THE PICTURE OF DORIAN GRAY, Oscar Wilde. 192pp. 27807-7 $1.00

A VINDICATION OF THE RIGHTS OF WOMAN, Mary Wollstonecraft. 224pp. 29036-0 $2.00

MONDAY OR TUESDAY: Eight Stories, Virginia Woolf. 64pp. 29453-6 $1.00

FAVORITE POEMS, William Wordsworth. 80pp. 27073-4 $1.00

EARLY POEMS, William Butler Yeats. 128pp. 27808-5 $1.00

For a complete descriptive list of all volumes in the Dover Thrift Editions series
write for a free Dover Fiction and Literature Catalog (59047-X) to
Dover Publications, Inc., Dept. DTE, 31 E. 2nd Street, Mineola, N.Y. 11501